NEW YORK
CLASSICS

MW00990296

THE SELECTED WORKS
OF CESARE PAVESE

CESARE PAVESE (1908–1950) was born on his family's vacation
farm in the country outside of Turin in northern Italy. He
graduated from the University of Turin, where he wrote a thesis
on Walt Whitman, beginning a continuing engagement with
English-language literature that was to lead to his influential
translations of *Moby-Dick*, *A Portrait of the Artist as a Young
Man*, *Three Lives*, and *Moll Flanders*, among other works. Briefly
exiled by the Fascist regime to Calabria in 1935, Pavese returned
to Turin to work for the new publishing house of Giulio Einaudi,
where he eventually became the editorial director. In 1936 he
published a book of poems, *Lavorare stanca* (*Hard Labor*), and
then turned to writing novels and short stories. Pavese won the
Strega Prize for fiction, Italy's most prestigious award, for his
novel *La luna e i falò* (*The Moon and the Bonfires*) in 1950. Later
the same year, after a brief affair with an American actress, he
committed suicide. Pavese's posthumous publications include his
celebrated diaries, essays on American literature, and a second
collection of poems, entitled *Verrà la morte e avrà i tuoi occhi*
(Death Will Come and Will Have Your Eyes).

R. W. FLINT translated, edited, and introduced *The Selected
Works of Cesare Pavese* in 1968 and *Marinetti: Selected Writings*
in 1971. He has contributed interviews, essays, translations, and
reviews on Italian writers to various journals including *Parnassus*,
Canto, and *The Italian Quarterly*. He lives in Cambridge,
Massachusetts.

THE SELECTED WORKS OF CESARE PAVESE

Translated and with an Introduction by

R. W. FLINT

NEW YORK REVIEW BOOKS

New York

This Is a New York Review Book
Published by The New York Review of Books
435 Hudson Street New York, NY 10014
www.nyrb.com

Library of Congress Cataloging-in-Publication Data
Pavese, Cesare.
 [Novels. English. Selections]
 The selected works of Cesare Pavese / translated and with an
introduction by R.W. Flint.
    p. cm.
 ISBN 0-940322-85-4 (pbk. : alk. paper)
 1. Pavese, Cesare—Translations into English. I. Flint, R. W. II.
Title.
 PQ4835.A846 A238 2001
 853'.912—dc21

                          2001005156

ISBN 978-0-940322-85-1

Book design by Lizzie Scott
Printed in the United States of America on acid-free paper.
10 9 8 7 6 5 4 3 2

CONTENTS

INTRODUCTION

Pavese's nine short novels make up the most dense, dramatic and homogeneous narrative cycle of modern Italy, and also—I will add for the benefit of those who think this factor important—the richest in representing social ambiances, the human comedy, the chronicle of a society. But above all they are works of an extraordinary depth where one never stops finding new levels, new meanings.

—ITALO CALVINO, in *L'Europa Letteraria*,
December 1960

When Italo Calvino's memorial essay appeared in 1960, all of it written in the same uncompromising spirit, I was a happy man. It gave me a solid native peg on which to hang a discussion of Cesare Pavese, whose work I had begun to love, admire, and translate some years before. Pavese was already a popular writer in Italy in 1960 and had been often praised, but Calvino's testimony came from a novelist I liked, a younger man who had known him well, enjoyed his company, and had joined the publishing house of Einaudi in Turin to work with him.

Digging Pavese out of his passionate, tormented era, the decade from 1940 to 1950, is like trying to find someone in Pompeii while the lava is still hot. It goes without saying that this was one of the bloodiest and most dramatic decades in Italian history since the Risorgimento. The neorealist movies of the Forties, *Open City*, *Bicycle Thief*, *Paisan*, *Shoeshine*, and others, were the first exported witness to the rejuvenating effect of those agonized years. A small miracle had happened. Part of an industry normally given over to kitsch had broken loose and become suddenly eloquent with reality, with a sober, delicate, and disabused affection for the real Italy of the moment, a country soaked in despair, riddled with hypocrisy, but a land of heroes nevertheless. In Italy, this short cinematic flowering was forgotten (except by the better directors) almost as soon as it faded from the screen. But many non-Italians must have wondered if there were not perhaps a literary equivalent of those films, a writer who dramatized the entire era with a freshness and inwardness beyond their scope. And one with the foresight and skill to project his work well ahead of his age.

There was indeed such a writer, and Cesare Pavese is clearly the man. He did his best work precisely between 1940 and 1950, and then, in August 1950, not long after winning his country's chief literary prize, committed suicide. Identification with an era could hardly go further than that.

This selection from Pavese's quite extensive *oeuvre* includes four novels, three of which—*The House on the Hill, Among Women Only,* and *The Devil in the Hills*—certainly make up the main body of his fiction. If Calvino's "homogeneous" has any force, it applies to these works, which belong to what Italian critics call Pavese's bourgeois novels (a term adopted here with no polemical intent whatever). Two ambitious novels that frame these three— *Paesi tuoi (The Harvesters)* of 1941 and the culminating *La luna e i falò (The Moon and the Bonfires)* of 1950—are of considerable interest and should be read, in better translations than any now available, in conjunction with *Dialoghi con Leucò (Dialogues with Leucò)* of 1947, contemplative dialogues "spoken" by characters from classic mythology, elegantly translated by Professors William Arrowsmith and D. S. Carne-Ross; and with *Lavorare stanca (Hard Labor)*, his poems of 1936, also translated by Professor Arrowsmith. That Pavese was among other things what can be called a mandarin cannot and should not be denied. But a cultivated Italian highbrow, especially one devoted like Pavese to Giovanni Battista Vico, the first great modern theorist of history and culture, is never satisfied unless he can revive the purest classic terrors and ferocities, at least once in his career, in some contemporary form. *Paesi tuoi* and *La luna e i falò* approach that goal in radically different but related ways. Vico had written, as Pavese records in his diary, that the peasant agriculturalists of classic times were the most cruel of all social classes. Agreeing with this judgment on the basis of his wanderings among the Turinese hills, Pavese undertook to illustrate it in ways that seem irresistibly melodramatic to modern readers both inside and outside Italy. In *Paesi tuoi* there's a certain affected monotony; a young writer's stagy crassness, in *Luna*, plot rather than language is finally self-defeating—a jumble of effects and genres each exquisitely handled, but each stubbornly separate from one another. Pavese's vital interests belonged to the urban middle and working classes, and this bears crucially on the choice of language throughout his work.

> Turin is as he was: industrious, clenched in a feverish and stiff-necked preoccupation, and, at the same time, indolent and given to wandering and daydreaming. Wherever we go in the city that resembles him we find our friend starting back to life; in every angle, on every street corner we expect to meet his tall figure in its dark cloak, his face barricaded behind his collar and his cap pulled over his eyes.

Thus the novelist Natalia Ginzburg in an affectionate memoir of her old colleague at Einaudi, Pavese, "whose conversation could be pointed and invigorating like nobody else's." And to commence with Turin, the city that he made into one of the absolute places in modern literature, is to commence with politics. In the general helplessness of any Italian city to throw off Fascism without aid from outside the country, Turin thought it had a mission to win with the pen what nobody could win with the sword.

In that most industrialized and therefore, in many ways, most turbulent city under Fascism, politics were the heart of the matter. Antonio Gramsci, Italy's first and still most important Communist writer, won a scholarship to the University of Turin in 1911 from his native Sardinia and spent most of his active life in the city. An eloquent liberal, Piero Gobetti, started a vigorous polemic against the Fascists in Turin as early as 1922, as a result of which he suffered a violent physical reprisal and died soon afterward in Paris, in 1926. But the movement he founded in Paris, *Giustizia e Libertà*, continued to be a rallying point for Pavese and his friends. Gobetti had become a local legend when intellectuals elsewhere hardly knew what was going on, when Mussolini was still pinning medals on Gabriele D'Annunzio, the rapidly fading hero of Fiume, a once remarkable poet luckless enough to have taken Fascism almost as seriously as he took himself.

Throughout Pavese's boyhood there had been fierce labor troubles. Later, at secondary school (the *liceo* is often an Italian's real education, after which comes specialization at a university), at the university, at work as a tutor, as a translator from English, and eventually as a member of the new leftist publishing house of Giulio Einaudi, he naturally fell in with the most active younger anti-Fascists. One of these was Leone Ginzburg from Odessa, a schoolmate like most of his friends, later a professor of Slavic at the university and husband of Natalia Ginzburg; he was arrested in 1934 for clandestine activities, released for a time, arrested again, and died under torture in prison in 1944.

Pavese's literary studies in secondary school—in the class photograph he sits well front and center, the moody young genius —took place under a forceful old-fashioned Risorgimento liberal, Augusto Monti, himself a novelist of merit, who shaped the minds of two decades of young middle-class Turinese. Some of Pavese's working-class tutees and friends were early casualties in the war. The unrelenting heat of all this turmoil, its constant upshot in the direst action as war threatened and eventually arrived, helps explain the air of drivenness, of impending trouble and enforced prudence, in much of his work.

In 1914, when Pavese was six, his father, a former judge in the city, died of a lingering brain tumor. In 1918 the vacation farm at Santo Stefano Belbo where the novelist was born had to be sold. His capacity for worry seemed to have been further increased by an absence of much emotional support from his widowed mother and his married sister, although he lived with his mother until her death in 1931 and then with his sister's family. (In the diary he gallantly exonerates his parents from any faults in his upbringing, but a typically Piedmontese diffidence in both women can be read between the lines. Family feeling among the Piedmontese is often a matter of what one doesn't do, the freedoms one allows, rather than what one does.)

Pavese emerged from the conditioning of the Thirties, an era when the better part of Italian decency went gradually underground, speaking in his books a new language of his own: a terse, pungently oblique domestic language of "small" people living apparently small lives, the inflections of whose speech carry the full weight of the times. This kind of vigorous disguise, too vigorous for the muddled heads of officialdom, is an old Italian specialty, particularly in the north. During the Thirties and Forties, Pavese had translated some ten contemporary American novels, as well as *Moby-Dick*, *Benito Cereno*, *Moll Flanders*, *David Copperfield*, and Joyce's *Portrait of the Artist as a Young Man*.

To shape his language and summon up a new social class both to speak the language in his books and later to read it, he made use of many literary devices for keeping distance, lyric, elegiac, and panoramic. But from the beginning he had very positive and (for Italy) original ideas about the shift of interest from the nineteenth-century novel of character to the twentieth-century novel of "static essentials," where character is a relatively fixed quantity that doesn't so much change as slowly reveal itself under stress. This theory perfectly suited Pavese's temperament in any case. He accomplished all this on a new, mysteriously hypnotic, subterraneanly moving, telescoped scale that freed him in turn to loosen and roughen his syntax, to mimic Piedmontese speech without resorting to dialect, to compress, scramble, and foreshorten at will—to fuse the homely, the lyric, and the panoramic with extraordinary tact.

Pavese had chronic asthma, sometimes painfully at night, which took the place of traditional TB in stimulating his appetite for reality, *pari passu* with his keen and growing sense of language. He was more in love with Joyce's "pathos of small circumstances" than any Italian novelist since Svevo. And capable of rising to a dry, quietly powerful eloquence, verbally but not emotionally understated, that condenses "an extremely sheer and compact richness of inner motivations and universal ideas," in Italo Calvino's words. Sometimes it may be an overwhelming image, like the looming outline of the hill Superga outside the window in the last paragraph of *Among Women Only*; or the whole last chapter of *The House on the Hill*, which immensely deepens and expands nearly every motion (except comedy) that his prose has made in the earlier chapters.

The key to Pavese's stamina must lie in this vital tension between the (now) self-evident demands of anti-Fascist decency and
the ambitions, always somewhat exotic in Italy, of a full-scale novelist. But as a matter of plain fact, of the four works collected in
this volume, three of them—*The Beach*, *Among Women Only*,
and *The Devil in the Hills*—contain no politics at all in the usual
sense. The last two are usually treated, in varying tones of approval or disdain, as his "bourgeois" novels. *The Beach* is in many
respects a trial run for *The Devil in the Hills* of seven years later. A
quick survey of the longer novels may provoke the conclusion that
Pavese gives the upper classes a pretty rough time. He liked Scott
Fitzgerald so much that he once confided in a letter that he didn't
dare translate him, as he had not translated Hemingway for the
same reason. He was also fond of Proust. But he lived in an atmosphere far less smitten with the glamour of wealth than Proust's or
Fitzgerald's. In *Among Women Only*, the upper classes are repre-
sented by a fumbling pair of industrialist parents, assorted demi-
lesbians, and half-vicious hangers-on. In *The Devil in the Hills*,
their spokesman is a drug addict far gone with tuberculosis. In *The
House on the Hill*, we see them through the eyes of an elderly
pietist, Elvira, an adolescent prig, Egle, and others of their kind.
Pavese's class prejudice is the truly Arcadian feature of his work—
pure, arbitrary, and selfless. He often ignored it in his life—he had
several prosperous friends—and argued against it in his fiction; but
it was always there when he needed it most.

When someone asks the narrator of *The House on the Hill* if he
believes in Italy, the narrator answers: "Not in Italy. In the Italians."
Everything Pavese touches in the novels is seen chiefly as it affects
his narrators' lives, and they in turn "speak" for the newly mobile,
newly restless, supposedly rootless peasant-proletarian class of the
cities, often established in middle-class jobs like teaching; a "class"
he created virtually single-handedly for Italian fiction.

Needless to say, Pavese did not, one fine morning, suddenly notice this class and begin writing about it. His literary beginnings
followed all the usual steps. But the igniting spark was American:

> You are the peach of the world! Not only in wealth and ma-
> terial life but really in liveliness and strength of art which

means thought and politics and everything. You've got to predominate in this century all over the civilized world as before did Greece, and Italy, and France. I'm sure of it.

(Letter, April 1930)

Pavese's "English" letters in 1929 and 1930 to a Piedmontese friend in Chicago, who sent him American books by the several dozen, were certainly his quaintest, the sort of English the first really literate Italian computer will write after it has been liberally programmed with Americans from Walt Whitman to Damon Runyon. He had written his doctoral thesis on Whitman in 1930 ("I succeeded barely in finding something I wanted for my degree's thesis about Walt Whitman. You don't know, I'll be the first Italian to speak at some extent and critically of him. Look me over, I'll almost reveal him to Italy"—in a letter to the same friend).

But Pavese intended to be as subversively heterosexual as Whitman had been the opposite. His whole sense of a new age, of movement, civilization, and true ease depended, as he wrote in a letter, on "overcoming our sacrosanct Piedmontese misogyny." Whitman inspired him with visions of mixing the lyric and the panoramic, of exploring a new private self that might become a new national self; a documentary art that might be poetically liberating. As a chronic walker, Pavese also shared Whitman's, so to speak, locomotor sympathies. His first book of poems, *Lavorare stanca*, saw him beginning to use his newly stretched "American" senses to celebrate the misfits, the workers without hope —farmhands, sand diggers, beggars, seamstresses, whores, etc.— whom he had begun to see and meet during his constant walking and bar-sitting on the city's outskirts.

His middle-classness is important, however, in the light of a common literary faith of the day, expressed by Alberto Moravia in an essay on Verdi, that everything good in Italian life comes from either the peasantry or the nobility. This romantic creed seems even shakier when one remembers that Italy itself was essentially bourgeois vis-à-vis the rest of Europe during the high Renaissance. Moravia, to be sure, has made himself abundantly clear about his own definition of Italian middle-classness, in *The Time of Indifference*, in nearly everything he has written. His version of the petty vanity and pusillanimousness that opened the road to Fascism differs very little from Pavese's in books like *Among Women Only*. But Moravia's middle class always has two strikes against it; Pavese's is a far less predetermined quantity. Like many others at the time, uneasily, ambiguously, without much illusion (vide *The Devil in the Hills*), Pavese shared this feeling for the peasants, the peasants of Verga and D'Annunzio at any rate. He kept scanning his own nature for telltale hints of peasant origin. But in a crisis he invariably took the city man's part, and this required courage and imagination. In the best books, his theme was often a city man's or woman's education at the expense of a latent savagery in the peasants; something that destroyed continuity and made intelligent contemplation—Pavese's true love—a feeble and spasmodic affair.

Turin is one of the best cities in Europe for framing this drama, a city laid out by the Romans in their Augusta Taurinorum, whose straight-lined gracefulness and alpine changeability are shot with memories of half a dozen pasts. It is also the city where class distinctions are most fluid, where workers are constantly streaming into the factories from the country, where the oldest families don't mind soiling their hands with commerce and management. Add to its normal restlessness the violence of Fascism and the war and you can see why Pavese's endlessly debated middle position was a very live option. He often chose the outskirts as his theater and starting point (see the opening of *The Devil in the Hills*) because it symbolized his contempt for the twin official cults of *strapaese* (super-country) and *stracittà* (super-city). What wonderfully silly names! The cultural battle under Fascism was mostly a pillow fight of empty counterpositions in which, however, every third, fifth, or ninth government pillow might contain a bomb. Hence his reluctance to deal with even the normal politics of the factories. Like a traveling mountebank from Fellini's *La Strada*, he set up his booth on the periphery and controlled his action from that relaxed retreat.

Pavese's conversion to Communism was an extremely reluctant, hesitating affair, caused as much by personal loyalties as by intellectual persuasion. He wrote a few inspirational pieces for the Third Page of the Communist paper, *L'Unità*, and even won a

Communist literary prize. But the discomfort of his allegiance becomes positively comic in some passages of Davide Lajolo's biography, *Il vizio assurdo* (*An Absurd Vice*), when this gentleman, as intellectually doctrinaire as he is personally generous, nearly flays the hide off Pavese—most fraternally—for his petty evasions. It should be no surprise, since choices had to be made, that this volume passes over his two most overtly Communist novels, *The Companion* (1948) and *The Moon and the Bonfires* (1950). Although the latter especially has many fine things in it, both of them show how Pavese's peculiar center of gravity was disturbed whenever he thought he should paraphrase an official line or veer too close to socialist realism or create an ideological hero like Nuto, the sententious carpenter-clarinet-player in *The Moon and the Bonfires*. It matters little that this character was taken from a living model (who, incidentally, was interviewed by Norman Thomas di Giovanni and claimed to have found Pavese an utterly baffling character). Nuto is still a bore when he preaches.

If one overlooks these doctrinaire excesses—and who during those years avoided them?—one finds in Pavese a novelist lucky in nearly everything essential for the kind of fiction he was born to write. He was even fortunate in two periods of exile that took him away from the city at critical moments. The first, in 1935, was to Brancaleone Calabria in the extreme south, where he was sent as a punishment for his editorial role at the anti-Fascist Einaudi magazine, *La Cultura*—a rather mild chastisement as reprisals went in the Thirties. It separated Pavese from an apparently hard-boiled young woman whom he had fallen in love with and hoped to marry, and who, from her effect on the novelist during his winter months in a tiny Calabrian village (all his letters from that time survive), sounds like very bad medicine indeed. She had used his mailbox in her clandestine work for the Communist underground and was obviously a prime model for his fictional women in many of their traits.

Pavese's sentence was commuted from three years to ten months, and he came back to Turin to learn from a friend that his *innamorata* had married someone else the day before—at which point he passed out cold on the station platform. Later that year, his book of poems, *Lavorare stanca*, for which he entertained great hopes and on which he had worked exclusively for several years, was published in Florence, sponsored by the novelist Elio Vittorini. It met with complete silence. Professor Arrowsmith explains this failure at length and quite plausibly in his introduction to his above-mentioned translation, *Hard Labor*. Knowing the poems in the Arrowsmith translation, or better still in the original, adds immeasurably to the experience of reading the fiction. They are, in any case, something in the nature of short atmospheric sketches or stories. Many are reminiscent of nothing so much as the poetic naturalism of Edward Hopper—an ultimate narrative austerity for Italian poetry, but scarcely a problem for Americans.

Between his Calabrian interlude and his self-decreed exile in 1944, Pavese's only significant publication was *Paesi tuoi*, in 1941, a solid popular success whose innovations were beautifully calculated to offend nice-minded critics and bring down a verdict of "Americanism" that stuck to him for the rest of his life.

After a short stint in Rome for Einaudi, Pavese returned to Turin late in 1943 to find the Einaudi office closed and his friends dispersed. His second year-long exile, to a family farm high in the hills at Serralunga, was another subtle mixture of the voluntary and the involuntary. He had tried to enlist in the army before the guerrilla war but was turned down for physical reasons. These same reasons were enough in themselves to discourage his joining the guerrilla war later. To stay in the city during the bombing seemed pointless. But joining his sister's family out of danger, in a longed-for rustic setting, brought on a series of inner crises—Leone Ginzburg's death in 1944 contributing to them—that eventually worked themselves out in his masterpiece, *The House on the Hill*, and supplied the germ of all his later work. Of this *Wunderjahr* he wrote on January 9, 1945: "A strange, rich year . . . with much deep thought about the primitive and savage, which has begun some notable work. It could be the most important year of your life so far." It could indeed.

There are two moderately distinct clusters of ideas in Pavese's work which are worth discussing. During his last year he often told correspondents that they could find a summary of his life in "La Belva" ("The Wild Beast") from *Dialogues with Leucò*. It evokes the meeting of Endymion and Artemis on a mountaintop in moon-light. Pavese's Artemis signifies many things in his intimate life:

She stands there before me, a lean, unsmiling girl, watching me. And those great transparent eyes have seen other things. They still see them. They *are* those things. Wild berry and wild beast are in her eyes, and the howling, the death, the cruel turning of the flesh to stone. I know the spilled blood, the torn flesh, the voracious earth, and solitude. For her, the wild one, it is all solitude. For her the wild animal is soli-tude. Her caresses are like the caresses one gives a dog or a tree. But, stranger, she looks at me, looks at me—a lean girl in a short tunic, like a girl from your own village.

Pavese assumes that you, the reader, the stranger, know the girls of your "village" as he knows his shy and decisive Piedmontese, that women are not the merely generic creatures of not-so-distant French ancestry that they so often prove to be in Italian novels. Antonioni knew his business when he chose *Among Women Only* as the basis of his first ambitious movie, *Le Amiche* (*The Girl-friends*). Fundamentally, I think, Pavese was defending the Italian woman's right to be independent without needing to be omnis-cient, neither sheep nor bully nor Earth Mother.

Sex. Love. Death. Pavese's suicide in 1950 soon after a very briefly happy affair with a young American actress was supposed to imply that he had something, if not original, at least extremely touching, to say about this holy triad. He lit up this murky ground with bright aphoristic flashes (W. H. Auden called him "one of the masters of the aphorism" in a review of the diary) but worked no miracles; the ground remains murky. What we have is an impres-sive account of a characteristic modern dilemma that spares no one, not even Italian geniuses.

His sufferings are continually being defused and disinfected by a very genuine hostility to *all* cults of suffering, whether literary, religious, military, or what have you. In that, Pavese was original and sane on the Italian scene. Otherwise the love-sex-death triad was largely humus for his work, a subplot that he could hardly have avoided if he had wanted to. His life and work followed a clearly visible curve of energy that reached its peak in 1944 at Serralunga and declined rapidly after 1949. Nearly everything he did in 1950 suggests a man beyond help. And how natively Piedmontese it was that work should have been his undoing, the very ecstasy of work he was forever denouncing in his fellow townsmen.

A chief source of suspense in the fiction is the hope Pavese arouses from the first paragraph of each book that his narrator will sooner or later rise to the occasion with a genuinely magnanimous word or act. The moral warts and blemishes he endows his narrators with are themselves engines of suspense, craftily deployed. Nowhere is this more entertaining than in *The Beach*. In his later, more committed years, he tended to look down on this novella. Structurally it may break apart into two only distantly related sections. Every page, however, is needed to establish the Pavese voice in its peculiar rough-hewn delicacies, to prepare the reader for the wonderfully edgy, funny, and pathetic final episodes. The last nine chapters are as resonant as anything he did later.

What to say about *The House on the Hill* in a short space? Too much or too little. It's altogether the least mannered of Pavese's novels, but events that move the action and affect the narrator directly may now require some explanation. The "Republic," of course, was the abortive Republic of Salò under Mussolini and the Germans that opposed the legal government of the King, Marshal Badoglio, and the Allies from September 1943 until April 1945. As a novel almost free of melodramatic devices (such as Poli's TB in *The Devil in the Hills*), the least dependent on overarching symbolism, the most deeply felt in the lengths to which every theme and sequence is carried well beyond craft into the higher reaches of art while the author's feet stay firmly planted on the ground (indeed, they seem to grow into the ground), *The House* is a thoroughly noble book whose nobility is its least obtrusive feature. If ever, the cool breeze from Arcadia that sometimes blows at the height of such overwhelming human breakdowns can be felt in this novel. A sign of its mastery is one's lack of objection to the way he casts off fully realized people like Cate, Dino, Elvira, Fonso, and the others. Much as we like them, we are drawn into the argument until we agree to its final need for a swept stage. The egotism of his procedure, like Dante's, emerges as the ground of his strength.

Among Women Only is nearly, but not quite, the inversion of everything in *The House on the Hill.* Yet the choice of a feminine theater is also his most energetic pledge of faith during the general postwar collapse. The two books have very similar heroines. No doubt Cate of *The House* would turn out to be as complete a cultural philistine as Clelia (Pavese's closest friend for many years was a painter; not all of Clelia's opinions are his own). Whether these are real women, or, as Calvino jocularly complained in a letter to Pavese, a stable of Houyhnhnms, of Paveses got up in wigs, false breasts, and breath reeking of pipe tobacco, the reader must decide for himself.

The Devil in the Hills requires a short excursus about Pavese's classicism as it bears on his Americanism of the Forties:

> Your classical knowledge stems from the Georgics, D'Annunzio, and the hill of Pino. To that background you added America because its language is rustic-universal . . . and because it's the place where town and country meet. Yours is a rustic classicism that could easily become prehistoric ethnology.
>
> (Diary, 1943)

To Pavese, D'Annunzio meant two distinct things: first, the kind of cultural adolescence he wanted to conquer in himself and which, for literary purposes, he did conquer; second, on a more vital level, the elegant and precise sexualizing of nature and country life for which Italian literature is much in his debt. In rural matters D'Annunzio has been the Italians' pocket Freud. And if Pavese had so little to say about Freud, it was because he himself wanted to carry D'Annunzio a stage further into urban rationality. Pavese read the Jungian ethnologists, but Jung himself was not in his line. In *The Devil in the Hills* we watch him weave with D'Annunzio-trained finesse a tent of poetic-symbolical speculations within which his loose summer carnival can take place.

"Where town and country meet . . ." This doesn't seem an exciting prospect until his "Americanized" late adolescents start talking, and then one realizes that whatever he may do with the theme, he is not going to sentimentalize it. By 1948, when the book was planned, Pavese thought he had pretty well worked his way through Marxism proper and was embarked on the most serious utopian ideas for the post-Marxist world. But he was conservative even about Marxism and tried to keep all he had learned. How can town and country meet was now his theme.

In the elegiac potency of the long Greppo sequence—he begins his farewell-to-the-Greppo cadence as early as Chapter 24 of a thirty-chapter novel—one is reminded of how much of his fiction is an elaborate series of leave-takings and strategic withdrawals. A clear autumnal frost seems to mark the whole *oeuvre*. In *The Devil in the Hills*, a book drenched in echoes from literature of every period, I think one can see that Pavese is being elegiac about fiction itself, in a way that strangely combines the clarity of Joyce's *Dubliners* and the all-accepting spirit of *Finnegans Wake*. In other words, he seems aware that fiction has little more to divulge except its own essence, the continuing possibility of writing it well, of broadening and simplifying its effects until it becomes the permanent possession of whoever reads it early enough in life. Fiction, in Pavese's view, is passing out of the realm of revelation into that of initiation—but it must keep at least the full potency of that ideal.

The Devil in the Hills is his answer to the charge of "decadence" that followed closely the charge of Americanism. In Poli he drew what he hoped was a credible young Milanese who would also have a little of Dostoevsky's Myshkin and Mann's Hans Castorp in his nature but whose fate would relieve the author of the suspicion of being an irresponsible "Nietzschean." There is, however, a parallel to Nietzsche in the alpine air of looking down from a height on Europe that Pavese has, of composing something at once prophetic, instructive, entertaining, and devoutly nonviolent at heart. Should we listen? Fifty years after Pavese's death, I don't know how not to.

—R. W. FLINT
First printed 1968, revised 2001

CHRONOLOGY

1908	Cesare Pavese born at his parents' vacation farm in Santo Stefano Belbo near Turin
1914	Death of father. Due to sister's illness, Pavese spends an entire year at Santo Stefano, going to a local school
1918	Mother sells farm at Santo Stefano and buys summer house at Reaglie
1930	Takes degree at University of Turin with a thesis on Walt Whitman. Death of mother
1931	Translation of Sinclair Lewis's *Our Mr. Wrenn*
1932	Translation of Melville's *Moby-Dick* and Sherwood Anderson's *Dark Laughter*
1933	Publishing house of Giulio Einaudi founded. Pavese contributes to Einaudi review, *La Cultura*
1934	Arrest of Leone Ginzburg for clandestine activities in connection with underground movement, *Giustizia e Libertà*. Pavese takes over direction of *La Cultura* for a year. Translates Joyce's *Portrait of the Artist as a Young Man*
1935	Arrested and exiled for ten months to Brancaleone Calabria. Translation of Dos Passos's *42nd Parallel*
1936	Returns to Turin. Tutors and works for Casa Einaudi. *Lavorare stanca* (Hard Labor) (poems)
1938	Translation of Defoe's *Moll Flanders*
1939	Translation of Dickens's *David Copperfield*

1940 Translations of Gertrude Stein's *Three Lives* and
Melville's *Benito Cereno*

1941 *Paesi tuoi* (The Harvesters) (novel)

1942 Translation of Faulkner's *The Hamlet.*
La spiaggia (The Beach) (novella)

1943 Director for a short while of Einaudi office at Rome,
return to Turin, removal to Serralunga

1944 At Serralunga all year

1945 Becomes editorial director at Einaudi in Turin and joins
Communist Party

1946 *Feria d'agosto* (stories and miscellaneous prose
writings)

1947 *Dialoghi con Leucò* (Dialogues with Leucò) (prose
dialogues)
Il compagno (The Companion) (novel)

1949 *Prima che il gallo canti*, collective title for *La casa in
collina* (The House on the Hill) (novel), and *Il carcere*
(The Political Prisoner) (novella).
La bella estate, collective title for *La bella estate*
(novella), *Il diavolo sulle colline* (The Devil in the Hills)
(novel), and *Tra donne sole* (Among Women Only)
(novel)

1950 *La luna e i falò* (The Moon and the Bonfires) (novel).
Strega Prize for fiction.
Suicide, August 26

POSTHUMOUS WORKS

1951 *Verrà la morte e avrà i tuoi occhi* (Death Will Come and
Will Have Your Eyes) (poetry).
La letteratura americana e altri saggi (American
Literature and Other Essays)

1952 *Il mestiere di vivere* (The Burning Brand) (diary
1935–1950)

THE SELECTED WORKS
OF CESARE PAVESE

THE BEACH

1. For some time my friend Doro and I had agreed that I would be his guest. I was very fond of Doro, and when he married and went to Genoa to live, I was half sick over it. When I wrote to refuse his invitation to the wedding, I got a dry and rather haughty note replying that if his money wasn't good for establishing himself in a city that pleased his wife, he didn't know what it was good for. Then, one fine day as I was passing through Genoa I stopped at his house and we made peace. I liked his wife very much, a tomboy type who graciously asked me to call her Clelia and left us alone as much as she should, and when she showed up again in the evening to go out with us, she had become a charming woman whose hand I would have kissed had I been anyone else but myself.

I happened to be in Genoa several times that year and always went to see them. They were rarely alone, and Doro with his free and easy manner seemed entirely at home in his wife's world. Or perhaps I should say that his wife's world had seen their own man in Doro and he had played along, careless and in love. Once in a while he and Clelia would take the train and go off somewhere, a kind of intermittent honeymoon. This went on for about a year. But they had the tact not to say much about it. I, who knew Doro, appreciated this silence, but I was envious too. Doro is one of those people who stop talking when they are happy, and to find him always contented and absorbed in Clelia made me realize how much he was enjoying his new life. It was rather Clelia who told me one day, after she had begun to feel easier with me, when Doro had left us alone: "Oh, yes, he is happy"—with a furtive but irrepressible smile.

They had a small villa on the Genoese Riviera, where they often went on their expeditions. This was the villa where I was supposed to be their guest, but during that first summer my work took me elsewhere, and then I must add that I felt a little embarrassed at the idea of intruding on their privacy. On the other hand, to keep on seeing them as usual, always among their Genoese friends, passing breathlessly from one conversation to another, to have to keep up with them on these hectic evenings was scarcely worth the trouble; going all that way just to get a glimpse of him or exchange a few words with her. My trips became fewer and I began to write letters—formal notes with a little gossip added now and then, to serve as best they could in place of my old companionship with Doro. Sometimes it was Clelia who answered—a quick, open handwriting, cheerful bits of news intelligently chosen from a mass of varied thoughts and events that belonged to another life and another world. But I had the impression that it was in fact Doro in his indifference who left the responsibility to Clelia, which irritated me, so that without even any special pangs of jealousy I neglected them even more. In the space of a year I may have written perhaps three more times, and one winter I had a surprise visit from Doro, who for a whole day didn't leave me alone for one hour, talking about his affairs—he came for this—but also of our good old times together. He seemed more expansive on this occasion, logically enough, considering our long separation. He renewed his invitation to spend my holidays with them at their villa. I told him I would accept on the condition that I live by myself at a hotel and see them only when we were all in the mood for it. "Fine," Doro said, laughing. "Do what you like. We don't want to eat you." Then for almost another year I had no news, and when midsummer came, I happened to be free and without any special plans. So I wrote to see if they wanted to have me. A telegram shot back from Doro: "Stay where you are. Am coming to you."

2. When he was there in front of me, looking so sunburned and summery that I almost didn't recognize him, my anxiety changed to annoyance.

"This is no way to behave," I told him.

He laughed.

"Have you quarreled with Clelia?"

"What do you mean? I have things to do," he said. "Keep me company."

We walked all that morning, discussing even politics. Doro talked strangely. Several times I asked him to keep his voice down: he was behaving aggressively and sardonically, in a way I hadn't seen in him for a long time. I tried to steer the conversation back to his own affairs, hoping to hear something about Clelia, but he immediately began laughing and said: "Hands off. I think we'll let that pass." Then we walked a little more in silence, until I started to feel hungry and asked if he would let me treat him.

"We might as well sit down," he said. "Have you something to do?"

"I was supposed to be going to see you."

"In that case, you can keep me company."

He sat down first. The whites of his eyes as he talked were as restless as a dog's. Now that I saw him closely, I realized he seemed sardonic chiefly because of the contrast between his face and his teeth. But he didn't leave me time to mention it, saying suddenly: "How long it's been."

I wanted to know what he was getting at. I was annoyed. So I lit my pipe to let him see I had plenty of time. Doro pulled out his gold-tipped cigarettes, lit one and blew the smoke in my face. I kept quiet, waiting.

But it was not until it began to get dark that he let himself go. At noon we had lunch in a trattoria, both of us dripping with sweat. Then we continued our walk, and he kept entering various shops to let me know he had errands to take care of. Toward evening we took the old road toward the hill that we had walked together so often in the past, ending up in a little room halfway between a restaurant and a brothel that had seemed the *ne plus ultra* of vice when we were students. We strolled under a fresh summer moon that revived us a little from the day's sultriness.

"Are those relatives of yours still living up here?" I asked Doro.

"Yes, but I'm still not going to look them up. I want to be alone."

From Doro this was a compliment. I decided to make peace with him.

"Forgive me," I said quietly. "Can I come to the sea?"

7

"Whenever you like. But first keep me company. I want to escape to the old places."

We talked about this as we ate. One of the owner's daughters served us, a pale, disheveled girl, maybe the same one who had lured us up so often in the past. But I noticed that Doro paid no attention to her or to her younger sisters, who appeared from time to time to serve couples in the corners. Doro drank; this he did, and with gusto, egging me on to drink, growing enthusiastic as he talked about his hills.

He had been thinking about them for some time, he told me; it had been—how long?—three years since he had seen them; he needed a vacation. I listened and his talk got under my skin. Many years before he married, the two of us on foot and with knapsacks had made a tour of the region, carefree and ready for anything, around the farms, below hillside villas, along streams, sleeping sometimes in haylofts. And the talks we had had—I blushed to remember, they seemed hardly believable. We were at the age when a friend's conversation seems like oneself talking, when one shares a life in common the way I still think, bachelor though I am, some married couples are able to live.

"But why don't you make the trip with Clelia?" I asked innocently.

"Clelia can't, she doesn't want to," Doro stammered, putting down his glass. "I want to do it with you." He said this emphatically, furrowing his brow and laughing as he used to during our wilder discussions.

"In other words, we are boys again," I muttered; but perhaps Doro didn't hear.

One thing I couldn't get straight that evening was whether Clelia was aware of this escapade. From something in Doro's manner I had the idea that she wasn't. But how to get back to a subject my friend had dropped so conclusively? That night I made him sleep on my sofa—he didn't sleep very well—and I wondered why the devil, just to suggest a project as innocent as a trip, he had waited until evening. It bothered me to think that perhaps I was merely a screen for a quarrel between him and Clelia. I have said already that I had always been jealous of Doro.

This time we took an early-morning train and arrived while it was still cool. Deep in a landscape so vast that the trees seemed tiny, Doro's hills rose up; dark, wooded hills that stretched long morning shadows over their yellow lower slopes dotted with farmhouses. Doro—I made up my mind to watch him closely—was taking things very calmly now. I had been able to make him concede that the trip would last no more than three days; I had even persuaded him not to bring his suitcase.

We walked down, looking around us, and while Doro, who knew everybody, entered the station hotel, I stayed in the empty square—so empty I glanced at the clock hoping it might already be noon. But it wasn't yet nine, so I carefully examined the cool cobblestones and the low houses with their green shutters and balconies bright with wisteria and geraniums. The villa where Doro used to live stood outside the village on a spur of a valley open to the plain. We had spent a night there during our famous expedition, in an ancient room with flowered panels over the doors, leaving our beds unmade in the morning and giving ourselves no more trouble than to close the gate. I had not had time to explore the surrounding park. Doro had been born in that house; his people had lived there the year round and died there. Doro sold it when he married. I was curious to see his face in front of that gate.

But when we left the hotel to walk, Doro took a completely different route. We crossed the tracks and went down the bed of the stream. He was obviously looking for a shady place the way one looks for a café in the city. "I thought we would be going to the villa," I muttered. "Isn't that why we came?"

Doro stopped and looked me up and down. "What's got into your head? That I'm returning to my origins? The important things I have in my blood and nobody is going to take them away. I'm here to drink a little of my wine and sing a little—with anybody. I'm going to have a good time, and that's all."

I wanted to say: "It's not true," but kept quiet. I kicked a stone and pulled out my pipe. "You know I can't sing," I muttered between my teeth. Doro shrugged.

The morning and afternoon we spent in peaceful exploration, climbing and descending the hill. Doro seemed to like paths that led nowhere in particular, that petered out by a sultry riverbank, against a hedge, or beside a locked gate. Toward evening when a low sun reddened the fine dust of the plain and the acacias began to shiver in the breeze, we went up a stretch of the main road that crossed the valley. I could feel myself reviving and Doro also became more talkative. He told about a certain peasant notorious in his day for driving his sisters out of the house—he had several—and then making the rounds of the farms where they used to take refuge, working himself into a lather and demanding a supper of reconciliation. "I wonder if he's still alive," Doro said. He lived in a farmhouse down below which one could see, a small dry man who spoke little and was feared by everyone. Still, he had a point; he didn't want to marry because he said he would hate to have to drive his wife away too. One of his sisters actually escaped altogether, to the general satisfaction of the countryside.

"What was he? A representative man?" I asked.

"No, a man born for something quite different, a misfit, one of those people who learn to be sly because they don't care much for their lives."

"Everybody should be sly, at that rate."

"Exactly."

"Did he marry?"

"No, he did not. He hung on to one sister, the strongest, who bore him sons and worked the vineyard. And they did well. Perhaps they are still doing well."

Doro spoke sarcastically, and as he spoke swept the hill with his eyes.

"Did you ever tell Clelia this story?"

Doro didn't answer; he seemed distracted.

"Clelia is the kind to enjoy it," I went on, "especially since it isn't your sister."

But I only got a smile in reply. Doro, when he liked, smiled like a young boy. He stopped, putting his hand on my shoulder. "Did I ever tell you that one year I brought Clelia up here?" he said. Then I stopped, too. I said nothing and waited.

Doro resumed: "I thought I told you. She asked me herself. We came in a car with friends. We were always driving around in those days."

He looked at me, and looked at the hills behind me. He began to walk again and I moved off, too.

"No, you didn't tell me," I said. "When was it?"

"Not long ago. A couple of years ago."

"And she asked you?"

Doro nodded.

"Still, you waited too long," I said. "You should have brought her here earlier. Why did you leave her at the sea this year?"

But Doro went on smiling in that way of his. He looked meaningfully at the steep slope of the highest hill and didn't answer. We climbed in silence as long as there was still light. From high up we stopped to look down on the plain, where we thought we could just make out in the dusty haze the dark crest of the forbidden villa.

When night came, cheerful faces began to appear at the inn. Billiards were played. Doro's contemporaries—some clerks and a bricklayer splashed all over with lime—recognized him and made much of him. Then an old gentleman showed up. He had a gold chain across his vest and said he was very happy to make my acquaintance. While Doro was playing billiards and horsing around, the old man had a coffee with *grappa* and, leaning confidentially across the table, started to tell me Doro's history. He told me about the villa, bought by a certain Matteo when it was only a hay barn, together with all the surrounding land. This Matteo was some mysterious ancestor, but then Doro's grandfather had started to sell off the grounds to build the house, and finally there was this big house with no grounds left; and he, my ancient friend, prophesied to his friend, Doro's father, that one fine day his sons would sell the house too and leave him in the cemetery like a tramp. He spoke a homely Italian, flavored with dialect; I don't know why I got the impression he was a notary. Then bottles appeared and Doro drank on his feet, leaning on his cue, winking here and there. Finally the only people left were the bricklayer—Ginio by name— the two of us, and a big lout in a red necktie whom Doro had not met before. We left the inn to stretch our legs, the moon showing us the way. Under the moon we all looked like the bricklayer; his coat of plaster made him seem dressed for a charade. Doro had begun talking his dialect. I could understand them but not reply easily, which made us all laugh. The moon drenched everything, even the great hills, in a transparent vapor that blotted out every memory of the day. The vapors of wine did the rest. I no longer

11

bothered to wonder what Doro had in mind. I just walked beside him, surprised and happy that we should have recovered the secret of so many years before.

The bricklayer led us to his house. He told us to keep quiet so as not to wake the women and his father. He left us on the threshing floor in front of the big dark openings of the hayloft, in a streak of shadow from a haystack, and showed up again in a few minutes with two black bottles under his arm, laughing like an idiot. Taking the dog with us, we all lurched down the field behind the house and sat on the edge of a ditch. We had to drink from the bottle, something that bothered the young man with the necktie; but Ginio said with a laugh: "All right, you s.o.b.'s . . . drink," and we all drank.

"Here we can sing," Ginio said, clearing his throat. He let go with a solo, his voice filling the valley. The dog couldn't contain himself any longer: other dogs answered from far and near, and ours also kept up his barking. Doro laughed in a large, happy voice, took another swig, and joined in Ginio's song. The two of them together soon silenced the dogs, which was at least enough to make me realize the song was melancholy, with much lingering on the lowest notes and words oddly gentle in that rough dialect. It may well be that the moon and the wine played their part in making them seem so. What I am sure of is the joy, the sudden happiness I felt as I stretched out my hand to touch Doro's shoulder. I felt a catch in my breath, and suddenly loved him because we had come back together after such a long time.

That other character—a certain Biagio, it turned out—every so often yowled a note, a phrase, and then dropped his head and picked up the conversation with me where he had left it. I explained to him that I was not from Genoa and that my work was paid by the state because of my university degree. Then he told me he wanted to get married but wanted to do it up brown, and to do it up brown one needed Doro's luck, who at Genoa had picked up both a wife and an agency. The word "agency" gives me the creeps; I lost patience and said sharply: "But do you know Doro's wife? . . . If you don't, keep your mouth shut."

It's when I talk like that to people that I know I'm over thirty. I thought about this a while, that night, while Doro and the bricklayer started on their army stories. The bottle came around to me, after lime-stained Ginio had wiped the mouth with the palm of his hand, and I took a long pull, the better to relieve in wine the feelings I couldn't relieve in song.

"Yes, sir, excuse me," Ginio said as he took the bottle back, "but if you come back next year I'll be married and we'll crack one in my house."

"Do you always let your father order you around?" Doro said.

"It's not me who lets, it's he who orders."

"He's been ordering you around for thirty years now. Hasn't he broken his neck yet?"

"It would be easier for you to break his," said the type with the necktie, laughing nervously.

"And what does he say about Orsolina? Will he let you marry her?"

"I don't know yet," Ginio said, drawing back from the ditch and squirming on the ground like an eel. "If he doesn't, so much the better," he grumbled, two yards away. That little man as white as a baker, who did monkeyshines and used the familiar *tu* with Doro —I remember him every time I see the moon. Later I made Clelia laugh heartily when I described him. She laughed in that charming way of hers and said: "What a boy Doro is! He will never change."

But I didn't tell Clelia what happened afterward. Ginio and Doro started another song and this time we all bawled it out. It ended with a furious voice from the farmhouse yelling to shut up. In the sudden quiet Biagio shouted back some insolence and took the song up again defiantly. Doro began again too, when Ginio jumped to his feet. "No," he stammered, "he recognized me. It's my father." But Biagio didn't give a damn. Ginio and Doro had to jump him to stop his mouth. We were still swaying and sliding around on the same spot of grass when Doro had an idea. "The Murette sisters," he said to Ginio. "We can't sing here, but they used to sing once. Let's go see Rosa." And he set off right away, while the Biagio character grabbed my arm and whispered in a panic: "Oh, my God. That's where the *brigadiere* lives." The situation looked bad, but I caught up with Doro and pulled him back. "Don't mix wine and women, Doro," I shouted. "Remember we're supposed to be gentlemen."

13

But Ginio came up in a determined manner, admitted that the three girls must have put on weight, still, we weren't going for that but only to sing a little, and suppose they *are* fat, what the hell? a woman should be well-rounded. He yanked and hauled at Doro, saying: "Rosa will remember, you'll see." We were on the main road under the moon, all milling excitedly around Doro, who was strangely undecided.

Rosa won, because Biagio said nastily: "Can't you see they won't want you because you're filthy with lime?", at which point he got a punch in the face that sent him stumbling to the ground three yards away. He then disappeared as if by magic and we heard him calling out in the silence of the moon: "Thanks, engineer. Ginio's father will hear about this."

Doro and Ginio had already started up again, and I with them. I couldn't make up my mind what to say. If I had second thoughts, it was only that this dirty bricklayer would shame me in front of Doro in the intensity of their common memories, which they ran through excitedly as they approached the village. They talked at random, and that rough dialect was enough to restore to Doro the true flavor of his life, of the wine, flesh, and joy in which he had been born. I felt cut off, helpless. I took Doro's arm and joined them, grumbling. After all, I had drunk the same wine.

What we did under those windows was rash. I realized that Biagio must have hid himself in some corner of the little square and said so to Doro, who ignored it. Laughing and grinning like an idiot, Ginio led off by knocking at the worm-eaten door, under the moon. We were talking in stage whispers, amused and half cocked. But nobody answered; the windows stayed shut. Then Doro began to cough; then Ginio collected pebbles and began throwing them up; then we argued because I said he was going to crack the windows; then Doro finally let himself go with a terrible howl, bestial, like country drunks at the end of a song. All the silences of the moon seemed to shudder. Various distant dogs from who knows what courtyards joined in hideously.

Doors slammed and shutters creaked. Ginio started singing, something like the earlier song, but Doro's voice soon joined in and blanketed his. Someone was shouting from the other side of the square; a light glimmered at a window. A chorus of curses and threats had just begun when the bricklayer threw himself against the door, raining kicks and thumps with his fists. Doro grabbed my shoulders and pulled me into the belt of shadow from a nearby house.

"Let's see if they douse him with a washbasin," he whispered hoarsely, laughing. "I want to see him drenched like a goose."

A dog howled from very close by. I began to feel ashamed. Then we were silent. Even Ginio, who was holding one bare foot in his hands and hopping around on the cobblestones. When we shut up, so did the voices from the windows. The light disappeared. Only the intermittent barking kept on. It was then we heard a shutter up above being carefully creaked open.

Ginio squatted in the shadow between us. "They've opened," he breathed in my face. I pushed him away, remembering he was dusted with lime. "Go on, introduce yourself," Doro told him dryly. Ginio shouted from the darkness, peering up. I felt his cold, rough neck under my hand. "Let's sing," he said to Doro. Doro ignored him and gave a low whistle as if he were calling a dog. They were chattering among themselves up there.

"Come on," said Doro, "introduce yourself," and shoved him out into the moonlight.

Ginio, lurching into the light, kept laughing and raised his arm as if to ward off some missile. All was quiet at the window. His trousers began falling, tangled a foot, and nearly toppled him. He stumbled and sat down.

"Rosina, O Rosina." He stretched his mouth but choked back his voice. "Do you know who it is?"

A low laugh came from topside, then suddenly stopped.

Ginio went back to playing the eel, this time on hard ground. Pushing with his hands, he wriggled back toward the edge of the shadow. Doro was now standing, ready to give him a kick. But Ginio jumped out quickly, shouting meantime: "It's Doro, Doro of the Ca Rosse, come back from Genoa to see you all." He seemed out of his mind.

There was a movement above and a creak of lighted windows being opened. Then a heavy thump from behind the door, swinging it out, splitting the moonlight that soaked it. Ginio, nailed to the spot in the middle of his dance, was two steps from the doorway. A thickset man in shirtsleeves had appeared.

15

Just at that moment a harsh, insolent voice sounded from the bottom of the square—the voice of that Biagio. "Marina, don't open; they're drunk as beasts." Exclamations and scufflings came from the window. I could vaguely see waving arms.

But already the man and Ginio had collided on the stairs and were crashing around, panting like mad dogs. The man had black trousers with red piping. Doro, who was gripping my shoulder, let go suddenly and joined the fight. He kicked out at random, trying to find an opening, circling around. Then he quit and stood under the window. "Are you Rosina or Marina?" he said, looking up. No reply. "Are you Rosina or Marina?" he yelled, his foot on the doorstep.

A crash followed; something had fallen, a vase of flowers as we discovered later. Doro jumped back, still looking up to where at least two women were fussing around. "We didn't do it on purpose," said a sharp-voiced woman in exasperation. "Did we hurt you?"

"Who is speaking?" Doro shouted.

"I'm Marina," a softer, rather caressing voice answered. "Are you hurt?"

At that point I left the shadow, too, to speak my piece. Ginio and that other man had broken apart and were circling each other, grunting and fanning the air. But suddenly the carabiniere jumped over to the door, pulled Doro away, and shoved him back. The women upstairs squealed.

All around the square, windows opened again; there was a cross fire of hard, angry voices. The man had shut the door and one could hear him slamming down the wooden bar behind. A rosary of insults and complaints cascaded around us, dominated by the sharp voice of the first of the two women. I heard—and this is what finally sobered me—Doro's name running from window to window. Ginio set up a new storm of shouting and kicking the door. From windows around the square, apples and other hard projectiles—peach stones perhaps—began to rain down, and then, when Doro was seizing hold of Ginio and pulling him away, a flash from the window and a great explosion that silenced everybody.

THE BEACH

$3.$ The first evening, walking along the seashore with Clelia, I told her what I could about Doro's exploit, which wasn't much. Still, the extravagance of the thing brought a grudging smile. "What egotists," she said. "And me bored down here. Why didn't you take me with you?"

Seeing us arrive the afternoon after our escapade, Clelia showed no sign of surprise. I had not seen her for more than two years. We met her on the stairs of the villa, she in her shorts, sunburned and chestnut-haired. She held out her hand to me with a confident smile, her eyes under the tan showing brighter and harder than when I last saw her. Right away she began to discuss what we were going to do the next day. Just to please me, she postponed her descent to the beach. I jokingly pointed out how sleepy Doro was and left them alone to make their explanations. That first evening I went looking for a room and found it in a secluded back alley, with a window that gave on a big, twisted olive tree unaccountably growing up from among the cobbles. Many times afterward, coming home alone, I found myself contemplating that tree, which is perhaps what I remember best from the whole summer. Seen from below, it was knotty and bare, but made a solid, silvery mass of dry, paperlike leaves. It gave me the sensation of being in the country, an unknown country; often I sniffed to see if perhaps it might smell of salt. It has always seemed peculiar to me that on the outer rim of the coast, between land and ocean, flowers and trees should grow and good fresh water should run.

A steep, angular stone stairway led up the outside of the house to my room. Underneath, on the ground floor, every so often, while I was washing or shaving, an uproar of discordant voices broke out, one of them a woman's. I couldn't quite make out if they were cheerful or angry. I looked through the window grating on my way down, but it was too dark by then to see in. Only when I was a good distance away did one of the voices gain the upper hand, a fresh, strong voice I couldn't quite identify but which I'd heard already. I was about to go back and clear up the mystery when it occurred to me that, after all, we were neighbors and one always meets one's neighbors too soon in any case.

"Doro is in the woods," Clelia said that evening as we walked along the beach. "He's painting the sea." She turned as she walked, widening her eyes a little. "The sea is worth it. You watch it too."

We looked at the sea, and then I told her I couldn't understand why she was bored. Clelia said, laughing: "Tell me again about that little man under the moon. What was it he shouted? I was also looking at the moon the other night."

"Probably he was making faces. Just four drunks weren't enough to make the woman laugh."

"Were you drunk?"

"Evidently."

"What boys!" Clelia said.

Ginio's night became a joke between the two of us; all I had to do was allude to the little white man and his monkeyshines for Clelia to brighten up and laugh. But when that night I told her that Ginio was not a little bald old man but a contemporary of Doro's, she looked alarmed. "Why didn't you tell me? Now you've spoiled everything. Was he a peasant?"

"A bricklayer's assistant, to be precise."

Clelia sighed. "After all," I told her, "you had seen that place, too. You can picture it. If Doro had been born two doors up, you might be Ginio's wife right now."

"What a horrible idea!" Clelia said, smiling.

That night, after we had dined on the balcony, while Doro was stretched in the armchair smoking and silent and Clelia had gone to dress for the evening, my mind kept going over our previous conversation. A certain Guido had been mentioned, a forty-year-old colleague of Doro's and a bachelor, whom I'd already met at Genoa and found again on the beach in Clelia's circle. He was one of her friends and it came out that he had been with them on that auto trip when they had passed through Doro's village. Clelia, without being asked, and stirred by a fit of malice, told the whole story of that expedition, speaking with the air of answering a question I hadn't asked. They were coming home from some trip to the mountains; the friend Guido was at the wheel and Doro had remarked: "Did you know that I was born in those hills thirty years ago?" Then all of them, Clelia most of all, had pestered Guido until he agreed to take them up there. It had been a crazy business; they had to warn the following car of the delay and it never did keep up with them. They waited for it more than an hour at the crossroads. Night was falling when it finally caught up; having eaten as best they could in the village, they had to wind through mysterious little roads not on the map and cross so many hills it was nearly dawn when the cars rejoined on the Genoa road. Doro sat next to Guido to point out the places, and nobody managed to sleep. A real madness.

Now that Clelia had left, I asked Doro if he had made peace again. As I spoke, I thought to myself: "What they need is a son," but I had never brought the subject up with Doro, not even as a joke. And Doro said: "You can only make peace if you've made war. What kind of war have you ever seen me make?" At first I kept still. For all our openness, Clelia had never been a subject to discuss. I was about to say that one could, for instance, make war by catching a train and escaping, but I hesitated, and just then Clelia called me.

"What's Doro's mood?" she asked through the closed door.

"Fine," I said.

"Sure?"

Clelia came to the door, still fixing her hair. She looked for me in the shadow where I was waiting for her.

"What, you're friends and you don't know that when Doro doesn't rise when I tease him it means he's bored, fed up?"

Then I began on her. "Haven't you two made up yet?"

Clelia drew back to the bedroom and fell silent. Then she reappeared quickly, saying: "Why don't you turn on the light?" She took my arm and we crossed the room together in shadow. As we were about to emerge on the lighted landing, she gripped my arm and whispered: "I'm desperate. I wish Doro could be with you a lot because you're friends. I know you're good for him and distract him . . ."

I tried to stop and say something.

". . . No, we haven't quarreled," Clelia added quickly. "He isn't even jealous. He doesn't even dislike me. It's only that he's become someone else. We can't make peace because we haven't fought. Do you understand? But don't say anything."

That night, in Guido's car as usual, we arrived at a spot high over the sea at the end of a winding road that swarmed with bathers. There was a small orchestra and a few people dancing. But

the charm of the place lay in the small tables with shaded lamps
scattered around in niches of the rock, looking sheerly down on the
water. Flowers and aromatic plants added their scent to a breeze
off the sea. Way below, along the shore, one could make out a tiny
rim of lights.

I did my best to be alone with Clelia, but without success. First
it was Doro, then Guido, then one of her female friends, who
showed up one by one but kept changing partners so often that
no real conversation was possible. Clelia was always busy. Finally
I caught her and said: "I dance, too, you know," to her mild surprise, and took her off under the pines away from the floor. "Let's
sit down," I said, "and you can tell me the whole story."

I tried to get her to explain why she didn't have it out with
Doro. One has to bring things to a head, I told her, the way one
shakes a watch to get it started again. I refused to believe that a
woman like her couldn't with a simple tone of her voice bring to
his senses a man who, after all, was only behaving like a boy.

"But Doro *is* open with me," Clelia said. "He even told me
about the serenade to Rosina. Was it fun?"

I think I blushed, but more from irritation than embarrassment.

"And I am open, too," Clelia continued, smiling. She sounded
sulky. "Our friend Guido tells me, in fact, that my fault is to be
open with everybody; I never give anyone the illusion of having a
private secret with him alone. Sweeties! But that's how I'm made.
It's why I fell for Doro . . ."

Here she stopped and gave me a swift glance. "Do you find me
improper?" I said nothing. I was bothered. Clelia fell silent, then
resumed: "You see that I am right. But I *am* improper . . . like Doro.
That's why we are fond of each other."

"Well then, peace . . . What's all the fuss about?"

Clelia groaned in that childish way of hers.

"See, you're like all the others. But don't you understand that
we can't quarrel? We love each other. If I could hate him the way
I hate myself, then of course I would abuse him. But neither of us
deserves it. See?"

"No."

Clelia fell silent again. We listened to the shuffling on the dance
floor, the orchestra stopping and someone starting to sing.

"What advice did your Guido give you?" I asked in the same tone as before.

Clelia shrugged her shoulders. "Selfish advice. He's making love to me."

"For instance? To have a secret from Doro?"

"To make him jealous," Clelia said, embarrassed. "That fool. He doesn't realize that Doro would leave me alone and suffer in silence."

At this point, one of Clelia's female friends arrived, looking for her, calling her and laughing. I stayed by myself on the stone bench. I was finding my usual perverse pleasure in keeping apart, knowing that a few steps away in the light someone else was moving around, laughing and dancing. Nor did I lack for something to reflect upon. I lit my pipe and smoked it through. Then I got up and circled among the tables until I met Doro. "Let's have a drink at the bar," I suggested.

"Just to have things straight," I began when we were alone. "May I tell your wife that to avoid a beating we had to run off the next morning?"

We stood there laughing, and Doro answered with the shadow of a snicker. "Did she ask you that?"

"No, I'm asking you."

"Go ahead. Tell her anything you like."

"But aren't you fighting?"

Doro raised his glass and stared at me thoughtfully. "No," he said quietly.

"Well, why is it then that every so often Clelia looks at you with that scared, doglike expression? She has the look of a woman who's been beaten up. Have you been beating her?"

Just then Clelia's voice reached us. She was walking across the dance floor with a man. "Drunks . . ." We saw her waving at us. Doro followed her with his eyes, vaguely nodding until she was hidden again by her partner's back.

"As you can see for yourself, she's happy," he said quietly. "Why should I beat her? We get on better than a lot of people. She's never tried to anger me. We even agree about amusements, which is the hardest thing."

"I know you get on well." I stopped short.

Doro said nothing. He looked at his glass with a depressed air, lowered his head, held the glass away, then emptied it quickly, half turning around as if to clear his throat.

"The trouble is," he said brusquely, getting up, "we trust each other too much. One of us says certain things just to make the other happy."

Clelia and Guido were approaching us among the tables.

"Does that apply to me?" I asked.

"To you, too," Doro muttered.

4. When I came to the sea, I was afraid I might have to spend whole days with hordes of strangers, shaking hands and passing compliments and making conversation—a regular labor of Sisyphus. Instead, except for our inevitable evenings with friends, Clelia and Doro lived reasonably calm lives. Every evening I had dinner with them at the villa, and their friends didn't arrive until after dark. Our little trio was gay enough. However much the three of us had to disguise our worries, we discussed many things quite freely and openly.

I soon began to have some little adventures of my own to tell— gossip of the trattoria where I had lunch, peculiar episodes and stranger conjectures that a sloppy seaside existence seems to encourage. That voice I had heard ringing through the window bars the first evening I went upstairs—the next morning I made its owner's acquaintance. A sunburned young man passed me on the beach, gave me a polite wave of the hand, and passed on. I recognized him as soon as he had passed. None other than one of my students of the year before. One fine day he had passed up his usual lesson in my study and never showed up again. That very morning I was baking in the sun when a black and vigorous body plumped down on the sand next to me; the same boy again. He showed his teeth in a smile and asked if I were on vacation. I answered without raising my head: I happened to be a good distance from my friends' umbrella and had hoped to be alone. He explained to me, quite simply, that he had come by mere chance and liked it here. He didn't mention the lesson business. I was irritated enough to tell him that the evening before I had heard his family quarreling. He smiled again and said it was impossible because his family wasn't there. But he admitted he was living in a street with an olive tree. As he got up to go, he spoke of friends who were waiting for him. That evening I looked into the ground floor—a pungent smell of frying—and saw children, a woman with her head wrapped in a handkerchief, an unmade bed and a stove. When they noticed me, I asked about him, and the woman—my landlady—came to the door and, jabbering away, thanked heaven I knew her tenant because she rued the day she had taken him in and wanted to write to his family—such nice people, who had sent their son to the beach to give him a good time—and only the evening before he had brought a woman into his room. "There are some things . . ." she said. "He's not eighteen yet."

I told Clelia and Doro this incident and described the visit Berti paid me the morning after, when he met me at the top of the stairs, held out his hand, and said: "Seeing that now I know where you live, it's better to be friends."

"That fellow will be asking for your room next, you'll see," Doro said.

Encouraged by Clelia's attention, I went on. I explained that Berti's brass was merely timidity become aggressive in self-defense. I said that the year before, before disappearing and probably squandering the money he was supposed to spend in lessons, that boy showed signs of being in awe of me and gave an embarrassed nod when he saw me. What happens to everyone had happened to him; the truth was masquerading as its opposite. Like those sensitive spirits who pretend to be tough. I envied him, I said, because, being still a boy, he could still delude himself about his real nature.

"I think," said Clelia, "that I ought to be a closed, diffident, perverse character myself."

Doro smiled to himself. "Doro doesn't believe it," I said, "but he's the same; when he plays gruff is when he wants to cry."

The maid, who was changing the plates, stopped to listen, blushed, and hurried off. I went on. "He's been like that since he was a boy. I remember him. He was one of those people who are offended if you ask them how they feel."

23

"If all this were true, how easy it would be to understand people," Clelia said.

These conversations stopped after dinner when the others arrived. Guido came as usual—if he left his car, it was only to play cards; some older women, some girls, an occasional husband—in other words, the Genoese circle. It was no surprise to me that more than three people make a crowd, that nothing more could be said that was worth the effort. I almost preferred the nights we took the car and drove along the coast looking for fresh air. Sometimes, on some belvedere, when the others were dancing, I could get in a few words with Doro or Clelia. Or exchange some serious nonsense with one of the older women. Then all I needed to feel alive again was a glass of wine or a breeze off the sea.

On the beach in the daytime it was another story. People talk with an odd caution when they are half naked; words no longer sound the same. When they stop talking, the very silence seems to contain ambiguities. Clelia, stretched on a rock, had an ecstatic way of enjoying the sun. Offering herself to the sky, she seemed to sink into the rock, answering with faint murmurs, a sigh, a twitch of her knee or elbow, whatever might be said to her by the nearest person. I soon realized that Clelia really didn't hear anything when she was stretched out like that. Doro understood and never spoke to her at all. He sat on his towel, hugging his knees, gloomy and restless. He never sprawled like Clelia. If he ever tried, before long he was twisting around, turning on his stomach or sitting up again.

But we were never alone. The whole beach swarmed and babbled. So Clelia preferred the rocks to the common sand, the hard and slippery stone. Now and then she would get up, shake out her hair, dazed and laughing, would ask us what we had been talking about, would look around to see who was there. Someone might be leaving the water, someone else trying it with his toes. Guido in his wrapper of white toweling was always turning up with new acquaintances and dropping them at the foot of the beach umbrella. And then he would climb to the rock, tease Clelia, and never go in swimming.

The best time was the afternoon or sunset when the warmth or color of the sea persuaded the most reluctant to take a dip or walk along the beach. Then we were almost alone, or there was just Guido talking cheerfully. Doro, who found a dark distraction in his painting, sometimes planted his easel on the rock and drew boats, umbrellas, streaks of color, happy enough to watch us from above and overhear our gossip. Once in a while, one of the group would appear in a boat, carefully beach it, and call out to us. In the silences that followed, we would listen to the slapping of the waves among the stones.

Friend Guido was always saying that this wave rustle was Clelia's vice, her secret, her unfaithfulness to all of us.

"I don't think so," Clelia said. "I listen to it when I'm naked and stretched out. I don't care who sees us."

"Who knows?" Guido said. "Who knows what conversations a woman like that carries on with the waves? I can imagine what you say, you and the sea, when you're in each other's arms."

Doro's seascapes—he finished two in those few days—were done in pale, fuzzy colors, almost as though the very violence of the sun and air, dazzling and deafening, had muted his strokes. Someone had climbed up behind Doro, followed his hand, and given him advice. He didn't reply. Once he told me that one amuses oneself the best one can. I tried to tell him that he wasn't painting from life because the sea was a good deal more beautiful than his pictures; it was enough just to look at it. In his place and with the talent he had, I would have done portraits; it's satisfying to guess at people's natures. Doro laughed and said that when the season was over he would close his paintbox and think no more about it.

We were joking about this one evening and strolling with Doro to a café for apéritifs when friend Guido observed in that crafty tone of his that nobody would have said that under the hard, dynamic shell of a man of the world there slumbered in Doro the soul of an artist. "Slumbers is right," Doro answered, careless and happy. "What doesn't slumber under the shells of us all? One just needs courage to uncover it and be oneself. Or at least to discuss it. There isn't enough discussion in the world."

"Out with it," I told him. "What have you discovered?"

"I've discovered nothing. But do you remember how much we talked when we were boys? We talked just for the fun of it. We knew very well it was only talk, but still we enjoyed it."

"Doro, Doro," I said. "You're getting old. You should leave these things to those children you don't have."

Then Guido burst out laughing, a pleasant laugh that screwed up his eyes. He put his hand on Doro's shoulder and held himself up, laughing. Incredulously, we looked at the half-bald head and hard eyes of a handsome man on vacation.

"Something is slumbering in Guido, too," Doro said. "Sometimes he laughs like a half-wit."

Later I noticed that Guido laughed this way only among men.

That evening, after we had left Doro and Clelia at the gate of their villa, we dropped the car at the hotel and took a short walk together. Following the shore, we talked about our friends, almost against our wills. Guido explained Doro's trip and his unexpected return, making fun of the restless artist. Curious how Doro had succeeded in convincing everyone of the seriousness of his game. Our little circle was even talking about encouraging him to show his work and make of his art something one might call a profession. "But of course," Clelia chimed in later, "that's what I always tell him myself."

"Bunk!" Guido said that evening.

"But Doro is fooling," I said.

Guido shut up for a while—he was wearing sandals and we shuffled along like a couple of monks. Then he stopped and declared sharply: "I know those two. I know what they are doing and what they want. But I don't know why Doro paints pictures."

"What's the harm in it? It distracts him."

What was wrong was that like all artists Doro was not satisfying his wife. "Meaning?" It meant that all this nervous brainwork was weakening his potency, the reason why all painters suffer periods of tremendous depression.

"Not sculptors?"

"All of them," Guido grumbled, "all those idiots who force their brains and don't know when to stop."

We were standing in front of the hotel. I asked him what kind of life, then, ought one to lead. "A healthy life," he said. "Work but not slavery. Have a good time, eat and talk. Above all, have a good time."

He stood in front of me, hands behind his back, swaying from side to side. His shirt, open and pulled back, gave him the air of a wise adolescent who knows the whole story, of a forty-year-old who has stayed adolescent out of sheer laziness. "You've got to understand life," he added, narrowing his eyes with an uneasy expression, "understand it when you're young."

5. Clelia had told me that every morning Doro escaped and went swimming in the milky sea of dawn. That was why he lazed behind his easel until noon. Sometimes she went along too, she said, but not tomorrow because tonight she was too sleepy. I promised Doro to keep him company and on that particular night I happened not to sleep. I got up with the first light and walked the cool and empty streets down to the still damp beach. I had to stop and watch the golden sunlight picking out and setting on fire the little trees along the mountain ridge, but as soon as I had sat down I saw a head coming ashore in the still water and then there emerged the dark, dripping figure of my young friend, the boy.

Naturally he came up to speak to me, rubbing his short, lean body dry with a towel. I looked out to sea, trying to discover Doro.

"How is it you're alone?" I asked.

He didn't reply—he was absorbed in drying off. When he finished, he sat down a short distance away, with his back to the water. I swung around sideways to watch the mountain burning with gold. Berti poked around with his fingertips in a little bundle, took out one cigarette, and lit it. Then he excused himself for having only one.

I said I was amazed to find him up so early. Berti gestured vaguely and asked me if I were waiting for somebody. I told him that by the sea one didn't wait for people. Then Berti slid down on his stomach, propped himself on his elbows, and looked at me while he smoked.

He told me he was disgusted with the carnival air the beach took on in the sun—all those babies, umbrellas, nurses, families. For his part, he would prohibit it. So I asked him why he came to the sea; he could stay in the city, where there weren't any umbrellas.

"The sun will come up soon," he said, twisting to look at the mountain.

We were quiet for a while in the almost complete silence.

"Are you staying long?" he asked me. I told him I didn't know, and looked out to sea again. A black spot began to appear. Berti also looked out and said: "It's your friend. He was on the buoy when I first came down. How well he swims! Do you swim?"

After a short while he threw away his cigarette and got up. "Will you be at home today?" he said. "I want to talk to you."

"You can just as well talk here," I said, raising my eyes.

"But you're expecting people."

I told him not to play the fool. What was the trouble, lessons?

Then Berti sat up and contemplated his knees. He began to talk like someone being cross-examined, stumbling every so often. The gist was that he was bored; he had no company and would be very, very happy to talk to me, to read some book together—no, not lessons—but just to read the way I sometimes had at school, explaining and discussing, telling them a lot of things he knew he didn't know.

I squinted at him coolly but interested. Berti was one of those boys who go to school because they are sent, who watch your mouth as you talk and pop their eyes at you vacantly. Now, bronzed and naked, he clasped his knees and smiled restlessly. Who knows, it occurred to me, perhaps these types are the most wide awake.

By this time Doro's head had almost reached the shore. Berti got up suddenly and said: "Goodbye." Other bathers were beginning to circulate among the bathhouses and I had the impression that Berti was chasing a skirt that had disappeared behind these cabins. But here was Doro coming out of the water, head down as if climbing a slope, smooth and dripping, his head glistening under the cap that made him look quite professional. He stopped and stood swaying in front of me, panting hard. His lungs were still heaving under his ribs from the swimming. Irresistibly I thought of Guido, and our conversation of the previous night. I must have smiled vaguely because Doro, pulling off his cap, said: "What's up?"

"Nothing," I replied. "I was thinking of that fine fellow Guido who is getting fat. Great thing not to be married!"

"If he took an hour's swim every morning, he'd become a new man," Doro said and fell to his knees on the sand.

At noon in the trattoria Berti showed up again looking for me. He paused among the tables with his jacket on his shoulders over a dark blue sports shirt. I beckoned him over. Grabbing a chair from one of the tables, he came over, but my look must have embarrassed him because he stopped, his jacket slipped to the floor, he reached for it and dropped the chair. I told him to sit down.

This time he offered me a cigarette and began immediately to talk. I lit my pipe without answering. I let him say whatever he wanted. He told me that for family reasons he had had to stop studying but had not yet found a job—and now that he'd stopped studying and seeing me he understood that studying, not like a schoolboy but on his own, was a smart thing to do. He said he envied me and had known for some time that I wasn't merely a teacher but also a good man. He had many things to discuss with me.

"For instance?" I said.

For instance, he replied, why didn't they talk things over with the teacher at school and perhaps even take walks with him? Was it really necessary to waste one's time because a few dumb clucks keep holding up the class?

"In fact, you wanted so much to study that school wasn't enough for you and you took lessons."

Berti smiled and said that was another matter.

"And I'm sorry to hear," I went on, "that your parents are not millionaires. Why do you make them spend money on private lessons?"

He smiled again, in a way that had something feminine about it and also contemptuous. It's women who answer like that. Some woman had taught him the trick, I thought.

Berti kept me company part of the way back—I was going on an expedition with Clelia's friends that day—and told me again that he understood very well that I had come to the sea for a rest and that he had no intention of forcing me to give him lessons, but at least he hoped I might tolerate his company and might exchange a few words with him sometime on the beach. This time I was the one to give him a womanly smirk. Leaving him in the middle of the road, I said: "By all means, if you are really alone."

That day's trip—we were all packed into Guido's car—had a sorry outcome. One of the women, a certain Mara, a relative of Guido's, slipped on a rock while she was gathering blackberries, and broke a collarbone. We had climbed along our usual mountain road beyond the night spot, beyond the last little scattered houses, among pines and red cliffs, to the level place where I had seen the sun breaking out the morning before. When we carried the poor girl to the road, it was plain that we couldn't all get in the car. A very worried Guido wanted to stretch the groaning Mara out on the cushions. There was still room for Clelia and two other women, who grinned back at Doro and me; so it ended with the two of us walking back on foot. A couple of hundred yards along, we saw the second of the two girls sitting on a heap of gravel.

Doro wound up our conversation in a hurry: "This is what it means to live in a crowd of women."

They had obliged the other girl to get out to make more room for Mara, who might really have broken her back for the fuss she made. It fell to her because she was the only girl in the bunch. "We others aren't women," she grumbled. "Mara has had her fun for this year. They are taking her back to Genoa." She gave us sidelong looks as she walked. Doro smiled her a welcoming smile. They talked about Mara, about how her husband was going to take it, a man so energetic that he left his office at Sestri only on Sundays. "He'll be happy his wife had an accident," Doro said. "Finally he'll get to spend a summer with her."

The girl—her name was Ginetta—laughed spitefully. "Do you think so?" she said, fixing us with her gray eyes. "I know that men like to have their wives a good way off. They're egotists."

Doro laughed. "What *wisdom*, Ginetta! I'll bet that right now Mara is thinking of something else." Then he looked at me. "It takes boys or bachelors to make remarks like that."

"I'm not saying anything," I muttered.

That Ginetta was a handsome girl. She walked vigorously and had a habit of tossing back her hair like a mane. She was about to say something when Doro cut her short.

"Is Umberto coming this year?"

"Bachelors are hypocrites," she replied.

"Oh, I don't know," he said.

"You're getting the best of both worlds, Ginetta, marrying a bachelor who is already leaving you alone. What will he do to you next?"

Half serious, Ginetta gazed in front of her and tossed her head.

"It's quite usual for a husband to have been a bachelor first," I observed quietly. "One has to begin somewhere."

But Ginetta was discussing Umberto. She told us that he wrote that at night the hyenas howled like babies who refuse to go off to sleep. Darling Ginetta, he told her, if our children make so much noise I'll go sleep in a hotel. Then he told her that the chief difference between the desert and civilization was that in the first you couldn't shut your eyes because of the noise.

"What an idiot!" Ginetta laughed. "We're always joking."

Ginetta's chatter and the way the road twisted among the pines, allowing frequent glimpses of the sea, made me cheerful and light-headed. It seemed as if the sea, way off below, were drawing us on. Even Doro swung along more freely. Evening came almost at once.

"Poor Mara," Ginetta said. "When will she be able to swim?"

That evening we found the umbrella deserted and the beach already empty. We went into the water, Ginetta and I, and swam side by side as if racing, not daring to part company in the silence of the empty sea. We returned without a word, and I could see between my strokes the pine-covered hillside we had descended a short while before. We reached shallow water; Ginetta emerged gleaming like a fish and went to her bathhouse. Doro threw away the cigarette he had been smoking while he waited.

We walked together up to the villa. Clelia had already gone. At dinner that evening I learned that Mara had returned to Sestri with Guido and that we would be alone without a car for several days. The news pleased me, because I loved to spend the nights in peaceful conversation.

"That fool," Clelia said. "She might have waited for the end of the season before breaking her collarbone."

"Ginetta says that we men are the egotists," Doro observed.

"Do you like Ginetta?" Clelia asked me.

"She's a very healthy girl," I said. "Why? Is there something else?"

"Oh, nothing. Doro maintains that I looked like her when I was a girl."

I ventured the opinion that all girls look alike. One had to see them as women to tell them apart.

Clelia shrugged her shoulders. "I wonder how you judge me?" she murmured.

"I lack the necessary evidence," I said. "Only Doro could judge you properly."

Doro surprised us by joking about it, saying that a man in love has lost the use of his eyes, that his judgment doesn't count. The way he talked, he sounded like Guido. I stared at him in amazement. The best of it was that Clelia ignored us and merely shrugged her shoulders again, grumbling that we were all the same.

"What's the matter?" I said with a laugh.

Nothing was the matter, and Clelia began to complain in a small voice that it was like listening to some old fossil talking, that just to think of her girlhood, her childhood rather, when she was a schoolgirl and went to her first dance and put on her first long stockings, made her shudder. Doro listened abstractedly, barely smiling. "I was an overanxious child," Clelia said gloomily. "I kept thinking that if tomorrow Papa should suddenly lose his money and if the kitchen should burn down, we wouldn't have enough to eat. I made a little cache of nuts and dried figs in the garden and waited for disaster so that I could offer Papa my provisions. I would have said to Papa and Mama: 'Don't despair. Clelia thinks of everything. You've punished her, but now forgive her and never do it again.' What a fool I was!"

"We are all fools at that age," I said.

"I believed everything they told me. I didn't dare poke my face between the bars of the gate for fear that someone passing might put my eyes out. Still, from the gate you could even see the water; I had no other distractions because they always kept me shut up. I used to stand on the garden bench and listen to the passers-by, listen to the noises. Whenever a siren sounded in the harbor, I was happy."

"Why are you telling us these things?" Doro said. "To bear someone else's childhood memories, one must be in love with her."

"But he does love me," Clelia said.

We talked a long time that night and then went to see the ocean under the stars. The night was so clear that one could make out a thin foam breaking along the promenade. I said that I really didn't believe in all that water and that the sea made me feel as if I were living under a glass bell. I described my olive tree as some kind of lunar vegetation, even when there wasn't a moon. Clelia, turning between me and Doro, exclaimed: "It sounds lovely! Let's go see it."

But crossing the square, we met some acquaintances to whom we had to tell the story of Mara. It wasn't long before Clelia had forgotten the olive tree, and we all went back to the villa to play cards. Slightly annoyed, I left them, saying I was tired.

At the other side of the square I met Berti, who wasn't quick enough to get back into the shadow out of sight. I walked on. Berti spoke first.

"What's all this spying?" I said finally.

An hour before, I'd noticed him below the villa. He had been hanging around on the promenade a short distance away. His white jacket showed up too well against the sports shirt. He told me—bold in the darkness—that he'd heard there had been an accident in the pine woods and wanted to find out if it were true.

6. "As you see, I'm alive," I said. "Did you really need to shadow me all evening?"

He asked if I were going to bed. We stopped under the olive tree, a black stain in the darkness. "They said that a woman was killed," Berti said.

"Are you interested in women, too?"

Berti looked up at my window. He spun around quickly and said that an accident could make a vacationer decide to leave. He had thought that I and my friends would be leaving.

"And that relative of theirs?" he asked.

I realized that evening that when he mentioned my friends he was thinking of Clelia and Doro. He asked once more if Mara were a relative of theirs. Just the suspicion of his interesting himself in the thirty-year-old Mara made me smile. I asked him if he knew her.

"No," he said. "So what?"

I arranged to meet him next day on the beach, teasing him about his discovery of the pleasures of reading in company. "If you imagine I'm going to introduce you to girls, you're mistaken. You seem able to make out pretty well on your own."

That night I sat by the window smoking, thinking over Clelia's confessions, bothered by the thought that Ginetta would never have made similar ones to me. A familiar depression took hold. The memory of my talk with Guido, added to that, sank me completely. Luckily I was by the sea where the days don't count. "I'm here to have a good time," I told myself.

The next day we were sitting on the highest seaside rock, Doro and I, and beneath us Clelia was spread out flat, covering her eyes. The beach umbrella was deserted. We discussed Mara again and decided that a beach is composed of women, or at any rate of children. A man may be missing and nobody notices; if a Mara is missing, a whole circle disbands. "Look," Doro said, "these umbrellas are so many houses; they knit, eat, change their clothes, pay visits: those few husbands just stand there in the sun where their wives have put them. It's a republic of women."

"One might deduce that they had invented society themselves."

At that moment a swimmer came up below the rocks. He lifted his head from the water, getting a handhold. It was Berti.

I watched him without saying a word. Perhaps he hadn't noticed me up there—I can't see two yards ahead myself when I first leave the water. He swayed back and forth in the surf, hanging on. On a level with his forehead, a few inches away, Clelia was basking, motionless on her back. Berti's hair kept falling over his eyes; to keep it in place he made those tentacular gestures of the arms that suggest the instabilities of swimming. Then he suddenly broke away and paddled on his back, circling a submerged reef at the point where the sand gave way to rock. He called something to me from out there. I waved at him and went on talking to Doro.

Later, when Clelia had shaken herself out of her blissful state and the other girls and acquaintances showed up, I scanned the beach and saw Berti standing among the bathhouses reading a newspaper. It wasn't the first time, but that morning he was obviously waiting for something. I signaled him to come up. I insisted.

Berti moved a bit, folding his paper without looking at us. He stopped below the rocks. I said to Doro: "Here is that enterprising type I was telling you about." Doro looked and smiled, then turned in the direction of the bathhouse. So I felt I had to go down and say something to Berti.

To introduce a boy in black trunks to girls coming and going in swimsuits, or to men in beach robes, is no great affair; in other words, no apology was required. But Berti's solemn, bored face irritated me; I felt silly. "We all know each other here," I brought out curtly, and coming up to Ginetta as she was about to go in the water, I said: "Wait for me."

When I got back to the shore—Ginetta stayed in for more than an hour—I caught sight of Berti again sitting on the beach between our umbrella and the next, hugging his knees.

I left him alone. I wanted to talk a while with Clelia. She had just emerged from her bathhouse, putting on a white bolero over her suit. I went up to her and we gave each other a mock bow. We walked slowly away, talking, and when Berti had disappeared behind the umbrella, I felt better. We made our usual tour of the beach, between the foam and the noisy, sprawling groups of people.

"I've just been swimming with Ginetta," I said. "You're not going in?"

From the first day I had hinted at my readiness to swim with her out of politeness, but Clelia had stopped to look at me with an ambiguous smile. "No, no," she had said. I looked at her, surprised. "No, no, I go swimming alone." And that was that. She explained that she did everything in public, but in the sea she had to be alone. "That's peculiar," I said. "Peculiar it may be, but that's how it is." She was a good swimmer, so there was no embarrassment for her there. She had just made up her mind. "The company of the sea is enough. I don't want anybody. I have nothing of my own in life. At least leave me the sea . . ." She swam away, hardly moving the water, and I was waiting for her on the sand when she came back. I started the conversation again; Clelia just smiled at my protests.

"Not even with Doro?" I asked.

"Not even with Doro."

Next morning we joked about her mysterious swim as we

picked our way among the bodies, laughing at fat bellies and criticizing the women. "That red umbrella," said Clelia. "Do you know who's underneath?" One could make out a bony nakedness clad in a two-piece suit of the bikini variety. It was tanned in streaks; the bare stomach showed the mark of an earlier, normal bathing suit. Toes and fingernails were blood red. Over the back of the deck chair hung a luxurious pink towel. "It's Guido's friend," Clelia whispered, laughing. "He keeps her on the string and lets nobody see her, and when he meets her he kisses her hand and pays her all the compliments." Then she took my arm and leaned forward.

"Why are you men so vulgar?"

"It seems to me that Guido has all sorts of tastes," I said. "As for vulgarity, he's got plenty of that."

"But no," Clelia said, "it's that woman who's vulgar. The poor fellow is very fond of me."

I started explaining to her that nothing is vulgar in itself but that talking and thinking make it so, but Clelia had already lost interest and was laughing at a child's little red beret.

We strolled to the end of the beach and stopped for a smoke on the rocks. Then, dazed by the sun, we went back. Looking blankly around, I noticed Berti walking away from our umbrella—burned back and shorts—talking nervously to a strange little woman in a flowered dress, high sandals, and bright, powdered cheeks. Just then Clelia shouted something to Doro, waving, and the two turned around, Berti hurriedly escaping as soon as he saw us, the little woman sauntering along behind, calling his name none too respectfully.

"That geisha who was following you," I said when he came to meet me at the trattoria. "Was she by any chance the woman you took to your room that day?"

Berti smiled vaguely around his cigarette.

"I see you have good company," I continued. "Why are you looking for more? Lucky thing I didn't introduce you to those girls."

Berti looked at me hard, the way one does when one is pretending to think about something. "It's not my fault," he burst out, "if I met her. Excuse me to your friends."

Then I changed the subject and asked him if his parents knew about these undertakings. With his usual vague smile he said slowly that that woman was worth more than many well-brought-up girls, as, for that matter, was true of all her sort, who at least had one advantage in their hard lives over the proper ones.

"And that might be?"

"Yes. Men all agree that by going to prostitutes and letting off steam they are protecting the others. So prostitutes should be respected."

"Very well," I told him. "But you, then, why do you run away and act ashamed of her?"

"I?" Berti stammered. That was another story, he explained. He was repelled by women; it made him furious that all men lived just for that. Women were stupid and affected; the infatuation of men made them necessary. One should agree to leave them alone, to take them all down a few pegs.

"Berti, Berti," I said, "you're a hypocrite, too."

He looked surprised. "Making use of a person and then cutting her the next minute; no, that is out." I noticed that he was smiling and ostentatiously crushing his cigarette. He said in his mildest tone that he had not made use of that woman, but—he smiled —she had been making use of him. She was alone, she was bored by the sea; they found themselves together on the beach—she herself had begun by joking and swapping stories. "You see," he told me, "I couldn't say no because I felt sorry for her. She has a little pocketbook with the mirror all broken. I understand her. She's only looking for company and doesn't want a penny. She says that by the sea one doesn't work. But she's malicious. She's like all women and wants to embarrass men by making them look foolish."

We went home through the deserted streets at two in the afternoon. I had made up my mind to give no more advice to that boy: he was the kind one must give a long rein, to see where they end up. I asked if that woman, that *lady*, he had not by chance brought from Turin himself. "You're crazy," he replied snappishly. But the snap left him when I asked who had taught him to apologize for things that nobody cared about one way or the other. "When?" he stammered. "Didn't you ask me a short while ago to excuse you to my friends?" I said.

He told me that, considering I was with the others, he was

sorry we had seen him with that woman. "There are people," he said, "in front of whom one is ashamed to be ridiculous."

"Who, for instance?"

He was silent a moment. "Your friends," he said carelessly.

He left me at the foot of the stairs and walked off under the sun. Because Doro liked to rest during the hottest hours and I am unable to sleep during the day, I went inside merely to rid myself of Berti. Now the daily tedium of the hot and empty hours began. I wandered through the village, as always, but by now I knew every corner by heart. Then I took the road to the villa in the hope of talking to Clelia. But it was still very early and I stayed for a while ruminating on a low wall behind some trees that were silhouetted against the sea. Among other things I thought for the first time that somebody not knowing Clelia well and seeing the two of us strolling and laughing together would have said there was something between us a little stronger than friendly acquaintance.

I found Clelia in the garden, lying back in the shade on a wicker chair. She seemed glad to see me and started talking. She told me that Doro was sick of always painting the sea and wanted to stop. I couldn't hold back a smile. "Your friend Guido will be happy," I said. "Why?" Then I tried to explain that, according to Guido, Doro was thinking more of his painting than of her and that this was the reason for their quarrels.

"Quarrels?" Clelia said, frowning.

I was irritated. "Come now, Clelia, don't try to make me believe that you haven't been fighting a little. Remember the evening when you asked me to keep him company and distract him . . ."

Clelia listened, slightly offended, and kept shaking her head. "I never said a thing," she muttered. "I don't remember." She smiled. "I don't want to remember. And don't you play the homewrecker."

"Ye gods," I said. "The first day I was here. We had just got back from that trip where we were shot at . . ."

"Wonderful!" Clelia exclaimed. "That little white man and his monkeyshines?"

I had to smile, and Clelia said: "Everyone takes me literally. You all remember what I say. And you grill me, you want to know." She clouded over again. "It's like being back in school."

"For my part . . ." I grumbled.

"People should never remember the things I say. I talk and talk because I have a tongue in my head, because I don't know how to be alone. Don't you take me seriously too; it's not worth the trouble."

"Oh, Clelia," I said, "are we tired of life?"

"Of course not. It's so beautiful," she said, laughing.

Then I said that I no longer understood poor Doro. Why should he want to stop painting? He had become so good at it.

Clelia grew pensive and said that if she weren't what she was—a bad child who didn't know how to make anything—she would have painted the sea herself, she liked it so much. It was something of her own; not only the sea but the houses, the people, the steep stairs, all of Genoa. "I like it all so much," she said.

"Perhaps this is why Doro ran away. For the same reason. He likes the hills."

"That might be. But he says his country is beautiful only in his memory. I couldn't be like that. I have nothing beyond myself."

We were waiting for Doro, facing one another across a small table. Clelia went back to telling me about her girlhood and laughed a great deal about the ingenuousness of that life—in the closed atmosphere of elderly men who wanted to make her a countess and bounced her around between three houses: a shop, a palazzo, and a villa. What pleased her was the triangle of streets that linked them together through all that mass of city. Her uncle's palazzo was an ancient building with frescoes and brocades, full of glass cases like a museum. From the road its big leaded windows seemed to jut out over the sea. As a child, she said, it had been a nightmare to enter that immense hallway and spend her afternoons in the gloomy darkness of the small rooms. Beyond the roof was the sea, the air, the busy street. She had to wait until her mother had finished whispering with the old lady, and endlessly, martyred by boredom, she used to raise her eyes to the dark pictures where mustaches glimmered, cardinals' hats, pale cheeks of ageless, doll-like women.

"You see how silly I am," Clelia said. "When the palazzo was almost in our hands, I couldn't stand it. Now that we're poor and transplanted, I would give anything to see it again."

Cesare Pavese

Before Doro appeared on the balcony, Clelia told me that her mother didn't want her to stay at the shop where Papa was because it wasn't nice for a little girl like her to hear arguments behind the counter and learn so many awful words. But the shop was full of things and had shining showcases—the same that filled the palazzo—and here people came and went; little Clelia was glad to see her father happy. She was always asking him why they did not sell the pictures and lamps at the palazzo so as not to go always deeper into trouble. "I had an anxious childhood," she told me, smiling. "I would wake up at night in a panic at the thought that Papa might become poor."

"Why were you so afraid?"

Clelia said that in those years she was a little bundle of apprehensions. Her first inklings of love had come to her in front of a picture of St. Sebastian, the martyr, a naked youth lurid with blood and peeling paint, arrows stuck in his stomach. The sad, amorous eyes of that saint made her ashamed to look at him. This scene came to represent love.

"Why am I telling you this?" she said.

Doro soon appeared on the balcony, intent on drying his neck with a towel. He nodded to me and went in again. I asked Clelia if she had changed her ideas about love.

"Naturally," she said.

7. When I got back at night, I used to stand at my window smoking. One supposes that smoking promotes meditation, whereas the truth is that it disperses one's thoughts like so much fog; at best, one fantasticates in a manner quite different from thinking. Real discoveries or inspirations, on the other hand, arrive unexpectedly; at the table, swimming, talking of something entirely different. Doro was aware of my habit of dropping off for a moment in the middle of a conversation to chase an unexpected idea with my eyes. He did the same thing himself; in the old days we had taken many walks together, each of us silently ruminating. But now his silences, like mine, seemed distracted, estranged; in a word, unusual. I had been only a short while by the sea and it

seemed a hundred years. And nothing had happened even so. But tonight when I went home I had the idea that the whole past day—the banal summer day—required of me goodness knows what effort of mind before I could make sense of it.

The day after Mara's accident, when I saw friend Guido with his cursed automobile, I divined more things in the few seconds it took me to cross the road and shake his hand than during an entire evening of pipe smoking. That is to say, I realized that Clelia's confidences were an unconscious defense against Guido's vulgarity, a man otherwise very courteous and well-bred. Guido was sitting there, bronzed and glowing, holding out his hand and showing his teeth in a smile. Guido was rich and bovine. Clelia was reacting against him but without showing it; therefore, she took him seriously and began to resemble him. Who knows what inspiration would have turned up next if Guido had not started laughing and obliged me to talk. I climbed into the car and he took me to the café where everybody would be gathered.

While they were discussing Mara, I went on exploring my thoughts and asked myself if Doro understood Clelia's complaints as I did and why it didn't seem to bother him that Clelia kept no secrets even from me. Meanwhile, the two of them arrived, and after the first greetings Guido told Clelia that when he was crossing Genoa he had been thinking of her. Clelia looked at him archly, in fun, but it was enough to make me suspect that sometime before she had told Guido the same girlhood secrets—and I felt put out.

After dinner Guido arrived at the villa; he was in high spirits and had brought Ginetta with him in the car. While Doro and Guido were talking about their work, I listened to Clelia and Ginetta. I remembered what Doro had said as we went down the mountain, that the characteristic thing for someone who marries is to live with more than one woman. But was Ginetta a woman? Her frowning smile and some of her busybody opinions made her seem more like a sexless adolescent. Still less could I imagine how Clelia was supposed to have resembled her as a girl. There was a certain tomboyishness in Ginetta, restrained most of the time, that every so often seemed to shake loose her whole body. She was certainly not given to confessing herself with friends;

still, to look at her talking, one had the sense that there was nothing there to hide. Those gray eyes were as clear and candid as the air itself.

They were discussing some scandal or other—I don't remember what—but I recall that Ginetta was defending the people involved and appealed to Doro, interrupting all the time, while Clelia very gently reminded her that it wasn't a question of morals but rather of taste.

"But they will get married," Ginetta said.

That was no solution, Clelia put in; marriage is a choice, not a remedy, a choice that should be made calmly.

"Damn it, it *will* be a choice," Guido interrupted, "after all the experiments they've made."

Ginetta didn't smile; she repeated that if the purpose of marriage was to have a family, all the better to make up one's mind right away.

"But the purpose isn't just to have a family," Doro said. "It's to prepare a background for a family."

"Better a child without a background than a background without children," Ginetta said. Then she blushed and caught my glance. Clelia got up to serve the drinks.

Then we played cards. It was late when Guido finally drove us home. After dropping Ginetta in front of the garage, we walked back to the hotel. I would have liked to walk alone, but having said little all evening and played cards with aggressive indifference, Guido wanted to keep me company. I brought up Mara again, but Guido didn't seem interested. Mara was in good hands and in no danger. When we reached the hotel, he kept on walking.

We arrived at the end of my little alley in silence. I made as if to stop. Guido went on a few steps, then turned and remarked casually: "Let them wait. Come as far as the station with me."

I asked him who would be waiting for me, and Guido replied indifferently that, what the devil, I must have company of some sort. "Nobody," I replied. "I'm a bachelor and alone."

Then Guido muttered something, which started us walking again.

Who would be waiting for me, I asked again. Perhaps that boy of the beach?

"No, no, professor, I meant some relationship . . . some affair."

"Why? Have you seen me in company?"

"No, I don't say that. But, after all, one needs some relief."

"I'm here to rest," I said. "My relief is being alone."

"I see," Guido said absent-mindedly.

We were on the little square, before the café, when I spoke. "And you have a friend?"

Guido looked up. "That I have," he said belligerently. "That I have. We're not all saints. And she costs me a pile."

"Engineer," I exclaimed, "you manage to keep her well hidden."

Guido gave a self-satisfied smirk. "That's why it costs me a pile. Two accounts, two establishments, two tables. Believe me, a mistress is more expensive than a wife."

"Get married," I said.

Guido showed his gold teeth. "It would always be a double expense. You don't know women. A girl is modest enough while she's still hoping. She has everything to gain. But the fool who marries is at her mercy."

"And you marry the lady."

"We're fooling. Leave those things to old men."

I dropped him in front of his hotel, promising to meet his woman the next day. He shook my hand enthusiastically. Entering my place, I thought of Berti and looked around, but he wasn't there.

The next morning I was busy writing until the sun was well up, then I wandered the streets chewing over the last evening's conversations. Now, in the noise and brilliance of the day, they seemed off-color and inconsistent. I aimed for the beach, where everybody was gathered by now.

But I met Guido at the entrance to the bathhouses, this time in a maroon wrapper. He drew me aside and steered me without a word toward that certain umbrella. When we were there, Guido broke into a boyish smile and exclaimed: "Nina darling, how did you sleep? Allow me . . ." and he told her my name. I touched the fingers of that skinny hand, but between the glare and obstruction of the umbrella, I saw chiefly two long, blackened legs and the complicated sandals in which they ended. She got up to sit in the deck chair and looked me over with eyes as hard, as fleshless as the voice she directed at Guido.

We exchanged a few compliments. I asked how she had enjoyed her swim. She said she only went in toward evening, when the water had warmed. She honored my joke with a few barks of laughter and held my hand a good while when I said goodbye, asking me to come back. Guido stayed with her.

I reached the rocks and saw Berti sitting back, chatting with a sixteen-year-old friend of Ginetta's. Doro, stretched on the sand between them, left them alone. By this time Clelia was in the water.

8. One morning Doro took me by the arm and explained why he was tired of painting. We were slowly leaving the village on the road that climbed above the sea.

"If I could be a boy again," he told me, "I'd do nothing but paint. I'd leave home and slam the door behind me. It would be something definite."

This show of feeling pleased me. I told him in that case he wouldn't have married Clelia. Doro said laughing that that was the only thing he hadn't been mistaken about. Yes. Clelia was a true vocation. Still, he said, it wasn't those stupid paintings he did to pass the time that made him furious; it was his having lost the enthusiasm and will to discuss things with me.

"What things?"

He paused and looked at me rather haughtily and said that if this was how I was going to take it he would complain no more. Because I was also getting old and obviously it happened that way to everybody.

"It could be," I said, "but if you have lost the desire to talk, I don't come into it."

I didn't warm to this line of speculation. The fuss was ridiculous, but I kept silent and Doro dropped my arm. I looked down at the sea beneath us and an idea occurred to me: Could his quarrels with Clelia have consisted of nonsense like this?

But here was Doro talking again in the same careless tone as before. I saw that my annoyance had made no impression. I answered in the same vein, but my rancor grew into a quite genuine anger.

"You still haven't told me why you quarreled with Clelia," I finally said.

But Doro eluded me again. At first he didn't understand what I was getting at, then he looked at me quizzically and said: "Are you still thinking about that? You *are* stubborn. It happens every day between married people."

The same day I told Clelia, after she had been complaining about a boring novel, that in such cases the fault lies with the reader. Clelia raised her eyes and smiled. "It always happens," she said. "One comes here for a rest and ends up being impertinent."

"Everybody?"

"Guido, too. But Guido has the excuse that his mistress torments him. You, no."

I shrugged my shoulders and looked foolish. When I told her I had met the aforesaid lady, Clelia blushed with pleasure and almost clapping her hands begged me: "Tell me, tell me, what's she like?"

I knew only that Guido had half a mind to get rid of her—palm her off on me, for instance. I said this in a quiet way that Clelia seemed to like; she was pleased. "He complains that she costs too much," I added. "Why doesn't he marry her?"

"That's all we need!" Clelia said. "But that woman is a fool. Look at the intelligence she shows in letting herself be shut up in a cupboard like a Christmas present."

"So far I've only seen her legs. Who is she? A ballerina?"

"A cashier," said Clelia. "A witch whom everyone in Genoa knew before Guido fell into her clutches."

"She's a clever one, is she?"

"It doesn't take much with Guido." Clelia smiled.

"I think she's putting on this submissive act the better to snare him," I said. "It's a good sign when a woman lets herself be kept in a closet. It must mean she already considers herself at home."

"If you like to think it a good sign," Clelia said sulkily.

"But surely he can't do better than marry her?"

"No, no," Clelia bridled. "I wouldn't receive her in my house."

"Would you rather that a brute like him should marry a Clelia or a Ginetta?" I eyed her to see how she would react to the word, but she let it pass.

45

"It's iniquitous," Clelia said, "that a girl should be defenseless before you men. I congratulate those women who take you for a ride."

One afternoon I had a visit from Guido at my house. He put his face in the door with an apologetic laugh and said he didn't want to disturb my reading. I made him come in, embarrassed myself because of my little iron bedstead, and offered him a seat by the window. He fanned himself with his hat and finally asked me to make his apologies to Doro and Clelia for not being able to go and fetch them in the car. He had an engagement.

We passed some very uncomplimentary remarks about Guido on the beach that evening. The most spiteful were the girls, who had been counting on a ride. Berti, established now and circulating among us, seemed the only one who didn't care. I heard him saying to Ginetta that after all you came to the seaside to swim and not to go around looking at tourist attractions.

"Well, now," I said to him, sitting down nearby on the sand, "you're not thinking any more about readings?"

"Certainly I am," he replied.

"Even with these girls around?"

He gave me a black look. "I?" he said. Sitting there against the rock, he seemed really annoyed. Yet, not long before, he had been standing up to them all in the most condescending, detached manner.

"You're not going to tell me that you dislike us too. After all, you came here to see us."

Berti smiled. Ginetta passed in front of us, fixing her bathing cap before going in. From where I was sitting, as I watched her loping along in the act of covering one ear, she seemed very tall, more than a woman. Berti looked down at his knees and muttered: "They bother me. Who can understand them—girls?"

Doro loomed over us, about to throw himself on the sand. "This is the student," I told him. I introduced them. They knelt up and shook hands.

Then Doro began chatting with me inconsequentially, in one of those brusque, bizarre moods we used to have as students. It was clear that Berti was out of it. One part of me was listening to Doro, the other keeping an eye on my young friend.

Suddenly Berti asked point-blank: "Engineer, will you be staying here long?"

Doro looked through us and didn't answer. Berti waited, blushing right through his tan. After a long pause, I said that I was leaving at the end of August. But Doro remained implacably silent. All three of us looked out to sea, where Ginetta was just going in and Clelia unexpectedly emerging. We watched her approach and I couldn't decide whether to smile. She made a grimace; her foot had slipped on the shingle.

"Come now, the sea is yours," she called out to us, waving, and made for the umbrella. Doro got up. "How about a short walk?" he said. I got up, hardly noticing Berti, who was still gazing at the horizon with a stoic air.

Later, fresh and rested, we were gathered around the umbrella, Clelia smoking a cigarette, I my pipe.

"Who knows where Berti has gone?" I said. Doro didn't move. Stretched between us, he looked up at the sky. "You are real friends," Clelia said. "You're inseparable."

"I make a screen for his loves," I said. "There's a woman who otherwise would be jealous."

Clelia loved this kind of talk and I had to relate the whole business, including our conversation in the trattoria. Doro said nothing; he went on staring into space.

9. The next time I saw Berti he was sitting moodily in the trattoria. He had obviously entered for lack of something better to do. He told me he wanted to visit me in the afternoon so that we could read something together.

"Don't you like girls any more?" I asked.

"Which ones? I hate them," he answered.

"You don't mean to say it's the engineer's company you're after?"

He asked me if Doro were really my friend. I said yes, he was, he and his wife were the dearest friends I had.

"His wife?"

He didn't realize that Clelia was Doro's wife. His eyes gleamed.

"Really?" he repeated and lowered his eyes with that impassive and irritated air that was his way of being serious. "What did you think?" I murmured. "That she was a ballerina?"

Berti crumpled the tablecloth and heard me out. Then he raised two bright, ingenuous eyes, his boy eyes, and asked once more if he could come up to my room that afternoon.

"Nobody will break in on us?" he asked, evidently thinking of Clelia.

"What's this?" I asked. "You hate women and blush just thinking about them?"

Berti made some idiotic reply and we fell silent. Finally we got up. He was taciturn along the street, but he answered with increasing animation, like a person talking at random to ease his mind of some great thought. I stopped a moment under the olive tree to speak to the landlady. He waited for me at the foot of the stairs, eyeing and caressing the smooth stone which formed the balustrade; a half-tender, half-disdainful smile on his lips. "Come up," I said, rejoining him.

When we were inside, he went to the window, leaned his back against the wall, and watched me pace around the room.

"Professor, I am happy," he burst out unexpectedly. I had turned my back to rinse out my mouth.

I asked him why and he replied with a wave of the hand, as if to say: "That's how it is."

Even that afternoon we did no reading. He began telling me how every so often he felt an urge to work, a mania, a need to do something; not so much to study as to have some responsible position, some real work to give himself up to, day and night, so as to become a man like the rest of us, like me. "Well, work then," I told him. "You're young. I wish I were in your place." Then he said he didn't see why people made so much of being young; he would rather be thirty—it would be so much time gained—the intervening years were stupid.

"But all years are stupid. It's only when they're over that they become interesting."

No, Berti said, he couldn't really find anything interesting in his fifteen, in his seventeen years; he was glad they were behind him.

I told him the good thing about his age was that the foolishnesses didn't count, for the very reason that displeased him, because he was still considered a boy.

He looked at me with a smile.

"Then the things I do aren't foolish?"

"It depends," I said. "If you annoy the wives of my friends, it will certainly be a piece of foolishness as well as a discourtesy."

"I don't bother anyone," he protested.

"That remains to be seen."

He confessed in the course of our talk that he had stupidly assumed that the lady was my friend's mistress and that to learn she was his wife instead had pleased him, because it made him furious that women, just because they were women, should offer themselves to the first comer. "There are days when the world and life itself seem like one big cathouse."

At that moment a shrill voice I recognized interrupted him, an exasperated woman. It rose from the street, talking back to our landlady. We looked at each other. Berti fell silent and lowered his eyes. I knew it was the woman of the beach, his mistress in a manner of speaking. Berti stayed put.

The landlady said: "He's not here; I know nothing about it." The woman shrilled back, declaring that nobody ever showed *her* such lack of respect—it would take more than holy water to rinse the landlady's mouth out, she proclaimed.

When they had shut up as someone walked by, I waited for Berti to speak, but he was looking off into space, glum and distracted.

As he went off, I told him to behave so that these things wouldn't happen. I cut our meeting short and closed the door.

He didn't show up at the rocks that evening. Guido did, mopping sweat off his face. Clelia teased him by asking when we would be going dancing on the hill again.

"Do you hear that?" he said to Doro. "Your wife wants to dance."

"Not me," Doro said.

Clelia was telling me about a small loggia in her uncle's old palazzo that she had just thought of that evening and wanted to see once again. Guido listened for a while, then said that I was just the man to appreciate those voices from the past.

Clelia smiled, taken aback, and replied that we all were await-
ing our news of the present from him. We looked at Guido, who
winked—for my benefit, I imagine—and said to Clelia that at least
she should tell us about something interesting: her first ball, for
instance—a woman's first ball is always full of surprises.

"No, no," said Clelia. "We want to hear about *your* first ball.
Or maybe about the last, yesterday evening."

Doro got up and said, "Take it easy. I'm going swimming."

"Exactly," I said. "People are always talking about the first
balls of young girls. What about those of little boys? What happens
to future Guidos the first time they embrace a girl?"

"There isn't any first time," Clelia said. "The future Guidos
don't begin at a given date. They've been at it even before they
were born."

We kept it up like this until Doro returned. Clelia enjoyed aggressive jokes like that, adding, unless I am mistaken, a teasing
sous-entendu, a touch of malice that Guido sometimes missed. Or
rather he had an air of being too preoccupied to notice it. But the
mock-angry pleasure he took in the game made me smile.

I said: "You seem like husband and wife."

"Clod!" said Clelia.

"What else can you do but joke with a woman like Clelia?"
Guido said.

"There's only one man you can't joke with," I said in my turn.

"Naturally," Clelia agreed.

Doro turned around and flung himself on the sand in the sun's
last rays. After a while Guido got up and said he was going to the
bar. He walked off among the poles of closed umbrellas, threading
his way through the coming and going of the evening beach. Some
distance away, Ginetta and her young friends were noisily greeting
an arriving boat. The three of us were quiet; I listened to the thud
of the waves and the muted cries.

"Do you know, Clelia," I said finally, "that after seeing you my
student decided to change his life?"

Doro raised his head. Clelia opened her eyes in amazement.

"He has chucked that lover of his and damns all women. It's an
infallible sign."

"Thanks," Clelia murmured.

Doro lay back again. "Considering that Doro is present," I went on, "I can tell you. The boy's in love with you."

Clelia smiled without moving. "I'm sorry for that woman . . . Isn't there anything I can do?"

I smiled.

"When you think of all those hungry girls," Clelia said, "it's a nuisance."

"Why then?" I said. "He is happy. He's happier than we are. You should see him caressing trees . . . He's drunk with it."

"If it takes him like that . . ." Clelia said.

Doro turned over on the sand. "Oh, cut it out . . ." he said.

We told him to keep quiet because he had nothing to do with it. Clelia looked down awhile without speaking. "But is it really true?" she asked suddenly.

I laughed and reassured her. "What does that fool see in me?" she asked. She looked at me suspiciously. "You're all fools," she said.

I repeated that my student was happy and that was good enough; I wouldn't mind being a fool on those terms.

Clelia smiled and said: "That's true. It reminds me of when I stayed in the loggia and instead of studying I threw twists of paper down at the necks of passers-by. Once a man looked up and scared me to death. He wanted to know what I had written to him. It was a Latin composition."

Doro laughed, stretched out with his face in the sand.

"And that man was Guido," I said.

Clelia stared at me. What did I have against Guido, she asked. I stuck to my guns. "I know him," I said.

"Guido doesn't do those things," Clelia said. "Guido respects women."

10. Somewhat hesitatingly Guido invited me to go up there one evening in the car. "Nina will be there. Sure you won't mind?" He glanced at Berti, who had been dawdling a few steps behind to let me talk, then looked questioningly at me. I asked him to bring Berti along, a young lad of spirit who could dance, which was more

than I could say for myself. Guido frowned and said: "Of course."
Then I introduced them.

It was an evening of silences. Berti had expected to find Clelia
and instead had to dance with Nina, who looked him up and down
and lost her tongue in the process. The rest of us sat silently at the
table watching the couples. It was not that Guido wanted to get
rid of Nina; the remarks he dropped seemed to me only his way of
letting off steam. "I've reached the age, professor, when I can't
change my way of life, but if Nina wants to have some fun, see
new places, new company to distract her, I would look favorably
on the idea."

"You've only to tell her."

"No," Guido said. "She feels lonely. You understand; a man
has friends, relationships to keep up. He can't always give her all
his time."

"Wouldn't a frank explanation do the trick?" I suggested.

"With other women, but not with her. She's a friend, an old
friend, you see . . . a demanding woman, do I make myself clear?"

Then Nina had a few dances with him; Berti smoked cigarettes
at the table, glancing around. He asked me if the woman was
Guido's wife.

"Not she," I told him. "She belongs to the world you dream
about. Who are you looking for?"

"No one."

"My friends aren't coming. When this woman is here, they
stay away."

That night under the stairway by the olive tree I asked him
if Nina had appealed to him, and seeing his smirk I said that he
would have done Guido a great favor if he had amused her for
a while. "But if he is tired of her, why doesn't he chuck her?" Berti
said.

"Try and ask him," I said.

Berti did not ask him, but instead, the evening after, having
discovered that we would be going up to dance with Clelia and
Guido, he went up on foot—I don't know if he had eaten or not.
We saw him threading down among the tables to a seat in the back.
He had a soft drink in front of him and threw a cigarette away. But
he didn't move.

Ginetta didn't happen to be in the party. Now that I seemed to be able to read his mind, I realized that he had expected Ginetta to be there to lead off the dance with. Guido, very much rejuvenated by his evening of freedom, was looking around, pleased with himself. He waved vaguely in Berti's direction. Berti got up and came over. Being a coward, I stared at the floor. "How is the signora?" Berti asked.

Clelia broke the embarrassment with an irrepressible burst of laughter. Then Guido answered: "We are all very well," in a tone of voice and with a large wave of the hand that made us all smile, except Berti, who blushed. He stood there looking at us until I, squinting at Clelia, couldn't resist saying: "This is the famous Berti." Doro made him a bored sign to sit down, grumbling: "Stick with us."

Naturally it fell to me to entertain him. Berti, sitting on the edge of his chair, gazed at us patiently. I asked him what he was doing alone up here; he answered like someone trying hard to listen to the orchestra.

"My friend tells me you have stopped studying," Doro put in. "What are you doing, working?"

"I am unemployed," Berti retorted, somewhat fiercely.

"My friend tells me that you're enjoying yourself," Doro went on. "Have you made friends?"

Berti merely said no. We were all silent. Clelia, half turned toward the orchestra, said: "Berti, do you dance?"

I was grateful to her for those words. Berti forced himself to meet her eyes and nodded. "It's a shame that Ginetta and Luisella haven't come," Clelia said. "You know them, don't you?" Without looking away, Berti replied that he did. "Aren't we going to dance?" said Clelia.

None of us said anything as they moved off. Guido made a fuss to get a coffee spoon; meanwhile I looked over at Doro. He must have seen an anxious question on my face, because as I was about to hide my embarrassment by staring off in another direction, I noticed him frowning, then smiling halfheartedly.

"What is it?" Guido asked, getting up.

Clelia and Berti came back almost at once. Whether the band was playing faster than usual or whether my nervousness had

53

distracted me I can't say, but back they came, and Clelia said something I can't recall, something she might have said climbing out of a taxi. Berti followed her like a shadow.

They danced once again in the course of the evening. I think Clelia had encouraged him with a look. Berti rose without saying anything and, scarcely looking at her, waited for Clelia to join him. During the intervals when I was sitting at the table either with Doro or with Guido, occasionally one of us would address a word to Berti, who answered condescendingly, in monosyllables. Guido danced often with Clelia, returning to the table with sparkling eyes. Then we all stayed at the table for a while, gossiping. Berti made an effort not to look at Clelia too much, watching the orchestra in a bored, absent-minded way. He said nothing. At this point Guido spoke to him: "Are you taking makeup exams this autumn?"

"No," Berti muttered calmly.

"Because you have more the face of an exam-taker than of an educated person."

Berti grinned foolishly. Clelia smiled, too. Doro stayed put. Seconds passed and nobody spoke. Guido scowled at us and mumbled something. Most offensive of all was the half-scornful grin he dedicated to Berti. As if to say: "That's done. Let's forget it."

Berti said nothing. He went on smiling vaguely. All at once Clelia said: "Shall we dance?" I raised my head. Berti got up.

Clelia came back to the table, calmly nodding to someone she knew on her way. She sat down; there was a tired, almost sulky expression on her face, and without looking at us, she murmured: "I hope that now you're going to be more entertaining." A number of her friends emerged from the shadow and distracted her.

During our ride home in the car, Clelia replied, to a hint of mine, that Berti had not said a word while they were dancing. But Guido, on the other hand, said a great many when the two of us went later for a last trip to the bar. He explained that he couldn't stand boys and especially couldn't allow them to put on the air of reading him a lesson. "They too have to live," I said, "and learn from experience."

"Let them wait until they've run through as many as we have," Guido said stubbornly.

Nina was waiting for him at the bar. I was expecting her. She was sitting at a low table, her chin on her fist, watching the smoke from her cigarette. She nodded to us, and while Guido was ordering at the bar, she asked me in her husky, uneven voice, but without moving her arm, why I hadn't shown up sooner.

"What about yesterday evening?" I said.

"You don't dance, you don't sunbathe, you don't eat with anyone, why don't you come with us? Oh, Guido's friends! What has that woman got to seduce you all? Don't tell me it's the engineer's company you're after."

"I'm not saying anything," I stammered.

It was so warm that evening it was a shame to go inside. I had no idea whether or not Berti was waiting for me at the foot of the stairs. Probably he had gone to sit on the beach and mull over his shame. I wouldn't have wanted to see him. Back in my room, I stood for a long time at the window.

Berti called me from the street early the next morning. Our lane was still completely in shadow. He asked if I weren't coming with him to swim. He was quiet awhile, then asked if he could come up. He entered aggressively, his eyes shining and tired. "Does this seem the right time?" I said. He looked as if he hadn't slept and told me as much right off, very casually. He seemed actually proud of it. "Come to the sea, professor," he insisted. "There's nobody there."

I had to write a letter. "Professor," he said, after a short pause, "all you have to do is turn the night into day and everything becomes beautiful."

I looked up from my paper. "Troubles at your age are light."

Berti smiled with a certain hardness. "Why should I have troubles?" He looked down.

"I thought you had quarreled . . ." I said.

"With whom?" he interrupted.

"All right, then," I grumbled.

"Come in swimming, professor," Berti said. "The sea is huge."

I told him I would be coming later with my friends and to leave me in peace. He went, with an expression half serious, half irritated, and immediately I blamed myself for having treated him so meanly. But patience, I thought, you are learning something at his expense.

I met Guido at the bar. He was wearing white shorts and an open-neck shirt as usual; the bogus virility of his tan made me smile. Guido smiled and held out his hand, raising his eyes to the roofs, sly and severe at once. "What a day!" he said. It was indeed a wonderful sky and a splendid morning. "Have a glass of Marsala, professor. Last night, eh?" He winked, I don't know why, and refused to let me go. "And what is the beautiful Clelia doing?" he said.

"I've just come from my room."

"Always the sober one, eh, professor?"

We walked off. He asked me if I were staying much longer. "I'm beginning to have enough," I said. "Too many complications."

Guido was not listening, or perhaps he missed the point.

"You don't have company," he said.

"I have my friends."

"Not enough. I share the same friends, but I wouldn't be in such fine form this morning if I'd slept in a single bed."

As I didn't reply, he explained that he also enjoyed Clelia's company, but the smoke was not the roast.

"And the roast would be . . ."

Guido laughed loudly. "There are women of flesh," he said, "and women of air. A deep breath after dinner is great. But first you have to eat."

Actually, I said, I was at the sea for Doro's sake.

"Incidentally," I added, "he's not painting any more."

"It's about time," retorted Guido.

But neither Clelia nor Doro came to the beach that morning. Neither Gisella nor any of the others knew why. I got impatient by noon, and taking advantage of the others' plans for a boat trip, I went home to dress and climbed up to the villa. No one in the street. I was about to open the gate when Doro and an elderly gentleman with a cane and a panama hat came out on the walk. The latter walked slowly toward the road, nodding at things I couldn't hear. Doro, when we were alone, looked at me with dancing eyes.

"What's going on?" I said.

"It happens that Clelia is pregnant."

Before showing my pleasure, I waited for Doro to give the lead. We went up the walk toward the steps. Doro seemed amused and unbelieving. "The truth is, you're happy," I said.

"I want to see how it works out first," he said. "It's the first time it's happened to me."

Then Clelia came out of her room, asking who was there. She smiled at me, almost as if to excuse herself, and put her handkerchief to her mouth. "Don't I disgust you?" she said.

Then we talked about the doctor, who had run on a good deal about responsibility and wanted to return with all sorts of instruments to make a scientific diagnosis. "What a nut!" Clelia said.

"Nonsense," Doro retorted. "Today we are going to take the train to Genoa. You've got to see De Luca."

Clelia looked at me. "You see," she said. "Paternity has started already. He's giving orders."

I said I was sorry they would have to cut off their vacation; but otherwise it was a fine thing.

"And you think I'm not sorry too?" Clelia grumbled.

Doro was counting on his fingers. "It'll be more or less . . ."

"Knock it off," Clelia said.

Instead of going by train, they went in Guido's car. Doro kept me company as far as the village, confiding a certain distaste for having to discuss it all with everybody; he would have preferred a dislocation or a fracture. He chattered and joked about trivialities.

"You're more worked up than Clelia," I told him.

"Oh, Clelia is resigned already," Doro returned, "so resigned it gives me a pain."

"Didn't you expect it?"

"It's like a lottery," Doro said. "You put your ticket in your pocket and forget about it."

That afternoon I was with Clelia, saying goodbye, when Guido brought his car to the gate. I watched her circulate through the rooms, as she did up parcels, the maid running about. Every so often Clelia would sigh and come to the window where I was leaning, like a hostess making the rounds of her guests who reserves for one of them the privilege of hearing about her tiredness and boredom.

"Happy to be going back to Genoa?" I asked.

She gave a distracted smile and nodded.

"Doro likes unexpected journeys," I said. "Let's hope this is the last."

Even this allusion escaped her. She merely said that in these things one couldn't be sure of anything; then she blushed as she got the point, saying: "You brute."

I told her that I, too, would be leaving the coast. I was going home. "I'm sorry," she said. At the least, I told her, I was happy to have spent with her her last summer as a girl. For a second Clelia became that girl of past days: she stood still and straight and said softly: "It's true. What a nuisance I was. You must have been very bored, you poor boy."

They left halfway through the afternoon with a joking Guido. Clelia wasn't exactly in the mood for badinage, so I imagine he soon left off. They told me to wait for them because they meant to return in a few days; I felt a bit sad watching them go. The truth is that I had wanted Doro to take me with them.

The next morning I was with Ginetta on the beach, and after talking a while about Clelia I didn't know what more to say, when some young men came to take her away. I circulated among the umbrellas. I caught sight of Nina and turned toward the sea. I expected Berti to show up any moment.

But instead, on my way back to the road, I met Guido. He had already dropped the car at the garage. He told me the couple were staying on at Genoa. Their doctor was away, and Clelia hadn't taken the trip very well. "It's a bore," he said. "Everybody's leaving this year."

Berti, as usual, put in an appearance at the trattoria. He crept in like a shadow; I was conscious of him standing in front of the table before I raised my eyes. He seemed quite calm.

Judging by his bored and empty expression, I would have said that he knew about the departure. Instead he asked me if I had gone to the beach that morning. As we talked, I worried about what I should say to him. I asked him when he was going back to the city.

He made an irritated gesture.

"They are all going back," I said.

When he heard Clelia's news, he fiddled with his box of matches. I had not explained the reason for her departure. He seemed rather cast down; then it occurred to me that perhaps he might be thinking that he was the reason, because of the dance incident, so I told him that the signora, according to his own lights, had been a good wife and conceived a child. Berti looked at me without smiling, then smiled unaccountably, threw away the matchbox, and stammered: "I expected it."

"It's annoying," I told him, "that these things happen. Women like Clelia should never fall."

Without my having noticed the transition, Berti had become inconsolable. I remember that we returned to the house together. I was silent; he was silent, staring vacantly around.

"Are you going back to Turin?" I said.

But he wanted to go to Genoa. He asked me to lend him the money for the trip. I told him he was mad. He replied that he might have lied and told me he wanted the money to pay off a debt, but that sincerity was wasted on me. He merely wanted to see Clelia again and say hello.

"What are you thinking?" I exclaimed. "That she remembers you?"

He fell silent again. I was thinking how strange the situation was: I had the money for the trip but wasn't going. Meanwhile we arrived at our lane and the sight of the olive tree rubbed me the wrong way. I began to see that no spot is less habitable than a place where one has been happy. I understood why Doro, one fine day, had taken a train to his hills and the morning after had returned to his destiny.

The same evening we met at the café. Everyone was there, even Guido—Nina, too, at her table—and I persuaded Berti to return with me to Turin. Guido wanted to take us dancing; he was even willing to take Berti. But that night we both left.

THE HOUSE
ON THE HILL

1. For a long time we had talked of the hill as we might have talked of the sea or the woods. I used to go back there in the evening from the city when it grew dusk, and for me it was not just another place but a point of view, a way of life. For instance, I saw no difference between those hills and these ancient ones where I played as a child and where I live now: the same broken, straggling country, cultivated and wild, the same roads, farmhouses, and ravines. I used to climb up there in the evening as if I too were fleeing the nightly shock of the air-raid alarms. The roads were swarming with people, poor people who scattered to sleep even in the fields, carrying their mattresses on their bicycles or on their backs, shouting and arguing, obstinate, gullible, and amused.

We began to climb, everyone discussing the doomed city, the night, and the terrors to come. I who had lived up there for some time watched the others gradually thin out as they left the main path, until a moment came when I was climbing alone between the hedges and the low wall. Then I walked with my ears open, looking up at familiar trees, sniffing the earth and everything around me. I was happy enough; I knew that during the night the whole city might go up in flames and all its people be killed, but the ravines, houses, and footpaths would wake in the morning calm and unchanged. I would still look out on the morning from the orchard window. I would still have slept in a bed, no question of it. Like me, the refugees of the fields and woods would go back down to the city, only more tired and numb than I was. It was summer and I remembered other evenings when I was sleeping in the city, evenings when I also came back down late at night, singing or laughing, when thousands of lights outlined the hill or the city at the end of the road. The city was a lake of light. We were living in the city then. We didn't realize how short a time we had. Friendships and long days to spend in the most casual meetings, we had plenty of both. We were living, or so we thought, with others and for others.

I should say—as I begin this story of a long illusion—that blame for what happened to me cannot be laid to the war. On the contrary, the war, I am certain, might still save me. When the war came, I had been living for some time in the villa up there where I was renting those rooms, but if my work had not kept me in Turin I would already have gone back to my parents' house in the other hills. All the war did was to remove my last scruple about keeping to myself, about consuming the years and my heart alone; and one fine day I realized that Belbo, the big dog, was the last honest confidant I still had. The war had made it legitimate to turn in on oneself and live from day to day without regretting lost opportunities. It was as if I had been waiting for the war a long time and had been counting on it, a war so vast and unprecedented that one could easily go home to the hills, crouch down, and let it rage in the skies above the cities. Things were happening now that justified a mere keeping alive without complaining. That species of dull rancor that hemmed in my youth found a refuge and a horizon in the war.

Once again, that evening, I climbed the hill; it was growing dark and beyond the low wall distant ridges began to appear. Belbo was waiting for me at the usual place, crouched on the path; I heard him whimpering in the dark. He trembled and scratched the earth. Then he rushed at me, leaping to touch my face, and I calmed him, spoke words to him until he dropped and trotted ahead and stopped to sniff a tree, happy. When he realized that instead of taking the footpath I was going on toward the wood, he jumped for joy and disappeared among the trees. It's fun to circle the hill with a dog. While you walk he sniffs and makes you aware of roots, hollows, gullies, hidden existences; he multiplies the pleasure of discovery. Since childhood it has seemed to me that a trip through the woods without a dog means losing too much of the life and hidden parts of the earth.

I wanted to stay away from the villa until late evening because I knew that my landladies and Belbo's would be waiting for me as usual to make me talk, to make me pay for the trouble they took on my account, for the cold supper and their affability, with the tortuous, casual opinions on the war and things in general that I kept at hand. Sometimes a new turn in the war, a threat, a night of bombs and flames, would give the two women an excuse for confronting me at the door, in the orchard, around the table; for chattering, shouting, throwing up their hands; for dragging me to the light to find out who I was, to make certain I was one of them. I liked to eat alone and forgotten in the darkened room, listening, alert to the night outside, hearing the time pass. When the siren wailed in the dark over the distant city, my first emotion was annoyance at the loss of solitude, at the nervousness and fuss that penetrated even our lives up here, my two women putting out a lamp already dimmed, the anxious hope for something momentous to happen. We all went out to the orchard.

Of the two I preferred the old woman, the mother. Her bulk and infirmities had something calm and earthy about them; one could imagine her under the bombs resembling a darkened hill herself. She had little to say but knew how to listen. The other, her daughter, a forty-year-old spinster, was buttoned-up, bony, and named Elvira. She lived in terror that the war might arrive up there. I knew that she was anxious about me; she told me so. She suffered when I was in the city, and once when her mother was rallying her in my presence, Elvira answered that if the bombs destroyed a little more of Turin I would have to stay with them day and night.

Belbo ran back and forth on the path and invited me to plunge into the woods. But that evening I wanted to stay on a turning of the path, bare of trees, where I could look down to the broad valley and the hillsides. That is how I liked the big hill, winding its slopes and ridges in the dark. It was the same before, but sprinkled with many lights; life was peaceful, the houses populated; there was rest and pleasure. Even now, one sometimes heard voices, bursts of laughter in the distance, but the great darkness weighed down, covered everything, and the land had grown wild again, lonely, as I had known it as a boy. Behind the tilled fields and the roads, behind the human houses, under one's feet, the ancient indifferent heart of the earth cowered in the darkness, lived in hollows and among roots, in hidden things and childhood fears. I began in those days to enjoy my childhood memories. One might

65

have said that beneath bitternesses and uncertainties, behind the need to be alone, I was finding my boyhood just to have a companion, a colleague, a son. I saw this country where I grew up with new eyes. We were alone together, the boy and myself; I relived the wild discoveries of earlier days. I was suffering, of course, but in the peevish spirit of someone who neither recognizes nor loves his neighbor. And I talked to myself incessantly, kept myself company. We were two people alone.

Again that evening a buzz of voices came up the slope, mixed with songs. They came from the other side, where I had never explored, and sounded like an echo of earlier times, a voice from my youth. I recalled for a moment the bands of refugees who swarmed over the hillside like trippers. But the sound stayed put, came always from the same place. It was strange to know that under the threatening darkness, facing the muffled city, some group of people, perhaps a family, were killing the long wait by singing and laughing. I did not even stop to consider that it required courage. It was June, the night was beautiful, one had only to let oneself go. But for my part I was happy to have in my life neither any real affection nor embarrassment, to be alone, tied to no one. I seemed always to have known that I would come to this sort of backwater between city and hill, to this continual anxiety that confined one's horizon to the next day, the next awakening; indeed, I'd have been very close to admitting it aloud if there had been anyone to listen. But only a close friend could have listened.

Belbo stood on the embankment and barked at the voices. To hear better myself, I grabbed him by the neck and made him stop. Among the drunken voices a few were clear; there was even a woman's. Then they laughed, all talking at once. Finally a very beautiful man's voice rose up alone.

I was about to return the way I had come when I said to myself: "You fool. The two old women are waiting for you. Let them wait."

In the dark I tried to discover the exact location of the singers. "Perhaps they are people you know." I took Belbo and pointed to the other slope. I sang a phrase of the song under my breath and said: "Let's go there." He sprang away.

Then, guided by the voices, I walked down the path.

2. When I came out on the road and stopped to look around, I heard the alarm sounding on the other side of the ridge, almost drowned by the noise of the crickets. I could sense as if I were there the city freezing up, the trample of feet, the slamming of doors, the scared and empty streets. Here the stars poured light. Now the singing in the valley had stopped. Belbo barked a short way off. I ran up to him. He had found a courtyard and was jumping about among some people who had come out of a house. A light showed faintly through a half-closed door. Someone shouted: "Close the door, ignoramus," and they all laughed loudly. The light went out.

Belbo was no stranger there; someone joked about the two old women; they accepted me without asking who I was. They came and went in the darkness, some children among them. They all looked at the sky. "Are they coming or aren't they?" They spoke of Turin, of troubles, of smashed houses. A woman was sitting apart, moaning to herself.

"I thought you all were dancing," I ventured.

"Good idea," said the shadow of a young man who had been talking to Belbo before. "But nobody remembered to bring a clarinet."

"Would you have dared?" said a girl's voice.

"Oh, him! He would dance while his house was burning down."

"Oh my, yes," said another girl.

"We can't, we're at war. *Italians!*" here his voice changed, "*I have created this war for you. I give it to you; you are worthy of it. There will be no more dancing or sleeping. Like me, you must only make war.*"

"Keep quiet, Fonso. What if they hear you?"

"What do you want to do? Let's sing."

And the voice took up the song again, but low, muffled, almost as if afraid of disturbing the crickets. Some girls joined in; two young men ran to the field. Belbo began barking furiously.

"Be good," I told him.

Under the trees there was a table with a bottle and glasses. The innkeeper, a big old man, poured me a glass. It was a sort of inn; all of them were more or less related, and they came up from Turin in a group.

"As long as the weather lasts, fine," an old woman said. "But with the mud and rain?"

"Don't be afraid, granny, there's always a place for you here."

"Now it's nothing, it's this winter."

"This winter the war will be over," a little boy said and ran away.

Fonso and the girls were singing, always in muffled voices, ready to catch a hum or a distant roar of engines.

I, too, was straining to hear anything from minute to minute above the chorus of crickets, and once when the old woman opened the door again, I also shouted at her to close it.

There was something in these people, the young men, their joking, their easy friendliness of wine and company, that I knew from the city in earlier times; other evenings, expeditions on the Po, entertainments in country inns and city taverns, old love affairs. In the cool air of the hill, that emptiness, that tense anxiety, I recovered an older and more remote flavor of peasant life. I let myself listen to the girls and women and was silent. I laughed quietly and wholeheartedly at Fonso's jokes, sitting with the others on a beam under the open sky.

A voice said to me: "And you, what are you doing? On vacation?"

I recognized the voice. Now, thinking back, I am sure I did. I recognized it but didn't ask myself whose it was—a somewhat hoarse, abrupt, and challenging voice, the typical voice, I thought, of the women of this region.

I said jokingly that I was looking for truffles with my dog. She asked me if they ate truffles at the school where I taught. "Who said that I was a teacher?" "One can tell," she answered out of the darkness.

There was a trace of mockery in her voice. Or was it the game to pretend that we were masked? I ran quickly through everything we had said before; I didn't seem to have given myself away and decided that perhaps the people who knew my old women knew about me as well. I asked her if she were staying at Turin or up here.

"Turin," she answered quietly.

I made out in the shadow that she must have a good figure. The curve of her shoulders and knees was attractive. She sat clasping her knees, her head thrown back with a self-satisfied air. I tried to get a better look at her face.

"You're not going to eat me, are you?" she threw in my face.

Just then we heard the all-clear. For an instant everyone was silent in disbelief, then a great uproar broke out; the boys jumped up and down, the old women thanked God, the men grabbed their glasses and beat time on the table. "It's over for tonight." "They'll come again later." "*Italians! I have done it for you!*"

She had remained where she was, leaning back against the wall, and when I said: "You are Cate. You're Cate," she said nothing. I think she had closed her eyes.

I had to move because they were all going indoors. I wanted to pay for my wine, but they said: "Nonsense." I waved, shook hands with Fonso and someone else, called Belbo, and as if by magic found myself alone on the path looking at the black face of the inn.

Soon after, I was back at the villa. But meanwhile night had come, full night, and Elvira was waiting almost on the doorstep, her hands tightly clasped and her lips compressed. All she said was: "You were caught by the alarm tonight. We were worried." I shook my head and smiling into my plate began to eat. She glided silently around in the circle of light, disappeared into the kitchen, began closing cupboard doors. "Would that every evening were like this," I murmured. She said nothing.

As I ate I thought of the meeting, what had happened. I was more struck by the interval, the years, than by Cate. It was incredible. Eight, ten? I seemed to have reopened a room, a forgotten cupboard, and to have found another man's life inside, a futile life, full of risks. It was this that I had forgotten. Not so much Cate, not the poor pleasures of those days, the rash young man who ran away from things thinking they might still happen anyway, who thought of himself as a grown man and was always waiting for his life to begin in earnest; this person amazed me. What did the two of us have in common? What had I done for him? Those banal, emotional evenings, those easy adventures, those hopes as familiar as a bed or a window—it all seemed like the memory of a distant country, of a life of agitation; thinking back, one wondered how it could have been possible both to enjoy and betray it in that fashion.

Elvira took a candle and stopped at the end of the room. She was outside the cone of light from the central lamp and told me to turn it off when I came upstairs. I saw that she had hesitated.

69

The switch was next to the switch for the outside lamp; once in a while I mistook them and flooded the courtyard with light. I said sharply: "Peace. I'll turn off the right one." She coughed with her hand on her throat and forced a laugh. "Good night."

Well, I thought as soon as I was alone, you are not that boy any longer, you aren't taking the old chances. This woman would like to tell you to come home earlier, she would like to have it out with you but doesn't dare; so she wrings her hands, holds tight to her pillow, and clutches her throat. She has no pleasures to promise, and knows it. But she deludes herself seeing you living alone and hopes your whole life will take place here under this lamp, in your room with its pretty curtains, between the sheets she has washed for you. You understand all this but still don't take the old chances. You're not interested in her; if anything, it's your hills you're after.

The next thing I asked myself was if Cate, the old Cate, had been deluded as I had been. Eight years ago, what was she like? A thin, indolent, mocking girl, a bit awkward and violent. She went out with me, went to the movies or out to the fields with me. If she twisted her arm in mine, hiding her broken fingernails, it didn't mean she was expecting anything. It was the year I rented a room in the Via Nizza, when I was giving my first lessons and eating often in milk bars. They were sending me money from home, so little was I able to make out on my own in those days. I had no future beyond the horizon of an average country boy who has finished studying and moved to the city. You look around. Each morning is an adventure and a promise. I saw many people then, made the rounds and lived in a crowd. There were school friends, there was Gallo, who died later from a bomb in Sardinia—women, everybody's sisters, Martino the gambler who married a cashier— the big talkers, the ambitious ones who wrote plays and poems, carrying them around to read aloud in cafés. We went dancing with Gallo, went out to the hill—he came from my part of the world; we talked of opening a country school, he to teach agriculture and I the sciences; we would have bought lands, planted market gardens, remade the countryside. I forget how Cate fell in with us; she lived in the suburbs, on the edge of the meadows that border the Po. Gallo had hangouts apart from ours; he played billiards at the end of the Via Nizza. Once when we passed in a boat he stopped and called Cate from the yard. Then in the summer I took her out alone.

We pulled the boat up on the bank when we took Cate out, went into the fields and played Indians among the bushes. Many women used to intimidate me, but not Cate. With her you could easily lose your temper without losing her. It was a little like asking for something to drink at a country inn: you don't expect a great wine but you know what you're getting. Cate sat still and let you make love. Then she would get panicky lest anyone see us. We didn't have much to say, and this encouraged me. It wasn't necessary for me to talk or make promises. "What's the difference," I used to ask her, "between fighting and making love?" So we did it once or twice on the grass, badly. Then a day came when we began to plan while still on the trolley to go and make love. One morning a thunderstorm broke when we had just arrived and made us curse our lost opportunity.

One evening Cate came upstairs to my room to smoke a cigarette in peace and that time we made love with more enthusiasm on the bed, and she said how nice it was when it was cold or raining to come around and be together, to discuss things and relax. She stroked my books and sniffed at them in fun and asked if I really had the use of the room day and night without anyone coming to disturb me. She lived with her family, six or seven of them, in two rooms over a court. But that was the only evening she came to see me. She came to the café instead where I saw my friends, but in spite of Gallo's being there and everyone's friendliness toward her, she sat depressed and no longer laughed as she used to. I was wobbling then between the satisfaction of having a girl of my own and embarrassment at the rather slovenly and awkward person she was. She told me she would like to learn typing, work in a big store, and earn enough to go to a famous spa. Several times, to her great delight, I bought her a stick of rouge, and it was then I understood that one can support a woman, educate her, give her a good life, but as soon as one knows too much about what her elegance is composed of, then goodbye magic. Cate's dress was threadbare and the leather of her handbag cracked; it was touching to listen to her, so great was the contrast between her life and her desires. But her joy in the rouge got on my nerves, made me realize that for me it was all mainly sex. Graceless, tiresome sex. It was a pain to know that she was so dissatisfied and ignorant. She improved at times, but she kept having foolish enthusiasms, sudden moods of revolt, and maddening fits of ingenuousness. The idea of being tied to her or of owing her something for the time she had given weighed on me always. One evening, under the station arcade, I held her by the arm and asked her to come to my room. Summer was nearly over and my landlady's son was returning from camp the next day; with him in the house it would be impossible to entertain a woman. I begged, I implored her to come; I clowned and cracked jokes. "I'm not going to eat you," I told her. Nothing doing. "I'm not going to eat you." That stubborn bashfulness shook me up. She hugged my arm and kept repeating: "Let's go for a walk."

"Then let's go to the movies," I said, laughing. "I've got money."

And she, angrily: "I don't go with you for the money."

"But I, on the other hand," I said point-blank, "go with you to go to bed." We looked daggers at each other, both red in the face. The shame I felt later; I think that later I might have wept with anger if it had not been for the pride and the joy that swept over me because now I was free. Cate was crying, tears streaming down. She said quietly: "All right, I'll go with you." We reached the outer door without speaking; she clung to me and leaned all her weight on my shoulder. At the door she made me stop. She hesitated, said: "No, I don't trust you," squeezed my arm hard, and ran away.

After that evening I never saw her again. I thought little about it because I was sure she would come back. When I realized she was not coming, the sting of my meanness had already faded. Gallo and my friends were my whole horizon again, and, to be brief, I was enjoying that satisfaction of appeased bitterness, of an occasion well lost, that later became a habit with me. Not even Gallo mentioned her again; there wasn't time anyway. He left with a commission for the African front and I didn't see him for some time. That winter I put his agriculture and the country school out of my mind, became a complete city man, and discovered that life was really worth living. I visited many houses, talked politics, tried new pleasures and adventures, and managed not to let them hurt me. I took some jobs in science, saw people, got to know my colleagues. I studied hard for some months and imagined a future for myself. That shadow of doubt in the air, that fever in everybody, the menace of war about to break out made the days more vivid and our adventures more futile. One could let oneself go and then recover; nothing really happened and everything had a savor. Tomorrow, who knows?

Now things were happening and the war had come. I hashed it all over at night, seated in the cone of light while my old women slept; composed, pathetic, and at peace. What did the air raids matter on the hill when everyone was safely back and no lights were showing? Even Cate was asleep, in the house in the middle of the woods. Was she still thinking about my old harshness? I remembered as if it were yesterday and wasn't sorry that our meeting had been so brief and in the dark.

Working at Turin, walking, coming home in the evening, talking to Belbo, I ruminated on all this for several days. One night when I was in the orchard a new alarm sounded. The antiaircraft began firing immediately. We retired to the parlor, which shook with the explosions. Outside, dead splinters hissed among the trees. Elvira was trembling, her mother silent. Then a roar of engines and more explosions. Over and over the window glowed red or flashed brilliantly. It lasted more than an hour, and when we went outside amid the last sporadic firing, the whole valley of Turin was in flames.

3. The next morning I returned with many others to the city to a distant reverberation of crashings and boomings. People with bundles were running about everywhere. The asphalt of the streets was pitted with holes, covered with leaves and pools of water. It looked as though a hailstorm had passed. The last fires were still crackling, red and shameless, in the bright sun.

As usual, the school was untouched. Old Domenico, eager to escape and see the sights, welcomed me. He had been out already before dawn, after the all-clear, at the moment when people are emerging from their holes and running around, when some student-teacher half opens the door, letting in light from the many large fires outside, when one takes a drink and enjoys merely being alive. He told me what it had been like in our air-raid shelter where he slept. No classes today, naturally. Even the trolleys stood still with their doors open, empty, where the catastrophe had found them. The tracks had all been damaged. The walls were all scored as if by the maddened wing of a bird of fire. "Awful street, nobody goes by," Domenico kept repeating. "The secretary hasn't shown up yet. Fellini hasn't come. You can't find out anything."

A cyclist stopped, put a foot down, and told us that Turin had been entirely destroyed. "There are thousands of dead," he told us. "They have smashed the station, burned out the markets. They said on the radio they were coming back tonight." He pedaled off without looking back.

"He knows how to talk," Domenico grumbled. "I don't understand Fellini. He's usually here by now."

Our street was truly peaceful and solitary. The tuft of trees in the schoolyard crowned the high wall like a provincial garden. Today one couldn't hear even the usual noises, the rattling of trolleys or human voices. Not hearing the pounding of boys' feet this morning was not so strange, but it seemed incredible that even against this calm sky between the houses the apocalypse had raged in the dead of night. I told Domenico to go if he wanted and look for Fellini. I would stay at the porter's office and wait for them.

I spent half the morning getting the class register up to date for the coming inspections. I added up figures, wrote summaries. Now and then I glanced down the corridors or into the empty classrooms. I was thinking of the women who lay out a corpse, wash and clothe it. Any moment the sky might roar again, burst into flames, and nothing remain of the school but a cavernous hole. Only life, naked life, mattered. Registers, schools, and corpses were things already discounted.

Mumbling the names of the boys in the silence, I felt like an old woman mumbling her prayers. I had to smile. The faces came back. Had any of them been killed last night? Their excitement on the day after a raid—the disorder, the novelty, the hope of a holiday—was like my own pleasure in escaping every evening from the alarms, in finding myself in my cool bedroom and stretching out in safety on the bed. How could I smile at their innocence? We all had an innocence in this war; for all of us these frightful circumstances had been made banal, routine, unpleasant. Whoever took them seriously and said: "It's war," was worse off; he was a fool or a cripple.

Nevertheless, someone had died last night; if not thousands, at least tens. Enough, anyway. I thought of those who stayed in town, of Cate. The idea that she didn't go up to the hill every evening had got stuck in my head. I thought I'd heard something of the sort in the courtyard. As a matter of fact, after that night's alarm they hadn't sung again. I wondered if I might have something to say to her, if I feared something from her. I seemed only to be missing that darkness, that air of a house and woods, the young voices, the novelty. Perhaps Cate had been singing with the others that night. If nothing has happened, I thought, tonight they will go back up.

The phone rang. The father of one of the boys. He wanted to know if there really were no classes. What a disaster last night . . . and were the professors and the headmaster safe and sound? Was his son studying his physics? Of course, war is war. I should be patient. One must try to understand and help the boys' families. Humble respects and apologies.

From then on there was no peace from the phone. Boys called, teachers and the secretary called. Fellini called. "Are you functioning?" he said, surprised. I imagined the discontent that had crumpled half his face. "There's nobody in the porter's office, what do you think? that it's a picnic? Come down here right away and give Domenico a hand." I hung up and went out. I'd talked enough. After a night like that, it was all ridiculous.

I used up the morning strolling at random in the confusion and sunshine. Some ran around, some stood and stared. Gutted houses were still smoking. Intersections were blocked. High up, amid the newly opened walls, strips of wallpaper and kitchen sinks were dangling in the sun. It wasn't always easy to distinguish between the new and the old ruins. One noticed the general effect and concluded that a bomb never fell twice in the same place. Excited, sweating cyclists put down a foot, gaped, and pushed off for other sights. Wherever a fire had raged, children, mattresses, broken furniture seemed to pile up on the sidewalk outside. An old woman was emptying out a boarding house by herself. The others stood around watching. Every so often we studied the sky.

It was strange to see the soldiers. When they passed in patrols with helmets and shovels, one knew they were going to dig out the shelters, to bring out the dead and the living, and one wanted to stir them up, yell at them to run, to hurry, for the love of God. That's all they were good for, we said among ourselves. We took it for granted that the war was lost. But the soldiers marched slowly, skirting the holes, they too staring all around at the houses. A moderately pretty woman walked by and they cheered her in chorus. They were the only ones, the soldiers, who seemed aware that women still existed. In a city disorganized and always expecting trouble, nobody noticed women any more, no one followed them, not even in their summer dresses, not even when they were laughing. Even in this I had anticipated the war; this peril had been absent from my life for some time. If I still had desires, I had no more illusions.

In a café where I stopped to read a paper—newspapers were still being printed—the patrons were talking in low voices. The paper said that the war was grim but that it was something all our own, made out of faith and passion, the only riches we still had. It had happened that bombs fell even on Rome, destroying a church and violating some tombs. This deed called even the dead to our side; it was the last of a series of bloody acts that had angered the whole civilized world. One must draw faith from this final insult. We were at a point beyond which there could be nothing worse. The enemy was losing his head.

A patron I knew, a fat and jovial man, said that at bottom the war had been won already. "I look around and what do I see?" he shouted. "Crowded trains, business booming, a black market, and plenty of money. Hotels are open, industries are functioning, everywhere people are working and spending. Is anyone giving in, does anybody think of surrender? All right, a few houses destroyed mean suffering. But the government will pay for them anyway. If we have reached this point in three years of war, there's good reason to hope it will last a little longer. After all, we all might die in our beds."

"The government isn't to blame for what happens," said someone else. "Ask yourself where we would be with another government."

I left because I had heard this all before. Outside, a large fire that had damaged a palazzo on the avenue was dying down. Porters were carrying out lamps and armchairs. They had heaped a great shambles of furniture in the sunshine: little tables with mirrors, thick chests. This elegant stuff made one think of a store window. It reminded me of houses I used to know, of our evenings and discussions, and my frenzies. Gallo had been in Africa for a while and I was working at the Institute. That was the year I believed in science as the crux of city life, in academic science with its laboratories, congresses, and professorships; the year of great adventures, when I knew Anna Maria and wanted to marry her. I would have become her father's assistant. I would have taken trips. There were cushions and armchairs in her house; one discussed the theater, planned mountain vacations. Anna Maria knew how to appeal to my peasant side; she said I was different from the others, praised my project for country schools. Except that whenever she mentioned Gallo she made him out as some kind of boring hayseed. Anna Maria taught me how to speak, how to hold my tongue, to send flowers. We went out the whole winter, and one night in the mountains she called me into her room. From that moment she had me by the nose, and pretended to be my loving slave without doing anything to bolster my self-confidence. Every day she had some new whim and jeered at my patience. When scenes broke out—threatening, portentous looks from dark-rimmed eyes—she became sullen, too, and would cry like a baby. She said she didn't understand me; I gave her the shudders. To stop all this nonsense I wanted to marry her. I asked her everywhere, on staircases, at dances, in doorways. She played mysterious and smiled.

This went on for three years and brought me almost to suicide. Killing her wouldn't have been worth the trouble. But I lost my enthusiasm for advanced science, for the beau monde, for scientific institutes. I felt like a peasant. Because the war didn't begin that year (I was still expecting the war to settle something), I became a teacher and started my current way of life. Nowadays I mostly smile at flowers and cushions, but when I first discussed them with Gallo I was still smarting. In uniform on another occasion,

Gallo said: "Foolishness. It hits everybody sooner or later." But he didn't realize our being hit is rarely a matter of chance. In a sense I continued to suffer, not because I missed Anna Maria, not at all, but because every thought of women had this threat. If I shut myself up little by little in bitterness, it was because I was looking for bitterness, because I had always been looking for it, and not just with her.

This is what I was thinking as I stood in front of the gutted palazzo. At the end of the avenue, amid trees, one could see the great ridge of hills, green and deep in the summer. I wondered if I should stay in the city and not return until evening. Usually the raids came at night, but yesterday's at Rome had been at noon. The first days of the war I kept out of the shelters, forcing myself to stay in the classroom, walking nervously about. Those early raids were a joke. Now they had become heavy and fearful; the siren alone struck terror in one's heart. There was no good reason to stay until evening. A whole class of people, the lucky, the top drawer, were going, or had gone, to their villas in the mountains or by the sea. There they lived pretty much as usual. It was left to their servants, their doormen, the poor, to take care of their mansions in town, to pull their chestnuts out of the fire. Left to the porters, the soldiers, and the mechanics. Then even those others began to get away at night to the woods and inns. There was little sleeping. Mostly they drank or argued, ten in a hole. Shame at not being one of them had stayed with me; I wanted to meet them in the road and talk. Or perhaps I was only enjoying that easy danger and doing nothing to change. I liked to be alone and to imagine that no one was waiting for me.

4. That evening I came home under a sliver of moon and gossiped after dinner in the orchard as my old women liked me to. From the villa nearby, Egle had come over, a little fifteen-year-old student whom Elvira was taking care of. They said the schools ought to close, that it was a crime to keep the children in the city.

"And the teachers. And the porters," I added. "And the trolley conductors. And the bar cashiers."

My sallies annoyed Elvira. Egle's little eyes narrowed on me.

"Do you mean what you say?" she asked suspiciously. "Or are you joking even tonight?"

"The soldiers have to fight the war," Elvira's mother said. "It's never been like this before."

"It touches everyone," I said. "Everyone will have his turn to complain."

The moon went down behind the trees. In a few nights it would be full and would flood earth and sky, would light up Turin and bring on the bombs.

"Someone," Egle put in, "said that the war would be over this year."

"Over?" I said. "It hasn't even begun."

I stood still, listened hard, and saw a startled look in the others. Elvira recovered and they all were silent. "Someone is singing," Egle broke in, relieved.

"Good for them."

"What idiots."

I left Egle at the gate. Alone among the trees, I couldn't find the road at first. Belbo was on a path of his own, panting among the bramble bushes. I wandered vaguely, as one does in the moonlight, fascinated by the tree trunks. Once again Turin, shelters and sirens, was like a distant fantasy. But so was the encounter I hoped for, so were those voices in the air, even Cate was unreal. I wondered what I would have said if I could have discussed them, for instance with Gallo.

When I reached the road, my thoughts were back on the war, on the useless dead. The courtyard was empty. They were singing in the field behind the house. Belbo had lost himself halfway back and no one knew I was there. In the shadowy blur I made out the window gratings, the little stone tables, the half-open door. Corncobs from the year before were hanging from a balcony. The whole house had an abandoned, almost rustic look.

"If Cate comes out," I thought, "she may tell me everything, to get revenge."

I was on the point of leaving and going back to the woods. I hoped Cate wasn't there, that she had stayed in Turin. But a small boy turned the corner on the run and stopped dead. He had seen me.

"Nobody here?" I asked him.

He looked at me doubtfully, a white boy dressed in a sailor suit, a funny sight in the dim moonlight. I had missed him the other evening.

He went to the door and called inside: "Mama." Cate emerged with a platter of vegetable peelings. Just then Belbo hurtled up, rolled over, and plunged into the shadow. The frightened boy clung to Cate's skirts.

"Silly," Cate said to him. "It's nothing."

"Are you all still alive?" I asked Cate.

She had turned toward the grating to throw away the peels. She stopped in her tracks. She turned her head—taller than before—I recognized her mocking smile. "Are you playing some trick?" she said. "Do you come here to make fun of us?"

"Last night," I said, "I didn't hear singing, so I thought you had stayed in Turin."

"Dino," she said to the boy. She threw out the peels and sent him inside with the platter.

Alone, she stopped laughing. She said: "Why aren't you with the others?"

"Is he your boy?" I asked.

She looked at me without a word.

"Are you married?"

She shook her head hard—this I remembered too—and said: "What does it matter to you?"

"He's a good-looking boy, well set up," I told her.

"I take him to Turin. He's going to school. We come back here before dark."

I could see her clearly in the moonlight. She was the same but seemed someone different. She spoke with self-possession, though it seemed yesterday when she and I were walking arm in arm together. She wore a short skirt, country style.

"You don't sing?" I asked.

Again that hard smile, again that headshake. "Have you come to hear us sing? Why don't you go back to your café?"

"You child," I said with a smile she hadn't seen on me before. "Are you still thinking of those days?"

I noticed the familiar sensual lips, but they were firmer, more compact. The boy came back into the yard and Belbo began to bark. "Here, Belbo," I shouted. Dino flew by, ran behind the house.

"You won't believe it," I told Cate, "but my only companion is this dog."

"It's not yours," she said.

Then I asked her good-humoredly if she perhaps knew everything about me. "About you I know nothing at all," I said. "What kind of life have you had, how are you living now? Did you know that Gallo was killed in Sardinia?"

"It's not true!" Cate said, upset. I told her how it had happened and she was almost in tears. "It's this war," she said then, "this stinking business." She was beside herself; she stared at the ground.

"And you, what have you been doing?" I asked. "Did you get your job in the store?"

She twisted her mouth again and said again what did I care. We were close; I took her hand. But I didn't want her to think I was playing with her feelings. I held her wrist gently. "Don't you want to tell me what your life has been?"

A bulky old woman came out of the house. "Who is it?" she said. Cate told her about me; the old woman had come to talk. Just then the moon went down.

"Dino has joined the others," Cate said.

"Why don't you change him out of his sailor suit?" the woman said. "Don't you know the grass will stain the seat of his pants?"

Cate answered something. I spoke of the moon. We walked together toward the field. They had stopped singing and were laughing. In the short interval I learned that the old woman was Cate's grandmother, that the house was an inn, Le Fontane, but after the war began, people stopped coming there. "If this war doesn't end," the woman said, "your grandfather will sell and we'll all go live under a bridge."

This time there were few people behind the house: Fonso, another man, two girls. They were eating apples under a tree, pulling them off the low branches. They ate and laughed. Dino had stayed at the edge of the field to watch.

Cate went up and spoke to him. I stayed with her grandmother in the shadow of the house.

"More people were here the other night," I said. "Did they stay in Turin?"

The old woman said: "Not all of us have automobiles. Some of them work until night. The trolleys aren't running." Then she looked closely at me and dropped her voice. "The people in charge are scum," she muttered. "Dirty blackshirts. Do they think of us? Look who they handed us over to."

I waved at Fonso in the distance. He had yelled something to me, gesturing. They were shouting among themselves, throwing apples and running. Cate turned back.

They were calling from the house. A darkened door had opened and someone said: "Fonso, it's time."

Then everybody, girls, young men, the boy, hurtled toward us, passed, and disappeared.

The old woman sighed. "Oh, well," she said, moving off. "Those people. Let them make their own peace. They won't eat each other, that's for sure. It's us who get caught."

I stayed alone with Cate. "Aren't you coming to listen to the radio?" she asked.

She took a few steps with me, then stopped.

"You're not a Fascist, are you?" she said.

She was serious and laughing. I took her hand and snorted: "We all are, dear Cate. If we weren't we would revolt, throw grenades, risk our necks. Whoever lets things go and takes it easy is already a Fascist."

"It's not true," she said. "We're waiting for the right time. Wait till the war is over."

She was very angry. I held her arm.

"Once," I told her, laughing, "you didn't care for these things."

"You're not doing anything? What are your friends doing?" So I told her I hadn't seen my friends for some time. One had married, another had been transferred to goodness knows where. "Do you remember Martino? He was married in a bar."

We laughed at Martino together. "It happens to everybody," I went on. "You spend months, years together, then it happens. Someone misses an engagement, someone moves, someone you saw every day changes so much you no longer know who he is."

Cate said that the war was to blame.

"This kind of war is nothing new." I said. "A day comes when we all find ourselves alone. It's not so bad." She looked me up and down. "Every so often one finds someone again," I added.

"And what does that mean to you?" she said. "You don't want to do anything. You want to be alone."

"Yes. I like being alone."

Then Cate talked about herself. She had worked, had been in a factory, maid in a hotel, counselor at a summer camp. At the moment she went to work every day in a hospital. The old house on the Via Nizza had been hit the year before and everyone in it killed.

"That evening," I said, "were you offended, Cate?"

She looked at me with an ambiguous half smile. More from obstinacy than anything else, I asked, "Well then, are you married or not?"

She shook her head slowly.

There's been someone more of a stinker than I was, I thought, and I said: "The boy is your son?"

"And if he is?"

"Are you ashamed of him?"

She shrugged the way she used to. I thought she was laughing. Instead she said in a low, hoarse tone: "Corrado, let's leave it there. I don't want to talk about it. May I still call you Corrado?"

Then I felt at peace. I saw that Cate was not thinking of taking me on again. She had her life and that was enough. I had been afraid that she might be dramatic and humiliated, as she had been once before. I said: "Goose. You can call me what you like." Belbo sidled up and I took him by the neck.

Then everybody came out of the darkened house, chattering and laughing.

5. June ended, the schools closed, and I stayed on the hill all day. I explored it in the sun, down the wooded slopes. Behind the inn the land was laid out in fields and vineyards where I often went, to certain sheltered hollows, to collect herbs and mosses, my old passion from a boyhood study of botany. I used to prefer farmland and

its outer edges where wildness took over to villas and gardens. Le Fontane was ideally situated; the woods began right there. I saw Cate other times, morning and evening, but we didn't talk about ourselves. I got to know Fonso and the others fairly well.

With Fonso it was mainly jokes. He was really a boy, not yet eighteen. "In this war," I told him, "we will all take part somehow. They will call you up at twenty and me at forty. How are we doing in Sicily?"

Fonso worked as a messenger in an engineering firm. Each evening he arrived with his mother and sisters and in the morning raced off like a demon on his bicycle. He was cynical, a great joker; he got worked up easily.

"Word of God," he said, "if they draft me I'll blow up headquarters."

"You too! Only if you get burned. Everybody waits to get burned before they come to life."

"If all those people they've called up so far would come to life," Fonso said, "we might get somewhere."

At night school the year before, Fonso had developed a taste for statistics, the newspapers, all the obvious things. He must have had fellow workers at Turin who were opening his eyes. He knew everything about the war; he never let the subject drop; he asked a question and cut your answer short with another question. He was also hot on science and scientific theory.

He asked me while I was talking if as a civilian I was ready to come to life myself.

"One has to be on the ball," I said, "to be younger. Talk gets you nowhere. The only way is terrorism. We're at war."

Fonso said it wasn't necessary. The Fascists were scared. They knew they had lost the war. They didn't dare any longer to draft people. They were only looking for an opportunity to give in, disappear in the crowd, and say: "Now *you* take over." The whole thing was a house of cards.

"Do you think so? They've got everything to lose. They won't give in until they are dead."

The others, Cate's grandmother, the women, were listening.

"If he says they are scum," the innkeeper broke in, "believe him. He knows. Drop it."

All of them at Le Fontane knew I was a teacher, a scientist. They treated me with considerable respect. Even Cate was submissive sometimes.

"This government," the old man continued, "can't go on."

"But that's exactly why it lasts. Everyone says, 'It's dead,' and nobody does anything."

"You, what do you say? What would you do?" a serious Cate asked me. They all stared at me in silence.

"Murder them," I said. "Stop them where they live. Continue the war here at home. Otherwise nothing will touch them. Only when they know that every move they make will set off a bomb will they stay quiet."

Fonso grinned and tried to interrupt.

"Would you do it?" Cate said.

"No," I answered. "I can't."

Cate's grandmother looked at us with her reproachful eyes. "You people, you don't know what it costs. Don't overwork your consciences. Even those people will die some day."

Then Fonso explained to her what the class struggle was.

I went now to Le Fontane nearly every evening to listen to the radio with the others. My two women were deeply shocked to learn that we were listening to London. "It's forbidden," Elvira said. "They might hear you from the road." She bemoaned my walking the woods at night during the raids. There had been another murderous raid on Turin. The two of them found a piece of shrapnel in the orchard the next morning, sharp and heavy as the blade of a hoe. They called me over to look at it. They begged me not to expose myself. So I said there were plenty of inns; one could take cover anywhere.

Arriving at Le Fontane in broad daylight gave me a sense of adventure. From the embankment I came out on the empty road, which had once been tarred over. Only the year before, it had been crowded with cars, cyclists, pedestrians. Now a pedestrian was an event.

I lingered in the courtyard to eat fruit or drink a glass of wine. The old woman offered me coffee, water, and sugar. To pay her back I ordered wine. At that hour I wasn't expecting Cate or anyone else. If Cate was there, I watched her bustle around, asked for

the gossip of Turin. In truth, I stayed there chiefly for the pleasure
of being at the edge of the woods. In the July sun, savage and still,
the familiar little table, the well-known faces, and that drawn-out
leavetaking satisfied me deeply. Once Cate came to the window
and said: "Oh, it's you," and didn't even come down.

The one who was never missing in the yard or behind the house
was her son, Dino. Now that school was over, the grandmother
was in charge and let him play, washed his face with a rag, and
called him to meals. Dino was no longer the pale and silent boy he
had been that night. He ran, threw stones, wrecked his shoes—
a lean little monkey. I don't know why, but he almost always gave
me a pain. Looking at him, I thought of Cate's unhappiness years
ago, her awkward body, the shame of those days. It must have been
the year of Anna Maria. Cate, alone and humiliated, didn't know
how to defend herself; somehow she must have given in, at some
dance or in a field, to someone who despised her, some poor fish,
some suburban Romeo. Or maybe it had been a great, transforming
love affair. Would she ever have told me? If we hadn't parted that
evening at the station, perhaps this monkey would have never
been born.

Dino's hair flopped in his eyes and he wore a patched-up knitted vest. He preened himself a lot with me about school and his
colored notebooks. I told him I hadn't studied as many subjects
as he was studying, but that I had also done a little drawing in
my day—small stones, hazelnuts, rare plants. I made him a few.

That same day he followed me up the hill to gather mosses. Dis-
covering the little Veronica flowers made him happy. I promised to
bring my glass, and he wanted to know how much it magnified.

"These little specks of violet," I told him, "look like roses or
carnations."

Dino trotted behind me and wanted to come to the villa to try
the magnifying glass right away. He talked easily, sure of himself,
as if with his playmates. But he used the formal *voi*.

"Listen here," I told him, "you've got to use *tu* or *lei* with me.
Voi is for Fascists. Use *tu* like your mother."

"You're just like my mother," he said sharply. "You want us to
lose the war."

Then I said: "I get all the *voi* I can take at school."

I said: "So you like the war?"

Dino looked pleased. "I'd like to be a soldier. To fight in Sicily." Then he asked: "Are they going to fight here, too?"

"You bet your boots," I said. "Are you afraid of the sirens?"

Lord, no. He had been to see where the bombs had fallen. He knew all the airplane engines and types and had three incendiary bomb sticks at home. He wondered if one could go collect bullets in the fields after a battle.

"The real bullets," I said, "may land anywhere. All that stays in the fields are the cartridge cases and the dead."

"In the desert there are vultures," Dino added, "who bury the dead."

"They eat them," I said. He laughed.

"Does your mama know that you want to fight in a war?"

We came into the yard. Cate and her grandmother were sitting under the trees.

Dino lowered his voice: "Mama says the war is a disgrace. That it's all the Fascists' fault."

"Do you love your mother?" I asked.

He shrugged his shoulders, as if between two men. The women watched us come up.

I couldn't tell in those days whether Cate liked me to be with Dino. The old woman did—I kept him from under her feet. Cate seemed surprised to see him hanging around me collecting flowers, snatching the glass out of my hand; she snapped at him occasionally as one does with children who lack respect for their elders. Dino shut up, hunched over comically, and went on talking in a whisper. Then he ran to show her his drawings of the parts of a flower. He shouted to her that I was going to bring a book about plants. Cate held him, fixed his hair, said something to him. I almost preferred the times when Cate was away.

I thought that Cate was jealous of her son. One evening I caught her looking at me with a shadow of contempt. "Cate, do I upset you sometimes?" I asked her lightheartedly. The question caught her off guard; she dropped her eyes and voice. "Why?" she stammered, she who usually cut such questions short.

"We were being boys together," I said. "One never learns things in time."

But by then she was looking up and shouting across the court-yard.

Shortly afterward she said to me: "Do your women know you are lowering yourself to talk to us? Do you tell them when you come home at night that you've been to the inn? What's the name of that bandy-legged woman who wants to marry you? Elvira?"

I had told her all these things in fun. "What's the trouble?" I said. "I like to be with you. I like everyone here. I explore the woods and roads. I like you all, the same way I like the hill."

"But do you tell Elvira?"

"What has Elvira to do with it?"

"Elvira is the mother of your dog," she said emphatically. "Doesn't she deserve to know where you've been all day?"

"Elvira is an idiot."

"Still, you're well off there. As you are with us."

"Are you jealous, Cate?"

"Of whom? You make me laugh. Am I jealous of Fonso?"

"But Fonso is a boy," I shouted. "So what?"

"We're all children to you," she said. "We're like your dog."

That was all I had from her that evening. Fonso arrived, and the girls and Dino. We chattered, listened, someone sang. There were new faces. Some friends of Fonso—newlyweds bombed out of their apartment—were drinking. Then, when it was time, Cate chased after a reluctant Dino, to bring him to bed. They all chased him around in the dark, and somebody said: "Corrado." "Corrado," they kept saying—and the one called Corrado obeyed.

6. Cate had just come back to the yard when I went up to her. She hadn't noticed anything. Perhaps she thought I wanted to talk some more about Elvira. She gave me a cool look and stopped.

"His name is Corrado," I said.

She looked at me, surprised.

"It's my name," I said.

She twisted her head in that stubborn way of hers. She looked at the others, at the tables, in the shadow. "Go away, they'll see us," she whispered, scared.

I swung around to stay near her. She walked fast and said lightly: "Didn't you know that was his name?"

"Why did you give him that name?"

A shrug and no answer.

"How old is Dino?" I stopped her.

She pinched my arm. "Later. Behave yourself."

They gossiped a long time about the war and the raids. Fonso's friend had been wounded in Albania and told what everybody had known for some time. "I got married in order to sleep in a bed," he went on. "And now the bed has gone." And the little wife: "We'll sleep in the fields, don't worry." I sat next to the old woman and was examining Cate's profile in silence. I had the feeling that I had rediscovered her that night, that I had been talking to her without knowing who she was. Each time a little more obtuse; that's how I had been. It had taken me a month to discover that Dino was short for Corrado. What was Dino's face like? I closed my eyes but failed to visualize it.

I leaped up suddenly to walk in the yard. "Will you go in behind with me?" Cate asked, jumping up also. I walked with a slight feeling of nausea; my life seemed to be crumbling. It was like an air-raid shelter when the walls are shaking; when one says to oneself: "So many things I might have done."

We walked in the dark. Cate kept silent. She took my arm, stumbling and making small jumps. "Hold me up." I did so. We stopped.

"Corrado," she said. "I was wrong to give Dino that name. But you see it doesn't matter. Nobody ever calls him that."

"Then why did you do it?"

"I was still in love with you. You don't know that I was in love with you?"

I thought to myself that she would have said so long before if it were true. "If you love me," I said brusquely, pulling her arm, "whose son is Dino?"

She freed herself. She was strong, stronger than I. "Don't worry," she said. "Have no fear. It wasn't you who did it."

We looked at each other in the dark; I felt weak and sweaty. She had just a touch of sarcasm in her voice.

"What did you say?" she asked quickly.

"Nothing. Nothing. If you love me . . ."

"Not any longer, Corrado."

"If you gave him my name, how could you have gone to bed with someone else that winter?"

In the dark I got control of my voice again; I felt humble and generous. I was speaking to the old Cate, the desperate girl.

"You made love with me," she said quietly, "and you didn't care a damn one way or the other."

That was something else, but what could I answer? I told her as much. She said that one could make love and think of something entirely different. "You know it's true," she repeated. "You don't love anyone, though you must have done it often enough."

I told her again, softly, that I hadn't been thinking of those things for some time.

She went back: "You did it anyway."

"Cate," I was getting angry. "At least tell me who it was."

She smiled again, ignoring my question. "I've already told you how I lived during those years. I always worked harder than I needed to. At the beginning it was ugly. But I had Dino. I couldn't afford to mess around. I remembered what you told me once, that life is worthwhile only when you live for something or someone."

This, too, I had taught her. The phrase was mine. If she asks for whom are you living now, I thought, what would you say?

"Come now, you don't despise me?" I forced a smile. "There was something good between us? You can think of those days without spite?"

"You weren't bad in those days."

"But now I am?" I said, taken by surprise. "Now I give you the creeps?"

"Now you seem unhappy and make me feel bad," she said gravely. "You live alone with a dog. You bother me."

I looked at her, amazed. "Am I no longer any good, Cate? Even with you, am I worse than before?"

"I don't know," Cate said. "You're sort of nice in a feeble way. You let things slide and don't inspire much confidence. You have nobody, you don't even get worked up about anything."

"I was worked up about Dino," I said.

"You don't love anybody."

"Do I have to kiss you, Cate?"

"Fool!" She kept calm. "That's not what I meant. If I'd cared, you would have kissed me some time ago." She paused a moment. "You're like a boy, a conceited boy. One of those boys in whose lives something has gone wrong but they don't want anyone to know about it, to know they are suffering. That's why you bother me. When you talk to the others you are always resentful, malicious. You're afraid, Corrado."

"It's the war, the bombs."

"No, it's you," Cate said. "You live that way. Just now you were afraid about Dino. Afraid he might be your son."

They were calling us from the courtyard, calling Cate.

"Let's go back," Cate said, submissively. "Don't worry. No one will disturb your peace."

She had taken me by the arm and I stopped her short. "Cate, if it is true about Dino, I want to marry you."

She looked at me, not laughing or otherwise disturbed. "Dino is my son," she said quietly. "Let's go."

So I passed another night like the one before, when I first found her again. This time Elvira had gone to bed early. Now that I was spending all day on the hill, she knew she had me safely in hand and let me indulge my whims. She laughed at me because, with all my mosses and poking around in the fields, I didn't know the names of her garden flowers; of some of them—scarlet, fleshy, and obscene—I didn't even want to hear. Her eyes danced when she talked about them.

"Evil night thoughts," I told her, "turn into flowers. No name could describe them. Even science stops at a certain point." She laughed, hugging her elbows, flattered by my game. I was reminded of it that evening because there were some of those flowers in the bunch on the table. I wondered if Cate, had she seen them, would have appreciated the joke. Maybe so, but not expressed that way, not so obliquely. I had discovered something that evening, another proof that I had been stupid and blind even on this occasion. Cate was serious and in control of herself; she understood things better than I did. The arrogant, superior tone I used to take got me exactly nowhere with her now. It haunted me all night; her sarcasm loomed portentously over my long night's insomnia. I even found some comfort in it. If Cate said that Dino was hers, I would have to accept her word. My mind was busy until dawn, and at breakfast when Elvira returned from Mass, I said to myself with a laugh: If you only knew what's going on. She, instead, had heard at Santa Margherita that the war couldn't last much longer because the Pope had made a speech advising everyone to live together in peace. One had only to wish it with all one's heart and peace would be made. No more bombs, no fires or bloodshed. No more vendettas or hopes for a second flood. Elvira was restless and happy. I said I was going for a walk and left her busy around the oven.

It was Sunday and all the Saturday-night people were still at Le Fontane. I saw Nando, the bombed-out husband, at the window, and Fonso's sisters, who were shouting something at him. I waved at the girls, asked if Dino had gone to the woods. They pointed to the field behind. I meant to leave everything to chance and told Giulia to tell him I had gone to the spring. Belbo, big and excited, was already nosing in the woods. I called him, made him crouch on the path, told him to wait for Dino. He growled and showed his teeth.

When I was on the slope and the voices were dying away, I imagined the two of them running among the trees, the fine adventure. Perhaps in twenty years Dino would remember that hour, the odor of the sun, the distant voices, sliding down rocks. I heard a panting and rustling and Belbo appeared. He stopped and looked at me. He was alone. I waved and said: "Go. Come back with Dino. Go on!" I stooped to pick up a stone. Then Belbo leaped and began barking at me. I took up a stone. Belbo went slowly back the way he had come.

I came up below the spring, in a hollow of thick, muddy grasses. Patches of sky and airy hillsides showed among the trees. The coolness there smelled of the sea, almost briny. What did the war, what did the bloodshed matter, I thought, when this kind of sky shone amid the trees? One could arrive on the run, throw oneself on the grass, play hide-and-seek or Indians. That was how snakes, hares, and boys lived. The war would end tomorrow. Everything would be as before. Peace would return, the old games, the rancors. The earth would drink up the spilled blood. The cities would breathe again. Only in the woods would nothing change, and where a body had fallen roots would take hold.

Dino arrived with his stick, whistling, preceded by Belbo. He said that Giulia hadn't told him; he had figured it out for himself that I was waiting. I asked him: "What's that on your face?" and holding him steady I looked at him carefully, ran my fingers over his features—eyes, eyelids, profile. But can one say that a child resembles an adult? I had laughed over it countless times. Now I was paying. Dino rolled his eyes, puffed his cheeks, sighed heavily. This, if anything, this stubborn withholding, was like something in me. I tried to see my own boyhood in that contortion. I thought that I had also had a neck as thin as that when I explored the vineyards in these regions.

Then we started off. "Today we will really get to the top." I told him about the times I had squeezed grapes in my village. "Everybody, man and boy, has to wash his feet. But the barefoot ones had cleaner feet than we had."

"I go barefoot myself sometimes in the fields," Dino said.

"You're no good for squeezing grapes. You weigh too little. How old are you, exactly?"

He told me. He was born at the end of August. But Cate, had I left her in November or in October? I couldn't recall. It was cool that evening by the station. There was fog; was it winter? I couldn't remember. All I remembered were struggles in the August heat by the Po.

Once we reached the road along the ridge, we went faster. It was the village of Pino. From here, from balconies of houses that jutted out in midair, one could see the plain of Chieri, smoky and endless.

"My father," I told Dino, "used to cover a stretch of road like this every morning before dawn, in a little cart, on his way to the market."

Dino trotted along, not opening his mouth, rapping the asphalt with his stick.

"You didn't know your father?" I said.

"Mama, she knew him," he replied. "She says they haven't seen each other again."

"You don't know who he was?"

He looked at me confidently but impatiently. It was clear he had never thought about it.

"If not, he must be dead," I said. "Isn't his name on your school report?"

Dino looked ahead and pondered. "It only says mama." He frowned. "I'm an orphan."

We glanced in at the door of the inn. There was a Sunday feeling in the air. Loafers playing billiards looked at us, fell silent. "It's politics," I whispered to Dino. "Do you want some bread and salami?"

Dino ran to the billiard table, circled around to the big window at the back where one could see the sun-baked plain. The players, surveyed by Dino, had begun playing and talking again. They passed close to him, brandishing their cues.

Country boys, they were discussing other matters. Some wore black shirts.

"What do you expect?" a blond, bundled-up young man said. "It's Sunday for everybody."

They laughed heartily, too heartily, uneasy. Recalling it later, I suddenly realized that this Sunday of sunshine had been the last time a stranger's arrival necessitated a change of subject at the inn. While that brief summer lasted, at any rate. But none of us knew it then.

Dino was crunching his bread and following the game. Belbo too had come in. It wasn't easy to get them out of there. Belbo was sniffing around under the table. I told Dino I was going and would leave him there to get drunk. I was almost outside the village when they caught up with me on the run.

That afternoon Egle came with her brother, an air-force officer, a handsome, lean, dark boy who made a little bow when he shook hands. I left my room at the sound of voices and found them in the orchard with my old women. The young man was bored, disgusted; he wore civilian clothes, talked of flying over the sea and of gulls. "Say it, then," he remarked to me. "We aviators are the fools. We're always on the job, but who wanted this war less than we did?"

"You only *fight* it, you simpletons," his sister interrupted.

Elvira was listening, lost in admiration for him. "At your age," I told him, "life was a parlor for us, an antechamber. It was a great thing to go out in the evening, to jump on the train in the country and go back to the city. We were waiting for something that never came." The boy got my meaning. He said: "And now something has happened."

Then Elvira made the tea. The old woman asked timidly whether, now that the English had landed, there was danger the war in Italy might flare up again.

"From our point of view," the young man said, "it's better to fight in Italy than on the sea or in the desert. Then at least we know we'll fall in our own country."

"You have clean things and hot food in your quarters, at least, don't you?" Elvira asked him. "A cup of tea like this?"

"I don't understand why they don't want us in the war," Egle said. "We could do so much at the bases and at the front—amuse you, help you. Not only as nurses." Her brother said: "It's true."

Then evening came and for some reason I stayed to look at the black sky. I went over the night and the morning, the past, many things. I thought of my strange immunity in the midst of everything. Of my idiotic grievances. From time to time I caught a distant singing, shouts. I thought of Dino, the aviator, the war. I thought of how old I was and that I would always go on the same way.

7. The next day we heard the news. Beginning at dawn, radios had been blaring from the nearby villas. Egle called me from the yard. People were streaming into the city talking at the top of their voices. Elvira knocked at my door and shouted at me through the door that the war was over. Then she came in and, looking the other way while I dressed, told me, red in the face, that Mussolini had been thrown out. I came down, found Egle, and we listened to the radio—this time London as well. No question, the news was true. The mother said: "But is the war over?"

"Now it will begin," I said, incredulous.

Now I understood those noises during the night. Egle's brother had run to Turin. Everyone was running to Turin. Heads popped out of villa windows; everybody was talking. It was the beginning of that frenzy of meetings, words, gestures, and incredible hopes that could end only in terror and blood. All eyes were excited, even those of the self-absorbed. From that time on, solitude as well, even the woods, would have a new flavor. I needed only a simple glance among the trees to find this out. I would have liked to know everything, to have read the papers already, so as to escape among the tree trunks and contemplate the new horizon.

Fonso, Nando, and the girls stopped at the gate with a chorus of shouts. "There's work to do," Nando called out. "The Fascists are resisting. Come with us to Turin."

"The war is continuing," Fonso said. "We were looking for you last night."

"You look as if you were going on a picnic," I replied. We stalled around until the girls said: "Come on."

"Kill them. Get the upper hand," shouted Fonso. "We are needed."

They left, saying they would be back at night, when peace was made. I stayed up there, not because I was afraid of a few bullets (the air raids were worse), but because I could foresee demonstrations, processions, wild discussions. Egle wanted me to accompany her to another villa, where she was going to shout out the news and the rumors. We took a small lane among trees that led us behind the slope to a mysterious little world of birds and dried brook beds. "They have broken into the prisons." "There's a state of siege." "All the Fascists are hiding." Turin, two steps away, seemed very remote. "Maybe tomorrow we'll find a fleeing bureaucrat in the woods," I said.

"Horrible!" Egle said.

"Eaten by worms and ants."

"As he deserves," said Egle.

"If it weren't for them," I told her, "we wouldn't have lived quietly on the hill for so many years."

We had arrived and she had begun calling her friend. I told her I had to leave. She made a disapproving face.

"The lady Elvira," I said, "doesn't like our walking together in the woods."

She looked at me narrowly, reached out her hand to me like a grown woman, and burst out laughing.

"You devil," she said.

The friend, a girl with plaited hair, came to the window. I had already taken the road back to the inn and could hear them laughing in the distance. Now I knew I was really alone. Even Belbo had run off to Turin. I imagined the silent inn, Dino in the field, the two women in the kitchen. "Now that the war is ending, perhaps Cate will tell me the truth," I thought as I climbed.

It wasn't necessary to go all the way up. Cate was coming down in the sunshine, colorfully dressed, skipping.

"How young you are," I said to her.

"I'm happy," and she grabbed my arm without stopping, like a dancer. "I'm so happy. Aren't you coming to Turin?"

Then she stopped and her voice changed. "It would be just like you not to know anything. You probably even slept all night. Nobody has seen you."

"I know everything," I said. "I'm as happy as you. But you know perfectly well the war is still going on. Now the real troubles will begin."

"And so? At least now one can breathe. We'll make out all right."

We went down together, arguing. She wouldn't let me mention Dino. She said that now we had to unite—shout, strike, make ourselves felt. For a while, she said, there shouldn't be any raids and we had to make the most of it, force a peace from the government. She already knew how little the government was worth. "They're all the same," she said. But this time they were afraid, had to save their skins. All they needed was a shove.

"And the Germans," I said, "and those others?"

"You said yourself that we should wake up and make a clean sweep . . ."

"Cate, you really have a passion for all this," I said suddenly. "You've become a revolutionary."

She told me to go to hell, and we arrived at the trolley stop. I hadn't spoken of Dino. It seemed odd for us to be talking politics so ardently, but on the trolley everyone talked in low voices. The columns of the porticoes and walls were covered with proclamations; people crowded around. They were walking the bloodless, festive streets in a numbed sort of stupefaction, an antlike bustle like the morning after a heavy raid.

97

Cate was going to her hospital and we parted. She said that perhaps neither she nor the boys would return that evening.

"And Dino is staying alone?"

"Dino has gone on with Fonso and the others. We'll join them
this evening."

I was not too pleased. While they were joking by the gate, Dino
had not even spoken to me, hadn't even shown himself. Cate said,
"Where will you eat?"

Alone again, I circled through Turin. It did in truth look like a
day after the fires. Something immense had happened, an earthquake, for which only the old ruins and rubble scattered through
the streets and haphazardly piled up could make a suitable back-
drop. One could say or do nothing that didn't seem ridiculously in-
adequate. A band of boys went by, dragging a big tin wall insignia
by a rope. They howled in the sun and the thing rattled like an old
kettle. Dino, after all, was a boy like these and only yesterday
imagining himself in the war.

A cordon of soldiers, part of the "state of siege" force, surrounded Fascist headquarters. They carried helmets and rifles,
guarding a street of burned papers, broken windows, doors off their
hinges. Passers-by gave them a wide berth. But the soldiers were
bored and laughing among themselves.

I ran into Egle's brother at a street corner. He had on his uniform
with ribbons and belt and was staring indignantly at the street.

"Oh, Giorgi," I said, "is your leave over?"

"All this should never have happened. This is the end."

"What do they say in the army?"

"Nothing. They're waiting. Nobody has the courage to come
and attack us. They're a pack of cowards."

"Who should be attacking you?"

Giorgi stared at me, surprised and offended.

"They all run away, all afraid, and they have been waiting
for twenty years to revenge themselves. I put on my uniform, the
uniform of the Fascist war, and nobody dares to come and pull it
off. There are only a few of us. These children don't know how few
we are."

Then I told him that the king was his master and orders came
from him. He had to obey.

He smiled in disgust. "You, too. Don't you see that we're only at the beginning? That we must defend ourselves?"

He walked off, his mouth tight shut. I watched his back until he disappeared in the crowd. How many were there like him? I wondered if all the Giorgis, all the handsome boys who had fought the war, were going to look at us like that all day.

"It may be lost, but it's not over," I muttered to myself. "There'll be some dying yet." And I looked at the faces, the houses. "Before the summer is over, how many of us will still be here? How much blood splashed on the walls?" I stared at the faces, the dark-ringed eyes of people coming and going, the peaceful confusion. "It will touch that fair-haired boy. It will touch that trolley conductor, that woman, that news seller. That dog."

It ended with my going to the Dora quarter, where Fonso's shop was. I strolled along the avenues beyond the bridges. The hill rose to my right, clear and huge. This is a quarter of large, cheap apartment houses, fields, low walls, and little straggling houses from the time when it was still country. The sky was warmer and more open; the people—women, boys—swarmed the sidewalks, the grass, and the shops. Big, rash, enthusiastic slogans had blossomed on the walls during the night.

A rumble and heavy boom of machinery came from Fonso's shop: a gate and a long low shed at the end of a meadow. So they are working? I thought; truly, nothing has changed. The day was passing peacefully in those streets that had seen so much suffering and hope, where so much blood had been spilled in the streets when we were boys. The workmen, the bombed-out were working as before, as always. Who knows, they may have thought it was all over.

As I waited, I thought of Cate, of the logic of her existence that had returned to take hold of me just then. All that was left of the violent, satirical gusto I had shared with Fonso for the hard-boiled humanity of the suburbs, of the useless rage that had driven me to Anna Maria's salon, was shame and secret blushes. All those adventures had been so futile that I was reduced to telling myself: "Bravo. You're well out of it."

But had I really escaped? There was the war's end, there was Dino. As threatening as the immediate future was, the old world was rocking; my life was completely tuned to that world, to the terror and bitterness and disgust that world aroused. Now I was forty and here were Cate and Dino. No matter whose son he was, what mattered was that we were together again this summer after the absurd harshnesses of before, that Cate now knew what she was living for and for whom. Cate had a purpose, the will to be outraged, a full life and her own. Was I being futile once more, hanging around her half-lost, half-humiliated?

Things were starting to move in the factory yard. Others were waiting, groups forming, some leaving—solid men, girls, youngsters with jackets over their shoulders. They started calling each other, shouting. Then I recognized my friends. Here the evasive suspicion that reigned in the city amid the disorder and celebration was submerged in a very different openness; a naïve, reckless uproar. Even the solitaries who glanced at you and went off whistling had a boldness in their walk. The girls made the most noise. They asked and gave the news, shouting with gusto things prohibited only the day before.

The sun burned down. I saw Fonso in the middle of a circle. I didn't move. He was really just a boy. Next to him were a huge man in overalls and a skinny one, all laughing. I hoped that Cate or one of the others would come to the gate; but none did.

"The professor," Fonso shouted.

I joined them. They were discussing the news. "The *cavaliere* Mussolini," the thin man said scathingly, chewing his cigarette, "the *cavaliere* . . . Fancy that! Now they remember."

"They're afraid of the Germans," Fonso said.

"Nuts! We're all numskulls," the other sneered. "Do you want to know? The brass began to smell the stink themselves so they ran to the king and said: 'Listen. You must give us a rest, get us out of the soup. Meanwhile you carry on the war; the Italians will have a vacation and break their necks, and tomorrow we'll come back and give you a hand. Agreed?'"

"Let him rave," grumbled the giant in overalls. "If he can't be an ass today, when can he? Did you tie one on last night?"

"Four of them did," said Fonso, amused.

"Enough then. Let's go home."

"Just watch them come back," the thin one shouted.

I stayed alone with Fonso and the big man. We walked around among the shouting, waving crowd.

"Still, Aurelio is right," Fonso said. "They have filled the barracks with soldiers."

The giant, intrigued, turned around. "The soldiers belong to the people, don't they?" he said. "They're the people armed. Who can tell who they will fire at?"

"They're afraid of the Germans," I interrupted. "They will fire on the Germans."

"One thing at a time," the other said slowly. "Their time will come too. Not now."

"Hell," said Fonso. "Let them shoot now. That's what war is."

The big man shook his head.

"You don't know politics," he said. "Leave it to older men."

"We left it to you once," Fonso said.

The radio was beginning to crackle inside when we reached the house. We stopped; everyone stopped. "Quiet. The news." There followed news of the state of siege, good order in all of Italy, exultant processions, our decision to fight and win ourselves honor to the last drop of blood.

"Leave it to those who know," the giant kept repeating.

"It's all shit," Fonso said. "Long live Aurelio."

Behind the house the hill stretched into the sky, seeded with houses and woods. I wondered who of the people waiting, bustling, talking were noticing it then. Strange to say, the houses of that district were all intact. I asked Fonso if he were going back up that evening.

"Too much going on in Turin," he said. "Got to keep your eyes open."

The big man nodded approval.

"And where are the women?" I said. "Did Cate stay at the hospital?"

"Stick with us tonight," Fonso said. "Let's all go to the meeting."

"What meeting?"

Fonso grinned like a boy. "A meeting in the square, or in secret. Depends. With this government you don't know what the hell is up. Before, at least, the jail was secure."

I forced myself to arrange to meet them later. I shook the heavy hand of the other man. I left in the hot sun and ate in a central café where one could never have told from the conversation that anything had happened. One thing was sure—even the enemy radio said so—for several days there would be no bombs. I stopped at school; nobody there. Then I merely wandered through the streets and into cafés, turned over books in a store, stopped by houses that held old memories. Everything seemed renewed, fresh, beautiful, like the sky after a thunderstorm. I knew well enough it wouldn't last, and slowly turned toward the hospital where Cate worked.

8. At night I climbed the hill arm in arm with Cate, Dino trotting ahead half asleep. We had had dinner together on the fourth floor of Fonso's house, with sisters, neighbors; laughing, listening to the radio, cocking an ear to every suspicion of a riot or procession from the street below. The summer evening seething with hopes and rumors went to my head. Then we all descended to the paved court in the dark. People came—workers, fellow lodgers, girls—and there was one man, really a boy, who stepped out on the balcony and talked with a heat anything but naïve of the great fact of those days and of tomorrow. It was like dreaming to hear those public phrases. Enthusiasm took hold of me. "Neither propaganda nor terror has touched these people," I thought. "Man is better than what he believes." Then others joined loudly in the argument. The giant appeared and urged caution, was applauded. "He's been in prison," they told me. "Let the government explain itself," they yelled at him. "Let the rest of us speak!" A strident woman's voice started a song, and everyone joined. I was afraid the patrols in the street might hear us and stood watch at the door.

Now Cate and I were walking in silence, arm in arm like lovers, and between us walked a hope, a summer restlessness. We had crossed Turin together twice that day, and before dinner, on the open space by the Po in front of the hospital, I recalled that I had met Cate right here; it was from here we would set out in a boat. The day was ending in a fragrant coolness. The transparent air, the clarity—everything—recalled other evenings: innocent, peaceful evenings. Everything seemed resolved, promising, forgivable. I had talked about Gallo again with Cate, his melancholy heavy voice. The new thing that had entered the world that evening was canceling out all hardnesses, rancors, defenses. There seemed almost nothing to be ashamed of. We could talk.

Cate laughed, pretending not to believe in my furious love for Anna Maria. "She must have been a witch," she said, "one of those who work on men. Why weren't you married?"

"She didn't want me."

Cate frowned. "It was you who didn't want her. You made her realize it somehow. Why shouldn't she have married you?"

"I was too wrought up. I wanted to marry her as a way of escape. There was no other way."

"Well then. It was you. You're not able to love."

"Cate," I said, "Anna Maria was rich and corrupted. Don't trust anyone who takes a bath every day. They have another blood. They're people who enjoy themselves differently from us. The Fascists are better. The Fascists put them where they are in any case."

"So you know these things?" Cate said, smiling.

"If Anna Maria had had a son and called him Corrado, I'd have fled like the wind," I said.

Cate was silent, still happy, though she was frowning.

"Tell me, Cate, are you sure that Dino . . ."

We were alone among the houses, waiting for the trolley. On the Via Nizza only a few wrecked houses stood out. I took her hand.

"No," she said. "There's no need for you to pretend. We're not the same. What does it matter to you if Dino is your son? If he were, you'd want to marry me. But one doesn't marry for that. Also you would want to marry me to free yourself from something. Forget about it." She pulled my lapels, caressing me. She smiled at me. "I've said so before. He's not your son. Are you content?"

"I don't believe it, Cate," I mumbled over her fingers. "If you were in my place, what would you do?"

"I would let it go," she said cheerfully. "Who in these days wants a son?"

"Fool!"

103

Cate reddened and squeezed my arm.

"No, you're right. I would tear your eyes out. I'd wreck everything. But I'm his mother, Corrado."

It was dark now as we climbed. Dino stumbled alongside, half asleep. Tasting again the sweetness of our conversation, I walked along with Cate, and hoped restlessly. For what? I don't know, perhaps her sweetness, her firmness in handling me, the tacit promise not to hold a grudge—I had counted on these things for some time. I couldn't even get angry. She treated me as if we were married.

We began to whisper to keep Dino from hearing. He was stumbling, already asleep. He gasped as if dreaming on his feet. I took him by the head to hold him upright. I seemed to be holding myself as a boy: the same short hair and long shoulders. Did Cate understand these things?

"Who can say if Dino resembles his father?" I said. "He likes to roam the woods, to be alone. I'll bet that when you kiss him he wipes his face. How often do you kiss him?"

"He's a little mule, a stubborn animal," Cate said. "He grabs everything. At school he fights with everybody. He's not vicious at all."

"Does he like his schoolwork?"

"So long as I can help him," Cate said. "I'm so glad that next year they are going to change his schedule. He was studying and learning things he ought not to."

Her irritation made me smile.

"Pay no attention," I told her. "All boys want to be soldiers."

"But it's so beautiful," she said, "what has happened. It's as if we were reborn today, cured."

We were silent awhile, thinking our own thoughts. Dino breathed out, grunted something. I took his hand, pulled him to my side.

"And after next year, what school will he go to?"

"I want him to study as long as possible, to become somebody."

"But will he want to?"

"When you explained the flowers to him, he was happy. He likes to learn."

"Don't be too sure. In these things boys amuse themselves, like making war."

She looked at me, surprised.

"Take me," I said. "I also studied the sciences as a boy. And I haven't become anybody."

"What are you saying? You have your degree, you're a professor. I'd like to know the things you know."

"Being someone is something else altogether," I said quietly. "You can't even imagine it. You need luck, courage, willpower. Courage most of all. The courage to stand alone as if others didn't exist and think only of what you're doing. Not to get scared if people ignore you. You have to wait for years, have to die. Then after you're dead, if you're lucky, you become somebody."

"You're always the same," Cate whispered. "You make everything impossible so as not to have to do it. All I want is that Dino should have a good position in life, that he won't have to work like a dog and curse me for it."

"If you really hope for the revolution," I said, "you should be contented with a worker son."

Cate was offended. Her face clouded over. Then she said. "I just want him to study and become like you, Corrado. Without forgetting the rest of us."

That night Elvira was waiting for me at the gate. She didn't ask if I had eaten. I was treated coldly, as someone thoughtless enough to expose himself to danger and make others suffer. She didn't want to know what I had done in Turin. She said only that they had always treated me well and believed they had the right to some consideration, some thought. Of course I could go with anyone I liked, she said. But at least tell them.

"What right?" I replied. "No one has rights. We have a right to conk out, to wake up good and dead. With all that's going on."

In the dark Elvira was looking over my shoulder in silence. I saw that her cheeks were glistening with tears.

Then I lost patience completely. "We are born by chance," I said. "Father, mother, children; everything happens by chance. It's pointless to cry. One is born and dies alone . . ."

"It's enough just to feel a little love," she murmured in her assured tone.

9. I stayed away from Turin for many days, contenting myself with the papers and the new freedom to listen and declaim. New ideas, gossip, and hope flowed in every direction. The only thing that didn't occur to people up there in their villas was that the old world hadn't driven off its enemies but had committed suicide. But does any suicide really intend to disappear?

Elvira had herself in hand the next morning; she knew me too well. She only blushed a little when I appeared. Her mother tried to make fun of us; I answered somewhat dryly and Elvira froze up like a widow in mourning. Then she gave me her faithful-dog, patient-sister, victimized look. Poor soul, she wasn't faking; she was suffering all right. But what to do? be sorry for having teased her about those flowers; that must have been what was eating her.

While she was circling around the house at night, I was trying to get all the radio stations I could. It was obvious now that the war would continue, and without aim. The truce in the air was over; the Allies were threatening new attacks. I opened a door and found Elvira, who crossly asked for the news of the world. It was her great device for talking to me; at this rate she must have wanted the war never to end; but that day she must have realized from the threat of change that I was slipping away from her.

My relief was the daytime, Le Fontane—Cate and Dino. I didn't even need to appear in the yard: it was enough to stroll the usual paths and know that Dino was there. A few times I managed to keep Belbo crouched down while I peered unseen over the hedge. The old innkeeper was there, rinsing out demijohns and chewing his cigar stub. A short, stocky man, he came and went from the cellar, stooping to pick up a nail, to study the window grate, to fix a length of vine over the wall. One would scarcely gather from watching him that anything mattered more than the nail, the wall, the worked fields. His name was Gregorio. Cate's grandmother, on the other hand, often raised a voice, in the afternoons, as raucous as a magpie's, accusing Dino, the neighbors, and things in general. While Fonso, Nando, and the girls were spending their nights in Turin, this was the only sign of life at Le Fontane, even in the evening, when Cate arrived. It seemed an abandoned, lifeless place, a part of the woods. And what is true of woods also: one could only spy on it, sniff around it, not live there or really possess it.

When I asked if Dino were still making drawings, he shrugged and after a while brought me the sketchbook. Then we talked of birds, grasshoppers, geological strata. Why, I wondered, shouldn't I keep him company as I used to when I barely imagined this business? If nowadays Dino accepted me without much enthusiasm it was because I was too close to him, making myself act the father. Strange thing, I reflected, but children are no different from adults; they get fed up with too much attention. Love is a thing that bores. But was Elvira's infatuation with me, my sessions with Dino —making myself a boy for his benefit—were these love? Do loves exist that are not egotisms, that don't try to reduce a man or a woman to one's own convenience? Cate let me go ahead and take her place beside Dino and go walking with him. In the evening, as we came back, she gave us an impenetrable, mocking smile and listened contentedly to Dino's boasting. At times I suspected that she, too, was finding us a convenience. Dino was learning and profiting from our meetings.

One thing that excited him were prehistoric monsters and the life of savages. I bought him other illustrated books. We played at imagining our hollow on the Pino path with its mosses, ferns, and horsetails a cave of megatheria and mammoths. He was much in favor of scientific conspiracies and infernal machines, of masses of robots; he sopped them up from his comic books. A school friend of his in Turin, Cruscotto, spent the day cutting up tin and aluminum, stringing it on wires, assembling a whole underground system for defending the house. Just a few choice spirits, they were, who talked of Flash Gordon, the Yellow Men, Doctor Mysteriosus. When the air raids began, they made experiments, held councils of war. With them was Sybil, the Leopard Girl, but she was played by a number of little girls and there was no need to have her in the underground fortress; the enemy was raping Sybil and one had to rescue her. Dino described all this to Cate and the grandmother; he got excited, imitated all the voices and shots and laughed at everybody. He was especially cynical about the Sybil episodes. I knew why.

When we two were alone, it was another story. Dino didn't mention Sybil. I understood him. Between men a girl is always something indecent. So, once, it had been for me. We crept out between the trees, looking carefully about. Where Dino was intent on savages, pursuits, and spears from ambush, I was seeing the beautiful open spaces, the variety of the slopes, the intricate pattern of bindweed through a canebrake. But one thing we had in common: for us the idea of woman, of sex, that burning mystery, didn't belong in the woods. Too disturbing. For all that the ravines, roots, embankments reminded me each time of the bloodshed and ferocity of life, I never succeeded in conjuring up, in deep woods, that other savage thing, a woman's embrace. At the most it was Elvira's red flowers, which made me laugh. Dino laughed too—why? —at women, at Sybil. He grew awkward, hunched up, shielded himself. What did he know? Instinct or experience, we were alike. This tacit understanding pleased me.

The alarms and flights of planes soon started again. The first thunderstorms came, but from a sky washed clean the August moon lit up even the mouths of roadside drains. Fonso and the others reappeared. "These English half-wits," they said. "They don't understand that one raid is enough to wreck a month's work in the underground. When the house is burning, we too have to get out."

"They know it perfectly well. They don't want our work," Nando said. "They all agree on that."

The big man of the overalls was also with us that night, Tono by name. He said: "War is always war."

"You make me laugh," I said. "We're a battlefield. If the English have smashed the Fascist barracks, it was not to make a villa out of it for us. They just don't want obstacles in their line of fire, that's all."

"But we're here," Fonso said. "It's not easy to get rid of us."

"Not easy? Just burn over the stubble. They're doing it now."

Nando said: "War is the work of moles. Get down underground."

"Just do it then," I shouted. "Hide yourselves and that's it. But while there's a German in Italy it will be pointless."

Giulia or some other girl said: "The professor is angry."

Cate said: "Who's asking *you* to move?"

All the faces turned toward me, Dino's too.

Each time I swore to keep quiet and listen, just shake my head and listen. But that careful balance of anxieties, waits, and futile hopes in which I was spending my days was made for me; I would have liked it to last forever. The impatience of the others might destroy it. I had long been used to staying put while the outside world went crazy. Now a gesture of Fonso and his friends was enough to throw doubt on everything. That's why I got worked up and talked.

"Since Fascism fell," I said, "I don't hear you singing any more. How come?"

"Cheer up, we'll sing then," the girls said. Someone said: "Old songs of yesteryear!" Dino burst into "The Red Flag." We all sang a stanza of it, uneasy and laughing; but the discussion was already beginning again. Tono the giant said: "There'll be plenty to do when the elections come up."

It was on one of those evenings that Cate's grandmother spoke her piece to me while we were waiting for the all-clear in the courtyard. I had just said to Fonso: "If the Italians mean to take things seriously, they will have to use bombs." The old woman said: "Go and tell that to someone who works. If you have your loaf of bread and can stay on the hill, the war is a pleasure. It's people like you who brought on the war." She said it quietly, without a trace of rancor, as if I were her son. At first I didn't react. "Would they were all like him," Cate said. I kept still. "Skin is skin—what nonsense!" Fonso put in.

"We too, Mama," Cate said. "We come up here to sleep."

The old woman was muttering now. I wondered if she knew how justly and deeply she had reached me. The excuses the others made for me didn't count; in a sense they only made things worse.

Tono the socialist said: "Everyone tries to save himself. We are fighting because everyone, even the bosses, our enemies too, knows where salvation lies. That's why the socialists oppose war."

And Fonso: "Just a minute. You don't say why the working class always has to defend itself. The bosses keep their control with war and terror. They advance over our dead bodies. And you are wrong to expect them to be understanding. They've understood all too well. That's why they keep on."

Then I joined in again. "I'm not speaking of this. I'm not talking of classes. Fonso is right, of course. But we Italians are made like that: we obey only force. Then, with the excuse that it is force, we laugh it off. Nobody takes it seriously."

"Certainly not the bourgeois."

"I'm talking about all the Italians."

"Professor," Nando broke out gravely, "do you love Italy?"

Again I had every face looking at me: Tono, the grandmother, the girls, Cate. Fonso smiled.

"No," I said slowly, "not Italy. The Italians."

"Shake!" Fonso said. "We understand each other."

10.

Nights afterwards Turin went up in flames. It lasted more than an hour. The engines and explosions seemed to be right over our heads. Bombs fell on the hill and in the Po. One plane made savage machine-gun attacks on an antiaircraft battery—we learned the next day that several Germans were killed. "We're in the hands of the Germans," everyone said. "They're defending us."

The next evening, another attack, worse still. One could hear the houses crumble, the earth shake. The people ran off to sleep in the woods again. My women prayed until dawn, kneeling on a rug. I went down to Turin the next day among the fires, and everywhere they were calling for peace, the end. The newspapers were exchanging insults. A rumor was spreading that the Fascists were returning, that the Veneto was filling up with German divisions, that our soldiers had orders to fire on the crowd. Political prisoners were coming out of the jails and camps. The Pope made another speech invoking love.

A quiet night passed, in fearful tension (Milan was hit this time), then another night of fire and ruins. The enemy radio said the same thing each evening. "It will be like this every evening until the end. Surrender." Now in the streets and cafés one only discussed how it might be done. All of Sicily was occupied. "We'll negotiate," the Fascists said, "but first let the enemy leave the soil of the fatherland." Others cursed the Germans. All of us expected a landing below Rome, below Genoa.

Going back to the hill, I sensed how precarious our refuge had become. The silence of the woods had an expectant air. Even the sky was empty. I would have liked to be a root, a worm, and sprawl underground. Gloomy Elvira irritated me with that voice and those dark looks. I well understood Cate's hardness, why she would no longer talk about all this. It wasn't the season for love; for us it never had been. All the past years had brought us here, to these straits. Without knowing it, each in his own way, Gallo, Fonso, Cate, everyone had been waiting for this hour, preparing ourselves for it. People like Elvira who had let themselves be taken unawares only annoyed me. I preferred Gregorio, who at least was old, was like the earth or trees. I preferred Dino, the dark seed of a closed future.

The girl Egle told me that her brother had gone back to fighting. This, too, was a just fate. What else could that boy do? There were many like him who didn't believe in the war, but the war was their destiny—war was everything and nobody had taught them how to do anything else. Giorgi was taciturn. He had said only: "My job is up there," and rejoined the fighting. He didn't protest or even try to understand.

The protest came from his family, who understood no better. I learned it from Egle, who passed by the gate every morning looking for milk, eggs, and gossip. She stopped to talk to Elvira or the mother and I could hear an echo of the Giorgi parlor in their whispering voices, a world I knew well: the study of her rich industrialist father. How was the war going? Worse than before. What had the Fascists done to let themselves be ruined? They had done a great, a generous act, made a sacrifice to bring harmony back to their country. And how did the country respond? It responded with strikes, treachery, sabotage. Just let them keep it up! They were being watched. Everything would be straightened out again sooner than one might think.

Thus did Elvira's mother carry on; thus Egle, who noticed everything and knew everyone's affairs. "The rest of us," she said, and the rest of us were her father, her parlor, the villa, "who has suffered from the war more than we have? Our Turin house was smashed; only the doorkeeper survived. We have to live up here. My brother has gone back to fighting. For two years he has risked his life. What have these subversives got against us anyway?"

"What subversives?"

"But all of them! The people who still don't know why we are fighting. Hoodlums. You know some of them."

She cocked her head and squinted narrowly at me.

"I know no hoodlums," I cut in. "I only know people who work."

"There, he gets mad." She looked at me quizzically. "We know you go to the inn, we know who you see there."

"Nonsense," I said briefly. "And who might these hoodlums be?"

Egle was silent, smugly lowering her eyes.

"The only hoodlums I know," I said, "are those who got us in the war and still hope to gain from it."

She gave me a dirty look, breathing hard; she looked like a guilty schoolgirl in a temper.

"Your brother doesn't come into it," I told her. "Your brother is deluded, one of those who is paying for the others. But at least he is brave—unlike those others."

"A lot of courage you've got," Egle said, furious.

We parted on that note. But the story of the inn was only just beginning. One day I went to the kitchen while Elvira was beating whipped cream (her kingdom was the kitchen and she meant to seduce me with sweet things, but her mother took a dim view of the waste) and said: "No starvation here."

She looked up. "You can't get anything now. Not eggs or butter, not at any price. All those people who used to eat boiled potatoes get it all now."

"We always have plenty," I answered.

Elvira frowned, turned her back on me, and went to the oven.

"Those inns where people spend the night celebrating are buying everything up."

"Where one has to sleep on the ground," I added.

"I don't want to hear about it," Elvira blurted, turning around. "They are just not our kind of people."

"That I can believe," I said. "They're worth much more than we are."

She grasped her throat, her eyes flashing.

"If it's wine and women that bother you, ask Belbo. Nobody like a dog for judging one's neighbor."

"But they are . . ."

"Subversives; yes, I know. All the better. Do you imagine there are only priests and Fascists in the world?"

I can't remember now why I said those things. I only know that Cate was right in saying that I was bad-tempered, proud, and afraid. She had also said that I was generous against my will. This I don't know. But I was contradicting everybody, always putting on a new mask. I sensed how time was pressing; that everything was useless, vain, already discounted. The morning of my quarrel with Elvira there was a sudden alarm, at noon. The hill, the valley, distant Turin; all was silent in the sunshine. I was standing in the orchard. I wondered how many hearts had skipped a beat just then, how many leaves were rustling, how many dogs flattening themselves on the ground. The ground as well, the hill and its skin must have shuddered. All at once I saw how foolish this indulgence of mine in the woods had become, that pride in the woods I didn't forget even with Dino. Under a summer sky turned to stone by the howling of sirens I saw that I had been playing like an irresponsible child. What was I for Cate but a baby like Dino? What for Fonso, the others, myself?

I waited anxiously awhile for the hum of engines. The anxiety of days, nearly unbearable at that moment, could only be cancelled by some immense, irreparable event. But wasn't this my usual game, my vice? I thought of Cate, Fonso, Nando, the poor of Turin, waiting in air-raid shelters, piled as if in so many catacombs. Some joked, some laughed. "It will be a long worm before it turns," they were saying.

Blood and ferocity, underground life, the woods; these things were not a game? Were they not like Dino's savages and comic books? If Cate should die, who would think of her son? Who would know any longer whose son he was?

The creak of a pump gave me a start. Elvira came out to announce lunch.

In silence—the radio didn't function during alarms—we sat down, Elvira at the head of the table, the old woman at the side, as always. The mother crossed herself. No one spoke. To spread out my napkin, handle the silverware, and eat seemed a game, a pointless game. At one o'clock the all-clear sounded. We jumped up, half amazed. Elvira put another slice of pie on my plate.

11. Summer was ending. Peasant women began to be seen in the fields, and little ladders leaned against the fruit trees. Now Dino and I never left the meadow; there were pears, grapes, the field of Indian corn. We heard about the landing in Calabria. Heated discussions at night. The immense, irreparable event was taking place. Then why was no one doing anything? Were we to end like that?

The eighth of September took us by surprise when we were stripping walnut trees with Gregorio. First to pass was a military truck, screaming on the curve and raising a great dust. It came from Turin. After a pause, another roar and screech of tires; a second car. Five of them passed. Dust floated down among the trees in the limpid evening. We looked at each other. Dino was racing in the courtyard.

Cate arrived at dusk. "Don't you know?" she called from the road. "Today Italy asked for an armistice."

The monotonous, hoarse, incredible voice of the radio was repeating the news mechanically every five minutes. It stopped, then resumed again, each time with a menacing undertone. It never varied, never wavered, never added anything. It had the stubbornness of an old man or a child reciting its lessons. We were silent at first, except for Dino clapping his hands. We were too disconcerted, as we had been earlier by the five military trucks.

Cate said that in Turin Radio-London was blaring in cafés and on the streets and large groups were cheering. A landing at Salerno; fighting everywhere. "At Salerno? Why not at Genoa?" There had been processions, demonstrations.

"It's a mystery what the Germans are doing," Cate said. "Are they leaving or not?"

"Don't expect it," I told her. "They couldn't even if they wanted to."

"It's up to our soldiers," the old woman said. "Now it's up to them."

Old Gregorio said nothing but kept looking at me. He too was like a stupefied child. The comic notion flashed through my mind that even the old marshal who was hurling us against the barricades that evening, even his generals, knew as little as Gregorio and were hanging on the radio in roughly the same state of enlightenment as he and I.

"But at Rome," I said, "what's going on at Rome?"

No radio station told us. Cate had heard in the city that it was already occupied by the English, that all it needed was a few thousand parachutists to link up with our men and face the Germans. "They must be fools, those ministers, but they'll keep their skins. They will have foreseen all this, you can be sure," Cate said.

"And Nando and Fonso," I asked suddenly, "aren't they coming? This is what they have always waited for. They'll be happy."

"I didn't see them," Cate said. "I ran up to talk to you."

Nando and Fonso didn't come that evening. Giulia arrived panting. She said that in the factory a committee had been formed for collecting arms, that Fonso had made a speech, that they were talking of seizing the barracks. Gunfire had been heard on the outskirts. It was known that bands of thieves had ransacked a military store, that the Germans were selling their uniforms to the Fascists and escaping in disguise.

"I'm going back to Turin," Giulia said. "Goodbye."

"Tell those other girls to come up here," the old woman shouted. "Tell Fonso and those idiots. There are some rough days ahead."

"It's nothing," Cate said enthusiastically. "This time it is really ending. Just a few days more of resistance."

"There'll be no more air raids," I said.

When I was about to leave for dinner, Dino made all of us laugh. "Is the war over?" he asked in a thin little voice.

I was up at dawn the next day. No news from Rome. Our radio was broadcasting little songs. From abroad, the usual war bulletins. The landing at Salerno, a mirrorlike sea teeming with transports; the operation was still going on. Elvira stood listening nearby, tense and pallid. We made a little cluster around the radio. I said at one point: "I don't know when I'll be back"—and left.

To fill the empty morning I set out for Turin. I met very few people on the way—one exhausted cyclist puffing up the hill. Way below, Turin was shimmering peacefully between slopes. Where was the war? Our nights of fire seemed remote, hard to believe in. I kept alert for the sound of trucks.

In the city all the headlines announced surrender. But people seemed preoccupied with their own affairs. Stores open, police at the crossroads, trolleys running. No one spoke of peace. At the corner by the station a little bunch of unarmed Germans were loading furniture on a van; some bystanders were helping. Our men are out of sight, I thought; they are all being held in barracks because of the "state of siege." I listened hard and peered in the eyes of passers-by. All were closed up, keeping to themselves. Perhaps yesterday's news has been denied and nobody wants to admit to having believed it, I thought. But two young men under the outer portico of a bar were shouting in the middle of a circle of people and setting fire to an unfolded newspaper which a waiter was trying to snatch away. Some were laughing.

"They're Fascists," a man said quietly.

"Hang them, murder them," a woman howled.

I learned the news from a notice on the doorway to the bar. The Germans were occupying the city. Acqui, Alessandria, Casale had been seized. "Who says so?" Arriving travelers.

"If it were true, the trains wouldn't be running," I said.

"You don't know the Germans."

"And at Turin?"

"They will come," another said, grinning, "in their own good time. Everything methodically. No useless disorders. They carry out their massacres calmly."

"But is nobody resisting?" I asked.

Under the portico the shouting and confusion increased. We went outside. One of the two young men, standing on a table, was haranguing a crowd that hung back and jeered. Two others were fighting against a pillar and a woman yelling insults was trying to get between them. "The government of shame," the orator shouted, "of treason and defeat, asks you to consummate the assassination of the fatherland." The little table rocked; the crowd yelled invective.

"Sold to the Germans!" they shouted.

There were old men, servant girls, boys, a soldier. I thought of Tono and what he might have said. I yelled something at the speaker myself, but just then the crowd wavered and broke up. Someone called out: "Make way or I'll kill you." Two shots rang out, reverberated under the portico; people dropped to the ground, melted away; broken window glass tinkled; and far off, in the middle of the square, I caught sight of those two still kicking each other while the woman attacked them both.

The two shots sang in my mind for quite a while. I left to escape being caught, but now I knew why people were silent and cautious. I went to my school through the quiet and empty streets, hoping to find someone I knew. Exams will begin in a month, I thought. Old Domenico poked his head out.

"News, professor? Are you bringing us peace?"

"Peace is a bird. It's just come and gone."

Domenico shook his head. He slapped his newspaper. "Some things are too bad to say."

He had heard nothing about the Germans. "They know what to do," he burst out. "They know. Oh, professor, what good times when we had the Duce!" He lowered his head and his voice. "Have you heard what they say? That he might come back?"

I went off with that new thorn sticking in me. Cate and I had an understanding that when she got off the trolley each day she would look around to see if I had perhaps come down to Turin. I stopped at the corner and waited. An hour passed and she didn't come. Instead I overheard other conversations to the effect that the Germans were occupying the centers and disarming our men. "But will we resist?" Who knows? At Novi there had been a battle. "You see. They're at Settimo. A whole armored division is advancing."

"But what is our Command doing?"

A nearby café turned on its radio and after a lot of static we heard dance music. "Tune in London," they cried. London came in, in French; then more exasperating crackling. An Italian voice, from Tunis, excitedly read the same old bulletin—the Russian advance, the landing at Salerno; the operation was still in progress. "What do they say at Rome?" we cried. "What's happening at home? Cowards!"

"The Fascists are in Rome," a voice shrilled.

"Cowards, whores!"

I felt someone taking my arm; it was Cate, smiling her old smile. We left the circle.

"You remembered," I said.

We crossed the square. Cate spoke quietly and smiled coldly.

"The situation is insane," she said. "It's the most tremendous day of the war. There's no government; we're in the Germans' hands. We've got to resist."

We passed beyond the Dora district. "What do you want to do?" I said. "It's a matter of days. Speed will help the English—more than us."

"Have you heard the German radio?" Cate said. "They are broadcasting Fascist hymns."

We came to the courtyard of the workers' committee. It seemed only yesterday, though a month had passed. Nobody there. Cate talked to the neighbors from a balcony.

Finally Giulia and Nando's young wife appeared. "Haven't the men got back?" Nando's wife sank against the door. "Don't worry," I told her. "Is this a day to expect a man to come home? It was worse in Albania."

She shouted: "They're boys, they're madmen."

We turned on the radio—no news.

"If they get themselves arrested," the wife groaned, "then the Germans have them where they want them."

"Fool," Cate shouted back at her, "they haven't been taken yet."

Then they said that during the night a patrol had broken up a meeting and Tono had been arrested. "They wanted to set him free," Giulia said. "You'll see."

Cate had to return to the hospital. We sat on the bed and had something to eat.

"I'm coming too," I told her. The wife wouldn't eat but walked up and down in the room. She seems the bravest, I thought; this is no time to get married. Better Cate, who at least doesn't love anyone.

We walked together toward the trolley. Cate asked: "Are you going home?" Then, looking around her: "Nobody is lifting a finger, not even a soldier. It makes me sick."

"We're a battlefield now, nothing else. Don't fool yourself."

"A lot you care," she murmured, looking away. "But you're

right. You've never seen people starving or had your house burned down."

"Are these the things that give one courage?"

"Grandmother told you the same thing. You people can't understand."

" 'You people' can't refer to me," I cut in. "I'm alone. I try to be as alone as possible. These are times when only a man alone can keep his head. Look at how Nando's wife is suffering."

Cate stopped and frowned. "No, you're not like Nando's wife. You don't put yourself out, not you. I'll see you this evening."

"Come back early," I called after her.

Again the street, the orchard, the women, the cool, quiet hill, the usual conversations. "Perhaps the Germans won't come this far," I said to Elvira. I asked about Egle, if she was as impatient as ever.

"Why?"

"You know well enough," I said.

I forced myself to listen to Radio Monaco. The Fascists were really raising their heads again. Furious, threatening voices. They were inciting the people. "They are still in Germany; it's a good sign." I was almost pleased that Radio Rome was silent. It must have meant that our people were resisting, that the Germans hadn't yet taken it. The old woman watched us silently, morose and scared.

At the inn I found Cate, who told me news of Fonso and Nando. "They have come back, they're all right," she said. "But they couldn't do anything. Tono and the others have been locked up in the Nuove prison."

But there was other news—that our soldiers were running away and nobody even dreamed of resisting.

12. I shrugged my shoulders this time too. It was a gesture that came easily in those days. The long-awaited catastrophe had come. It was clear that the quiet city in the distance, solitude in the woods, the orchard made no more sense. Still, everything kept going. The sun rose in the morning, set at night; the fruit ripened.

A hope, an anxious curiosity had taken hold of me; to survive the collapse, to do so in time to know the world that would follow.

I shrugged but drank in the voices. If I sometimes plugged my ears it was because I knew well, too well, what was coming and lacked the courage to look it full in the face. Salvation seemed a question of days, maybe hours; one glued oneself to the radio, examined the sky; one woke every morning with a surge of hope.

Salvation did not come. Instead, the first whispered rumors of bloodshed. I remembered that inn at Pino where on a July day I had last heard voices being lowered, and made my way there slowly, looking back over my shoulder. Now when you arrived somewhere, especially somewhere inhabited, you looked behind you and kept your ears pricked. The blockhouses hadn't been introduced yet, but the air was already thick with menace and surprise. Roads and fields swarmed with refugees, with soldiers bundled in raincoats, rags, jackets, fleeing the cities and barracks where the Germans and Fascists were raging. Turin had been occupied without a fight, as water drowns a village; Germans bony and green as lizards were manning the station and barracks; people went about stunned that nothing had happened or changed: no riots, no bloodshed in the streets; only, endless, subdued, subterranean, the flood of refugees, of troops, trickling through alleys, into churches, through the suburbs, on the trains. Other strange things were happening, as I discovered from whisperings and knowing winks between Cate and Dino. Fonso and the others were buying up arms, looting stores and storage depots, even hiding things at Le Fontane. In the suburbs civilian clothes were raining down from windows on fleeing soldiers. Where would these fugitives from the Germans end up? Some, of course, would reach their homes; but the others, those far from home like the Sicilians and Calabrians, backwash of the war, where would they spend their days and nights, where could they stop and live? "If the war doesn't end soon," I said to Egle and Elvira, "we'll all have to turn to brigandage." I put it this way to see them worked up. And I added: "Things are fine in the middle-class houses, at the villas of the generals who have thrown in with the Germans." But then Cate, when I talked to her, told me to shut up. I learned from Dino, who was always watching the road, that many people passed by the inn—I saw some of them myself—bearded, in rags, starving. Giulia or Nando's wife was always there, and the fugitives spoke, argued, and gnawed on lumps of bread. Dino swore that an Englishman, a prisoner of war, had come by; he knew only one word, *ciao*.

That now familiar disorder, that silent floundering and crumbling, was a sort of moral holiday, a crude revulsion from the intolerable news of the papers and radio. The war raged far away, methodical and futile. We had fallen, this time with no escape, into the hands of our old masters, now more expert and bloodstained. The jolly bosses of yesterday became ferocious in defense of their skins and their last hopes. Our escape was only in disorder, in the very collapse of every law. To be captured and identified was death. Peace, any kind of peace, at least imaginable during the summer, now seemed a joke. We had to see our fate through to the end. How far away the air raids seemed. Something worse than fires or ruins had started.

I heard it all discussed at the Pino inn, where I went surreptitiously because it was on a thoroughfare. I was particularly eager to know if Germans or Fascists had been seen locally. One morning I found a soldier there—he was still wearing his big boots and Fascist insignia—with a frayed raincoat over his naked torso. He was a Tuscan boy who laughed from the bottom of his eyes. He talked, chattered with the rest of us, describing his march from France, ten days of flight. He named his companions, laughed heartily, hoped to get to the Valdarno. He would neither eat nor drink. He was pale, half bearded, but must have been hitting it off with the maid, who, cross-eyed and bundled up, was smoldering at him from behind the bar.

"The valley bottom was watched by those bastards," he said. "You could never get by in open country. They fired at you. I saw plenty of burned villages."

"But there's not been any fighting in the mountains," someone said.

"Fighting—you mean reprisals," another said. "Let a village hide a soldier and the Germans will burn it."

"One night, on a bridge . . ." the Tuscan began, looking meaningfully at the maid.

We all drank it in, swallowing back our saliva. Amused, the

121

Tuscan begged a cigarette; other stories followed. The others there were mostly peaceable men from the country with stories of their own. Cruel, unbelievable stories they were: women and children taken as hostages for the husband, beatings ending with a leap from a staircase, harvests ruined, extortions, corpses in the street with a cigarette between their lips.

"The war was better," they said. But they all knew that this was the war.

"Let's hope the good weather will last," the Tuscan said.

I often walked the familiar roads alone, avoiding Le Fontane, Dino, Cate and her arguments. But the talk and anxiety to which we are hardened now was everywhere reborn in those days, stimulated by our unwillingness to believe, by a residual hope and a still justifiable egotism. Now, when even those days seem like a fantasy and salvation has lost nearly all meaning, all our meetings and wakings have a desperate peace, an amazement at having one more day for living, that keeps us cheerful. Nobody worries very much, either for himself or for others. One listens impassively.

But in those days I used to wake up, reluctantly, at dawn and run to the radio, never discussing it with Elvira or her mother. Each bulletin postponed the end for months. Turin, lying there in its valley, used to frighten me. Now not even fires and explosions —for they had ceased—could scare us. The war had come down among us, had entered our houses, the roads and prisons. I thought of Tono and his heavy, bowed head and didn't dare ask myself what had become of him.

Elvira and her mother treated me maternally, rather grimly, submissively. There was a peace, a refuge in that house, a warmth like infancy. Some mornings I stood by the window, looking at the treetops and wondering how long this immunity was going to last. Fresh white curtains opened to the deep foliage and toward a far slope where a field had been opened in the woods and maybe someone was sleeping by the sheepfold. For how many years had I seen it each morning, green or covered with snow? Would these things still exist—afterwards?

I tried to study, to read. I thought of teaching science to Dino. But Dino was also part of the new world; Dino was closed up, unreachable. I saw he would rather stay with Fonso or Nando than with me. I told Cate to send him to me every morning at the villa, not to leave him alone on the roads. Sitting by a table with me, he would at least be applying himself. Nobody had thought of reopening the schools.

"But yes," Nando told her. "Let him take Dino off your hands. Let him at least study while he can."

It was cool already, that evening. We sat in the kitchen between the pots and the sink. Fonso and the girls were away. Without Fonso, conversation dragged. Nobody talked any more just to talk. When we were together like that under the light, I stole glances at them—Dino's grimaces, the women's silences—and the brightest and liveliest things were Nando's confident eyes, those boyish eyes that showed no trace of what they had seen in the war. His wife was now pregnant—they had managed it without a bed or house of their own—and his restlessness about the war was added to the excitement of politics.

"Professor, will you give my son his schooling?" he said, laughing; but his cheerfulness seemed strained and vulnerable. His wife watched us with no enthusiasm.

I left the inn at the first song of the crickets. The curfew hadn't reached us yet, but the fact is that those paths scorched my feet after dark. During the night at Turin the streets crackled with random shots, with the "Who goes there?" of young toughs supposed to be keeping order—even their fleering humor had a whiff of blood in it. I thought of Tono, already fallen into their hands, of Fonso's sly smile when his name came up. Fonso appeared unexpectedly at Le Fontane, sometimes in daylight as well; I asked him if they had revised the work schedule just for him. He winked and pulled out a permit in two languages made out for him in his double capacity as night watchman also. He was the only one who hadn't become edgy in the last month; his sarcasms were more precise and funny. His restless outbursts and aggressive chatter of earlier days had hardened into a cutting smile. It was clear that he had something to do, a commission which completely absorbed him but about which he kept mum. With time on his hands he loved to talk, but now he was a man with a mission.

One evening when Fonso was away, we discussed the war,

using newspaper diagrams and an atlas I had brought to show Dino. Nothing else I could do would interest him; for a long time he had thought only of getting to the city where every evening Fonso and the other boys were, where there was the curfew, the Germans, the war. The secrets he shared with Fonso, Nando's stories of guerrilla war in the Balkans, cut him off from me and the women. Nando told us gruesome tales of ambushes and reprisals in the Serbian mountains. "Wherever the Germans come, it ends that way; people begin to cut each other's throats."

"It's not so much the Germans," I said. "Those are places where you bring a gun to market even in peacetime."

The old woman turned around from the sink to look at me.

"So it's not the Germans, then?" Fonso's sister grumbled.

The grandmother said: "It's not the Germans' fault?"

"It's not the Germans' fault," I said. "The Germans have only pricked the bubble, discredited their friends. This war is bigger than it may seem. The people have seen their former masters running away and now nobody is in charge. But you can take my word for it, they mean revenge not only on the Germans, not only on them; they have it in for the Fascists, too. It's not a war of soldiers that might end tomorrow; it's a war of the poor, the war of people desperate with hunger, poverty, prison, corruption."

Once again they were all listening to me, even Dino.

"Take our men," I said. "Why didn't they defend themselves? Why did they let themselves get caught and sent to Germany? Why did they believe the officials, the government, their former bosses? Now that we have the Fascists again, they're starting to move, and they'll escape to the mountains, they'll end up in prison. The war is beginning now, the real one, the war of desperate men. Thanks, of course, to the Germans."

"Still, we must kill them," Nando said.

Dino looked at me solemnly, impressed at everyone's attentive silence.

"If the English don't come soon," I muttered, "we'll become another Montenegro."

The old woman scowled as she rattled her plates.

"The day will come," I said, getting up, "when we will have our own dead in the ditches, here on the hill."

Cate looked at me gravely. "You know so much, Corrado, and you do nothing to help us."

"Send Dino to my house tomorrow," I said with a laugh. "I'll teach him all these things."

13. There was no more room for doubt. What had been happening all over Europe was now happening to us—cities and countrysides in equal terror, crossed by armies and by fearful voices. Not only the autumn was dying. On a pile of rubble in Turin I had seen a big rat, tranquil in the sunshine. So tranquil that it didn't so much as move when I approached. It sat up on its hind legs and watched me.

The winter came and it was I who was afraid. I was used to the cold—like the rats, like everybody—used to going down in the cellar and blowing on my hands. It wasn't discomfort or the ruins, perhaps not even a threat of death from the sky; rather it was a final grasp of the truth that sweet hills could exist, a city softened by fog, a comfortable tomorrow, while at any moment bestial things might be taking place only a few yards away, things people discussed only in whispers. The city had become more savage than my woods. That war in which I had been sheltering, convinced of having accepted it, of having made my own uncomfortable peace, grew more ferocious, bit deeper, reached into one's nerves and brain. I began to look about me as tremulously as a scared rabbit. I started awake in the middle of the night. I thought of Tono, Fonso's grins, of plots, tortures, the latest dead. I thought of villages where they had been living this way for more than five years.

Even the newspapers—there were still papers—admitted that there had been resistance here and there on the mountains, that it was continuing. They promised punishments, pardons, tortures. Disbanded soldiers, they said, your fatherland understands you and calls you back. Hitherto we were mistaken, they said; we promise you to do better. Come and save yourselves, come and save us, for the love of God. You are the people, you are our sons, you are scoundrels, traitors, cowards. I saw that the old empty phrases weren't funny any more. Chains and death and the common hope took on a terrible daily immediacy. What had once floated around in the void, mere words, now gripped one's insides. There is something indecent in words. Sometimes I wished I were more ashamed of using them.

I would have liked to disappear like a rat. The animals, I thought, don't know what is going on. I envied them. My women had the advantage of knowing nothing about the war. Elvira soon understood this power of hers. Now the cold as well was driving me indoors; and returning from Turin, from the orchard or from empty walks over the bare, yellow hill, and forgetting the eternal, monotonous anguish and fear for a moment in the cavelike warmth of the house, was almost sweet. But I would have liked to be ashamed of that, too.

Dino came, those November mornings, to study his books. But he would stop his lesson point-blank to tell me the latest rumors, what a traveler had said, news of the Germans or partisans in the maquis. He already knew the first stories of weird ambushes, spies being shot. If Elvira came in, he clammed up. With each new revelation I saw what an enormous legend was being built up in those days and how only a boy who was astounded by everything could live with it and not lose his head. It was a mere accident that I wasn't a boy like Dino; I had been one twenty years before and my amazements then had been picayune compared to his. So then, I said to myself, if you should die in this war, all that would remain of you would be a boy.

"Don't you wear your sailor suit any more?" I asked him.

"I wear it to school. When are the schools opening?"

Elvira too, when the lesson was over, called him to the sideboard and gave him candy, wanting to know if he was going back to school, if he had sisters, if he remembered his father. Dino answered clownishly, frowning and bored at the same time.

"He's like me," I told Elvira. "When I was a boy and anyone kissed me, I wiped my face with my shirtsleeve."

"Boys," she said, "modern boys. The mother works and the child grows up any old way."

"No peasant boy has a mother who doesn't work," I said. "It's always been so."

"And this one is a nurse?" Elvira said. "And they live at the inn?"

"Having an inn these days ..."

Since the famous weeping spell, Elvira hadn't betrayed herself again. It was too easy for me to get excited and shout that with everything else—the dead, the fires, the deportations, winter and hunger—it was no time to agonize over whims or heartaches. Of love, in any case, of her absurd love we never spoke again. Those scarlet flowers in the orchard were dead; the whole orchard was withered to the ground. A great wind came and swept it clean. I told Elvira she should thank her stars for having a house, a fire, a warm bed, and a bowl of soup. Should thank God. People were worse off.

"I've always noticed," she said, piqued, "that troubles happen to those who look for them."

"For example, Italy joining the war ..."

"I don't mean that. It's enough to do one's duty. To believe ..."

"Obey and fight," I said. "Tomorrow I will come home with a dagger and a skull."

She popped her eyes at me, terrified.

It was miraculous how the weather held up. A little mist and fog each morning, then a golden sun. It was November and I recalled that fugitive from the Valdarno, wondered whether he had got home. I thought of all the others, the desperate and homeless. It was good luck about the weather. The hill was beautiful in its winter aspect of hard, powdery, bare earth. There were mounds of crackling leaves in the woods. I often thought I might take refuge there if I had to. I didn't envy the boys of eighteen to twenty. Military posters appeared even at Pino. The Republic was making a new army. The war was tightening its grip.

Then the schools reopened. One of my colleagues came to see me, the French teacher, a fat and melancholy man whom I hadn't spoken to for quite a while. I found him in the parlor, seated, and Elvira sitting in front of him, waiting.

"Oh, Castelli ..."

Castelli looked around and said yes, this was a house indeed. He lived in a room in the city and his landlords had gone to the country, leaving him alone in the big boarding house. "At least you have a stove here," he said, without a smile.

Then Elvira left to make coffee. I said something about school, we joked. Castelli listened with the stolid air of someone with something on his mind. So fat and embarrassed, he troubled me even now.

When the coffee arrived, we still hadn't come to the point. Elvira said: "Just a little. I don't deserve it." I watched him while he sipped and I thought: "Poor soul, a family man. Why does he live alone?"

At the door I said: "Well now, Castelli, what is it?"

He opened up only outdoors in the cold. I put on my overcoat and we walked on the gravel. He asked me if the war would end soon. He had asked the same question in the parlor. "You're not up for the draft," I said. "You're older than I am."

But Castelli wasn't worrying about the draft. "Clowns," he muttered, half indignant. It wasn't a political judgment. Castelli cared nothing for politics. He lived alone. But they had told him that to teach school meant accepting the Republic, recognizing the new government. "Who can we trust?" he burst out. "If only we knew whose hands we are in."

"The same old hands," I told him. "What nonsense. Only now they're more energetic."

"But how will it end?"

"Who has put this bee in your bonnet?"

As I expected, it had been our colleague the gymnastics instructor, ex-Fascist, and former group leader. He made no mystery of his desire to resign to avoid compromising himself, and was already accusing the others of opportunism and a culpable light-mindedness in respect to the war. "You've got to make up your mind," he declared to the others. "The nation is above personal sentiments."

"So this is what Lucini is saying?" I asked Castelli. "Then either he is a spy or the war is really over."

Then I was sorry for having said it. Castelli left very down in the mouth. I saw that suspicions, fears, a hundred uncertainties were eating him. He went off bent over, reminding me of Tono the socialist.

No one mentioned any of this at school. I saw my colleagues again, saw Lucini. Classes were stealthily resumed; a few boys from the upper classes were missing. It seemed absurd to see caretakers at the school entrance again, to hear the shouting of boys, assign homework. The bell had the sound of the past in it and gave me a start each time it rang. Cold rooms forced us to keep our overcoats on; it was all like the day before a move, provisional. I went back to eating at my old restaurant, watched my step, kept out of the way, and met Cate.

In the evening she and I and Dino climbed the hill.

"To have money," I told Cate, "not to depend on others. To hole up deep in the country and stay put."

"You seem to have everything," Cate said. "Is anyone better off?"

I felt myself blushing. "They were wishes, not protests," I said quickly. "I was joking."

"You'd like to stop thinking about the war," she said. "But you can't."

We went on for a while in silence. Dino trotted along beside me.

"All I want is for it to end," I said.

Cate raised her head sharply. She said nothing.

"Oh yes, I know," I said. "The only way is to forget it and work. Like Fonso, like the others. Jump in the water so as not to feel the cold. But suppose you don't enjoy swimming? Or that you're not interested in getting somewhere? Your grandmother made sense: whoever has a loaf of bread doesn't move."

Cate was silent.

"Speak your piece, signora."

Cate gave me a swift glance and smiled faintly. "I've already told you what I want."

Lowering her eyes, she rested them on Dino. It was a suspicion, an accent, a sort of rapid allusion. Perhaps an unconscious reflex, a promise. "If you play your part," she might have been saying, "there is Dino too . . ." I ruminated for a while. But one can't put these things into words. The simple suspicion was already bothering me. After all, I thought, what is she thinking? I don't give a damn for Dino.

"Doing or not doing these things," I said aloud, "is simply a matter of chance. No one starts it. The patriots and partisans are all disbanded men, draft dodgers, men compromised for some time; people who have already fallen into the water. It's all the same."

"Many of them aren't compromised," Cate said. "Every day someone falls who could have stayed quietly at home. Take Tono . . ."

"Ah, but it's here that the old woman makes sense," I exclaimed. "It's a class fate. It's the result of the life you lead. It's not for nothing that the future is in the factories. That's why I like you all . . ."

Cate smiled and said nothing.

14.
I had stopped going to see them at the apartment in the Dora district where Cate spent an hour every afternoon. I stopped because Fonso and Nando were always away—outside the city, in fact—and because one either does these things thoroughly or not at all. To compromise oneself as a sort of game is stupid. But there was risk in everything now. We live in times when no one, however much a coward, is sure of waking tomorrow in his bed. And the old woman is right. The priests are right. We are all to blame; we all must pay.

The first to pay was the most innocuous, Castelli. Despite the restlessness of the boys and the mellifluous talks of the headmaster, despite a ferocious new air raid that drove us to the cellar like rats, the vast corridors of the building, the leafless courtyard, and the ritual silences still made the school a refuge and a comfort, like an old convent. It seemed peculiar that anyone should look elsewhere for peace and a good conscience. But Castelli, now a victim of that ridiculous Lucini, Castelli who was already giving some private lessons, never asked Lucini why he himself didn't leave. They would walk up and down in the lobby and Lucini, small and aggressive, would be working his eyebrows, showing his teeth, nodding. Castelli had a session with the headmaster and one fine day presented his resignation.

The secretary, dubious, told me the story, adding: "Blessed are the diabetics." But the matter didn't go smoothly. I was also called in for a conference. From the headmaster's tone I gathered that something was coming to a boil. Oh, not an investigation, for goodness' sake. It didn't seem a case for that. He only wanted to hear whether I knew anything about a colleague's decision, if there had been talk, if I thought that strange motives . . . Then he darkened. "We would all rather stay home. It would be nice for everybody in times like these. Beautiful thought! But we all can't. We headmasters are the most exposed. We have to answer for every word of yours and our own . . ."

I recalled the time the year before when he had spoken to us at a convocation about the beautiful trust which, in that difficult hour, should reign between us and the administration. At that time Lucini was still a Fascist.

I couldn't restrain myself and mentioned his name. Then I bit my tongue. The headmaster's face darkened and at the same time he laughed. "Lucini is Lucini," he said. "We all know Lucini."

"But weren't we talking about him?" I said sharply.

We looked at each other stupidly. Then the headmaster sighed, as if he had a very backward schoolboy before him.

"Castelli," he said. "Castelli. Come on, let's go."

"Castelli?" I said. "But he's a saint."

He got up and went to the door; he closed it and turned back quietly, stopped, and tapped his forehead. Another impatient sigh. "Castelli has spoken to me indiscreetly," he said. "Some trouble is brewing, I'm sure of that. The danger is the boys. You don't know if he has been talking to the boys?"

"Only Lucini can say. They're always arm in arm."

"Oh, drop it," he snapped. "We can't involve Lucini."

"Why not?" I said, amused.

Then the headmaster gave me a foxy look. He went back and sat down behind the table, clasped his hands, and held them across his paunch. He seemed resigned at last.

"I want to speak to you openly," he said slowly. "We are all nervous wrecks these days. What one teacher says to another, what we say to each other in the privacy of this room, goes no further. I dare to think that together we make one big family. But we have a duty, a mission to fulfill. Before the boys, before their families, yes, even before the nation, before this wretched country, we are obliged to set an example—do I make myself clear? Making rash gestures, taking dramatic attitudes . . . we'll talk about conscience later, if you like . . . may have consequences . . . involve . . . jeopardize us. The eyes of many, not only of the boys, are upon us. Is this clear?"

We didn't talk about conscience. Neither of us brought it up. I promised him only to try to persuade Castelli to retract his resignation. Instead I went to Lucini and very solemnly inquired about his health. Lucini understood and grew angry. He said that this was no time to wear slippers and that anyone with guts ought to be committed.

"Committed how?"

"This war," he said, "has not been understood. We began with a corrupt regime. Traitors they were and traitors they still are. But the ordeal by fire will sort us out. We are living a revolution. This belated Republic..."

He didn't conclude much, but he did conclude. His idea was that the time was urgent; one had to join the battle and save the country by standing by whichever of the two contenders would make the revolution and dictate the peace.

"But who will win?" I muttered.

He looked at me dumfounded and hugged his shoulders.

I went home with Castelli and described the headmaster's fears. He listened dutifully. I spoke of Lucini and asked him if they had handed in their resignation together. "A fat lot of good it did," I told him, "for you to stay away from school. What use is it for you to let everyone know that you're fed up?"

The use was that he needed that half pay. "Lucini," he told me, "can't resign because once he leaves the staff, to whom could he give lessons? Does anyone take fencing lessons today?"

This business was becoming more and more absurd. I told him that no one would ever dream of reproaching us for having served the present government. "Everybody would have to stop in their tracks," I said. "Trolleymen, judges, postmen. Life would come to a full stop."

Quietly and stubbornly he said that this was exactly what was wanted. "But then you must give up the salary. It's government money."

He shook his head and went off. I went home again agitated and unhappy. I could imagine the women's faces, or Cate's, if I had made such a gesture. But maybe it would have pleased her. Elvira would have liked it for another reason. So then, I thought all evening, someone takes risks, really acts, and that's what he's like —thoughtless. Like a boy who gets sick and doesn't know he might die. He doesn't look inside himself, doesn't even renounce his salary. Like anyone else, he thinks he is acting in his own interest.

Then I got Christmas letters from home. My sister wrote, told me about the farming and complained about my staying in the city during such a year. Certainly traveling was miserable, the trains uncomfortable, freezing. Life is ugly everywhere, she said; there's nothing new here. The letter was packed in a basket of fruit and meat; there was also the Christmas candy.

Half the basket I took to Le Fontane for a New Year's dinner that Cate and I had planned. Everybody was supposed to come. The grandmother and the girls worked all day in the kitchen: Dino and I went looking for teasels and chestnuts. The day was cold, full of sun; no snow at all so far. Dino told me he had seen the sidewalk in town where three patriots had been shot; the bloodstains were still there; if he had come the day before, he would have seen the corpses. Some passers-by had turned and stared at the spot. I told Dino to forget it and concentrate on the holidays. But he added that you could still see the signs of bullets in the wall.

A package of books and a flashlight were waiting for him at Le Fontane; he would find them when we got back. Cate had already thanked me. I wasn't sure that Dino would like his present. I had never given one to a boy before. But could one give him a pistol?

We entered the inn numb with cold but very cheerful. It was beautifully warm in the kitchen. The old people were there, Fonso, Giulia, Nando, everyone.

"This place is safe," they were saying. "Not the constant fear of Turin."

"To think," they said, "that there's enough in the cellar to have us all lined up and shot. You too, granny."

The girls laughed and brought food to the table. "Come on, it's Christmas. Knock it off," someone said.

We spoke of Tono. He was in Germany, at an extermination camp. They talked of other men I didn't know, of escapes and *coups de main*. "There are more people in the mountains than at home," Nando's wife said. "What kind of Christmas will they have?"

"Don't worry," Fonso said. "We've even sent them wine."

I watched old Gregorio eating quietly in his shirtsleeves, hunched over. He said nothing, but seemed to be listening, looking

133

on benignly as if he had been hearing these conversations every day since he was born. The restlessness behind our cheerfulness didn't touch him. He reminded me of my village; of us all, he alone had always lived on the hill.

"When the good weather comes," Fonso said, "we'll come down from the mountains."

"They'll soon ferret you out if you do," I said. "Better to stay in the mountains."

Even Cate agreed with me. "Last summer," Fonso said, "they came up there to find us. We can't afford to give them the time."

"Until the English begin helping us," Nando said, laughing, "we won't have decent weapons. Germans and Fascists supply us now. If they don't bring something up, we'll just have to go down and get it."

"What a war, what a war!" one of the girls cried out. "Whoever gets away first is the winner."

We laughed and shouted, and then Dino, who had been drinking, began to play the fool and race around the table, pointing his flashlight like a gun and shining it in our faces. I said that for four years the Germans had been training themselves as guerrillas and we shouldn't forget it.

"To think that we'll have to see them in our houses," Nando said.

"Better that than the way it was," Fonso cut in.

"You can say that again."

No one spoke of the end. Nobody reckoned the time element. Not even the old woman. They said "Another year" or "Next year" as if it were a matter of no importance, as if flight, bloodshed, and death by ambush had become our normal life.

When the fruit and dessert came to the table, we spoke about my home region and the partisan bands up there. Cate asked about my parents. Fonso, who was organizing in Turin and in the mountains, said something about the clandestine work in the hills. He had no special news; it was another sector, but he knew it was a wretched country where too many disbanded men had gone back to farming and forgotten the war.

"They are hills like these," I said then. "Can one hide in the hills in winter?"

"One can hide anywhere," he said. "It's necessary in order to divide the attacking forces. When every house, every village, every hill has its own people, tell me, how can the blackshirts form a front?"

"Every German we grab," Nando said, "is one less to fight at Cassino."

Incredulously I thought of the vineyards and hills up there. That even there there would be shooting and ambushes, that houses would burn and people die, seemed incredible, absurd.

"Perhaps you can tell me," snapped Nando's wife, "if the English would thank you for it."

"Come now," said Fonso. "We're not fighting for the English."

The room smelled of smoke and wine. Even Cate lit a cigarette. They turned on the radio. The room grew noisier. It was very pleasant to lean against the stove listening to the voices in that warmth. A moment before, I had gone out to the yard with Dino while he crouched down in the dark; I lost myself a moment in the starlit emptiness. The same boyhood stars, now also glistening over the cities and trenches, on the dead and the living. Was there somewhere in those hills a corner, a peaceful courtyard, where at least for that night one could watch the stars without terror? From the door we heard the noises of the dinner. Then Dino called me, we went back in and the warmth enclosed us. The girls started singing.

I went down to Turin the next day, stopped at the school and found Fellini with his beret over his eyes. He chattered about the holidays, then said: "There's someone who had shit for Christmas."

That's how Fellini talked, with an insolent grin. I waited for the rest and it suddenly came.

"Don't you know about Castelli? They've suspended him and locked him up."

15. The year ended without snow, and at the start of the new semester Castelli was the chief subject of conversation. "Lucky it's not cold," they said. "Still, if it's true he has incipient diabetes, he won't be with us long." What could we do for him? "Nothing,"

we whispered, "nothing." The partisans might get stirred up. Lucini was silent, upset and evil-tempered. Whenever I reached the door of the school I expected to find a carload of Germans or militia. "We will all be watched," another said. "The boys, our houses. What a mess. They'll take us as hostages."

Old Domenico said: "We're at the point where if you're sick you don't dare go to bed."

"Professor, watch out . . ." the most wide-awake of the boys would call to me.

Even the headmaster worried me in those days. He sighed heavily and twitched every time the phone rang. It was clear that Castelli had put the rope around his own neck by talking to the superintendent of schools. Nobody missed his soft, sad face. He had brought it on himself. Furthermore, to be honest about it, hadn't he already been living, stubborn and solitary, as if in a cell? But now we were all living like that, behind four walls in fear and expectation, and every step, voice, every unexpected move caught us by the throat. "Silvio Pellico," the headmaster smiled, "at least let himself be locked up without jeopardizing any of his colleagues."

"But aren't there any relatives?"

"For goodness' sake, let him think of that."

So finally we forgot Castelli. I mean to say, we stopped discussing him. But like Tono, like Gallo, like the soldier of the Valdarno and Egle's brother, Castelli would suddenly jump back into my mind in a moment of strain, during an alarm or a freezing, briny dawn; whenever the news was especially bad. I thought of them at night going to bed in the dark or in the morning going down to Turin when the sun was igniting some fourth-floor window with a bloody orange-gold. Winter and window dazzle, burnished morning fogs had always reconciled me to the world, given me a shiver of hope. During the early years of the war the knowledge that such pleasures still existed made me feel expectant. Now this was also ebbing away and I didn't dare raise my head.

Egle had been chattering volubly about her brother. She gave him out as having come to his senses. No, he hadn't gone over to the Germans, it wasn't worth the effort. But neither had he joined

our old enemies, he was too loyal for that; he was at Milan working as an engineer in a factory, in semi-hiding with certain friends.
He was back in civilian clothes.

Suppose I had to flee, I asked myself, had to hide, where would I
go, where would I sleep or find something to eat? Would I have
found another place like this house, a little warmth and respite? I
felt hunted and guilty, ashamed of my quiet days. But I thought of
the rumors and stories of people who had taken refuge in convents,
towers, sacristies. What could life be like between those cold
walls, behind stained-glass windows, among wooden benches? A
return to childhood, to the smell of incense, to prayers and innocence? Certainly not the worst feature of those days. I began to feel
a hankering, almost a mania, to be forced into this life. Earlier,
passing a church, all I thought of were spinsters and bald old men
on their knees; a tedious murmuring. Suppose all this might not
matter, that a church, a monastery might be a refuge instead,
where with one's face in the palms of one's hands one could listen
to one's heartbeat slowing down? But for that, I thought, there was
no need for aisles and altars. Peace was enough, the end of blood-
spilling. I remember I was crossing a square and the thought
stopped me dead. I froze; it was an unexpected joy, a happiness. To
pray, enter a church, I thought, is to live a moment of peace, to be
reborn into a bloodless world.

But my certainty wavered. Soon after, I found a church and went
in. I stopped near the door, leaning on the cold wall. Far in back,
below the altar, a little red light; on the benches, nobody. I looked
hard at the floor and groped for that thought; I wanted to experience again the joy and certainty of sudden peace. No luck. All I did
was wonder if they were sending Dino to Mass. We had never discussed it. I couldn't remember what he did on Sunday mornings.
Certainly the old woman went to Mass. Bored, I went out to the
open air.

I never mentioned that moment, that burst of joy; least of all
to Cate. I wondered if the churchgoers—my women, the priests of
Santa Margherita—had that experience, if in prison or under the
bombs, before firing squads, anyone enjoyed a peace like that.
Perhaps death was acceptable on such conditions. But to discuss it
was impossible. It would be like going back to church and joining

in some rite—an empty gesture. The best thing about the liturgy, the altars, the empty naves was the moment one came out to breathe under the open sky; the door curtain fell back again and one was free, alive. Only of this could one talk.

Under the lamp, in the warmth of the dining room, while Elvira was cooking and her mother dozed, my mind on the heavy frosts, the corpses and flights in the woods. Within two months at the most it would be spring, the hill would be dressed in green, something fresh and delicate would be born under the sky. The war would be decided. They were already discussing new offensives and new landings. It would be like coming out of a shelter under the parting fire of strafers.

I said nothing to Cate about my experiment, but I wanted to know what she thought about such things. She said she had believed in them once. She stopped on the path—it was dark already, we were coming back from Turin—said that at times she felt an impulse to pray but was able to control herself. Unless your nerves are in good shape, she observed, you're not much use in a hospital.

"But it's praying that calms your nerves," I said. "Look at the priests and nuns. They're always calm."

"It's not prayer," Cate said. "It's their profession. They see all kinds of people."

So I reflected that we were all living as if in a hospital. We started walking again. My moment of peace, the useless relief, now seemed absurd, discounted. Truly, one could not talk about it.

"One cannot," said Cate, "pray without believing. It does no good."

She spoke dryly, as if answering a speech.

"Still, one must believe something," I said. "You can't live unless you do."

Cate took me by the arm. "Do you believe in these things?"

"We are all sick people," I said, "who want to be cured. It's an inner sickness; it should be enough to convince ourselves that it doesn't exist and then we'd be cured. When you pray, you feel as if you were well."

Then Cate looked at me, surprised. I expected a smile that didn't come. She said: "The really sick, you have to take care of them, cure them. Praying does no good. It's that way in everything. Even Fonso says so: 'It's what you do that counts, not what you say.'"

Then we discussed Dino. It was easier. Cate admitted she should bring him up more courageously, teach him to understand things for himself, leave him the time to decide, but she had failed. The grandmother sometimes took him to Mass and sent him to catechism. I told her that, whatever one did, children could not decide for themselves and that to send them or not to send them to catechism was already a choice; it meant teaching them something they haven't asked for. "Not believing in anything is also a religion," I told her. "One can't escape these things."

But Cate said it should be possible to explain the two ideas to a child and ask him to choose. Then I had to laugh, and she smiled too, when I said that the best way to make a Christian was to tell him not to believe, and vice versa. "It's true," she cried. "It's really true." We stopped in front of the gate and the dog jumped all over me; it was the only time we talked in this vein. The next evening I didn't see her at the trolley stop.

It was just that day that I thought of showing up in the Dora district and visiting the others. Then, because of the cold and the long way, I didn't go. I came home beneath the stripped trees, going over the meat of our talks, thinking again of Castelli. Elvira told me that a young man had been looking for me at Le Fontane. She didn't know who. I left immediately, before sundown, annoyed that Elvira had found things out this way. She shouted after me to ask if I were coming back to supper.

They were all there, minus Fonso and Giulia. Nando, at the door, nodded to me, preoccupied. I noticed suitcases and bundles on the tables, in the yard. They were all milling around in the kitchen; Dino was gnawing an apple.

It was Cate who said: "Oh, there you are."

They wanted to warn me not to go to the Dora district. "They are flying low," Nando said. "It's beginning."

"No, Fonso is in the mountains," they told me. "It's Giulia. The Germans took her today."

I wasn't afraid. My heart didn't sink—I had waited months for that moment, that blow. Or perhaps, when something begins in earnest, it's less frightening because it removes an uncertainty. Not even the shock of their excitement frightened me.

"A woman," I said, "takes care of herself."

They didn't answer; that wasn't the question. It was whether they had taken her by chance or whether they had been watching the house for some time. Many had been arrested at the factory and much evidence confiscated. Giulia had been called with some other women into the yard and made to climb into a truck. Someone ran immediately to give the alarm. Probably they were searching the boarding house right then. Nando's wife screamed that it had been stupid to leave the house. Now they would come looking for them at Le Fontane.

Cate answered her dryly that nobody would say anything.

"Except Giulia," the younger sister said. We discussed Giulia's courage. A question was burning my tongue, but I didn't dare put it.

"If they knew anything," the old woman said, "they would have picked you all up by now."

"Poor Giulia," Cate said. "We must take her a change of clothes."

Then it occurred to me that nobody at school had thought of doing this for Castelli. I asked: "Can one take packages to prisoners?"

We heard a car coming, and everyone kept still. The motor roared, grew louder, we held our breaths. It passed quickly and we looked at each other like swimmers coming panting out of the water.

"Do they deliver the parcels?" I asked.

"Sometimes."

"But first they take what they want for themselves."

"It's not what you take, it's your remembering them."

No one mentioned what I was thinking, but Dino at one point jumped up. "Let's hide in the cellar."

"You keep quiet!" his mother snapped. We came back to Giulia. The danger, Nando said, was that she might lose her head and became insulting. She hated those people too much. "If they manage to get her mad..."

I left them at nightfall, making an appointment with Cate for

Turin. I went out into the dark with a sense of relief and found Belbo waiting in the yard. He made me jump. We're like hare and hound, I thought.

Carnival time came, and strange to say, the square I crossed every day on the way to school was filled with booths, a half-hearted crowd, merry-go-rounds and stalls. I saw shivering acrobats and carnival wagons. The little noise they made didn't depress me as usual. It just seemed a small miracle that there still were people ready to travel, whiten their faces, put on a show. Half the square had been gutted by bombs; a few idle Germans were wandering inquisitively around. The mild February sky was good for the soul. On the hill, under the rotting leaves, the first flowers must have been pushing up. I promised myself to look for them.

I was always keyed up to see if I was being followed. I let Cate get down from the trolley, let her walk a distance, then joined her halfway up the hill in the clear evening light. She gave me news of Giulia, of the others. One knew only that Giulia was alive; there were rumors of more German raids and reprisals—it was always possible that one day they might use a woman as hostage, put her up against the wall. Fonso stayed away from Turin; they were getting ready in the mountains for their spring offensive. Some night soon his men were coming to Le Fontane, Cate said, to pick up stores.

"Good," I said. "I hope they hurry. It's a crazy business."

She smiled and said: "I know."

16. A night of warm rain followed, releasing the spring. The next day one breathed an earthy smell in the dripping stillness. I spent half the morning in the woods, in the hollow by the Pino path, revisiting the old trees and mosses. It seemed yesterday I had come up with Dino. I wondered how much longer it was going to be my only horizon and I looked at the fresh sky as if it were a stained-glass window. Belbo ran alongside.

On my way back I went along the ridge from which one could look down on Le Fontane. That day the courtyard came suddenly into view between the leafless trees and I saw two stopped cars of a blue-green color and around them small human figures of the same color. I felt slightly chilled and nauseated, trying to tell myself they were Fonso's men; it was like a very sudden eclipse of the sun. I looked more closely; no doubt of it, I could see the guns in the soldiers' hands.

For several seconds I didn't move; I stared at the hollow, the clean sky, the little group below, not thinking of myself, not afraid. I was stunned by the way things happen; I'd seen that house so many times from above, had imagined myself in every kind of danger, but a scene like that—in the clear morning light—I had never imagined.

But time was pressing. What to do? Could I do anything but wait? I wished it could all be over, that it were still yesterday: the yard deserted, the cars not there. I wondered if Cate had left for Turin, whether they were arresting her there. I thought of going nearer and overhearing the voices. It was obvious that I should run immediately to Turin, should risk everything to warn her, in the vague hope that she had stayed there.

People milled in the courtyard: skirts, civilian clothes—but I couldn't make out faces. They got into the cars. Soldiers left the house and climbed in with them. I recognized the old woman. Will they burn the house? Then I caught the faint sound of motors starting and driving off.

Time passed. I didn't move. Again, everything was burnished and still. If they've taken the old woman, I thought, they've taken everybody. I became aware of Belbo crouched and panting at my feet. I held him up by his front paws and said: "Down there!" He jumped up and down, barking. Fear pushed me behind a tree. But Belbo was already off like a hare.

I watched him run down the road into the yard. I recalled that summer night when there was singing at Le Fontane and everything was still to happen. I listened with my heart in my mouth and looked to see if anyone was still down there. Belbo began barking again, angrily, against the door. A cockcrow went up from a great distance; I heard the rumble of trucks on the Pino road.

The yard stayed empty. Then I saw that Belbo was jumping and had ceased barking; he was jumping around someone; a small boy. Dino came out from under the hedge. I saw them go down to the road and take the path I had taken so many times on my way back. Without doubt it was Dino. I recognized the red scarf he wore with his overcoat, and his usual trot. I began running like a madman through undergrowth and rotting leaves, dodging or pushing aside dripping branches; fear, excitement, anxiety made it a blind plunge. I caught sight again of Le Fontane from a clearing: the peaceful courtyard. Nobody was there.

I caught up with Dino halfway down the hill. He was walking with his hands in his pockets. He stopped, red in the face and panting. He didn't seem frightened. "The Germans," he said. "They came this morning in cars. They hit Nando. They wanted to kill him . . ."

"Where is your mama?"

Cate had been taken too. And old Gregorio. Everyone. He and his mother were just going outside to leave for Turin and had seen them coming. They didn't have time to turn around before the Germans had jumped down and run across the yard. They shouted and pointed stubby guns. Mama trembled. Nando was eating breakfast and hadn't finished yet. His bowl was still on the table.

"Did they go down to the cellar?"

A German had taken a basketful of bottles. Yes, they had hit Nando in the cellar; you could hear yelling. They found the cases and the guns. They were shouting in German. A little man in street clothes, speaking Italian, was ordering them around. Nando's wife had fainted. Mama had told him he should try to hide, then come to me and tell me everything. But he wanted to stay with the others, to get in the car too; he tried, but the Germans wouldn't let him. Then his mama had made go-away faces at him and he had run to the field and the grandmother was calling out, shouting. One might as well hide, he thought.

"Did she give you a message for me?"

Dino said no and went back to describing what he had seen. The little man had asked what the upstairs rooms were for. How many came to the inn in the evening? Then he talked to the others in German.

We came to the gate. Dino said he had eaten already and filled his pockets with apples. Along the road I thought of the villas hidden in their parks and that none of them were safe just by hiding.

Cesare Pavese

Elvira was waiting for us at the door. She had put on her coat and was waiting. She looked solemn and nervous. She ran to meet me, her face flaming red. She stammered in a faint voice: "The Germans are here."

"I know it," I wanted to say, but her gesture of grabbing my arm and dragging me away with no attention to Dino frightened me. She was not blushing for shame; she had a wild look.

"Two Germans came," she panted. "They spoke your name . . . they came in . . . they looked at your room . . ."

It was more then nausea; it liquefied my legs. I tried to say something, but nothing came out.

"An hour ago . . ." Elvira said low and hoarsely. "I didn't know where you were . . . I didn't want them to wait. I wrote the school's name and address on a sheet of paper. They left . . . but they'll return, they'll return . . ."

Even today I wonder why those Germans didn't wait for me at the villa and send someone to look for me in Turin. It is because of their failure that I am still free and up here. Why I should have been saved and not Gallo, or Tono, or Cate, I don't know. Perhaps because I'm supposed to suffer for others? Because I'm the most useless and don't deserve anything, not even punishment? Because I went into a church that time? The experience of danger creates more cowards every day. It makes one stupid. I have reached the point of being alive only by chance, when many better men than I are dead; I don't like it, it's not enough. At times, after having listened to the useless radio and looked through the window at the empty vineyards, I think that living by accident is not living, and I wonder if I have really escaped.

That morning I didn't stop to think. A taste of death filled my mouth. I jumped to the path behind the boxwood hedge. Over the hedge I told Elvira to give my money and bankbook to the boy and I ran to wait for him in the hollow of the ferns. I told Dino to be sure no one was following him, to go to the gate and look around.

To the Germans I asked Elvira to say that I often spent weeks at Turin, she didn't know where.

Dino shouted. He said: "There's a man."

I flattened on the gravel, bathed in sweat. Elvira came back and whispered: "It wasn't anything. Just a wagon passing."

144

Then I said: "All right, we're agreed," and took off.

I was soaked through when I got to the bracken. I walked up and down to cool myself off. From between the bare trees the immense sky opened out. I understood what the sky must be for prisoners. That taste of blood that filled my mouth prevented me from thinking. I looked at my watch. I repented having promised to wait; the strain was horrible. I pricked my ears for the barking of dogs, knowing the Germans used police dogs. Don't let Belbo come looking for me, I said aloud; they can easily follow him.

Then my worries and questions began. If the Germans should arrest Elvira and her mother, her mother would surely say that I was here. I would have liked to return and beg her not to. The many wrongs I had done Elvira came back to me. I wondered if Dino had already told her of the arrests and the guns. I calmed down a little with the thought that they had not been looking for guns at my place.

So passed that period of waiting—leaning against trees, talking to myself, walking, following the sun. I grew hungry, looked at my watch again; ten minutes after eleven. I had been waiting a mere half hour. Of Cate, Nando, and the others I hadn't dared think, almost as if to give myself a testimonial of innocence. At one point I shuddered, sick of myself. I pissed against a tree for the third time.

Dino appeared two hours later, with Elvira, who was wearing the black veil over her head which she normally wore back from Mass.

"No one has come," they told me. They carried a bundle and a smaller package. "There's your things and something to eat," she said. Socks, handkerchiefs, my razor. "You're crazy," I cried. But Elvira told me she had thought it all out and found me a fine, safe retreat. It was beyond Pino, on the high plain, the College of Chieri, a quiet house with beds and a refectory. "There's a fine courtyard and a school. You'll like it. It's a priests' school. They take care of each other, the priests."

She spoke calmly, no longer frightened. Even her flush had gone. Everything came out naturally, routinely. It was like those evenings when I said my good night to her.

"And Dino?" I asked.

For now he would stay with her. "We worked it all out," she said, barely glancing at him, and he nodded agreement.

Exhaustion, the taste of blood, came over me again; my eyes began to fog. I was floating in a sea of goodness, of terror and peace. Even the priests, and Christian forgiveness. I tried to smile but my face wouldn't respond. I muttered something—that they should go home right away, that most of all they shouldn't come to see me. I took the bundles and left.

I ate in the woods and toward evening I reached the college by an out-of-the-way path. Nobody had seen me. I swore that if possible I would never leave.

17. That sweep of cloister around the courtyard, those little brick staircases by which one climbed from the corridors to the upper rooms, and the big shadowy chapel made a world that I could have wished even more closed in, isolated, and gloomy. I was well received by the priests, who, I gathered, were used to such guests. They talked of the outside world, of life, the war, with a detachment that pleased me. I saw the boys vaguely in the background, noisy and harmless. I could always find an empty classroom, a stairway, for killing a little more time, for prolonging my life, being alone. At first I started at every unusual movement, every voice; I kept my eye on pillars, passageways, porches, always ready to hide again or vanish. The taste of blood lingered for many days and nights. During the rare moments when I succeeded in calming down and remembering the day of flight and the woods, I shuddered at the idea of the danger I had escaped, at the idea of an open sky, roads, and encounters. I would have liked the college entrance, that cold, massive porch, to have been walled up like a tomb.

Days passed in a circling of the cloisters. Chapel, refectory, lessons, refectory, chapel. So reduced, the time shrank one's thoughts, passed, and became a substitute for living. I entered the chapel with the others, listened to the voices, bent over or straightened up, repeated the prayers. If Elvira could have seen me! But I thought, too, of the peace and discovery of that day in the church, and covering my eyes I brooded like a hen over my inner commotion. The chapel windows were meager and dark, the weather similar; it drizzled day and night. In the cold I nursed my terror and shrunken hope. While I sat in the refectory amid the racket of the boys, I went humbly to a corner, warmed my hands on a plate, and enjoyed thinking of myself as a beggar. That some of the boys grumbled about prayers, about the service, the food, made me uneasy, filled me with a superstitious irritation. But for all this silence, humility, and self-recollection, I didn't recover the peace of that day in church. A few times I went to the chapel alone, concentrated on trying to pray in the chilly darkness. The antique smell of incense and stone reminded me that death, not life, is important to God. To move God, to have Him on one's side—I reasoned as if I were a believer—one must have already renounced the world and be ready to shed blood. I thought of those martyrs we studied in the catechism. Their peace was a peace beyond the tomb; all of them shed blood. As I didn't want to.

In short, I was asking for a lethargy, an anesthetic, a certainty of being well hidden. I was not seeking the peace of the world, but my own. I wanted to be good in order to be safe. I realized this so well that one day I softened. Naturally I wasn't in church but in the court with the boys. They were playing a noisy game of soccer. In the clear sky—it had stopped raining that morning—I looked at rosy, wind-driven clouds. The cold, the uproar, the sudden opening of the sky swelled my heart and I understood that a burst of energy, a pleasant recollection, were enough to revive hope. I realized that every day that passed was a step toward salvation. The good weather was returning, as in so many past seasons; I was still free, still alive. This time also my certainty lasted little more than an instant, but it was like a thaw and a grace. I could breathe, look about, make plans. I prayed again that evening—I didn't dare stop—but I could think of Le Fontane with less pain while I did so, and told myself it was all chance, a game, and for just this reason I could still save myself.

The roughest time was dawn when I was waiting for the rising bell in my cot under the roof. I strained in the dark for the sound of motors, the rattle of arms and dry commands being snapped out. It was the hour of visitations, when fugitives were flushed from their hiding places. In the warmth of my bed I thought of the prison cells, faces I knew, so many dead. The past came alive in the silence; our discussions returned. I closed my eyes and imagined myself suffering with the others. Even this thin strain of courage startled me. Then I began to pick out distant noises, cheepings, vague thuds. I imagined the broad, high plain in the fog, the stiff woods, swamps, open country. I saw the blockhouses and patrols. When light began to show in the cracks of the shutters, I had been wide awake and restless for some time.

Gradually I began to join the college routine. In fifteen days I took charge of the boys' study period. I got a group of twelve-year-olds; it was lucky because one of the older boys, in the uniform of the voluntary blackshirts, might well have asked embarrassing questions. I noticed other assistants like me in the refectory and yard; officials in hiding, they said, young men from the south separated from their families. I tried to avoid them. During study hours I supervised the boys, who stayed quietly at the benches, at the worst quarreling over a pen. I browsed in their schoolbooks. The best hour was morning, when the boys left for classes and the college became empty and silent. Then the young assistants would also clear out and explore Chieri, its girls and cafés. To hear them, it was a bonanza. They thought of nothing else. "We're men," they said. Their rashness scared me. But the silent morning in the courtyard or in an empty classroom, browsing or watching shadows moving under the archways, gave me a breathing spell. A visit or a footstep was enough to send me into a corner to look nervously at the stairs leading to the attic. In any case, I had now had too many false alarms to react very much. The chapel would serve me well because it gave on a vestry and from there to a church that opened on the square. But not everyone left the college in the morning. Some priests came and went in the cloister; I often talked to them.

There was a Father Felice who listened to the radio, gave me news, and joked with a bland, infantile air. He ran through the newspapers with me. For him the war meant the scurrilities of "those people," a noisy and far-off mess, something that made very little difference in Chieri. "Nonsense," he said, "this land needs manure, not bombs." Once two or three enemy squadrons, gleaming in silver, passed overhead; the ground shook with their engines and the noise drowned our voices. Father Felice ran to see them, pulled the alarm bell himself. Some other priests dashed out, wanted to go down to the cellar. "If they should ever come to Chieri, we would be dead already," he said, tugging the rope. Then we heard explosions in the far distance. Father Felice listened disgustedly, moving his lips. One couldn't tell if he were praying or counting the bombs. I envied him because I realized that he saw no difference between this mortal danger and an earthquake or any other catastrophe. When he talked to me, he accepted me prima facie, didn't ask me why I was hiding. He said only: "It must be hard for a man like you to be caged up." Once I told him it suited me very well. He nodded agreement. "Of course, a quiet life. But a little air doesn't hurt." He was young, just thirty, the son of peasants. With boys and young peasants, many of them hard cases, he knew how to act, could calm them down, hold their attention. "They're like calves," he said. "I can't think why they are sent to school." I wondered if Dino were with other boys; if he were going to school as before, if Elvira were talking to him. I wondered what had happened at the villa, if they had looked for me in Turin. All this seemed remote, from beyond the tomb, and even the idea of receiving news alarmed me. Better this way, to stay in the dark.

Instead news arrived, unexpectedly. They called me to the parlor. "A woman is looking for you." It was Elvira, complete with veil and handbag, and Dino, flushed and freshly combed.

"Nobody has come," they told me. "They've other things to think about."

"Not even in the village?"

"Not even in the village."

"They must have looked for me at home," I said.

"Your sister has written."

They gave me the letter. I opened it with my heart in my throat. Those places, that past, still existed. It had been mailed only a few days before and said the usual winter things. It was clear that nobody had been looking for me even there.

Then I saw a suitcase on the ground and Elvira anticipated me. "They're Dino's things, we brought them in the cart."

Dino was staring through the window at the porch and high wall. A priest was crossing the courtyard.

"We went to Le Fontane the other day. They hadn't even closed the door, but everything is the same. One must admit that people are still honest."

She spoke aggressively, in a pointless whisper, flushed and excited. She turned suddenly to Dino and asked: "Do you like it here?"

A boy came to call Dino to the rector. I looked at Elvira, astounded. She told him to go and give good answers, then turning to me, she attempted a smile. "We came with our priest," she said. "He says the boy can't grow up on his own. He needs school and guidance. He can't go to Turin; who would take him? The priest hopes the college will take him in. They'll take him, he's almost an orphan."

The strange idea upset me because of the obvious danger. Dino could lose his head and betray me. The notion that now he was alone in the world took me by surprise.

"Here they make a special allowance," Elvira insisted, "for cases like ours. It'll cost little or nothing. It's a great kindness."

So Dino stayed at the college, and Elvira left, examining me worriedly, assuring me that she would bring me other things and that Dino was now a screen for us. She also gave me greetings from her mother and Egle. She said they had a plate for me every evening at dinner. Either she or her mother had dreamed that I was coming down the stairs, and such things always come true.

18.
Dino understood from a look and a nod from me that we had never seen each other before. On our way to chapel in the evening I asked him if he had ever been in a college before. He replied, without raising his eyes, that before he had stayed with his mother. He played the comedy better than I did; shunted about as he had been, he had no need to pretend. Boys swirled around us, some of them listening. Then I told him that to live in a college you had to forget your old life, not even mention it. "It's only girls who gossip, not men."

The next day I watched him running and shouting with the other boys. Good, I thought. He wasn't sulking in corners; I wondered if I would have been as brave. I even felt a certain angry pride and said to myself, all right, he's only a child, but we two are made of the same stuff. If Fonso had been shut up in a college, would he live as I was living? The idea was absurd; Fonso was ranging the mountains and risking his life. How was it possible? All his days were flavored with death, like mine the morning they came to take us. Never, not even as a boy, did I have Fonso's hot blood. I was different from Dino, too. And now Dino had no one except me.

I watched him running, pushing his companions in the chapel, squinting up at the chapel windows and praying. He wore a pullover under his jacket, had red, stubby hands, and an obstinate look in his eyes. He made a great effort to play our game well, to remain impassible, to be underhanded in his notice of me. My mind went back to the summer—Flash Gordon, the savages' hideout, the Yellow Men. Everything comes around, I thought, even the shapeless imaginings of a boy.

Fine spring weather had come. On Sunday the boys marched in a column to Chieri and open country. I breathed deeply in the sunshine and cool air of the yard. I wondered if the war would end under that sky, in April or May. The news and the radio became disturbing once again. Offensives were raging everywhere, mighty landings, hopes. Once I put my nose outside the main door. When I was certain that nobody had been looking for me, I went into the lane and as far as a small square, where I found a church and a bell tower. I saw the hill behind the roofs, the distant violet hill of Pino. But was it worth taking risks if the war might end tomorrow? I was better off in the yard. I didn't envy those who went walking; I heard what they said when they came back.

One learned from the militia barracks that blackshirts and desperate characters were combing the countryside and shooting into windows at night. Their enemies were the young draftees and disbanded troops. The southern boys hiding out with me in the college fooled around among them and stole their girls in the cafés. Grinning, they described their exploits. They wouldn't stop even when the blackshirts murdered a patriot in the square. "Stinker," they said. "He went around armed, of course." One day the rector called everybody in and gave us a sermon. We should stop chasing women—our good name, the boys. The times might be bad, but nothing excused such behavior. Health began with honest living. Not to mention the other risks.

Another day I found Dino discussing the guerrilla war with a group of his friends. They were baiting a tall, bony boy who was defending the Republic. They asked him sarcastically why he no longer came to school in a uniform. Someone shoved him. Dino, pint-sized among the more excited boys, shrilled: "Where's socialism then? Where is it?" But Father Felice had already entered the circle and damped it down. "Don't you know that socialism is a sin?" he said gruffly to the boys. He got a laugh and slapped one of them. Dino's expression annoyed me.

I met him later, seated on the base of a column. He saw me coming and kept his head down. I asked him if that was the way to act, the way he kept secrets. "If you were with Fonso," I said, "they would have shot you some time ago. You're like Giulia," I said quietly. "You can't keep your mouth shut."

He gave me a calm but puzzled look. "I want to go to Fonso," he said. "I don't want to go back to the old lady's house."

I expected this and let him talk. He knew a courtyard in Turin where Fonso's messages were delivered. The doorman knew him. He was fed up with women. He wanted to be in the mountains, with the others.

"It's not easy," I said. "If they wanted you, they would have sent for you. Who knows where their camp is now? The Germans are searching everywhere."

Then I told him to obey his mother and stay with me. "You can't keep your mouth shut. If you do it again, I'll send you back to the old woman."

Those were the days when one kept reading of clashes on the mountains, of German concentrations, of an offensive designed to wipe out the patriots. Posters showed up everywhere with a huge mailed hand strangling bandits, and the legend: "So the traitor dies!" The Fascists were also getting ferocious. From Turin, from all Piedmont, stories arrived every day of executions, unheard-of cruelties. If Nando is still alive, I thought, it's a miracle.

I walked each evening with Father Felice in a wide corridor where the boys would play awhile before their enforced silence. Now and then one of the assistants would stop to talk to us. One of their jokes was to ask suddenly: "Father Felice, you can tell us. Which of these boys is your son?"

"If it had been you," he answered, "I'd have put you on bread and water."

Dino was yelling among the others and sometimes taking a beating. "That boy," Father Felice said. "Do you see him? He's a true wolf-child, one of the fruits of the war. Father and mother in prison, he on the loose. Who's to blame?"

"Everybody is," I said. "We all brought it on in one way or another." Father Felice clutched his breviary more tightly, shook himself, and drew up: "However it may have happened," he said, "it's up to all of us to remedy it. He's not the only one."

Then he opened his breviary, eyeing the boys closely. We had talked about the breviary together one morning. I had asked him to let me look through it. I didn't understand much—it was full of Latin prayers, psalms and glorias, gospels and meditations. One read of festivals, of saints; each day had its own. I deciphered horrible stories of sufferings and martyrdoms. There was one about forty Christians thrown naked to die on the ice of a pond, but first the executioner had broken their legs; the one about women beaten and burned alive, of tongues torn out, of intestines wrenched away. It was astounding that the antique Latin of those yellowed pages, those baroque phrases as worn as the wooden pews, should contain so much convulsive life, should virtually drip with so much atrocious bloodshed. Father Felice told me that what should be recited was mostly the office. He said that nobody knew how much of the hagiography had got in there; it was pure legend; they had been waiting a long while for the authorities to prune and revise the text. It would take too long to read it properly every day.

"But the important thing," I said, "is not whether or not such and such a martyr really existed. The reader is meant to understand what the faith has cost."

Father Felice nodded.

"The question," I said, "seems to be what is gained by reading the same words over and over."

"As far as prayers are concerned," Father Felice said, "novelty doesn't count. One might as well deny that the day is made up of hours. Life is summed up in the changes of the year. The country is monotonous, seasons always return. The Catholic liturgy follows the year and reflects the work of the fields."

These talks calmed me. It was my way of accepting the cloistered life. The few times I wanted to see Chieri and had forced myself as far as the outer road, I had seen nothing but quiet squares, low arches and churches, rose motifs in terra cotta, doorways. How to believe that in this and other villages all over the province blood was being spilled, ambushes sprung, and the law defied? That old liturgical world and its symbols of wine and grain, of little women who prayed in Latin but understood in dialect, gave a sense to my cavelike existence. There was no real difference; I could see that I had merely passed from the woods to the sacristy.

But not even this state of things lasted. I overheard conversations in the refectory. The string-bean boy who had been in the Fascist Youth boasted of wanting to denounce the college, of having friends among the blackshirts, of being ready to give the names of traitors in hiding. That night I didn't close my eyes. I told Dino to be on guard. If I ended up at the barracks, I was a dead man. The panic of flight came back, my anxious dawns. I discussed it with Father Felice. Nothing could be done. It would be worse to punish the boy. Then one day the rector came back to the chapel with his cap pulled over his eyes, nodded to me to follow him, and took me beneath the stairs. "Don't let them see us," he whispered. "You'll do well to leave. There's danger—very much."

I left without a word to anyone. Dino was in class. I left with a bundle as I had come. I passed through Chieri, trembling and happy, and at sunset, with the sun in my eyes, on the crest of the hills bare and damp in the spring, I stretched my eyes as I hadn't for a very long time. I reached the villa without being seen. My first greeting was from Belbo bouncing on the gravel.

That evening we sat at dinner later than usual. We listened to the radio and discussed the war, Dino, and that other precocious delinquent. Elvira said, controlling her feelings, that the villas of the region were full of such people, and if the Germans hadn't looked for me hitherto, it was because their spies knew I was far away. Nobody should see me, the mother declared.

I stayed hidden several days, even from Egle, watching the orchard from behind curtains. What wouldn't I have given for news of Cate and the others. Elvira told me that Le Fontane had been locked up, nobody knew by whom. With Belbo I went out at night to the orchard to look down at Turin, where so much was going on. I had nothing to do. Every place reminded me of Cate, of Cate's conversation. I realized with dismay that if Cate didn't come out of it alive, I would never know whose son Dino was. Perhaps, I thought, she will be willing to tell me. Perhaps she is sorry she didn't before. Perhaps Father Felice is right and it's my duty, the duty of all survivors, to make up for the tragedy.

Once Elvira said: "They have asked about you in Turin. The secretary who knows Egle sends you greetings."

These trivialities pleased me, restored me, were like a pat on the head to a dog.

A week passed this way, but staying in the house became depressing. I still didn't dare return to Chieri. When I discussed it with Elvira, she said: "How do you suppose the boy is making out? We should at least bring him some apples."

So the next day she made the trip. I spent the day reading. Back again, she was outraged, breathless. Dino had been gone from the college for six days. I let her rage against the priests and the doorkeeper. I did not even ask if they had investigated or had any clues. I knew well enough where he had gone; I had suspected for some time. I kept quiet, imagining him setting out, close-mouthed, for Turin, throwing himself in ditches when necessary, finally arriving there.

Nothing else happened at the college. Ours had been a false alarm. The rector said that I could return.

We let two days go by. I told Elvira about the house outside the Dora district, where perhaps they knew something about him or his friends. I couldn't risk going. I often thought: If Cate should come back and ask where I am?

Then I decided to go back to Chieri. I asked Elvira to bring me all the news she knew. "If Dino doesn't find anyone," I told her, "he knows the road and will come back." During my whole return trip I imagined him materializing in front of me, my taking him by the hand and walking with him. Instead, at the outskirts of Chieri, I ran into a military patrol. They came out of an alley and headed toward me, looking sinister. One was a young man, a boy; the other three had dark, bad-tempered faces. They held rifles under their arms, muzzles up. They passed close by and said nothing.

$19.$ May arrived and even at college the days grew more lively and noisy. In the evening and in the cold, fragrant morning light, the cloister was a perennial shouting, running around, swapping rumors. The schools were closing in a few days. The Allied advance had started, with months and months of fine weather ahead of it. Some of my colleagues in hiding, those boys from the south, had left already to join the lines and save themselves.

Rooms and refectory gradually emptied; the boarders went home. After a while they had scattered over the countryside and I was left in the deserted college, listening for the rare steps of a priest or someone slow to get away. It was understood that we assistants could eat and sleep as before, but in that peace and silence I thought only of Dino. He had been missing nearly a month; I was so worried I would have gone looking for him, had I known how to begin. Now the war news had little to say of the mountains or the rebels. Perhaps the danger was over. But Elvira's expedition changed my mind.

She came to the college to tell me. She had been in Turin, beyond Dora, had been to the prisons, consulted priests. No news of the boy; if he had actually reached the mountains, who knew where he might be now? Some of the bands, they said, were hiding in France. It was no place for children, up there. All the others, the women, his mother and her relatives, had been deported a month ago. A chaplain who knew all about Le Fontane had told her; he assumed they had all been shot. "Anyhow, it comes to the same thing," he said. "No one ever comes back."

What else could I do now in the empty cloister but taste, morning and evening, my old panic? Of course I could go for walks, revisit the squares and country roads, but passing my time in that pointless waiting seemed more futile each day. Now that the past was only a small shadow of pain, a suffering I shared with many others, this sojourn at the college was becoming as tedious as life in prison.

I couldn't go back to the villa. It would only mean reliving the past, remembering the lost, one by one, hearing their voices, deluding myself into thinking that something of them was left to me. I seemed to have changed a great deal since the year before, since the time I had walked alone in the woods and my school was waiting for me in Turin and I was patiently waiting for the war to end. Now Dino had been with me in that cloister; his mother had sent him to me. Dino had been a clot of memories that I accepted, that I wanted; he alone could have saved me and I had not been enough for him. I was not even sure he would have cared now whether we met again or not. If I had vanished with his friends, he wouldn't have given me a second thought. Truly, the war was not going to end before it had destroyed every memory and hope. I had understood that for some time. And I realized that I would have to leave that cloister, root out my memories, and accumulate a new life. Thinking about all those who were going—the assistants, Dino, Elvira—was tantalizing. Impossible to stay at college without fear. I understood Dino. I understood Father Felice. I should have been a priest.

Elvira had brought me another letter from my parents, who asked me, as always, to visit them during the vacation. No one would look for me up there; it was certainly the safest of hiding places. I decided to go, even before I admitted it consciously. I thought about it day and night, repeating to myself: "There's still time." But I had already decided. The last time I'd been up there the year before the war, even then I'd said: "If only I could die up here," because when you imagine it in advance, war is a rest, a peace.

Elvira wouldn't hear of it. She didn't say I would run risks at home; she well knew I would not. She spoke of the trip, unforeseen events, machine-gunnings, ugly meetings, smashed bridges. If I went—I could read it in her eyes—would I ever come back? Then I told her I was short of money; I couldn't sponge any more on others. Sooner or later, I said, the kept person rebels. "But this war will end," she said indignantly. "It has got to end, and then you will pay your debts when you come back to live with us."

I asked her for a knapsack for the necessary things. I asked her to tell no one, not even her mother, that I was going. "Also," I observed, "there's no guarantee that I'll get there." She wanted an address. "There's no need," I answered. "I'm not changing my life, I'm changing my hideout. Better to erase the tracks."

When she left me alone with my pack, I breathed again. The first days I spent quietly, convinced that now I could take things easily; doing or not doing them depended on me. Poor Elvira assumed I had already left. I realized then that my plan for leaving had been a means of escaping her and her deepening interest. I well knew what she had in mind.

But one morning there were Germans everywhere. Father Felice and the rector had gone to Turin—I was waiting for them, to find out how safe the trains were. The Germans said nothing, just settled themselves in the college. Troops and a service corps, unloading and storing gear. But the doorman looked me up to ask what name I meant to declare. The German commander wanted a list of all residents. So I took my pack and left.

To board the train without returning to Turin, I had to put the hill behind me and use unknown roads. With my heart in my throat I headed toward the plain, knowing that by evening I would be seeing hills again, the right ones. But they appeared much sooner than that. I looked hard for blockhouses and saw, on the horizon's edge between telephone poles and low clouds, a thin, rather bleak patch of blue. I didn't stop until I had almost reached the hills—Villanova, where the railroad was. I sat on a little wall. Girls on bicycles passed; no Germans or soldiers. I ate my bread and enjoyed the trees, the rugged slopes, the open sky, envying Dino, who had been roaming for months. I hadn't been walking two hours.

I had ample time to get bored with the platform, station, and hillsides. As people accumulated, I felt better; for some time I'd forgotten that the world was teeming with faces and voices. They all talked of hunger, flight, war, laughing and greeting one another. I had even forgotten the train; when it jumped out from the acacia grove and didn't immediately slow down, it caught me up in its wake as if I were a child. Once on board, while it rattled through the woods, I learned that the bridge over the Tanaro had been wrecked, that one had to get off there. I also learned that patrols were combing the train and arresting anyone without a special permit.

20. But at Asti low clouds filled the sky again, the wind came up, and twilight fell suddenly. When we jumped off the train, nobody paid us any attention. I walked along the tracks and in the livid light of a rain shower I saw smashed railway huts and water tanks, big craters, broken telephone poles. I was soon in the country. One arch of the bridge had collapsed. I was in time to get my bearings and ducked into a covered courtyard under the first downpour.

Here there were people and horse carts; it was a portico for stabling; people sat on their bundles, laughing. In the coming and going, among the lamps, I heard cadenced, earthy voices, already thick with my native dialect. This encouraged me. "It's my fate always to find porticoes," I thought.

I ate something a big plate of soup and a little bread, bought in a smoky, greasy kitchen. Others were scattered around the big room, eating salad and drinking—women, travelers, carters. Beneath the portico they were discussing the rain and the state of the roads, truck convoys and something big that was going on in the Tanaro Valley. I said I was going to a certain village, asking only if it would be easy to climb the valley on the other side. I spoke dialect. A carter looked me up and down, from shoes to shoulders. "It's all right if you keep moving," he said. "It's staying here that's nasty." The Germans had been maneuvering up there for several days and only women were sleeping at home. "We're waiting," said another. "If the Germans go, we'll harvest. But if they bog down . . ."

I reflected that mine was a different valley; I had other hills to cross. Someone placed me from my accent and asked the others: "How are we doing on the Langa?"

There was steady fighting on the Langa, depending on the terrain. We had control of entire zones. The real danger was not on the roads but on the bridges and in the villages. I remembered my

iron bridge, where I had stamped as a child to hear the reverbera-
tions. I mentioned a nearby village that could only be reached by
crossing the bridge. "The Republic is up there," they said.

Confusion and a thunderstorm took up almost the whole night.
The curfew kept one from going anywhere; people leaving before
dawn didn't bother with a room. I threw myself on some sacks,
and a carter lent me a blanket. It was cold for June. During the
long windy night I could smell the wine that someone had spilled
nearby. Hoarse, sleepy voices talked interminably about meals and
past memories. The carter stirred at the first light. He was going
my way only for half the valley—a fat, silent man with an offended
look. He glanced at the cold, clear sky and said: "Let's go."

We traveled all morning, sitting on opposite sides of the cart,
dangling our legs. We didn't say much; to be polite I told him I had
come from Turin, where I had a job, and I was going back to my
family. He raised his eyes and said: "You should take the railway
through Alessandria." Could I explain that I was afraid of stations
that I preferred the creak of his cart? Living as he did, he would
have laughed at my troubles, though only his eyes ever laughed.
He wasn't gloomy or arrogant; he was alone. I squinted up at the
hill; it had a little church, a dark pine, on a spur. As always, I
thought what a good hiding place that church would make. Grain-
fields and vineyards alternated on the slopes, still fresh from the
rain. I didn't recall ever having seen such live and sweet hills
before.

The cart's slowness was making me impatient. I discussed the
weather, asking the fat man if at least at night or when it rained
the roads were safer. He said that for himself he preferred the sunlight; in the dark, somebody's shot might always get you; at least
day patrols or Germans looked you in the face. He spoke unemo-
tionally, a stubborn man.

We met some Germans, an automobile halfway up the hill.
Their greenish uniforms seemed the color of the wet road. The
carter jumped down; I stared at a group of trees on the hill.

Soon after, a large noisy truck overtook us and passed, filled
with all kinds of uniforms, boys with berets and rifles. "They're
sending the Republic ahead," the carter grumbled. "Tonight we
will eat our pig."

We found them stopped at the first village square. Germans on motorcycles halted and roared off, women looked on from doorways, one heard a rifle shot somewhere; no one paid attention to it.

Now the cart was rattling over the cobbles. I had to get down. A sailor jumped up with his gun at the ready. We stopped and while my friend rummaged in his box, the other, a freckled blond, raised the canvas covering of our load of plows and looked in. He waved us on.

When we were in open country again, I said suddenly: "Is there some boundary between these people and the Germans?"

He spat on the ground and said nothing.

"Have you seen them before? Are there others in the villages?"

"Yes, indeed," he said. "Up there on the hill. They keep watch day and night."

Now, I thought, I *am* in hot water. If they stop me, goodbye. I couldn't stay longer at Chieri or the villa. If I thought about my winter scares at the college, I felt rash, thoughtless, a boy. I well knew that in all the Langa there wasn't a German who knew my name but now I'd become hardened to it and everyone's terror had become mine; every fear served as an excuse.

We climbed back on the cart. I stopped talking, knowing I would always come back to the same subject.

"We are at Molini," my friend said at one point. "You should take off your shoes and cross here. I'm stopping down there."

While the cart creaked on, we parted company and I shouted that name, the road with the iron bridge. He pointed vaguely at a hill beyond the Tanaro, watched me get started, and spat on the road. Having waded across and climbed the gravel bank, I started up the hill as quickly as I could. I wondered where Dino had slept, had eaten; whether there was a regular carting traffic from Turin to the mountains. He had left with his overcoat and scarf. If he hadn't reached Fonso, I told myself, he would have returned. A boy doesn't run risks.

My road wound between fields and vineyards, very different from those on the Turin hill. Here the fields were bleached, well worked, and broken up—no woods. One heard oxen lowing, the flutter of hens. Even the air was soft and smelled of home. I was walking slowly, looking around, listening as when I explored the hollows of Pino with Belbo, listening to the earth's noises, the perennial terror that reigns in the undergrowth. Now I was truly fleeing, as a hare flees.

Before evening I had passed two or three villages and the road was climbing. Far on the hill crests, one could pick out churches, solitary farms. Since I had crossed the Tanaro, neither cars nor motorcycles had overtaken me or crossed my path; all I saw were a few oxcarts and on one village square a few barefoot idlers. I dined on bread and tomatoes sold to me by a shrill little woman. She asked me if I were lost.

"I'm going home," I told her.

"Ah, you do well, you do well," she shouted. "It's a hell of a life."

I realized afterwards that she had taken me for a partisan. This was scary. I couldn't ask where they were, lest I be taken for a spy. I had to keep going. That evening I covered the last stretch of road between empty fields, under the low clouds. I'd been climbing a good while and was out on a high ridge.

Where to sleep was settled for me by a barefoot young man who sat in a ditch in a field smoking a cigarette. He wore only a shirt and trousers shredded at the bottom, a knitted beret on his head. I stopped and asked: "Is it a long way, across the valley?"

"Do you want to make the station?" he said casually in my own dialect. "You shouldn't, it's a German post."

"I'm not afraid of the Germans," I said. "I have to get beyond the valley."

"Further up are the partisans," he added with the same coolness.

"I'm not afraid of anyone. I'm going home."

He shook his head and fastidiously threw away his cigarette. "It's an awful long way by the paths. But it's late now. Wait for tomorrow."

He took me across the field and through a stand of trees. Behind a cherry tree was a long blackish shed, a stable; mounds of hay and straw. Below the hilltop, at the level of the fields, were other low roofs. I had never seen buildings better hidden; all you could see from the road were ears of corn and the far slopes.

Otino—he didn't want to know my name—brought me under the cherry and asked if I were thirsty. We broke a branch and stripped it of fruit. He pursed his lips, spat out the stones, and asked if I had come from near Agliano.

"I saw its smoke this morning."

I said I was going to Rochetta, in the valley of the Belbo, and had come from Chieri. Otino jumped into the tree and began knocking down cherries with his long arms.

"Where is Rochetta?" he said.

"Do they burn villages here?"

He whistled instead of replying. It was some military tune; so I said: "Then you were a soldier?"

"I should be," he said.

I spent the night in the hay barn. The air was cold; mist or clouds, whichever it was, covered the fields. I burrowed deep in the straw. In the dark I saw a faint gleam from the sky and stood ready to burrow deeper at the first alarm. Not everyone had a bed of straw, I thought.

I was wakened by Otino removing his tools from a post. The light was blinding, sun and fog together. "You won't get there today," he said. I asked for something to eat. He called a woman who brought us two small loaves of bread. "May I wash my face?" I asked him.

We pulled a pail up from the well. In the bright foggy sunshine I examined Otino's bronzed skin and masculine features. "There's the road," he said. "Stay always on the path going down; look for the railway tracks; look for the Tinella; hide among the willows ..." I thought of when I used to play with Dino.

21.

By midday I was walking on the open hills, having left Germans and the Republic somewhere below in the valley. I had lost the main road. I shouted at some women turning hay in a field, and asked how one got to a village near my own. They signaled for me to go back to the valley. I shouted no, that my path was through the hills. They waved me on with their pitchforks.

One saw no settlements, only farms on wooded or chalky slopes. To reach any one of them, I would have had to waste time on steep paths under the low, sultry clouds.

I drank in the outlines of hills, watercourses, vegetation, open stretches. Colors, forms, the very feel of the humid heat, were very familiar; I had never been there, yet I was walking in a cloud of memories. Some small, contorted fig trees were like mine at home by the well gate. Before nightfall, I said, I'll be at Belbo.

A little roadside house, blackened and gutted, pulled me up short. It looked like a wrecked wall in the city. Nobody there. But the ruin wasn't new; on the wall where a vine had been, a thin blue smudge of verdigris was starting to show. I thought of the echoing explosions, the sniping. How much blood, I thought, has already soaked these lands and vineyards. It had been blood like mine, of men and boys who grew up in this air, this sun, speaking my dialect and having my own stubborn look. It was unbelievable that such people who lived in my veins and memory should have suffered the war, they too; the tornado, the world's terror. I couldn't take in the fact that fire, politics, and death had overwhelmed my own past. I wanted to find everything the same as before, like a room that has been shut up. That was why—not merely from an empty prudence—I hadn't given the name of my village for two days; I trembled for fear of hearing anyone say: "It was burned down. The war passed by."

The road began to descend, then went up another hill. Up there, God willing, there should be a settlement and a bell tower. I stopped a short distance from the houses, sat on a pile of gravel, and pulled out my bread. "A woman will pass, or a wagon."

I could hear noontime noises from the village; crashes from the stables, children shouting, water splashing into buckets. A chimney was smoking. By now the sun had broken up the clouds and was glistening on everything. Distant slopes steamed like fresh manure. A smell of stables, hot tar, and summer heat.

I was half through my loaf when someone appeared on the road. Two young men, sunburned and shaggy, carrying machine guns at the ready. They were standing in front of me before I could get up.

"Where are you going?" one of them said.

"To the valley of the Belbo."

"What for?"

They were wearing heavy berets and a tricolor cockade. They scrutinized my shoes while I talked. I felt one of them fingering my pack and stepped backward.

"Keep your hands still," the first one said.

I smiled faintly. "I've come from Chieri," I stammered. "I'm going home."

"Let's see your papers."

I started to put my hands in my pockets, but the first man stopped me with his gun barrel, smiling quietly. "I said keep them still."

He put his hand in my pocket, pulled out the papers. The other said: "What are you doing here?"

While they were going through the papers, I stared at the village. Swallows were swooping over the roofs. Behind that head and its thick beret was the sky and far, wooded slopes.

The first was looking at my identity card.

"On what day were you born?"

"Profession?"

"What village?"

He turned to the other and said: "Look."

Then I said: "My village is down there."

"It's not true you come from Chieri. It says Turin here."

"I was at Turin, then at Chieri."

They looked at me suspiciously. "Does anyone know you?"

"They know me at home."

They exchanged looks. The one behind, a bony face, shook his head. They didn't lower their guns.

"Look," I said irritably, "you're the first people I've met. I left Turin because the Germans were looking for me."

Again the cold smile. "To hear you people talk, the Germans are looking for all of you."

"Let's go," they said.

In the village I noticed a circle of women in front of the church. I was walking between the two men, looking neither at the windows nor at the haylofts. A small wagon had been stopped in a lane and two young soldiers in overalls were guarding it. A hen cut across our path.

In front of a doorway a tall man in high boots and leather jacket, a revolver in his belt, was talking to a girl who held a baby in her arms. He was laughing and amusing the child.

He turned and looked at us. He had a handkerchief around his neck, a curly beard and hair. It was Giorgi, Egle's brother.

He took a step and beckoned. I shouted: "Giorgi!"

"I know him," I told the two men.

When we were near, I laughed.

"So now this," he said.

"Our meetings are always historic," I said when we were seated apart on a low wall.

He gave me a cigarette. "What are you up to, still in street clothes, on the highways of the world?"

"What are you doing in my country?" I said, laughing.

We told our stories. I didn't let him know that I was a fugitive. I told him I was going to my parents, that I had seen his sister, that his family thought he was in Milan. He smiled, cupping his cigarette. "One doesn't know where anyone is these days," he observed. "That's the beauty of it."

A gray car shot out of a yard and pulled up by the entrance to the village. An armed boy was driving.

"Are there many of you up here?" I asked Giorgi.

"Don't you know the region?"

"Your two men are the first partisans I've seen in the flesh."

His face tightened. "Should I believe it?" he said. "No, I shouldn't," and he smiled.

He said he was after supplies. "Where is your village?" he asked, and waved toward the woods. "I think it must be there. We, though, are pouring down from up there." He motioned toward the west. "Our whole life is here; requisitions, trips, and so on. It's not dull; there's a beauty in that, too."

He blew out smoke. Then I risked the question. I said the last time I saw him he was talking of war, but the Fascist war. He had put on a certain uniform and had it in for certain people. Had he possibly been touched by grace?

"Disgrace, you mean," he said. "For my sins I've taken an oath."

"But the Fascist war was different. Who are the subversives now?"

"Everybody," he said. "There's not an Italian left who isn't sub-versive." He smiled dryly, abruptly. "You don't think we're fight-ing for those damned fool friends of yours?"

"What fools?"

"Those who sing 'The Red Flag.'" He threw his butt away in disgust. "Our work with the blackshirts is finished, now we begin with the redshirts."

"I thought you sympathized," I said.

We were silent and looked at the valley.

"Tomorrow I hope to reach home," I broke in, getting up from the wall. "If, of course, someone doesn't nab me on the road."

He shook his head, serious. "You should carry several safe-conducts," he said. "This isn't what you might call ideal hiking country."

I watched them setting off toward the west. I remembered watching that part of the sky at sunset as a boy, when I lived be-yond the woods, and perhaps in the fiery outline of that horizon there was a curve, a summit, a tree I could see now. The partisans mounted their cars—another car came out of an alley. There were perhaps ten boys with Giorgi. My two friends didn't flick an eye-lash when they saw me. They all left noisily, went over the rise and out of sight.

Alone in the early afternoon, I asked directions from the vil-lagers. I had taken a wrong turn; from crossroad to crossroad I had worked back to the Tanaro. I had to retrace my steps several kilo-meters, following the valley, and then climb once again, taking my bearings on a bell tower up among the woods where the road went and one could see the right hills beyond, my own. It would be very difficult to get there tonight. But I could sleep in the sanctuary, a woman said.

I asked if it would be dangerous. Someone smiled. "You belong here. A house might collapse on anyone's head." But the woman said no, not if I went to the sanctuary.

By mid-afternoon I had reached the bottom of the valley. Now that I had the bell tower to reckon by, I wasn't afraid of getting lost. I went cautiously, limping a little, dragging a foot, to appear more innocuous. I was doubling back on my tracks; I passed foot-paths, small gulleys, a wooden wayside cross. The sky was clear

167

and very high. Halfway up the hill a little group of neat houses was waiting for me along the road by which I was climbing. I had already overtaken a peasant and his yoke of oxen. The next thing I heard was the roar of a truck. I turned and saw a big cloud of dust. Then they appeared, two large vans lurching along, full of gray-green berets, cartridge belts, and dark faces. I turned away from their dust. If they had fired into my back, the noise and annoyance wouldn't have been greater.

No one turned to look at me; they disappeared while I mentally followed the progress of these Fascists—I wondered if they were going as far as the sanctuary, if something were going on up there. I was still stunned by their explosive passage.

Then there was a real explosion, very near, at the head of the road. Machine-gun bursts and an explosion. Then howls, more firing. The motors had stopped. The air was singing with the sad whine of bullets. "Halt!" a voice shouted. Then a pause, a deep silence, then more booms and crackles, and a sinister hum like steel wires vibrating on vine poles.

I had jumped behind some trees; at every explosion I backtracked, ducked, flattened on the grass. During the pauses I ran backwards down the road. The crackle of fire went on, crisp and deadly. At the bottom of the road I saw the peasant, motionless with his oxen.

When I reached him, the firing was worse than ever. Those heavy muffled booms were grenades. But the rifle shots whined like living voices.

The peasant had driven his oxen across the road and into a canebrake. He saw me come up. In the deadly silence that followed, he jumped to hide himself better; he was an old man and groped pathetically among the canes. Then an ox bellowed.

"Easy," I told him. "Hide yourself." I jumped into the brake, pushing the old man ahead.

But the clash was over. Everything was suddenly quiet on the road and above. I listened for the sound of motors starting up or human voices.

The peasant was bending forward between his oxen. To hide them better, he had driven them at random into the thick growth;

there was a great snapping of canes. I called to him in an undertone
to stop.

Then the old man sat down, holding the halter in his hand.

22. We remained like that for quite a while. A motor had
started again up ahead and voices were shouting among the trees.
Then the noises died away.

A woman appeared at the corner. She ran down. I waited for her
in the middle of the road and asked her what had happened. She
gave me a terrified glance. She had a shawl over her head. The old
man of the oxen looked out from the canes. The woman shouted
something, clutching her ears with her hands. I asked her: "Are
there people up there?" She nodded with her chin, not speaking.

A young man on a bicycle rounded the corner. He came down
at breakneck speed. "Can one get by?" I yelled at him. He threw
down one bare foot, miraculously keeping his balance, and shouted
back: "There are dead, many dead."

When I made my way cautiously to the turning, I saw the big
troop truck. It was stopped, empty, across the road. A trickle of gas
was darkening the road, but it was not only gas. Alongside the
wheels and in front of the truck, bodies were lying and the gas
grew redder as I approached. Some women and a priest were running around.

One soldier—gray-green streaked uniform—had fallen on his
face with his feet still on the truck. Blood and brains spilled from
beneath his cheek. A little man, his hands on his stomach, was
looking up, yellow, bloodstained. Then more contorted bodies,
sprawled facedown, of a dirty livid color. Some of them were short
men, looking like bundles of rags. One was off on the grass where
he had jumped from the road to defend himself by shooting; he
was kneeling stiffly against the barbed wire as if alive, blood flowing from his mouth and eyes, a boy of wax crowned with thorns.

I asked the priest if the dead all came from the truck. This
sweating, energetic man looked at me wildly and said that the
houses farther up were also full of wounded. "Who attacked?"

Partisans from above, he told me. They had been waiting for days.

"The Fascists had hung four of them," screamed an old woman, weeping and fingering a rosary.

"And this is the fruit," the priest said. "Now we'll have savage reprisals. It will be one bonfire from here to the high valley of the Belbo."

The ambush had been laid between two large protecting rocks. Not one of the blackshirts saved his skin. The partisans carried off prisoners in the other truck, after lining them against a wall and threatening: "We could murder you in your own style. We prefer to keep you alive for your shame."

The local people were bundling their things and driving out their animals. Nobody would have dared to sleep at Due Rocce. Some went up to the sanctuary, hoping in the virtue of the place; others went anyway, just to go. They had until nightfall, because the boy on the bicycle who had shouted to me was running to give news of the wounded on the telephone, at the blockhouse, to save what could be saved. Tomorrow the roads and lanes would be a death trap.

The priest was inside, where someone was dying. I stayed among the dead, not daring to climb over them. I looked off at the bell tower and knew I wouldn't get home before tomorrow. Some instinct pulled me back, down the road already walked, to put between me and the coming storm the guiltless village below, the Tinella and the railway. Otino was down there; he could at least hide me. If I could get by the German stations before nightfall, I could wait with him for the fury to blow itself out.

I left, passed the peasant of the oxen, waiting with his mouth open in front of the canebrake, kept straight on, and an hour afterward I was climbing the last rise under a cool sky, beyond which lay the Tinella. Again I saw some of the morning's horizons. The church towers and farms made sense; I wondered if I would always live among terrors like this at home. Meanwhile I kept to the road, tense at the corners and crossroads, never showing myself against the skyline. Now I knew what a rifle shot was, what it sounded like.

At dusk I reached the Tinella and the tracks. While I was waiting in the mud among alder bushes, I heard the puffing of a train. A long local freight train chuffed slowly by and I noticed several burly German soldiers standing between cars. That they were traveling seemed a good sign, meaning that the zone was still quiet.

I jumped the tracks and went to Otino's hill. It was difficult finding my way among the acacias, but the hilltop stood out clearly. I took a path that seemed right and went up and listened for footsteps or rustling leaves above the shrilling of crickets. The sky overhead was brilliant with stars.

Otino wasn't there, but it was the right hill. I was tired, hungry, and dragging my feet over the furrows. I came on a small shed in a vineyard, made of solid masonry and doorless—a shelter for the man who tended the grapes. I went in and threw myself on a sack.

When I woke up much later, my back and neck were stiff and aching. A dog was barking not far away; I imagined him a stray, crazed with hunger. Not enough light came in the opening for me to see the countryside. In that darkness the dog's voice was the voice of the whole earth. I tossed around in a half sleep.

Not to be seen leaving, I went out before dawn. The moon was rising. Turning back, I realized that the "shed" had been a simple abandoned chapel. The sky brightened behind the moon and I was cold, hungry, and scared. I was crouching in a grainfield, cursing the heavy dew, thinking of those dead. "To think of them is to pray for them," I thought.

At full light I found the low houses, gave the women the news. Otino had gone into the fields. I asked permission to wait for him in the hayloft. They gave me bread and soup; while I ate I calmed the women about the probable outcome of the killings. "They will only comb that side of the Tinella," I said, "or else I wouldn't have made it here."

Days followed of high winds sweeping the slopes; from up there one could pick out the successive crests, the smallest trees, houses, vines, to the distant woods. Otino showed me the sanctuary tower and a crook of the road where the slaughter had taken place. He roamed the hilltops, saw people, made them talk. One morning we saw a column of smoke rising from the woods: that evening we heard in the village of another clash toward the Tanaro. A division of Germans and Fascists had descended on the slope and had burned, shot, and robbed.

At night I slept in the hayloft; they had lent me a blanket. The gusty wind fell toward evening and I strained my ears for the crack of shots or human cries. All of us stayed with Otino in the fields, under brighter stars than I could remember; we were all searching out distant fires. We caught sight of an ominous glow against the deep blackness of the hills. "Remember that," Otino told me. "You'll pass near there. Where they have burned, there's no more surveillance."

I wanted to pay him something for the food I had eaten. His mother didn't say no; she only sighed and wondered why the war never ended. "If it lasts a century," I said, "who is better off than you?" Under the portico one could still see a streak of blood from a skinned rabbit. "There you are," Otino said, pointing at it. "That's how we'll end."

He brought me into the vineyard I had entered the first night; I told him it seemed a fine refuge. If all you needed was to sleep in a church to be safe, Otino said, the churches would be stuffed. "There isn't a church left here," I replied. "They've stripped the nut trees and burned over the ground."

"We came here to play when we were boys."

We went in, talking of life in the district, how everyone was afraid that even along the railway one could be shot at by a German or overtaken by a troop truck. "Have they burned any churches?" I asked. "If that's all they burned," he said, "it would be nothing."

One evening we collected all the branches we could find, and adding cornhusks, we lit a fire in the corner, beneath the window. Then, sitting before the flames, we smoked like boys. We said: "We can set fires too." I was nervous at first and went out to look at the window, but the little reflection was screened by a hillock in any case. "They can't see it, no, no," Otino said. Then we discussed once more the local people, those who were more afraid than we. "They, too, aren't living any longer. That's not living. They know the moment will come."

"We're all in the trenches."

Otino laughed. Gunfire was spitting a long way off.

"Now we're beginning," I said.

We listened. The wind was quiet and the dogs were barking.

"Let's go to the house," I said. I spent a bad night, trembling at my thoughts. The rustle of hay seemed to fill the world.

Again, the next day, I studied the barrier of hills that waited for me. They were white and dried by the wind and heat, clear-cut under the sky. Again I wondered if the terror had reached the forests and above. I walked up a lane to buy bread in the village. People, curious and suspicious, watched me from doorways; I nodded to some of them. From the high square one could see new hills behind, like pinkish clouds. I stopped in front of the church. The brilliant light and silence gave me a pulse of hope. The present seemed impossible; life would be taken up again as secure and solid as it was at that moment. I'd forgotten for too long that bloodshed and pillage couldn't last forever.

A girl came out. She looked around and went down the street. For a moment she also entered my hope. She stepped carefully in the wind on the rough cobbles, not looking in my direction.

On the little square there wasn't anyone to be seen, and the heaped-up, red-brown roofs that until yesterday had seemed a safe hiding place now seemed like caves from which the prey would be driven out by fire. The problem was merely to resist the flames until they were finally spent.

In the evening came rumors of action in the nearby valley, against a village of women and old men. They swore it was true. In fact, nobody had heard a single shot: the stables had been plundered and the hay barns burned. The people, huddling in ravines, heard their cattle lowing but couldn't get to them. It had been late morning, just when I had been looking out from the church.

Otino was reaping in the fields, heard the news, and went on reaping.

"Thank God," I said, "that you kept me here."

He straightened up and passed his hand over his eyes. "Go at night when it's cooler."

We talked it over again that night and I decided it would be better to follow the Tinella than to risk the hills. I left the next day and by evening was at home with my parents, beyond the woods and the Belbo.

23.

Nothing has happened. I've been at home for six months and the war still goes on. Rather, as the weather gets worse, the armies on the main fronts have begun to retrench again; another winter will pass, we will see snow again, we'll make a circle around the radio by the fire. Here the November mud in roads and vineyards is beginning to slow up the partisan bands. They say that this winter no one will have the will to fight; it will be hard enough merely to exist and wait to die in the spring. If then, as they say, we get heavy snows like last year's to stop up the doors and windows, it would be better if it never thawed.

We have had our dead here too. Apart from this and the scares and our uncomfortable flights into gullies behind the property (my mother or sister thrashing me awake, snatching up shoes and trousers, running hunched-down through the vineyard, then the wait, the demoralizing wait), apart from the boredom and shame, nothing happens. Throughout September there was no day without shooting in the hills or by the iron bridge—isolated shots as in the old hunting season, but sometimes bursts of machine-gun fire. Now it is less frequent. This is the true life of the forest the way one dreams it as a boy. And sometimes I think that only a boy's unawakened conscience, his genuine unaffected unawareness could manage to see what is going on without suffering fits of repentance. The heroes of these valleys in any case are all boys; they have the straight, stubborn look of boys. But for the fact that we—who are no longer young—nursed this war in our hearts and said: "Let it come then, if it has to come," even war, *this* war, might seem a clean business. Anyway, who knows? The war is burning our houses. It is sowing our squares and streets with the dead. It drives us like hares from refuge to refuge. It will end by forcing the rest of us to fight as well, extorting our active consent. A day will come when nobody is outside the war—not the cowards or the melancholy or the solitary. We will all have agreed to make war. And then maybe we'll have peace.

Nevertheless, the corn has been gathered on the farms and the grapes harvested. Obviously, not with the cheerfulness of the old days; too many are missing, some for good. Of the people in the neighborhood, only the old or middle-aged remember me, but for me the hill remains always a childhood land—bonfires, escapades, and games. If I had Dino here, I could still give him orders, but he has gone to play a more serious part. At his age it is easy. It is more difficult for the others who have played it before and are still doing so.

Now that the countryside is bare, I go back to my walking; I go up and down the hill, reflecting on the long illusion that gave me the impulse to write this book. Where the illusion will carry me I often wonder. What else is there to think about? Here every step, nearly every hour of the day, and certainly every sudden memory confronts me with what I was—what I am and have forgotten. Obsessed by the chance encounters of this year, I keep asking myself: "What is there in common between me and the man who fled the bombs, fled the Germans, fled from remorse and pain?" Not that I don't feel a pang if I think of those who have disappeared, if I think of the nightmare figures who run the roads like bitches—I finally tell myself that it's still not enough, that to end the horror we must enter it, we the survivors must enter, even to bloodshed —but it happens that the "I," this I who sees me rummaging cautiously through the faces and manias of these recent days, feels like someone else, detached, as if everything done, said, or suffered had been merely somewhere out there—someone else's concern, ancient history. This, in other words, is the illusion: here at home I find an older reality, a life beyond my own years, beyond Elvira, Cate, beyond Dino or school, all that I have wished or hoped for as a man; and I wonder if I will ever be able to escape. I see now that throughout this year and earlier too, even during the season of my meager follies, of Anna Maria, Gallo, Cate, when we were still young and the war a distant cloud—I see that I have lived a long isolation, a useless holiday, like a boy who creeps into a bush to hide, likes it there, looks at the sky from under the leaves and forgets to come out, ever.

It is here the war has seized me and seizes me every day. If I walk the woods, if at every suspicion of raiders I duck into the gullies, if I sometimes talk to passing partisans (Giorgi has been here with his men: he threw back his head and told me: "We'll have time to talk on evenings of snow"), it's not that I don't see that the war is no game, this war that has come even up here, which seizes even our past by the throat. I don't know if Cate, Fonso, Dino, and all the others will return. Sometimes I hope so, and it scares me. But I have seen the unknown dead, those little men of the Republic. It was they who woke me up. If a stranger, an enemy, becomes a thing like that when he dies, if one stops short and is afraid to walk over him, it means that even beaten our enemy is someone, that after having shed his blood, one must placate it, give this blood a voice, justify the man who shed it. Looking at certain dead is humiliating. They are no longer other people's affairs: one doesn't seem to have happened there by chance. One has the impression that the same fate that threw these bodies to the ground holds us nailed to the spot to see them, to fill our eyes with the sight. It's not fear, not our usual cowardice. One feels humiliated because one understands—touching it with one's eyes—that we might be in their place ourselves: there would be no difference, and if we live we owe it to this dirtied corpse. That is why every war is a civil war; every fallen man resembles one who remains and calls him to account.

There are days when, walking this naked countryside, I give a sudden start; a dry tree trunk, a knot of grass, a ridge of rock seems like a stretched-out body. It might still happen. I'm sorry Belbo stayed behind in Turin. Some of the day I spend in the kitchen, in the huge kitchen with its floor of beaten earth, where my mother, my sister, the women of the house, make the preserves. My father comes and goes in the cellar as slowly as old Gregorio. At times I wonder if a reprisal, a whim, some destiny will send the house up in flames and reduce it to four gutted and blackened walls. It has happened already to many. What would my father do, what would the women say? Their tone is: "If only they would stop awhile . . ."; and for them the guerrilla war, this whole damnable business, is a game for boys, like those that used to follow the feasts of our patron saint.

If the partisans demand flour or cattle, my father says: "It's not right. They have no right. Let them ask for it as a gift."

"Who has a right then?" I ask him.

"Wait until it's over and we'll see," he says.

I don't believe that it can end. Now that I've seen what war is, what civil war is, I know that everybody, if one day it should end, ought to ask himself: "And what shall we make of the fallen? Why are they dead?" I wouldn't know what to say. Not now, at any rate. Nor does it seem to me that the others know. Perhaps only the dead know, and only for them is the war really over.

AMONG WOMEN ONLY

1.   I arrived in Turin with the last January snow, like a street acrobat or a candy seller. I remembered it was carnival time when I saw the booths and the bright points of acetylene lamps under the porticoes, but it was not dark yet and I walked from the station to the hotel, peering out from under the arches and over the heads of the people. The sharp air was biting my legs and, tired as I was, I huddled in my fur and loitered in front of the shop windows, letting people bump into me. I thought how the days were getting longer, that before long a bit of sun would loosen the frozen muck and open up the spring.

That was how I saw Turin again, in the half light under the porticoes. When I entered the hotel, I thought of nothing but a hot bath, stretching out, and a long night. Especially since I had to stay in Turin for quite a while.

I telephoned no one and no one knew I was staying at that hotel. Not even a bunch of flowers was waiting for me. The maid running my bath talked to me, bent over the tub, while I was exploring the room. A man, a valet, wouldn't do such things. I asked her to go, saying that I would be all right alone. The girl babbled something, standing in front of me, wringing her hands. Then I asked where she came from. She reddened brightly and said she was Venetian. "One can tell," I said. "And I am from Turin. You'd like to go home, I imagine?"

She nodded with a sly look.

"Then remember that I've just come home," I said. "Don't spoil the pleasure for me."

"Excuse me," she said. "May I go?"

When I was alone in the warm water, I closed my eyes; they

ached from too much pointless talking. The more I convince myself that there's no point in talking, the more I seem to talk. Especially among women. But my tiredness and a slight feverishness soon dissolved in the water and I thought of the last time I had been in Turin, during the war, the day after a bombing raid. All the pipes were burst, no bath. I thought with pleasure: as long as life contains baths, living is worth the effort.

A bath and a cigarette. While I smoked, I compared the sloshing that comforted me now to the tense life I'd been leading, to the storm of words, my impatient desires, to the projects I'd always carried through, although this evening everything had come down to this tub and this pleasant warmth. Had I been ambitious? I saw the ambitious faces again: pale, marked, convulsed faces—did one of them ever relax for a peaceful hour? Not even when you are dying does that passion slow up. It seemed that I had never relaxed for a moment. Perhaps twenty years before, when I was a little girl playing in the streets and waiting excitedly for the season of confetti, booths, and masks, perhaps then I could let myself go. But in those years the carnival meant only merry-go-rounds, *torrone*, and cardboard noses. Later there was a fever to go out, to see Turin and run through it; there were my first adventures in the alleys with Carlotta and the other girls, when, hearts beating, we felt ourselves being followed for the first time: all that innocence had come to an end. Strange. The evening of the Thursday before Lent when father was growing worse just before dying, I cried with anger and I hated him, thinking of the holiday I was losing. Only mother understood me that evening, teased me and told me to get out from under her feet and go and cry in the yard with Carlotta. But I was crying because the fact that Papa was about to die terrified me and kept me from letting myself go at the carnival.

The telephone rang. I didn't move from the tub, because I was happy with my cigarette. I thought that it was probably on just that distant evening that I told myself for the first time that if I wanted to accomplish something, or get something out of life, I shouldn't tie myself to anyone as I had been tied to that embarrassing father. I had succeeded, and now my whole pleasure was to dissolve myself in warm water and not answer the telephone.

It began to ring again, apparently irritated. I didn't answer, but I got out of the bath. I dried myself slowly, seated in my bathrobe, and was rubbing face cream around my mouth when someone knocked. "Who is it?"

"A note for the signora."

"I said I'm not in."

"The gentleman insists."

I had to get up and turn the key. The impertinent Venetian handed me the note. I looked at it and said to the girl: "I don't want to see him. He can come back tomorrow."

"The signora is not going down?"

My face felt plastered, I couldn't even manage a frown. "I'm not going down. I want tea. Tell him tomorrow at noon."

When I was alone, I took the receiver off, but they answered right away from the office. The voice rasped helplessly on the table like a fish out of water. Then I shouted something into the phone; I had to say who I was, that I wanted to sleep. They wished me good night.

Half an hour later the girl had still not returned. This happens only in Turin, I thought. I did something I had never done before, as though I were a silly girl. I slipped into my dressing gown and half opened the door.

Out in the corridor a number of people—maids, patrons, my impertinent Venetian—had crowded in front of a door. Someone exclaimed something *sotto voce*.

Then the door opened wide, and slowly, very carefully, two whiteshirts carried out a stretcher. Everyone fell silent and gave way. On the stretcher lay a girl with a swollen face and disordered hair, shoeless but wearing an evening gown of blue tulle. Though her lips and eyelids were motionless, one could imagine her having had a lively expression. Instinctively I glanced under the stretcher to see if there were blood dripping down. I searched the faces—the usual faces, one pursed up, another apparently grinning. I caught the eye of my maid—she was running behind the stretcher. Over the low voices of the circle (which included a woman in furs, wringing her hands), I heard the voice of a doctor; he had come out of the door, drying his hands on a towel and saying that it was all over, to please get out of the way.

The stretcher disappeared down the stairs, as someone said:

"Easy now." I looked at my maid again. She had already run to a chair at the end of corridor and returned with the tea tray.

"She was taken sick, poor girl," she said, coming into my room. But her eyes were shining and she couldn't contain herself. She told me everything. The girl had come to the hotel in the morning —from a party, a dance. She had locked herself in her room; she hadn't gone out all day. Someone had telephoned; people were looking for her; a policeman had forced the door. The girl was on the bed, dying.

The maid went on: "Poisoning herself at carnival time, what a shame. And her family is so rich . . . They have a beautiful house in Piazza d'Armi. It'll be a miracle if she lives . . ."

I told her I wanted more water for my tea. And not to dawdle on the stairs this time.

But that night I didn't sleep as I had hoped to. Squirming in bed, I could have kicked myself for having stuck my nose into the corridor.

2.

The next day they brought me a bunch of flowers, the first narcissi. I smiled, thinking that I had never received flowers in Turin. The order had come from that owl Maurizio, who had thought of surprising me on my arrival. Instead, the thing had gone wrong. It happens in Rome too, I thought. I imagined Maurizio, unhappy, wandering aimlessly down the Via Veneto after our good-byes and between the last coffee and first apéritif filling out the order form.

I wondered if the girl of yesterday had had flowers in her room. Are there people who surround themselves with flowers before dying? Perhaps it's a way of keeping up one's courage. The maid went to find me a vase, and while she helped me to arrange the narcissi, she told me that the papers hadn't mentioned the at-tempted suicide. "Who knows how much they are spending to keep it quiet? They took her to a private clinic . . . Last night they investigated. There must be a man mixed up in it . . . There ought to be a law for getting a girl . . ."

I said that a girl who spends evenings at parties and instead of going home goes to a hotel is considered able to take care of herself.

"Oh, yes," she said, indignant. "It's the mothers' fault. Why don't they stay with their daughters?"

"Mothers?" I said. "These girls have always been with their mothers, they grew up on velvet, they've seen the world behind glass. Then, when they have to get out of a mess, they don't know how and fall in deeper."

After which Mariuccia laughed, as if to say that she knew how to get out of a mess. I sent her out and got dressed. In the street it was cold and clear; during the night it had rained on the sludge and now the sun shone under the arcades. It looked like a new city, Turin, a city just finished, and the people were running about, giving it the last casual touches. I walked under the buildings in the center, inspecting the big shops that were waiting for their first customers. None of those windows or signs were modest and familiar as I remembered them, not the cafés or the cashiers or the faces. Only the slanting sunlight and the dripping air had not changed.

And nobody was just walking, everyone seemed preoccupied. People didn't live in the streets, they only escaped through them. To think that when I used to walk those central streets with my big box on my arm they seemed like a kingdom of carefree people on vacation, the way I used to imagine seaside resorts. When one wants a thing, one sees it everywhere. And all this only meant suffering and barking my shins. What did she want, I wondered, that stupid girl who took Veronal yesterday? A man mixed up in it . . . Girls are fools. My Venetian was right.

I went back to the hotel and saw Morelli's lean, unexpected face before me. I had forgotten him and his note.

"How did you find me?" I said, laughing.

"It's nothing. I waited."

"All night?"

"All winter."

"That must mean you have plenty of time."

I had always seen this man in a bathing suit on the Roman beaches. He had hair on his thin chest, gray hair almost white. But now his silk tie and light-colored vest had changed him completely.

"You know you're young, Morelli?" I said.

He bowed and invited me to lunch.

"Didn't they tell you last night that I don't go out?"

"Let's eat here then," he said.

I like these people who joke without ever laughing. They intimidate you a little, and just for that you feel safe with them.

"I accept," I told him. "On condition you tell me something amusing. How's the carnival going?"

When we sat down, he didn't talk about the carnival. He didn't even talk about himself. Unsmilingly, he told me a little story about a Turin salon—he gave the name: nobility—where it happened that certain important gentlemen, while waiting for the mistress of the house, stripped down to their shorts and then sat in armchairs, smoking and talking. The hostess, astounded, forced herself to believe that this game was now the fashion, a test of one's spirit, and had stayed there joking about it with them a long time.

"You see, Clelia," Morelli said. "Turin is an old city. Anywhere else this stroke of wit would have come from boys, students, young men who had just opened their first offices or got their first government jobs. Here, however, elderly people, *commendatori* and colonels, play such tricks. It's a lively city . . ."

Expressionless as ever, he leaned forward, murmuring: "That bald head over there is one of them . . ."

"Won't he take me for the countess?" I said lightly. "I'm from Turin too."

"Oh, you're not in the same set; he knows that."

It wasn't entirely a compliment. I thought of his gray-haired chest. "Did you undress, too?" I asked.

"My dear Clelia, if you want to be introduced in that salon . . ."

"What would another woman do there?"

"She could teach the countess strip tease . . . Who do you know in Turin?"

"Busybody . . . The only flowers I got came from Rome."

"They're waiting for you in Rome?"

I shrugged. He was clever, Morelli, and he knew Maurizio. He also knew that I liked a good time but paid my own way.

"I'm free," I said. "The only obligation I recognize is the one you owe a son or a daughter. And unfortunately I have no children."

"But you could be my daughter...or does that make me too old?"

"It's me that's too old."

Finally he opened up and smiled with those lively gray eyes. Without so much as moving his mouth in a smile, he filled with high spirits, looked me over appreciatively. I recognized this, too. He wasn't the kind to run after dolls.

"You know everything about this hotel," I said. "Tell me about yesterday's scandal. Do you know the girl?"

He gave me another long look and shook his head.

"I know the father," he said. "A hard man. Strong-willed. A sort of buffalo. He motorcycles and goes around his factory in overalls."

"I saw her mother."

"I don't know the mother. Good people. But the daughter is crazy."

"Crazy crazy?"

Morelli darkened. "When they try once, they try again."

"What do people say?"

"I don't know," he said. "I don't listen to such talk. It's like wartime conversation. Anything may be true. It might be a man, a revulsion, a whim. But there's only one real reason."

He tapped his forehead with a finger. He smiled again with his eyes. He held his hand on the oranges and said: "I've always seen you eating fruit, Clelia. That's real youth. Leave flowers to the Romans."

That bald character of the story muttered something to the waiter, threw down his napkin, and left, fat and solemn. He bowed to us. I laughed right at him; Morelli, expressionless, waved.

"Man is the only animal," he said, "who labors to dress himself."

When the coffee came, he still hadn't asked me what I was doing in Turin. Probably he knew already and there was no need to tell him. But neither did he ask me how long I was staying. I like this in people. Live and let live.

"Would you like to go out this evening?" he asked. "Turin by night?"

"First I've got to have a look at Turin by day. Let me get myself settled. Are you staying in this hotel?"

"Why not come to my place?"

He had to say that. I let the suggestion pass. I asked him to call for me at nine.

He repeated: "I can put you up at my place."

"Don't be foolish," I said. "We're not children. I'll come and pay you a visit one day."

That afternoon I went out on my own, and in the evening he took me out to a party.

3. When I returned in the evening, Morelli, who had been waiting for me, noticed that I had gone out in my cloth coat and left the fur behind. I had him come up and while I was getting ready I asked him if he spent his days in the hotel.

"I spend my nights at home," he said.

"Really?" I was talking into the mirror, my back turned to him. "Don't you ever visit your estate?"

"I pass over it in the train on my way to Genoa. My wife lives there. Nobody like women for certain sacrifices."

"Married ones, too?" I murmured.

I could tell he was laughing.

"Not only them," he sighed. "It hurts me, Clelia, that you should go around in overalls bossing whitewashers ... However, I don't like that place in the Via Po. What do you expect to sell there?"

"Turin is really an old woman, a concierge."

"Cities grow old like women."

"For me it's only thirty. Oh, well, thirty-four ... But I didn't pick the Via Po. They decided in Rome."

"Obviously."

We left. I was glad that Morelli, who understood everything, hadn't understood why I went out that day in a cloth coat. I was thinking about it when we got into the taxi, and I thought about it later. I believe that in the hubbub of the party, when cherry brandy, kümmel, and meeting new people had made me restless and unhappy, I told him. Instead of going to the Via Po, I had gone to the hairdresser—a little hairdresser two steps from the hotel—and while she was drying my hair I heard the sharp voice of the manicurist behind the glass partition telling how she was awakened that morning by the smell of milk spilled on the gas stove. "What a mess. Even the cat couldn't take it. Tonight I'll have to clean the burner." That was enough for me to see a kitchen, an unmade bed, dirty panes on the balcony door, a dark staircase seemingly carved out of the wall. Leaving the hairdresser, I thought only of the old courtyard, and I went back to the hotel and left my fur. I had to return to that Via della Basilica and perhaps someone might recognize me; I didn't want to seem so proud.

I had gone there, after exploring the district first. I knew the houses, I knew the stores. I pretended to stop and examine the shop windows, but really I was hesitating: it seemed impossible that I had been a child in those crannies, and at the same time, with something like fear, I felt no longer myself. The quarter was much dirtier than I remembered it. Underneath the portico on the little square I saw the shop of the old woman who sold herbs; now there was a thin little man, but the bags of seeds and the bunches of herbs were the same. On summer afternoons the shop used to give off a pungent smell of countryside and spices. Farther down the bombs had destroyed an alley. Who knows what's become of Carlotta, the girls, Slim? Or of Pia's children? If the bombs had flattened the whole district, it would have been easier to face my memories. I went down the forbidden alley, passed the tiled doorways of the brothels. How many times had we run by those doorways? The afternoon I stared at a soldier who came out with a dark look . . . what had got into me? And by the time I was old enough to dare to discuss such things (and the district had begun to make me less afraid than angry and disgusted), I was going to my shop in another part of town and had friends and knew all about it because I was working.

I arrived in the Via della Basilica and didn't have the courage. I passed in front of that courtyard and caught a glimpse of the low vaulting of a second-story bedroom and of balconies. I was already in the Via Milano; impossible to go back. The mattress maker looked at me from his doorway.

I told Morelli something of all this at the height of the party when it was nearly morning and one kept on drinking and talking just to hold out a little longer. I said: "Morelli, these people dancing and getting drunk are well-born. They've had butlers, nurses, maids. They've had country vacations, all kinds of protection. Good for them. Do you think that any of them could have started from nothing—from a courtyard the size of a grave—and got to this party?"

And Morelli patted my arm and said: "Cheers. We arrived. If necessary we'll even get home."

"It's easy," I said, "for the wives and daughters of wealthy families to dress the way they're dressed. They've only to ask. They don't even have to sleep around. Give you my word, I'd rather dress real whores. At least they know what work is."

"Do whores still dress?" Morelli said.

We had eaten and danced. We had met many people. Morelli always had someone at his shoulder who was saying loudly: "Be seeing you." I recognized some names and faces of people who had been in our fitting room in Rome. I recognized some gowns: a countess wore one with a peplum which we had designed and which I myself had sent several days before. A little woman in ruffles even gave me a tiny smile; her escort turned around; I recognized him, too; they had been married the year before in Rome. He bowed deeply and gravely in recognition—he was a tall, blond diplomat—then he was jerked away: I suppose his wife brought him to his senses by reminding him that I was the dressmaker. That was when my blood began to boil. Then came a collection for the blind: a man in a dinner jacket and a red paper hat made a comic speech about the blind and deaf, and two blindfolded women ran around the room grabbing men who, after paying, could kiss them. Morelli paid. Then the orchestra began playing again and some groups got noisy, singing and chasing one another. Morelli came back to the table with a large woman in rose lamé with the belly of a fish; a young man and a cool young woman who had just stopped dancing and suddenly dropped on the divan. The man immediately jumped up.

"My friend Clelia Oitana," Morelli was saying.

The large woman sat down, fanning herself, and looked at me. The other, in a low-cut, clinging violet gown, had already examined me and smiled at Morelli as he lit her cigarette.

I don't recall what was said at first. I was watching the younger woman's smile. She had an air of having always known me, of mocking both Morelli and me, although she was only watching the smoke from her cigarette. The other woman laughed and prattled nonsense. The young man asked me to dance. We danced. He was called Fefé. He told me something about Rome, tried to glue himself to me and squeeze me and asked if Morelli were really my squire. I told him I wasn't a horse. Then, laughing, he pulled me closer. He must have had more to drink than I.

When we came back, there was only the fat woman, still fanning herself. Morelli was making his rounds. Fish-belly sent the bored young man off to find something, them patted me on the knee with a neat little hand and gave me a malicious look. My blood boiled again.

"You were in the hotel," she whispered, "when poor Rosetta Mola was taken sick last night?"

"Oh, you know her? How is she?" I asked immediately.

"They say she's out of danger." She shook her head and sighed. "And tell me, did she really sleep in that hotel? What girls. Was she in there all day? Was she really alone?"

Her fat, dancing eyes bored in like two needles. She was trying to control herself but didn't succeed.

"Imagine! We saw her the night of the dance. She seemed calm enough . . . Such distinguished people. She danced a great deal."

I saw Morelli approaching.

"Listen, did you see her, afterwards? They say she was still in her party dress."

I mumbled something: that I hadn't seen anything. A furtiveness in the woman's tone prompted me to hold back. Or perhaps just contempt. Everybody came up, Morelli, the brunette in violet, that unpleasant Fefé. But the old lady, opening wide her large sharp eyes, said: "I was really hoping that you had seen her . . . I know her parents . . . What a shame. To want to kill oneself. What a day . . . One thing is certain, she didn't say prayers in that bed."

The brunette smoked, curled up on the divan, and looking at us mockingly said to me: "Adele sees sex everywhere." She blew out smoke. "But it's no longer the fashion . . . Only servants or little dressmakers want to kill themselves after a night of love . . ."

"A night and a day," Fefé said.

"Nonsense. Three months wouldn't have been enough . . . As far as I'm concerned, she was drunk and mistook the dosage . . ."

"Probable," Morelli said. "Or rather, it's certain." He bent toward the fat woman. Instead of taking her by the arm, he touched her shoulder and they went off, he joking, she bouncing.

The brunette spun around in a whiff of smoke, gave me a hard look, and praised the cut of my dress. She said it was easier to dress well in Rome. "It's another society. More exclusive. Did you make it yourself?"

She asked this with her dissatisfied and quizzical air.

"I don't have time to make my dresses," I snapped. "I'm always busy."

"Do you see people?" she asked. "Do you see so-and-so? Do you see such-and-such?" There was no end to the names.

"So-and-so and such-and-such," I said, "don't pay by day the debts they contract at night. And as for *her*," I went on, "when too many bills come due, she escapes to Capri . . ."

"Stupendous!" the brunette shouted. "What nice people."

They called her from the crowd; someone had come. She got up, brushed the ashes off her dress, and rushed off.

I was alone with Fefé, who looked at me dumbly. I told him: "You're thirsty, young man. Why don't you circulate?"

He had already explained that his system of drinking was to stop at the various tables, recognize somebody at each, and accept a drink. "You mix your drinks. However . . . You dance, and there's your cocktail."

I sent him away. Morelli arrived, and that thin smile of his.

"Like the women?" he asked.

Then it struck me that the party didn't mean much to me, and I began to tell him what I really felt.

4. But before leaving me that evening Morelli gave me a lecture. He said that I was prejudiced—I had only one prejudice, but it was a big one: I thought that working to get ahead, or even just to get by, was as important as the qualities, some admittedly stupid, of well-born people. He said that when I talked enviously of certain

fortunes I seemed to be taking it out on the pleasure of life itself. "At bottom, Clelia," he said, "you wouldn't think it right to win a football pool."

"Why not?" I said.

"But it's the same as being well-born. Just luck, a privilege . . ."

I didn't answer; I was tired, I pulled his arm.

Morelli said: "Is there really this great difference between doing nothing because one is too rich or doing nothing because one is too poor?"

"But when you get there by yourself . . ."

"So . . ." Morelli said. " 'Get there.' A sporting program." He barely moved his mouth. "Sport means renunciation and an early death. Why not stop along the road and enjoy the day? If you can. Is it always necessary to have suffered and come out of a hole?"

I kept still and pulled him by the arm.

"You hate other people's pleasures, Clelia, and that's a fact. You're wrong, Clelia. You hate yourself. And to think what a gifted person you are. Cheer up, make other people happy, forget your grudge. Other people's pleasures are yours, too . . ."

The next day I went to the Via Po without announcing myself or telephoning the contractors. They didn't know I was already in Turin. I wanted to get an unrehearsed idea of what had been done and how it had been done. When I came into the wide street and saw the hill in the background streaked with snow, and the church of the Gran Madre, I remembered it was carnival time. Here, too, stands with *torrone*, horns, masks, and colored streamers filled the arcades. It was early morning but the people were swarming toward the square at the end of the street where the booths were.

The street was even wider than I remembered. The war had opened a frightful hole, gutting three or four large buildings. Now it looked like a big excavation of earth and stones, a few tufts of grass here and there; one thought of a cemetery. Our store was right here, on the edge of the blankness, white with lime, still a doorless and windowless shell.

Two plasterers wearing white paper hats were seated on the floor. One was dissolving whitewash in a bucket, and the other was washing his hands in a lime-caked can. My arrival didn't seem to affect them. The second of them had a cigarette stuck behind his ear.

"The supervisor is never here this early," they told me.

"When does he come?"

"Not before evening. He's working at Madonna di Campagna."

I asked if they were the whole gang. They surveyed my hips with mild interest, not raising their eyes very far.

I stamped my foot. "Who's in charge here?"

"He was here a minute ago," said the first. "He's probably in the square." He went back to his stirring. "Go get Becuccio," he said to the other.

Becuccio arrived, a young man in a heavy sweater and army trousers. He grasped the situation right away, a wide-awake type. He shouted at the two to finish the floor. He took me around by the stairs and explained the work that had already been done. They had lost several days waiting for the electricians; it was useless to finish the shelving when they didn't know where the wires were going. The supervisor wanted them covered up; the utility company said no. I looked him over while he talked: he was thickset, curly-headed, and showed his teeth when he smiled. He wore a leather wristband.

"I want to telephone the supervisor," I said.

"I'll do it," he said right away.

I was wearing my cloth coat, not the fur. We crossed the Via Po. He took me to a café where the cashier welcomed him with an obvious smile. When he got a reply, he handed me the receiver. The supervisor's heavy, rasping voice softened as soon as he learned who I was. He complained that Rome hadn't answered one of his letters; he even brought up the Building Authority. I cut him short and told him to get here in half an hour. Becuccio smiled and held the door open.

I spent the whole day in the smell of lime. I went over the plans and the letters, which the supervisor shuffled out of a frayed leather briefcase. Becuccio had improvised an office for us on the first floor with a couple of boxes. I checked on the work to be done, paid the bills, talked to the utilities man. We had lost more than a month.

"As long as the carnival is on . . ." the supervisor said.

I said curtly that we wanted the shop ready at the end of the month.

We went over the bills again. I had first questioned Becuccio and knew how things stood. And I had come to an agreement with the utilities man. The supervisor had to agree to get the job done.

Between discussions I walked through the empty rooms where the whitewashers were now working on their feet. Another pair showed up in the areaway. I went up and down a cold staircase without a railing, cluttered with brooms and cans; the smell of lime—a sharp mountain smell—went to my head so that I almost thought this was my own building. From an empty window on the mezzanine I looked down on the crowded and festive Via Po. It was nearly dusk. I remembered the little window in my first work-room from which you looked out in the evening when you were making the last stitches, impatient for closing time and your happy release. "The world is large," I said aloud, without exactly knowing why. Becuccio was waiting discreetly in the shadow.

I was hungry. I was tired from last night's party and Morelli was probably waiting for me at the hotel.

I left, saying nothing about the next day. I spent half an hour among the crowds. I didn't walk toward the Piazza Vittorio Veneto, noisy with orchestras and merry-go-rounds, because I had always enjoyed spying on the carnival from alleys and half shadows. Many Roman holidays, many buried occasions, many follies came back to me. Out of all this, only Maurizio remained crazy Maurizio, and a certain peace and equilibrium. There remained also my wandering idly about like this, mistress of myself, mistress of my time in Turin, stopping where I liked and arranging what I liked for the next day.

As I was walking, I began to think of that evening seventeen years before, when I had left Turin, having persuaded myself that a person can love another more than himself; yet at bottom I knew quite well that all I wanted was to leave, to step out into the world, and I used that excuse, that pretext, for taking the step. The absurdity, the blissful ignorance of Guido when he imagined he was taking me away to support me—I was aware of all that from the start. I let him argue, let him try, and finally let him do it. I even helped him, I left before closing time to keep him company. That would be my envy and bad temper, according to Morelli. For three months I was happy and made Guido laugh: Had it been any use? He hadn't even been able to ditch me. You can't love someone more than yourself. If you can't save yourself, nobody can.

But—and here Morelli was not wrong—in spite of everything, I had to be thankful for those days. Wherever he was, dead or alive, I owed my good luck to Guido, and he wasn't even aware of it. I had laughed at his extravagant language, at his way of kneeling on the carpet and thanking me for being everything to him and for liking him; and I said: "I don't do it on purpose." Once he said: "People do their biggest favors without knowing it."

"You don't deserve them," I said.

"Nobody deserves anything," he had answered.

Seventeen years. I had at least as many more ahead. I was no longer young and I knew what a man—even the best—was worth. I reached the porticoes and looked at the shop windows.

5. In the evening Morelli took me to the salon. I was astonished at the number of young people there: they always say that Turin is a city of the old. It's true that the young men and girls formed a circle apart, like so many children, while we grownups, clustered around a sofa, were listening to an irritable old lady with a ribbon around her throat and a velvet mantle tell some story I don't recall about Mirafiori and a carriage. We all fell silent before the old lady; a few were smoking rather furtively. Her caustic little voice would stop whenever anyone came in, to allow greetings to be exchanged, then resume again at the first pause. Morelli, his legs crossed, was listening very attentively, and another man stared at the rug with a wrinkled forehead. But after a while I realized that you needn't pay attention to the old lady. No one thought of answering her. Half-turned on her chair, some woman would be whispering *sotto voce*, or another would get up and walk across the room to others.

It was a beautiful room, with glass chandeliers and a Venetian floor that you felt under your feet through the rug. A fire was burning to one side of the sofa. I sat motionless, examining the walls, the upholstery, the elaborate candy dishes. There was a bit too much of everything, but the room was all of a piece, like a jewel box; heavy curtains covered the windows.

I felt someone touching my shoulder, speaking my name, and saw in front of me, tall and gay, our hostess's daughter. We exchanged a few words and then she asked me if I knew various people.

I said no in a low voice.

"We know you come from Rome," she said loudly into an unexpected silence, "but last evening you met a friend of mine. Don't deny it."

"What friend?"

Those two women at the party—I knew now. But her aggressiveness bothered me.

"You must have met Fefé at least?"

"I'm surprised that he remembers. He was drunk as a carter."

This reply won her over completely. I had to get up and follow her to the circle of young people at the entrance. She told me their names: Pupé, Carletto, Teresina. They shook hands, either bored or very very serious, and waited for somebody to speak. The flood of words with which the blonde had torn me from the sofa did not keep me from feeling an intruder even here, although I had known for quite a while that in these cases there is always someone worse off. I cursed Morelli and felt my heart drop; I saw the life of Rome, last night's party, my face in the mirror that morning. I consoled myself with the Via della Basilica, knowing that I was alone in the world and that, after all, these were people I might never have met.

The blonde was looking at us blankly and, it seemed to me, disappointedly. Then she said: "Come on, somebody say something." For all her twenty years and such a desire to laugh, it wasn't much. But I didn't know Mariella and her tenacity—she was the granddaughter of the old lady on the sofa. She looked around and exclaimed: "Where's Loris? Somebody find Loris. I want Loris right away." Someone went to look for Loris. The others began to talk, one kneeling against a chair, another seated; a young man with a beard held the floor and defended an absent friend against the girls—a certain Pegi who had been shoveling snow on the avenues that winter, out of eccentricity the girls said, to engage himself the young man said.

"Engage himself, what does he mean by that?" I thought, as Loris arrived with his head down. He wore a black bow tie and was a painter. The suspicion crossed my mind that he owed his importance among those people wholly to his bow tie and heavy eyebrows. He had a sullen look, like a bull.

He smiled briefly. Mariella dropped into a chair and said: "Come on now, let's discuss the costumes."

When I finally understood what it was all about—a girl screaming a little louder than the rest set herself to explaining it—I pretended ignorance and smiled impassively. Mariella and the others were all talking.

"Without costumes and scenery, it just won't work."

"You're all a bunch of hams. What you want is *Carmen*."

"It would be better to have a masquerade."

"The poetic word should echo in the void."

"But how many of you have read it?"

I glanced across the room where the irascible old lady held forth to her circle. The men in the flickering firelight kept their eyes on the carpet; the women moved restlessly and the first cups of tea had appeared in their hands.

Loris was saying slowly: "We don't want to repeat the traditional theater. We're not so civilized. What we want is to give the naked word of a text, but we can't do it without a *mise-en-scène* because even now in this room, dressed like this, between these walls, we are part of a *mise-en-scène* that we have to accept or reject. Any ambiance at all is a *mise-en-scène*. Even the light . . ."

"Then let's give it in the dark," a girl shrieked.

While Loris was talking, Mariella got up and went off to supervise the serving, and then she called the girls. I stayed with the others and that Loris who was silent and smiling disgustedly.

"There's something to be said for the darkness idea," a young man put in.

We looked at Loris, who was staring at the floor.

"Ridiculous!" said a small woman in a slipper-satin gown that was worth more than a lot of words. "One goes to the theater to see. Are you or aren't you giving a show?" She had libidinous eyes that laughed in the boys' faces.

The painter wouldn't stoop to this conversation and changing expression said crossly that he didn't want tea, he wanted a drink. Meanwhile the teacups were being passed and Mariella put a bottle of cognac on the mantelpiece. She asked me if we had settled anything.

"Must I decide?" I said. "I'm in the dark."

"But you have to help us," Mariella shouted. "You know all about fashions."

A general movement around the sofa indicated that something was happening. Everyone got up and moved back and Mariella ran over. The old lady was leaving. I didn't hear what she said, but a pretty maid took her thin arm and the old lady jabbed her cane on the floor, looked around tiredly out of bright eyes, and as the others bowed, the two went out slowly, with hobbling steps.

"Grandmother wants us to keep the doors open so she can hear in bed," said Mariella, returning fresher than ever. "She wants to hear the records, the conversation, the people. She's so fond of our friends . . ."

At the first chance I cornered Morelli and asked him what he meant to do now. "Bad-tempered already?" he said.

"Less than you; you've had a good dose of the old lady . . . However . . ."

"Don't speak badly of her," Morelli observed. "You don't see many like Donna Clementina. They died out some time ago. Did you know that she's a concierge's daughter; she's been an actress, a ballerina, a kept woman, and of the three sons she gave the old count, one got away to America and another is an archbishop. Not to mention her daughters . . ."

"Poor old thing. Why doesn't she retire to the country?"

"Because she'd so full of life. Because she likes to run her house. You should get to know her, Clelia."

"She's so old . . . it scares me."

"That's a good reason for knowing her. If you're afraid of old people, you're afraid to live."

"I thought you brought me here to meet those others . . ."

Morelli looked around at the seated groups, the couples chattering at the other end.

He frowned and muttered: "Drinking already?"

6. There was no more talk of *mise-en-scènes* that evening. I saw Loris's bow tie fluttering about, but I drifted alone and Mariella must have understood because she took me among a group of women, including her mother, who were talking fashions. Did she think she was pleasing me? She went back to the subject of her friend at the first party, said that she would have liked to go but still felt too young. The stretcher and the tulle gown came back in my mind.

"Oh, you could have come," said the little woman in satin. "It was all quite proper. I know people who changed the place of their party right in the middle of it, for fun."

"Just a nice family evening?" Mariella said, grinning.

"Really, it was," another girl said.

"Playing post office in the dark, more likely," Mariella concluded, looking around. The older woman smiled, scandalized and happy. Mariella was by no means a fool; she was the presiding hostess and had been born to such talk. I wondered if she would have known how to make out if she had begun at the bottom like her grandmother. I remembered Morelli's lecture and stopped short.

We were talking about Morelli, as it happened, and the life he led. By mentioning Rome, some Roman villas, and a few carefully chosen big names, I silenced the most prudish of the group. I let them know that Morelli was at home in certain houses and that Rome was the only city it was never necessary to leave. Everyone came there. Mariella clapped her hands and said that we were having such a good time and that some day she would go to Rome. Someone spoke of Holy Year.

"Those poor things," Mariella said suddenly. "What are they doing? Shall we go and listen?"

So our circle broke up and the various groups swarmed around Loris's bow tie, who was holding forth to several eager girls. Just for sport, he and the others had drunk all the cognac and now were squabbling about some question or other—whether in life one could be oneself or whether one had to act. I was surprised to hear a thin girl with bangs, thick lips, and a cigarette mention the name of the brunette I had met the first evening, Momina "Momina said so, Momina said so," she repeated. After Mariella joined our group and all those distinguished gentlemen gathered around, a quavery voice went up: "When you make love, you take off your mask. That's when you're naked." While Mariella was passing drinks, I turned to Morelli. He looked pleased with himself, watching as though he wore a monocle. I caught his eye and when he was close I asked him *sotto voce* why they didn't send the drunks into the garden. "They'd be out in the open and wouldn't make trouble."

"You can't," he said. "The indecencies must be kept up only in company; the ladies and heavy fathers must hear them. More orderly that way."

I asked him who these awful children were. He told me names, giving me to understand that they weren't all respectable people, that the young were corrupted and getting worse: "It's not a question of social class, for God's sake, but after the war and even before it, what has any of that mattered?" According to him, one used to be able to mix with people only on condition of knowing who one was. "Now these people don't know any more who they are or what they want," he said. "They don't even enjoy themselves. They can't talk: they shout. They have the vices of the old, but not the experience . . ."

I thought of the girl in the hotel and was about to ask him if he had heard any more about her. But I didn't do it; I realized he was stubborn in such matters, that for all his manners he had hair on his stomach, was graying and getting old. "He's as old as my father," I thought. "He knows so much and doesn't know anything. At least Father kept still and let us alone."

Morelli was now in the crowd, arguing. He was telling the bearded fellow that they should learn how to handle women instead of discussing nonsense with them, that they should learn how to live and stop being children; while the other, naturally, wanted to convince Morelli and make him agree that in life people are only acting. I have never seen Morelli so annoyed. The women were amused.

I caught Mariella as she went by, smiling easily at a preoccupied gentleman; I took her aside and said that we—that is, I—wanted to say good night and thank her for the evening. She was surprised and said that she still wanted to see me again, we had many things to talk over; she wanted to persuade me to so something for them, Momina had told her how nice I was.

"She didn't come this evening," I said, just to say something.

Mariella brightened and excused Momina. She said Momina had telephoned saying she didn't know, she thought she would visit the Molas.

"You know . . . ?" she said, lowering her voice and raising her eyes.

"Yes," I said. "How is Rosetta?"

Then Mariella colored and, flustered, said that if I knew Rosetta we would have to talk about it; poor thing, her parents didn't understand her and made life impossible for her, she was strong and sensitive, she absolutely needed to live, to have things, she was more mature than her years and she, Mariella, was afraid that now their friendship wouldn't survive that terrible experience.

"But she, the girl, how is she?"

"Yes, yes, she's recovered, but she doesn't want to see us, she doesn't want to see anyone. She only asks for Momina and won't see anyone else . . ."

"That's nothing," I said, "provided she gets better."

"Of course, but I'm afraid she hates me . . ."

I looked at her. She seemed upset.

"It must be the nausea after the Veronal," I said. "When one's sick to the stomach, one doesn't want to see people."

"But she sees Momina," Mariella shot back immediately. "It makes me sick."

I thought: You've some growing up to do, my dear. I hope I could control myself better in your place.

I said: "Rosetta didn't take Veronal just to spite you." I said this with a goodbye smile. Mariella smiled and held out her hand.

I waved at the nearest people, leaving Morelli in his circle with the bow tie and the girls, and went off. It was drizzling outside and I took a trolley on the avenue.

7. Not two days had passed before Mariella telephoned me. I hadn't seen anyone since that evening and had spent the whole time in the Via Po. The girl's voice laughed, insisted, panted with volubility. She wanted me to see her friends, to see them for her

sake and help them. Would I be able to see her that afternoon for tea? Or better, could we stop a moment in Loris's studio?

"That way we'll encourage them," she said. "If you knew how nice they are."

She picked me up at the Via Po, dressed in a gay fur jacket in the Cossack style. The house was on the other side of the Via Po. We went under the porticoes around the square and Mariella drew away from the carnival booths without a glance. I thought of how only a few days' absence from Rome had settled me into new responsibilities and the company of true natives. Even Maurizio had sent no more narcissi.

Mariella chattered and told me many things about life in Turin and the shops. For having seen them only as a customer, she knew them well. To judge a shop by its show window is difficult for any-body who has never dressed one. Mariella, however, understood them. She told me that her grandmother was still the terror of the dressmakers.

We arrived at the top of a dirty stairway that I didn't much like. I would rather have continued talking. Mariella rang.

All painters' studios are alike. They have the disorder of certain shops, but studied and done on purpose. You never can find out when they work; there always seems to be something wrong with the light. We found Loris on the unmade bed—no bow tie this time —and the girl with bangs let us in. She had on a threadbare coat and glowered at Mariella. She was smoking. Loris was also smok-ing, a pipe; and both seemed put out of temper by our arrival. Mar-iella laughed warmly and said: "Where's my stool?" Loris stayed on the bed.

We sat down with forced gaiety. Mariella began her prattling, asked for news, was amazed, went to the window. Loris, black and taciturn, barely responded. The thin girl, whose name was Nene, looked me over. She was a strange, heavy-lipped girl of about twenty-eight. She smoked with impatient gestures and bit her nails. She smiled nicely like a child, but her abrupt manner was annoying. It was clear that she considered Mariella a fool.

As it happened, I expected what followed. They began to talk about their own affairs, about people I didn't know. There was the story of a painting sold before it was finished, but then the painter decided it was already perfectly finished as it stood and he didn't want to touch it again, but the client wanted it really finished and the painter wouldn't hear of it and wouldn't change his mind. Nene got heated, indignant and excited, chewed her cigarette and took the words out of Mariella's mouth. I understand how people talk shop according to their professions; but there's nobody like painters, all those people you hear arguing in the cheaper restaurants. I could understand if they talked about brushes, colors, turpentine—the things they use—but no, these people make it difficult on purpose, and sometimes no one knows what certain words mean, there's always somebody else who suddenly starts arguing, says no, that it means this other thing, and everything's upside down. The kind of words you see in the newspapers when they write about painting. I expected that Nene would also exaggerate. But no. She talked rapidly and angrily but didn't lose her childlike air: she explained to Mariella that one never stops a painting too soon. Loris sucked on his pipe in silence. Mariella, who cared nothing about painting, suddenly came out with: Why didn't we discuss the play? Loris turned over on the bed, Nene looked unpleasantly at both of us. She was aware of it herself and burst out laughing. It struck me that she laughed in dialect, as counter girls laugh, as I sometimes laugh myself.

Nene said: "But it's all up in the air now. After what's happened to Rosetta, we can't stage a suicide . . ."

"Nonsense," Mariella shouted. "Nobody'd think twice about it."

Nene looked at us again, provocatively and happy.

"That's all woman's stuff," Loris said, contemptuous. "It might interest the bourgeois husband, but as for me . . . Anyhow, we have to deal with the Martelli women, with the people putting up the cash. I don't know what Rosetta may have done . . . What I like, on the other hand, is this fantasia on reality in which the artistic situation jumps into life. The personal side of it doesn't concern me . . . But it would be too good if Rosetta had really acted under suggestion . . . However, the Martellis have backed out."

"What's all this have to do with it?" Mariella said. "Art is something else . . ."

"Are you sure?" Loris argued. "It's another way of looking at the same thing, if you like, but not another thing. As for me, I'd like to dramatize the dramatic suggestion itself. I'm sure it would be fantastic . . . a collage of theater news . . . to treat these clothes you wear, this room, this bed, as the stuff of theater . . . an existential theater. Is that how one says it?"

He looked at me, really at me, from that bed, with those hairy eyes. I can't stand these nasty-clever people and was about to tell him off when Nene jumped up, fresh: "If Rosetta had really died, one could do it. *Un hommage à Rosette* . . ."

Mariella said: "Who's not in favor?"

"Momina," the other said. "The Martelli women, the president, Carla and Mizi. They were Momina's friends . . ."

"That fool should have died, it would have been better . . ." Mariella cried out.

I'm used to hearing all the scandal and gossip of Rome in our shop, but this bickering between friends because a third one didn't succeed in killing herself impressed me. I was on the point of believing that the acting had already begun and that all that was going on was theatrical make-believe, as Loris wanted. Coming to Turin, I walked out on a stage and was acting now myself. "It's carnival time," I thought to myself. "You'll find that in Turin they play these tricks every year."

"As for me," Loris said, biting his pipe, "you agree among yourselves."

I studied Nene's bangs, her heavy lips, her faded coat. People live in strange ways. Listening to them talk about their work and the right they had to sell it unfinished, I understood that they were defending not so much the money as their arrogance. I wanted to say to her: My dear girl, you never know where the next meal's coming from, yet you put on these airs. Where do you sleep at night? Does someone keep you? Mariella, who doesn't paint, is well-born and has a fur coat.

They began to argue again about the play and said that there wasn't time to find another, and all right, they wouldn't do anything this year.

"That fool," Mariella said. "Let's read a single act, without action or scenery," Nene said, and then Loris jumped up, looked at them disgustedly, as the idiots they were, and said: "All right. Only leave me alone."

I looked again at a certain unframed picture against the wall under the window. It seemed dirty, unfinished: since I'd come in I'd been asking myself what it was. I didn't want anyone to notice my interest, lest Mariella should say: "Come on, show her your pictures." But that mess of violet and blackish colors fascinated me; I didn't want to look at it and yet I always returned to it; I thought to myself that it was like the whole room and Loris's face.

I asked when they planned to give the play. "Who knows?" Nene said. "Nobody's coughed up a penny yet."

"Don't you have an angel?"

"The angels," Mariella said nastily, "think they can impose their tastes even on us . . . That's why."

Loris said: "I'd be happy if anyone tried to impose a taste on me . . . But you don't find anyone nowadays who has a taste. They don't know what they want . . ."

Mariella gave a self-satisfied laugh, from inside her fur coat. Nene squirmed and said: "There are too many Martellis and too many Mizis mixed up in this. Too many hysterical women . . . Momina . . ."

"She overdoes everything," Mariella said.

"Momina knows what she wants. Let her do what she likes."

"So then who will come to hear us?" said Mariella, annoyed. "Who'll do the acting? The hysterical women?"

"Acting is out. We'll just read."

"Nonsense," Loris said. "We wanted to paint an atmosphere . . ."

They went on awhile. It was clear that the painter only wanted to daub some scenery to earn a little money. And that Mariella wanted to be an actress. Only Nene seemed without pretenses, but there was something at the bottom of her interest, too.

Then Momina arrived.

8. She came in with that discontented, dominating air of hers. Her gloves alone were worth more than the whole studio. Nene, opening the door for her, seemed like a servant. Everyone said a smiling hello.

"Why, you visit everybody," Momina said on seeing me.

"That's not difficult in Turin," I replied.

She moved here and there, going up very close to the pictures, and I saw that she was nearsighted. All the better. I watched Mariella closely.

"Put on the lights," she told us. "Don't you see it's night?"

When the lights came on, the window disappeared and the painting became a puddle of flayed faces.

"Everybody's dropping out," Nene said. "I'm dropping out, too. One loses time over a lot of dumb excuses and we still don't know What we're doing. Clara's right, let's recite in the dark, like a radio broadcast..."

Momina smiled in her dissatisfied way. She didn't answer Nene but instead told Loris that she had talked with somebody who had told her this and that, and Loris grunted something from the bed, holding his ankle; Mariella jumped in and they laughed and chattered and Nene said: "Crazy nonsense," and they forgot about the theater. Now Momina held forth, telling about a certain Gegé di Piovà who, meeting a girl he'd known as a child—they hadn't seen each other for years—went up to her in the bar of a big hotel: "Hello."

"Hello."

"They tell me you've developed," and slipping his hand down the front of her dress he brought out a breast and they both laughed with Filippo the bartender and the onlookers. Momina and Nene laughed; Mariella looked disgusted; Loris jumped up from the bed, saying: "It's true. She has magnificent tits."

"Slander," Mariella said. "Vanna's not like that."

"They're not magnificent?" Loris said.

They went on in that vein and Momina skipped from one subject to another, looking at me out of the corners of her eyes in her searching way, asked my opinion, tried to fascinate me. I was glad that the play didn't come up again. Only Mariella was restless, one saw that Momina had taken her place. Momina was younger than I, but not by much: she dressed very well, a gray suit under her beaver coat, her skin was massaged, her face fresh; she took advantage of her nearsightedness by passing it off as detachment. I recalled her violet dress on the first night and looked at her naked ring finger.

"We're leaving," Mariella said suddenly.

Momina told us to wait for her, that she had her car below. The three of us got into her green Topolino: I had expected something better. Mariella wanted to sit in the back. Lighting a cigarette, Momina explained: "This is all my husband allows me."

"Ah," I said.

"I live alone," Momina observed, putting the car into gear. "It's better for both of us."

I wanted to stop at the Via Po and take a last look. Momina said: "Stay with me, tonight."

Mariella, in the back seat, was silent. We dropped her at the gate on her avenue. At the last minute she took up the play again, complained about Momina, about us, accused us of having put a spoke in the wheel. Momina answered coldly; then they flew at each other while I looked at the shrubbery. Now they were quiet. "I'll tell you about it tomorrow," Momina told her. The two of us got back in.

She took me back to the center, saying nothing about Mariella. Instead she talked about Nene and said that she made such beautiful sculptures. "I can't understand why she wastes her time with that Loris," she smiled. "She's so intelligent. A woman worth more than the man who touches her is damned unlucky."

I asked her to take me to the Via Po.

When I emerged from the portico and went back to the car, Momina was smoking a cigarette and looking around in the dark. She opened the door for me.

We went to the Piazza San Carlo for an apéritif. We took two small armchairs in the back of a new gilded café, its entrance still cluttered with trestles and rubbish. An elegant place. Momina turned back her fur coat and looked at me. "Now you know all my friends," she said. "From Rome to Turin is quite a jump. It must be pleasant to work as you do."

What is she looking for, a job? I thought.

"Don't be alarmed," she went on. "The circle here in Turin is small ... I don't mean to ask your advice. You have taste, but my dressmaker is good enough for me ... It's a pleasure to talk to somebody who leads another life."

We talked a bit about Turin and Rome—she squinting at me

through the smoke—about how you can't find apartments, about the new café we were in; she had never been to Rome but she had been to Paris and didn't I think I should go to Paris for my work; I absolutely had to go; traveling for the sake of one's work was the only real traveling, and why should I be satisfied with Turin?

Then I said I had been sent here. "I was born in Turin."

She was born in Turin too, she said, but grew up in Switzerland and was married in Florence. "They brought me up a lady," she said, "but what's a lady who can't catch a train tomorrow for London or Spain or wherever you like?"

I opened my mouth, but she said that after the war only workers like myself could afford the luxury.

"When you work, you don't have time," I said.

She observed calmly: "It's hardly worth working just to come to Turin."

I believed I understood her and told her I hadn't been in Turin for nearly twenty years and had also come back to see my old home.

"You are alone, it seems."

"The house I lived in, the quarter . . ."

She looked at me with that discontented smile. "I don't understand these things," she said. "You probably have nothing in common with the girl who was born in Turin. Your family . . ."

"Dead."

" . . . If they weren't, they'd make you laugh. What would you have in common with them now?"

She was so cold and distant that I flushed and didn't know what to say. I felt a fool. After all, I thought, she's trying to pay you a compliment. She looked at me quizzically as if she had understood.

"Now don't tell me, like some people I know, that it's fine being born in a courtyard . . ."

I said that it was fine to think about the courtyard, comparing it with now.

"I knew it," she said, laughing. "Living is so foolish that one gets attached even to the foolishness of having been born . . ."

She knew how to talk, no question of that. I looked around at the gilding, the mirrors, the prints on the walls. "This café," Momina said, "was put up by a man like you, pigheaded . . ."

She made me smile. Are you on the ball because you've lived in Paris, I thought, or were you in Paris because you're on the ball?

But she said abruptly: "Did you enjoy the party the other evening?"

"Was that a party?" I murmured, disillusioned. "I wasn't aware."

"They say it's carnival time," she remarked ironically in a low voice, laughing. "These things happen."

"And pretty Mariella," I said, "why doesn't she go to these parties?"

"She's already told you that?" Momina smiled. "Why, you're real friends already."

"She hasn't asked me yet to run up a dress for her."

"She will, she will. We're all like that in Turin . . ."

9. I am a fool. In the evening I was sorry to have spoken badly of Mariella after she had defended that girl Vanna in Loris's studio. The bitterness stayed in my mouth. Of course I knew they were only words, that these people—all of them, including Morelli— lived like cats, always ready to scratch and snatch, but anyhow I was sorry and said to myself: "Here I am just like them." The mood didn't last, however, and when Momina asked what I was doing that evening I agreed to keep her company. We went to the hotel for dinner and naturally Morelli showed up and came over to our table to talk, showing no surprise at seeing us together. Halfway through the meal my telephone call from Rome came through. For a couple of minutes in the booth I discussed the Via Po, made projects, and breathed the old air. When I got back, Morelli and Momina told me to forget all that, we were going to enjoy ourselves, we would go out together and end up in Morelli's apartment.

That evening Morelli wanted to drive. He took us to the wine market, where he tried to get us drunk, as men do with inexperienced girls, but eventually he drank more than we did. And then, as a kind of game, we made the rounds of numberless places, getting in and out of the car; I kept taking off and putting on my fur, one dance and away—I seemed to recognize dozens of faces. Once we lost Momina and found her at the door of the next room, laughing and talking with the doorman. I had no idea there was so much going on in Turin. Momina stopped treating me absently, she laughed in Morelli's face and suggested we make the rounds of the dives along Porta Palazzo where you drink red wine and the whores hang out. "This isn't Paris, you know," Morelli said. "Content yourself with those four fairies over there." In a bar in Via Roma, near the little square with the churches, Morelli pretended to be bargaining for cocaine with the barkeep, they were great friends. He stood us drinks and then the drummer began telling us about the time he played in the Royal Palace. "His Highness ... because for me he is still His Highness ..." To get away, I danced with Momina. I don't like dancing with women, but I wanted to test a suspicion and this is still the quickest way. Nobody paid us any attention; Momina danced, talking into my ear, held me so tight it burned, rubbed against me, laughed and breathed in my hair, but it didn't seem to me she wanted anything else; she made no advances, was just a little crazy and drunk. Well and good; it would have been a very unpleasant mess.

And finally we arrived at the entrance to Morelli's place. He saw us a bit unsteadily into the elevator, talking a blue streak to both of us. As we went into his apartment, he said: "All this gabble lengthens your life. I'm glad I'm not old yet because if I were I'd be running after dolls ... You're not dolls, you're real women ... Vicious, bad-tempered: but women ... You know how to talk ... No, no, I'm not old yet ..."

We entered laughing and I liked the apartment immediately. It was obviously empty and very large. We went to the living room, which had big armchairs and was full of rugs and azaleas. The large window opening on the boulevard must have been pleasant in summer.

Brandy glasses in hand, we made plans. Momina asked if I were going to the mountains. There was still snow. Morelli talked stubbornly about Capri and the pine woods of Fregene; he tried to recall whether he had business in Rome that would justify a vacation or any kind of trip. I said it was odd that men should make such a fuss about appearances. "If it weren't for the men," I said, "we'd have had divorce in Italy long ago."

"No need of it, really," Momina observed tranquilly. "You can always come to an understanding with your husband."

"I admire Clelia," he said, "who hasn't even wanted . . ."

"It's not that I want to pry," Momina said, looking at me, "but, if you married, would you want to have children?"

"Have you had them?" I laughed. "That's what people get married for."

But she didn't laugh. "When you have children," she said, staring at her glass, "you accept life. Do you accept life?"

"If you live, you accept it, don't you?" I said. "Children don't affect the question."

"Yes, but you haven't had any . . ." she said, raising her eyes and looking at me.

"Children are a great nuisance," Morelli said, "but women are all for them."

"Not us," Momina shot out.

"I've always noticed that someone who hasn't wanted children usually ends by taking care of someone else's."

"That's not it," Momina interrupted. "The point is that a woman with a child is no longer herself. She has to accept so many things, she has to say yes. And is it worth the trouble to say yes?"

"Clelia doesn't want to say yes," Morelli said.

Then I said that arguing such matters made no sense because everybody likes a child but you can't always do what you want. If you want to have a child you have one, but you should be careful first to provide him with a home and money so that later he won't curse his mother.

Momina, lighting a cigarette, looked at me searchingly with her eyes half closed against the smoke. She went back to asking me if I accepted life. She said that to have a child you had to carry it inside, to become a sow, bleed and die—you had to say yes to so many things. That was what she wanted to know, whether I accepted life.

"Oh drop it now," Morelli said. "Neither of you is pregnant."

We drank some more cognac. Morelli wanted us to listen to some records; he said his maid slept like the dead. From the floor above came a reverberation of feet and a great uproar. "They're celebrating the carnival too," he said so solemnly that I broke out laughing. But I had been struck by this business of saying yes; Momina had taken off her shoes and had curled up in the armchair, smoking. We talked trivialities, she studying me with her discontented air, like a cat, listening; I talked but felt rotten inside. I had never thought about things in the light that Momina put on them; I knew it was all words—"we're here to have a good time"—but meanwhile it was true that not to have children meant you were afraid of life. I thought of the girl in the hotel and told myself: it will turn out that she was pregnant. I was a bit drunk and sleepy too, but Morelli, on the other hand, the later it got the more boyish he became; he walked around the room, amused us, talked of getting breakfast. When we went out—he had to come at any cost—they took me to the hotel in the car; and so we said no more that time about those things.

10. One of those days—it was drizzling—I had to return before evening from the neighborhood of the Consolata. I was looking for an electrician and it excited me a little to see the old stores again, the big outer doors in the alleys, and to read the names—delle Orfane, di Corte d'Appello, Tre galline—and recognize the signs. Not even the cobblestones had changed. I didn't have an umbrella and under the narrow slits of sky above the roofs I rediscovered the old odor of the walls. No one knows, I said to myself, that you're that Clelia. I hadn't dared stop to examine the old windows closely.

But when I was ready to go back I let myself go. I was in Via Santa Chiara and remembered the corner, the grated windows, the smeared, steamed glass of the shop front. I stepped firmly across the threshold to the sound of the old bell, as I used to, and passing my hand over my fur felt its wetness. The little shelves and their display of buttons, the little counter, the smell of cloth, were still the same in that close air.

A lamp with a green reflector still lighted the cash register. At the last minute I hoped the business had changed hands, but the bony, resentful face of the thin woman who got up from behind the counter was really Gisella's. I think I blushed and hoped that I, too, had aged like that. Gisella inspected me suspiciously, with a half smile of invitation on her thin mouth. She was gray, but neat.

Then she asked, in a tone that once would have made us both laugh, if I wanted to buy anything. I answered by winking. She didn't comprehend and began the phrase again. I interrupted her with my hand. "Is it possible?" I said.

After the first pleasure and surprise, which wasn't enough to give her color (she left the counter and we both went to the doorway to see each other better), we chatted and laughed and she looked at my fur and stockings with an appraising eye as if I were her daughter. I didn't tell her everything about myself or why I was in Turin. I let her think what she liked, mentioning Rome vaguely, that I had a job. When we were both girls, Gisella was raised so very strictly that she wasn't even allowed in the movies, but I used to tell her to come anyway.

She had already asked if I were married, and my impatient shrug had made her sigh, whether for me or for herself I don't know. "I'm a widow," she said. "Giulio is dead." Giulio was the son of the owner of the store, who had adopted the orphaned Gisella, and even in my time you could tell that she wanted Gisella to be her daughter-in-law. Giulio was a very tall, consumptive boy who wore a cape instead of an overcoat or sweater and always sunned himself in the winter on the steps of the cathedral. Gisella never talked about Giulio then; she was the only one who refused to believe that the old lady kept her in the house to marry the sick boy; she always used to say that he wasn't sick. Gisella was shrewd and lively in those days. In the house she was often held up to us as an example.

"And Carlotta?" I asked. "What is she doing? Still dancing?"

But Gisella had gone on talking about the shop and told me the usual story—she was glad to see me and relieve her feelings. I was struck by the rancorous tone she used in telling me that Carlotta had made her own way—she had been a ballerina in Germany during the war, then nobody had seen her. Gisella went back to the store, said that she had been bled white by Giulio's death, had been paying his sanatorium bills until three years ago. She told me about the old lady's death and of bad times even before the war. Her daughters—she had two, Rosa and Lina: one coughed, was anemic; the other one, fifteen years old; both were studying—they were a great trouble, life was expensive and the shop didn't bring what it used to bring in the old days.

"But you're well off. You still have that apartment."

Just trouble, she told me, nobody paid their rent; she had to throw out the previous tenants and now was renting to a group of girls. "It pays better. We're squeezed in upstairs." I recalled those two upper rooms, the stairway, the tiny kitchen. In the old lady's time, to climb those stairs was a risk, she was always in the middle of things, yelling at Gisella, telling her not to go out on the street. I was struck by the way Gisella now resembled the old lady, sighed, half shut her eyes; even the resentful smile she threw at my fur and stockings had a tinge of the rancor with which the old lady used to judge the rest of us.

She called her daughters. I would rather have left. This was my whole past, insupportable yet so different now, so dead. I had told myself so many times in those years—and later too, as a matter of fact—that my purpose in life was to make good, to become somebody, in order to come back some day to those alleys where I had been a girl and enjoy the warmth, the amazement, the admiration of those familiar faces, of those little people. And I had done it, I came back; and the faces, the little people had all gone. Carlotta had gone, and Slim, Giulio, Pia, the old women. Guido, too, had gone. Neither we nor those times mattered any more to the people left, like Gisella. Maurizio always says that you get the things you want, but when they are no more use.

Rosa wasn't there, she had gone to the neighbors'. But Lina, the healthy one, ran down the stairs, sprinted into the shop; she stopped, cautious and reserved, outside the cone of light. She was dressed in flannel, not badly, and was well developed. Gisella talked about making coffee and taking me upstairs; I said it would be better if we didn't leave the shop. In fact, just then the bell rang and a customer came in.

"Ah yes," Gisella said when the door closed again, "we were girls who worked, in those days . . . Other times. My aunt knew how to give orders . . ."

She looked at Lina with a faint smile of pleasure. It was plain that she had chosen the role of a mother who kills herself with work to keep her daughters from soiling their hands. She wouldn't even let Lina make the coffee. She ran upstairs herself to put it on. I exchanged a word or two with the daughter—she looked at me complacently—I asked about her sister. A woman came in, ringing the bell, and Gisella shouted down the stairs: "Coming."

I had said positively that I was just passing through Turin and leaving the next day: I didn't want obligations. But Gisella didn't insist; she brought the talk back to the old lady, made me talk about her in front of her daughter: about how the old lady ruled the roost and even gave advice to other people's daughters. That's how it always turns out. With the excuse of raising her, of giving her a house and a husband, the old lady had made Gisella into her own image—and now she, Gisella, was working on her daughters. I wondered if my mother had been like that, whether it is possible to live with someone, order her around, and not leave a mark on her. I had escaped from my mother in time. Or had I? Mother had always grumbled that a man, a husband, was a poor thing, that men are not so much bad as fools—and, as you see, I had pretty well accepted her preaching. Even my great ambition, my passion to be free and self-sufficient, didn't it come from her?

Before I left, Lina began to chatter about some friend of hers at school and found the opportunity to speak badly of her, to wonder where her family found the means to send her to school. I tried to remember myself at this age, what I would have said in a case like this. But I hadn't gone to school. I hadn't drunk coffee with my mother. I was sure that Lina would talk about me behind my back to her mother just as she had talked to me about her school friend.

11. Only the hours I spent at Via Po didn't seem wasted. I had to run around looking for this and that and met various people at the hotel. By Ash Wednesday, the masons and whitewashers were finished; the most difficult work remained, the furnishings. I was on the point of taking the train and going down to discuss everything again; you can't make yourself understood on the telephone to Rome. They said: "We trust each other—do what you like," and the day after, they telegraphed me to expect a letter. The architect designing the interiors came to dinner with me at the hotel: he had come back from Rome with a portfolio full of sketches. But he was young and liked to stall around; to avoid making decisions, he would agree to anything I said; from the look of things, all our nice Rome ideas had collapsed. You had to take account of the light under the porticoes and consider the other shops in Piazza Castello and Via Po. I began to agree with Morelli: the location was impossible. It was the kind of district you no longer find in Rome, or perhaps only outside the gates. People walked in the Via Po only on Sundays.

This architect was red, stubborn, and hairy, just a boy; he was always talking about villas in the mountains; as a joke he sketched me the plan of a little glass house for winter sunbathing. He said that he lived like me, out of a suitcase, but differently from me in that I could wear whatever I made or liked, whereas only those pigs who had money—nearly always stolen—could live in his villas. I got him talking about the Turin painters, about Loris. He got excited, steamed up, said that he preferred the whitewashers. "A housepainter knows color," he said. "If he studied, a housepainter could paint frescoes or make mosaics any day. No one can understand decoration unless he begins by painting walls. As for these artists, for whom do they paint and what do they paint? They can't spread themselves. What they do serves no purpose. Would you make a dress that isn't to wear but to keep under glass?"

I told him they didn't just make pictures or statues but had also talked about putting on a play. I told him some of the names. "Oh, great!" he interrupted sarcastically. "Great. What would you say if that bunch put on a fashion show and invited Clelia Oitana to see it?"

Then we went on in this vein and concluded that only we window dressers, architects, and dressmakers were true artists. He ended, as I expected he would, by inviting me to go to the mountains to see an alpine retreat that he had planned. I asked if he didn't have something a bit more comfortable to propose. Even a building in Turin. He gave me a one-eyed look, laughing.

"My studio . . ." he said.

I was sick of studios and talking. I almost preferred Becuccio and his leather bracelet. This other man was called Febo—he had signed all his drawings this way. I laughed in his face, with his own cockiness, and sent him to bed like an overly clever boy.

But Febo was red, stubborn, and hairy and must have decided that I would do for him. He managed to discover exactly how I stood with Mariella, Nene, Momina, with Morelli and his cognac, my visit to Loris's studio. The next day he came to tell me he wanted to take me to a gallery show. I asked if it wouldn't be better to decide on those curtains. He said that the show was the right atmosphere; you had a drink, you studied the furnishings of the place; it was a question of taste. We went, and even on the stairs I could hear Nene's laugh.

The rooms were a blend of Swiss chalet and twentieth-century bar. Girls in checked aprons served us. Inasmuch as the chairs and crockery were also part of the show, one was a bit uneasy and felt on show oneself. Febo wouldn't say if he had had a hand in it himself. There were paintings and small statues on the wall; I passed them up and looked at Nene instead, who, in her usual rags, laughed continuously, sprawled across a chair, crossing and uncrossing her legs, while a waiter lighted her cigarette from behind. Momina was there, with other women and girls. A little old man in a Chinese beard had settled in front of Nene and was sketching her portrait. A few people crowded to the door for a peek—the public viewing the artists.

But Nene soon noticed me and came over to ask if I had seen her work. She was happy, excited, she blew smoke in my face. Her thick lips and bangs really made her a child. She brought me to her statues—little deformed nudes that seemed shaped out of mud. I looked at them, bending my head from side to side, and thought—but didn't say—that Nene's womb might very well produce children like those. She looked at me avidly and open-mouthed, as if I were a handsome young man; I waited for someone to speak, bent my head to the other side. Febo came up from behind and said, catching us both by the waist: "Here we're either in heaven or in hell. It takes a girl like you, Nene, to reveal such terrors . . ."

A discussion sprang up in which Momina also took part. I paid no attention. I'm used to painters. I was watching Nene's face as she frowned or started at whatever was said, as if everything hung on someone else's opinion. Had she really lost her boldness, or was this another of her roles? Febo was the least believable of all. Only the other day he had said dirt of Nene and her things.

They talked good-naturedly about her and she played the bewildered child. Her insistence on showing me her things had bothered me. Couldn't she have let me see them by myself? But Nene was keeping up her reputation as a mannerless and impulsive girl. Perhaps she was right. Mariella's the only one absent, I thought. What would Becuccio say of these crazy women?

The idea of Becuccio started me laughing. Febo turned around genially, came closer, and whispered against my cheek: "You are a treasure, Clelia. You would make better children, I dare say."

"I thought you were speaking seriously before," I answered. "The most sincere one here is still Nene . . ."

"This gutsy art has given me an appetite," he whispered. "How about some sausage?"

Drinking *grappa* and eating sausage, he talked about the mountains again. Even the old painter with the beard was a competent climber. They were arranging a trip to some hut, assigning jobs, telephoning all over the place.

"You people go," Momina said. "I'm not going to the hut. Clelia and I will stop on the way . . . Have you ever been to Montalto?"

12. The Topolino stopped at a villa at the foot of the mountains. The two of us were alone. The other cars went on, they would wait for us at Saint Vincent. A few days of good weather had been enough to bring out the bloom in the hothouse flowers, but the trees in the garden were still bare. I hardly had time to look around when Momina cried: "Here we are."

Rosetta wasn't wearing her blue dress this time. She came to meet us in a skirt and tennis shoes, her hair bound with a ribbon as if we were at the seaside. She gave me a strong handshake, another to Momina, but didn't smile: she had gray, searching eyes.

Her mother came out also, in slippers, fat and asthmatic, wearing a velvet dress. "Rosetta," Momina cried, "you can come back now. The parties are over in Turin . . ."

Momina told her about friends, our outing, and who was going. I was surprised that Rosetta should accept her lightheartedness and answer in the same spirit; I wondered if I really had seen her on that stretcher—how many days ago? Fifteen, twenty? But perhaps Momina chattered that way to help her, to relieve her and us of embarrassment. They must have been close friends.

It was her mother, poor thing, who had tearful, frightened eyes, who was upset with Momina and looked at me apprehensively. She was so much the little lady that she complained of the hardship of living in the country, of staying at the villa out of season. But Rosetta and Momina didn't encourage her. It ended with Momina laughing at her. "That wicked father," Momina exclaimed, "imprisoning the two of you like this. You've got to escape, Rosetta. Agreed?"

"Agreed," Rosetta said quietly.

Her mother was afraid it wasn't a good idea. "You don't have skis, you don't have anything," she said. "Father doesn't know..."

"Who's talking about skiing?" Momina said. "Let those idiots ski if they like. We're going to Saint Vincent. Clelia hasn't come to ski..."

But first the mother wanted to give us tea, prepare the thermos, equip us. Not to waste time, Rosetta had already run off to dress.

We stayed with the mother. Momina murmured: "How is she?"

The mother turned around, her hand on her cheek. I could see her again in her furs, running down that corridor. "Please," she said, "don't let anything happen..."

"You've got to come back," Momina cut in. "You shouldn't hide like this. Her friends at Turin are beginning to talk..."

We reached Saint Vincent, keeping always to the mountains. Here, too, there was sun on the snow, and not many plants. I was amazed at all the cars in the Casino parking lot.

"You've never been here?" Rosetta leaned forward to ask me. She had wanted to sit in the back, in her fur jacket, and during the drive she and Momina had talked without looking at each other.

"It's nice," I said. "Three hours by car."

"Do you gamble?"

"I don't believe in luck."

"What else is there in life?" Momina said, slowing down. "People dream about having a car to come here to win enough for a car so they can come back . . . That's the world."

She was very positive, but also, I thought, mocking. In any case, neither of them laughed. We got out.

Luckily our friends had been scattered around the game rooms for some time and we three could sit alone at the bar. It was jammed and like a hothouse. Rosetta took an orangeade and sipped it quietly, watching us. Her gray, sunken eyes laughed very little. She seemed a quiet outdoor girl in her yellow sweater and slacks rolled up at the bottom. She asked who was with us beside Pegi and the girls.

The conversation turned to her friends, to the latest doings in Turin. Momina said at one point that the play was in deep trouble (she was smoking, eyes half closed in the smoke).

"Why?" Rosetta asked coldly.

"They don't want to embarrass you . . ." Momina said. "You know the play ends unhappily . . ."

"Nonsense," Rosetta cut in. "What does that matter?"

"Do you know who's in favor of the original version?" the other said. "Mariella. Mariella wants to give it and doesn't see any allusion in it. She says it doesn't matter to you . . ."

Rosetta glanced at me quickly. Getting up, I said: "Excuse me. I'm going to the ladies' room."

They both looked at me, Momina with amusement.

I had a feeling that I had said something one doesn't say. While I walked the corridors to calm down, I kept thinking: you stupid oaf. This is how you betray yourself. I imagine I was blushing.

I stopped in front of a mirror and noticed Febo coming out of one of the game rooms. I didn't turn until he had gone back.

When I returned, I said: "Excuse me." And Rosetta, with those steady eyes: "But you can stay. You don't bother us at all. I'm not ashamed of what I did."

Momina said: "You saw Rosetta that night. Tell us how she was. The waiters hadn't undressed her, I hope . . ."

Rosetta had a pained expression, as if trying to laugh. She even blushed. She realized it and her eyes hardened, looking intently at me.

I said something or other, that her mother and the doctor were standing around.

"No, no. I mean how Rosetta was," Momina said, not giving up. "The effect she made on a stranger. You were a stranger then. If she looked ugly, distorted, like someone else. The way one is, near death. After all, that's what she wanted."

They must have known each other very well to talk like that. Rosetta looked at me out of her deep eyes, attentive. I said that I'd only been there an instant but that her face seemed swollen, she was dressed in blue and didn't have shoes on. Of that I was certain. Everything was so in order and so little disturbed, I said, that I had looked under the stretcher to see if there was blood. It looked like an accident, an ordinary accident. After all, a person unconscious is very like a person asleep.

Rosetta breathed heavily, not attempting to smile. Momina said: "When did you take the pills?"

But Rosetta didn't answer. She shrugged her shoulders, looked around, and then asked in a low voice: "Did you really believe I had shot myself?"

"If you really wanted to do it," Momina said, "shooting would have been better. It worked out badly."

Rosetta gave me a deep look, intimidated—at that moment she seemed to be someone else—and she whispered: "Afterwards you feel worse than before. That's what's frightening."

13. There was no more time to talk about it. The girls saw us and came over, and common acquaintances, even some from my hotel, showed up. Now that they knew we were here, Febo, Nene, and that fellow Pegi shuttled between the game rooms, where they carelessly played and lost, and the bar, where they downed one drink after another. It ended with Nene and the boy Pegi, half drunk, squabbling so much that the old painter and Momina intervened because the rest of us were leaving. "We're coming, too," Momina said.

Meanwhile I wandered through the rooms, but the people packed around the tables got on my nerves, and there were big landscapes and nudes on the walls, almost as if to say that the aim of all the gamblers was to live well and keep nude women in furs. What makes you boil is that you have to admit that everything really does come down to this and the gamblers are right. They are all of them right, even those who live by it, even the impoverished old ladies whose avid eyes seem to cash in the other gamblers' winning chips. At least everybody is on a level, gambling—well-born or low-born, whores, pickpockets, fools or geniuses, they're all after the same thing.

The moment came when Nene, desperate, threw herself on a chair and cried: "Take me away, take me away." Then we went to the cars and piled the others in. It was only then that Nene noticed Rosetta and began calling her and wanted to kiss her. Rosetta obligingly calmed her by lighting her cigarette through the car window.

They left. Now it was our turn. But, looking at each other, we burst out laughing. "Let's have dinner at Ivrea," Momina said, relieved. "Then we'll go back to Montalto."

We returned to the rooms for a last look. Momina said she wanted to try to win the expenses of the trip, now that the jinxes had gone. "Stick with me," she said to Rosetta. "You're loaded with luck, like the rope from a hanged man's neck." Very solemnly they sat down at a table. I stood by, watching. In a couple of turns Momina had lost ten thousand lire. "You try," she said to Rosetta. Rosetta lost another five thousand. "Let's go to the bar," Momina said.

Here we are, I thought; now it begins. "Listen," I said as I was drinking my coffee, "I'll take you to dinner, but leave off."

"Lend me another thousand," Momina said.

"Let's go," Rosetta said. "There's no point."

I gave her the thousand, and we lost that too. While we were in the foyer and Momina was going on about her losses, who should show up but hard-nosed Febo, looking sly.

"And where are the beautiful ladies going?" he grinned.

He hadn't left. No one had thought of him. He had been in the room when we were playing. "You see," Momina said, "it's your fault. Go away, go away."

Instead, all four of us crammed into the Topolino. It wasn't easy to get rid of him, the more so because he joked bitingly about the common jinx and said: "You owe me something. We'll spend the night together."

Febo knew Ivrea well and took us to a place carters went to. "Nice," Momina said when we entered. We went on through to a sort of back room which had a large, hot terra-cotta stove, and the owner, a big man with hair in his ears and a big apron, came and helped us out of our coats, very attentive. "Be careful there," Febo said.

I was watching Rosetta throwing off her leopard jacket. "Put all your furs together and this man's hair would still be more than a match for them," Febo whispered.

"Our architect's not so bad either," Momina said.

"I'm not the only one," he came back. "How about Loris's hair? . . . How come he wasn't along?"

Momina turned to Rosetta: "You used to like Loris once. He was so amusing."

"In my opinion," Febo said, "hair's a great thing. Suppose Loris was *merely* degenerate? He would have had to give up his trade long ago. But with all that hair of his he gets off scot-free . . ."

"It's not funny," Rosetta said quietly. "It's not funny and it's not kind. You were friends once."

"Make her drink, make her drink," Febo shouted. "Then Rosetta can tell us about when everybody was friends with everybody . . ."

We ate the way you eat in such places, and drank likewise. The host suggested mysterious old wines from those regions; he and Febo winked at each other; after each dish he asked if it had been to our taste. Even Rosetta livened up and joked; there was no more talk about Loris. Instead we made fun of the alpinists, who at that moment were eating cold canned meat in the hut Febo had designed, and Febo said with his mouth full: "At least they're eating in tasteful surroundings."

"I wish Morelli were with us," Momina said. "He enjoys this kind of thing."

"Who's Morelli?" Rosetta asked.

"He's an old gentleman who's got his name linked with Clelia's," Momina said gaily. "But of course you know him."

"Oh, in other words," Febo said, "the handsomest aren't here. Take what you've got."

Closing time came, and with many smiles the host put us out. One good thing: we left it to Febo to pay him, by promise. I wanted to pay, but Momina said: "Nothing doing. He's already cost us too much, that character."

We took Rosetta to Montalto. Her mother was still up, waiting for her. She met us tearfully, and while Febo kept trying to pull me into the back seat, Momina stood outside arguing and made her promise they would return to Turin the next day. I said goodbye to Rosetta, who gave me her hand through the window and shot me a glance at once rebellious and grateful. We left.

"Why," Febo said, pushing his head forward between our shoulders, "why didn't they ask us to sleep at the villa?"

"Too many women for only one man," Momina said.

"Why be stingy?" he said. "Let's stop at Ivrea at least. I know a hotel..."

I was surprised when Momina accepted. "Tomorrow we're going back to Montalto," she said. "And if we'd gone to the hut, we would have slept outdoors, wouldn't we?"

When he was arranging for the rooms, Febo said: "Too bad they can't give us one for three."

Momina said: "They'll give one for Clelia and me."

We had hardly taken off our furs and washed (Momina had cold cream and perfume in her bag) when the door opened and Febo came in with a tray of liqueurs.

"Service," he said. "On the house."

"Put it down there," Momina said. "Good night."

We couldn't get rid of him. After a while Momina sat on the bed and I lay down on the other side and wrapped myself in the covers. Febo, seated beside Momina, talked away. They discussed women, nightclubs in Turin. They said everything—absolutely everything —with a freedom strange in two people who still used the formal "you" and had only met that day. Febo, with great bursts of laughter, had thrown himself on the bed two or three times and ended by staying there. Momina stretched out beside him. Resigned, I drowsed off a couple of times, and each time I woke there they were, chattering together. Then I realized they were wrapped in the same blanket. At one point, after a sudden spasm from Febo, I aimed a kick at him that got tangled in the covers. Then I sat up on the edge of the bed and lit a cigarette. Momina hurried to the bathroom; Febo, his hair mussed, handed me a glass from the almost empty bottle.

He was on me like a devil and tore off the covers. He squirmed a bit and it was soon over. Momina hadn't yet come back when Febo was on his feet beside the bed with his hair up like a dog's; he brushed it down with his hand.

"Now will you let us sleep?" I said.

When he was gone, I took off my dress and wrapped myself in the blankets. I drowsed off before Momina returned.

14.

The next morning I was already downstairs drinking my coffee when Momina came down. I had left her with her face sunk in the pillow and her back bare as I had seen her the evening of the first party. She came down all fixed up, but dark around the eyes. She seated herself smiling, put down her bag, and said quietly: "We're a couple of early birds."

She had some coffee and looked at me. "Shall we go?" she said, putting down the cup.

"Shouldn't we pay first?"

"It would be sweet, but do we have to?" She squinted at me with an absent air. "It would be a nice surprise when he wakes up. Brat."

So we left. She said no more. We got into the car in the garage and were immediately in the country.

"It's early to go to the Molas. Let's have a breath of air. Do you know the Canavese?"

So we drove around a Canavese completely hidden in fog and passed through two or three villages.

Her eyes on the road, she said suddenly: "A good girl, Rosetta, isn't she?"

"What's this story about Loris?"

"A year ago," Momina said, "when Rosetta was painting. She

took lessons from him. Then she quit. Loris was in the house all the time ... You know Loris."

"Like our friend last night," I said.

Momina smiled. "Not exactly."

"You don't mean he's ... ?" I ventured.

"What?" Momina exclaimed, looking at me closely. "Oh, that ... No. Old gossip. I would know."

"A difficult girl ... Suppose a farce like last night had happened to her."

"But she went to the hotel alone," Momina said. "She told me. She doesn't fake with me. Only Adele sees love at the bottom of everything ... Rosetta understands these things."

"Well, what did she poison herself for?" I asked. "At her age?"

"Not for love, I'm sure of that," Momina said, frowning. "She lives the same life I used to lead, the same all of us lead ... We know all about the Febos ..."

She was silent awhile, intent on the road.

"I don't know," I said, "but they make a lot of trouble. It would be better if there weren't any."

"Maybe. But I'd miss them. Wouldn't you? Imagine it. All of them sweet and dignified, all nice and respectable. No moments of truth. Nobody would ever need to come out of his den, to show what he really is, ugly and piggish as he is. How would you get to know men?"

"I think you like to enjoy them." I got that far and then stopped. I saw that I was being a fool, that Momina was worse off than I and laughed at these things.

But she didn't laugh now; she whistled, a light, contemptuous whistle. "Shall we go back?" she said.

The humming of the motor was making me drowsy and I thought about the night, about Febo's red hair. The light mist under the sun gave me a sense of freshness, and suddenly there came into my mind the tiled dairy bar I had entered alone so many mornings before hurrying to the shop, while Guido was sleeping satiated in my bed.

"Well, why do you think Rosetta did it then?" Momina suddenly asked.

Cesare Pavese

"I don't know," I said. "Perhaps . . ."

"It just doesn't make sense," she said curtly. "She looks at you with those frightened eyes . . . keeps closed up . . . She's never discussed things with us. You know what I want to say . . ."

When we got to Montalto the shutters were still closed, but a chilly sun was flooding the garden. Momina was telling me how strongly she was overcome at times by disgust—not just a nausea from this or that person, from an evening or a season, but a disgust with living, with everything and everyone, with time itself that goes so fast and yet never seems to go. Momina lit a cigarette and sounded the horn.

"We'll discuss it another time," she said, laughing.

The gardener opened the gate. We rolled up on the gravel. When we got out in front of the steps, the mother, frightened, appeared at the door.

"There's so damned much that doesn't make sense," Momina added.

We set off for Turin in a caravan, Rosetta with us; the mother with a maid and chauffeur in the big car sent up from Turin just for the trip. All morning, while waiting for the car, we had strolled around the villa and garden talking and looking at the mountains. Once I was alone with Rosetta; she took me upstairs to a terrace where as a child, she told me, she would shut herself up for hours at a time to read and look at the treetops. Down there—she said— was Turin, and on summer evenings she sat in that corner and thought of the seaside towns she had visited, about Turin and winter, the new faces she would some day meet.

"They often fool you," I said, "don't you think?"

She said: "You have to look them in the eyes. Everything's in their eyes."

"There's another way of knowing them," I said. "Working with them. When people work, they give themselves away. It's hard to fake on a job."

"What job?" she said.

So we rode to Turin while I thought to myself that neither she nor Momina knew what work was; they had never earned their dinner or their stockings or the trips they had taken and were taking. I thought of how the world is, that everybody works in order

228

to stop working, but if somebody doesn't work, you get mad. I thought of the old Mola woman, the signora, whose work was to agitate herself over her daughter, to run after her, see that she didn't lack anything; and her daughter paid her back with those terrors. I thought of Gisella and her little store—"we're squeezed in upstairs"—and all to keep them from doing anything, to keep them on velvet. I became nasty. I saw Febo's face. I started to think of Via Po.

I went there before evening, after first taking a bath in the hotel. Nobody had come looking for me, not even Morelli. But on the table was a bunch of lilacs with a telegram from Maurizio. This too, I thought. Doing nothing all day, he had time to think of such things. It was just a month since I had left Rome.

I found Becuccio supervising the arrival of the crystal chandeliers. He wasn't wearing his gray-green trousers or the heavy sweater any more, but a windbreaker with a yellow scarf. The leather wristband was there, as always. His curly hair and white teeth had a curious effect on me. While I talked I was very nearly on the point of reaching out and touching his ear. It's the mountain air, I thought, scared.

Instead I became very cold with him over the lateness of the shipments.

"The architect . . ." he said.

"The architect has nothing to do with it," I cut in. "It's your job to keep after the suppliers . . ."

Together we checked the crystals and I liked the way his large hands felt about in the straw for the brackets and pendants. In the newly plastered room, under an unshaded bulb, the prisms shone like rain in the beam of headlights. We held them up against the light. He said: "It's like when you're cutting tracks with an acetylene torch." He had been a worker on the night shift for the trolley line—the usual story. Once I felt him taking my hand under the straw. I told him to watch out. "It's expensive stuff."

He answered: "I know."

"All right then," I said. We finished the boxes.

15.

The people in Rome talked as though the shop would be ready by mid-March, but the vaulting on the first floor still had to be done. Working with Febo became difficult; he began saying that they didn't understand anything in Rome and that if I didn't know how to get my way he did. He came back from Ivrea with a foxy look; he never mentioned the bill at the hotel, but he began using the familiar *tu*. I told him I took orders in Rome but that in Turin I gave them, and how much did he want for his trouble. Keeping my voice down, I let him have it. The next day a bunch of flowers arrived, which I gave to Mariuccia.

But Rome was a headache. In a long evening phone call they gave me the news: the shop and windows were to stay the same, but the furnishings in the fitting rooms and the large salon on the first floor were to be changed; they were to be named according to the style of the decorations. We had to find mirrors, materials, lamps, prints, but they didn't know yet whether baroque or what. I had to tell the architect, make plans, take photographs, send someone to Rome. Suspend everything. Rugs and curtains, too.

"For the fifteenth?" I asked.

"Send the architect here."

I didn't send him, I went myself. The next evening, after a bath in my own apartment, and after airing the rooms, I was walking on familiar cobblestone. Two miserable days of sirocco followed during which I saw the usual bored faces and nobody came to the point. That was the Rome I knew. Halfway through a discussion some man, some woman would come in, start talking, jump up, and say: "But you have to think of this . . ." Somebody was always missing, the person who had called the conference. Madame was on the point of summoning Febo, then gave up the idea. We had our best talk at a table in the Columbia while the others were dancing. All I managed was to convince her that it was best to open definitely in May with the summer models, but I got an idea of what they had in mind. One of them had said that Turin is such a difficult city. I explained that there are limits to what you can do even in Turin.

Maurizio, too, got bored unexpectedly. He thought it was his duty to wait for me, stay beside me, follow me. He ostentatiously didn't mention Turin. I didn't mention Morelli. I was conscious of being much more alone in Rome, climbing those streets or dropping into Gigi's for coffee, than I had been in Turin in my hotel bed or in the Via Po. The last evening we came in late under a wind that shook the street lamps and rattled the shutters. I didn't tell him that certain hints from madame had made it clear that they were putting me in charge of the Turin shop and that I wouldn't be able to come back to Rome. I told him to stay in bed the next morning and not come to the station.

It was drizzling in Turin. Everything was chilly, melancholy, foggy; if it hadn't been March, I would have said November. When Febo heard that I had come back from Rome, there he was, grinning, with a cigarette in the corner of his mouth, but he wasn't very sure of himself. When I told him about this business of the baroque, he grinned happily again.

"So now, Clelia," he said softly, "what will you do?"

"I'll look for a decorator who knows baroque," I said.

"Turin is full of baroque. It's all over the place, but never baroque enough..."

"They know that in Rome," I said, "but they don't know what baroque is..."

"Let's do it like this," he said, and began throwing off sheet after sheet of rapid sketches.

He smoked and sketched all evening. He was good. I watched that red, bony hand, scarcely aware that it was his. It annoyed me that he should know so much, young as he was, and make light of it all, as if his talent were so much money he had accidentally found in his pocket. He told me earlier that he had gone to architecture school only on days when he knew a certain girl would be there. He had learned his trade while traveling the world with his mother, a crazy old lady who furnished and refurnished houses the way she would open and close a beach umbrella. He explained gaily that there was no need to change anything in the rooms, we had only to go to the antique dealers, and it needn't all be baroque —some could be provincial, in the worst taste—but we had to arrange the things well, give them proper stage lighting. He knocked himself out laughing and tried to kiss me. We were in the hotel lobby. I let him kiss my hand.

The next day Morelli appeared, excited, asking where I had

been for so long. I told him he had to help me because the young of Turin were really in poor shape and we old people had to stick together. I asked him if he knew the antique dealers, if he knew anything about style in furniture.

When he understood what I wanted, he asked if I were setting up house in Turin.

Then I took him to the Via Po and showed him the rooms.

"Your painter friends, what do they say?" he asked.

"If they only understood paintings . . ."

"Here the pictures will be the mirrors," he said seriously. "No need to let your customers disappear. There's no painting that's worth a beautiful woman undressing."

He accompanied me to the antique stores on the Via Mazzini and meanwhile we talked of Rome. "It would be easier in Rome," I said. "Rome is full of old houses being broken up . . ."

They weren't fooling in Turin either. Those shops were the honey and we the flies. You could hardly move among the mountains of stuff—ivory pieces, peeling canvases, grandfather clocks, figurines, artificial flowers, necklaces, fans. At first glance everything seemed old and decrepit, but after a while you could see there wasn't a piece—not a miniature, not an umbrella handle—that didn't make your mouth water. Morelli said: "They aren't showing us the best. They don't know who we are." He looked me over and said: "My wife should be here."

Crossing the street, he asked: "What do you think of all this stuff?"

"It hurts to think that when you die everything you own ends up like this in other people's hands."

"It's worse when it ends up like that before you're dead," Morelli said. "If our beautiful friend were here, she would say that we also pass from hand to hand, the hands of those who want us. The only thing that saves people is money, which passes through everybody's hands."

Then the talk shifted to women and houses and to Donna Clementina, who was a girl when some of those parasols and guitars and mottled mirrors were new. "She knew how to set herself up. No man could have claimed to have *her* in hand. These boys make me laugh, these girl friends of Mariella who have the vices but not the experience ... They think it's enough to talk. I'd like to see them in twenty years ... The old lady got where she wanted to go ..."

We went into another shop. We didn't talk baroque. I told Morelli that it was better to see a palace, a house, and find how things should look in their natural setting. "Let's go to Donna Clementina's," he said. "That evening there were too many people, but the porcelains alone are worth ..."

16.
We arrived just as some women were leaving; they stared at me. Twenty years ago my route never went through that quarter of Turin. We found Mariella and her mother, who had just had tea; the grandmother—unfortunately—was napping, she was preparing for the evening, when a certain Rumanian violinist was coming to play and she wanted to be present. A few friends were expected, would we care to join them?

Mariella looked at me reproachfully and while we were going into the room with the porcelains she scolded me for not having told her in time about the trip to Saint Vincent. "Come this evening," she said. "Rosetta and the whole crowd will be here."

"I haven't been seeing anybody. What are you all doing?"

"I can't tell," she said mysteriously. "You'll have to see to find out."

I pulled Morelli's coattail just in time to keep him from telling those gossips the story of my fitting rooms. Mariella's mother lit the showcase lights and told us something about each piece. She spoke of her great grandfather, of weddings, of aunts, of the French Revolution. Morelli told us the names of some of the pink, bewigged women in the miniatures hanging on the walls. There was a certain Giudetta—also in the family—who had lain under a tree in the royal gardens and the king of that epoch let cherries fall through the branches into her mouth. I looked closely and tried to understand these things, what they were made of and the artist's secret—the way you do with a dress—but I didn't get very far. The elegance of the figurines and the little painted portraits was made out of air, and without the names, conversation, and family stories that went with them, they weren't enough to create an atmosphere. I really had to rely on Febo.

So that evening we returned to listen to the violinist. I saw the fierce old lady again, with her shawl and her ribbon around the neck; I saw the circle of solemn old gentlemen, the lamps, the rug. Youth was less in evidence this time; they sat uncomfortably on the upholstered chairs. No Loris. Rosetta and Momina smiled at me from among the women.

The violinist played well, as violinists usually do on these occasions. He was a fat little man with white hair who kissed all the women's hands; it wasn't clear if he were being paid or had come as a friend. He laughed with his tongue in his cheek and looked at our legs. A lymphatic lady wearing glasses and a rose at her shoulder accompanied him on the piano. The women shouted: "Bravo!" All in all, I was bored.

Morelli clapped enthusiastically. When tea came, I looked for Rosetta and Momina. "As soon as the old lady gets up," we said, "we'll go too."

Mariella cornered me. "I'm coming too," she said. "Wait for me."

She ended by dragging along everyone, including the violinist. Outside the large entrance door the bespectacled lady started to shout. "The maestro wants to treat us." Everybody was speaking French.

In the car I found myself next to Rosetta. I said in the dark and confusion: "It's turned out badly. Ivrea was better."

"It's not morning yet," Momina said, getting in.

For the violinist, who was with the women and Morelli in Mariella's big car, treating us meant circling around the center of town, stopping in front of cafés, putting his head out, arguing, and then giving the signal to start off again. After three or four of these games, Momina said: "Go to the devil," and set off on her own.

"Where are we going?"

"To your hotel," she said.

We entered the salon gaily and noisily. Several people raised their heads.

"Doesn't it give you the shivers?" she said to Rosetta, who walked between us with clenched fists.

Rosetta smiled thinly. She said: "There's a possibility that nobody paid my bill. They might throw us out..."

"You never came back?" Momina asked.

Rosetta shrugged.

"Where shall we sit?" I asked.

The waiter brought us three cognacs. Behind the bar, Luis winked at me.

"Let's hope Mariella doesn't find us," I said. "I'm afraid the Rumanian won't do much treating."

"In all those people, somebody will offer to pay," Rosetta said.

Then I said it was funny but in Turin I had to avoid people. So many painters, inflated nobodies, musicians, a new one everywhere you turned—not even in Rome were people so continuously on holiday. And there was Mariella, too, who wanted to act at any cost. You wouldn't think there had ever been a war...

Rosetta, twirling her brandy glass, smiled from the chair. "She's talking about us too," she said quietly. "Why do we lead such lives?"

"I don't know," I said. "It seems to me that so much noise isn't worth the effort."

Momina, who hadn't yet sat down, paced restlessly between us and the bar. "Nothing's worth the effort," she said. "Before the war, you could travel at least."

Then she threw herself into a chair and put her hand down to take off her shoes.

"I'm afraid it's not done here," she said. "Haven't you got a couple of comfortable chairs in your room?"

We went up in the elevator. I watched Rosetta's movements. We came out in the corridor and she looked at me sideways; I nodded as if to say that it had happened here.

"All these corridors are alike," she said, keeping her eyes on Momina.

"Like the days of the year," Momina said. "All the doors are alike, and the beds, the windows, and the people who sleep here for one night... You need Clelia's courage to live here..."

"Or hers," I said, meaning Rosetta.

"Listen," Momina said, without turning around, "now that they're bringing up our cognac, if you like we'll put out the lights and you can tell us how you ended up here and made a mistake on the dosage . . . I still don't believe . . ."

Suddenly Rosetta stopped, very pale, clenched her fists and bit her lips. But we were at the door, and I said: "Let's go in." Rosetta went in silently. No one spoke between the moment we sat down (Momina threw off her shoes) and when the waiter put the tray on the table, and I became aware that Rosetta's eyes were filling with tears. Momina hadn't noticed anything.

"Aren't you going to sit down, Rosetta?" she said.

Rosetta shook her head angrily, went to the door, turned out the lights, and replied in a hoarse voice: "There, it's done."

For several moments, only the red tip of Momina's cigarette showed in the dark. One heard the distant rattling of a trolley. I began to make out the lighter rectangle of the window.

"Are you mad at me?" Momina said mockingly.

I could feel Rosetta's effort to control her voice. She didn't succeed. She stammered slowly: "You shouldn't laugh . . ."

"I do it to buck you up," Momina said coldly. "I do it for your own good. Try to be intelligent. You are, you know. What happened? I've done nothing. Have I insulted you? Have I told you to do this or not do that? I've only helped you to see clearly the messes you make . . . Does that scare you? I understand suicide . . . everyone thinks of it . . . but one has to do it right, make it real . . . Do it without recriminations . . . Instead, you act like a dressmaker's assistant who's been abandoned . . ."

"I . . . hate you," Rosetta stammered, breathing heavily.

"But why?" Momina said, serious. "What have you got to reproach me for? For having been too much to you, or too little? What does it matter, we're friends."

Rosetta didn't reply and Momina didn't continue. I heard her breathing. I put my glass down blindly in the dark. I murmured: "Sit down."

She sat down. I realized I could talk. Then I said that though it was no affair of mine, seeing that we were together I also had a right to talk. I had heard all kinds of stories about what she had done, and none was true. "If it's something between the two of you," I said, "say what you have to say and be done with it."

Momina twisted around in the armchair, looking for a cigarette. The light of her match nearly blinded me, I caught sight of her short hair over her eyes.

"What is it? Have you made love together?"

Neither replied. Momina began to laugh and cough.

17.

"You can't even say that's it," Momina took up again in a querulous voice. By that time I could finally make out their faces. "It's a good thing you put out the lights, dear. Can't you see that you've made a personal matter, a hysterical drama, out of something that might have been good and had some sense? Did you hear what Clelia said?"

She had heard, and must have been burning red. I don't think she was still crying or afraid. "You two have nothing to do with it," she said harshly, in her unreasonable voice. "I'm twenty-three, I know what life is. I don't have it in for anyone. Let's talk about something else, if you don't mind?"

"At least tell us what it feels like. Whom one thinks about at that moment. Did you look in the mirror?"

She didn't talk mockingly now, but with a baby voice, as if she were playing a part. Even before, when they put out the lights, it seemed like a scene in a play. Again the thought came to me that there had been absolutely no one on the stretcher that evening.

Rosetta said she hadn't looked in the mirror. She didn't remember if there were any mirrors in the room. She had turned out the lights then, too. She didn't want to see anything or anybody, just to sleep. She had a tremendous, a terrible headache. Which suddenly went away, leaving her stretched out and happy. How happy she was. It seemed a miracle. Then she woke up, in the hospital, under a lamp that hurt her eyes.

"Disgusted?" Momina murmured.

"Uh," Rosetta said. "Waking up is horrible ..."

"I knew a cashier in Rome," I said, "who went crazy from seeing herself all the time in the mirror behind the bar ... She got to thinking she was somebody else."

Momina said: "One should look at oneself in the mirror ... You've never had the courage, Rosetta."

We talked on like that, about mirrors and the eyes of a person killing herself. When the waiter came with another tray, we turned on the lights. Rosetta's face was calm and hard.

The telephone rang. It was Mariella and she wanted to know what had happened. She couldn't make out what I said because at her end an orchestra was blaring. I looked questioningly at the two women. I shouted into the phone that I had come home because I was tired. That they should dance and enjoy themselves. That it had been a pleasant evening.

Then Rosetta used the phone. She called her house. She said: "Mama, I'm coming home now." Momina put on her shoes and they went away.

The next day Rosetta paid me a visit in the Via Po. She came in smiling uneasily, in her leopard coat. Febo was upstairs with Becuccio, taking measurements. "You certainly don't want to meet our friend," I said. "Will you go shopping with me?" She waited for me in the large room while I shouted upstairs that I was going out. Seeing Rosetta so young, standing there beside the window, I thought of Mariella: "Mariella would make a first-class cashier."

Walking under the porticoes, I told her that I had thought of giving her a job. She smiled. "I've got an idea," I said. "A shop staffed by your most distinguished friends. Would you come in on it? The best names in Turin ... One at the cash register, one behind the showcases, others in the fitting rooms ..."

She took up the joke. She said: "Who would come to buy? There'd be nobody left."

"Your servants, perhaps ... People without names."

"We wouldn't know how to do anything ..."

"Who knows? Like charity parties ..."

"Oitana, I envy you," she said. "It's nice to work as you do."

"Sometimes it's hell. There's always a boss."

"Maybe that's what work is. Having someone to tell you what to do or not to do. It's a salvation."

"Try telling your maid that."

She hesitated. "Yesterday," she said. "I was a fool." I didn't interrupt. ". . . One says and does many false things ... You know what I mean. I'd like to be someone else, like that cashier in

Rome . . . even crazy like her. You shouldn't believe what Momina says . . . Momina is exasperating at times."

"She's been more discreet than I have." I hesitated, holding her eye.

"You, Oitana, know a lot about life . . ." She searched for words. "You wouldn't think much of two women who talked the way we did last night, would you?"

She had stopped stubbornly and was devouring me with her eyes. Yesterday evening, in the dark, she must have been as red as this.

I made her move on. I said that as long as a woman can still blush, you can't say much against her. (She excused herself, saying: "I blush over nothing.") I told her that everything is all right as long as you don't impair your health and don't get ugly ideas in your head. I asked her if that was why she had taken the Veronal.

We had stopped in front of the florist on the Via Pietro Mica. It was easier to talk. I said: "Shall we send Mariella some flowers, for yesterday?"

"Let's," she said.

We chose lilies of the valley. While the woman arranged the green, I said to Rosetta: "At your age they aren't vices. Vices come later."

"I don't think I have any," she said wryly. "It would be better if I did."

When we returned under the porticoes, I asked her what game we were playing now. She hadn't tried to kill herself for that?

Rosetta, surprised, said that she had no idea herself why she went to the hotel that night. In fact she had gone in happy. She was feeling relieved after the dance. For a long time, nights had made her shudder, the idea of having got through another day, of being alone with her disgusts, of waiting for morning, stretched out in bed—all became unbearable. That night, anyhow, was nearly over. But then, precisely because she hadn't slept but paced around the room thinking of night, of all the stupid things that had happened at night, and now she was alone again and couldn't do anything, little by little she became desperate, and finding the Veronal in her bag . . .

"Wasn't Momina at the dance?"

No, Momina wasn't, but at the hotel she, Rosetta, stretched out in bed, had thought about her a great deal, had thought about many things Momina had said—Momina who was even more fed up with life than she, but who laughed and said: "I'll wait for good weather before killing myself. I don't want to be buried in the rain."

"I," Rosetta said, "didn't have the patience to wait any longer."

"But you haven't quarreled with Momina?"

"No, we argue sometimes, like last night, but we're good friends. Momina's the only friend I have."

For what that was worth. I said sharply: "Only a friend?"

She looked at me, thin, with her cat's eyes. She began to blush faintly, then nervously got control of herself.

"What are you trying to make me say, Oitana?" she said. "Is it necessary? But I'm not ashamed. You know how it is with girls. Momina was my first love. A long time ago, before she got married ... Now we're just friends, believe me."

18.

I had to believe her. I asked her why she didn't think about marriage. She shrugged her shoulders, said that she knew men. "Perhaps not all of them," I observed.

"It's not necessary," she said.

"Don't tell me you're like Momina—afraid of having children."

"I like babies," she said. "But they ought to stay babies. When I think that afterwards they grow up and become people like us, I get mad ... Don't you think?"

"I don't have any," I said.

We left, promising to meet again, but I was sure she wouldn't come back. Rosetta had come to see me either from ingenuousness or because she didn't think much of me, but now she must have realized that it was impossible to keep our distances. We always came back to the same subject.

I went to Milan to inspect some glass tables and shelves with Febo, who borrowed a car for the trip. Everything went well, except that on the way back, when we stopped to light our cigarettes, Febo, with the look in his eyes of that night in Ivrea, let his hands start wandering. I gave him such a black eye that I thought I had blinded him, but starting off again, he behaved himself; I told him the world was large and one shouldn't make love with the people one works with. He watched the road sheepishly. I asked why he didn't try again with Momina, or even find himself a wife among Momina's friends. Rich and educated people who knew how to paint and put on plays. He looked at me, amused. He stopped the car. Oh, oh, here we are again, I thought. "Clelia, Clelia," he said, without touching me, "be my wife this evening."

"Is that a serious proposal?"

"We're already husband and wife. You socked me."

"I can be your mother, if you like."

"Yes, yes." He clapped his hands. "Yes, Mama. Will you take me to the fields to gather snails?"

However, we stopped to dance at a pavilion in a town outside Turin and Febo began to quarrel good-naturedly with a young couple who were dancing and had blocked our way. They threatened to give him another black eye. It was astounding the way Febo, blond and hairy, took chances in that country place where he didn't know the dialect. I told him to cut it out, and had to pull him away. Then he suggested dinner in some dive and asked me if I didn't like to break out sometimes and raise hell.

"That's not hard," I said. "What's ugly is making a dive the center of your life."

"Well then, let's do something ugly," he said.

We found a little joint at the end of Corso Giulio Cesare in Turin. At first Febo kept quiet and thought only of eating. But the host wasn't the hairy fellow at Ivrea and didn't have much in the kitchen. A red-eyed girl in slippers brought us our food, looking hard at my stockings, while the others there, an old woman and some truck drivers, watched us. The room was cold, freshly plastered, and already dirty; I thought how in my time this was all countryside, open roads and countryside.

"The things we do are truly unpleasant," I told Febo.

He tried to liven up and find the wine good. Behind the bar, the girl kept her red eyes on us. The others were now playing cards, smoking and spitting.

When we had finished the omelet, I suggested we go. "But there must be a place near here . . ." he said. When we went out, it was dark. A wind blew against the red neon signs along the avenue. "This city has its own kind of beauty," Febo said. "You don't understand, you live too much with the gentry."

I got into the car mad enough to throttle him. "It's you people, those stupid girls, the Mariellas and the Mominas, who like to act like gentry," I said. "I was born in Turin. I know what it's like to see someone else wearing silk stockings and not to have them yourself . . ."

While we were still arguing, and he was cackling derisively, we stopped again, in front of a café with an illuminated garden.

"Blood flows here at night," he said.

The light came from the windows of a large room lit by naked bulbs. There wasn't an orchestra. A radio played, and several couples were dancing and shouting on the cement floor. I knew those places.

"If you don't like the main room," Febo said in my ear, "there's a place upstairs."

I said I'd have a cup of coffee but wouldn't stay. We weren't the right company for each other in such a place. "I might very well drop you," I said, "and go with that type wearing the big silk neckerchief."

Febo looked at the boy in the foulard chattering at a table with two women with smeared lipstick. The boy raised an eyebrow, not answering, leaning back against the bar.

"That boy," I said, "doesn't dream of coming to see you or me to spend an evening. He doesn't have this itch to move around. Elegance for him is the perfume he buys in the tobacco stores and red and green neckties. He works with those girls. Why amuse yourself at his expense?"

Febo planted his elbows on the bar behind him and looked at the fellow. Not yet drunk, he grumbled: "Who's talking now? The woman or the colleague?"

I called him a clown and said I was serious.

Then, looking up, he asked me what sort of place I had been born in.

"Like this, more or less," I said dryly.

The young man with the foulard had discovered that Febo was

staring at him and had begun to stare back. "And you," Febo said, still looking brassily around the room, "you got out of your environment, put on silk stockings, and now you amuse yourself at the expense of us respectable and educated people. Who asked you to?"

As he spoke, he stared at the foulard, who had started to come over. I felt something brewing in the room and was blinded by anger, fear, and an instinct to stop the foulard. I slapped Febo in the face with everything I had, yelled something, and dragged him off by the arm. Everyone laughed and made way. We reached the car in a shower of laughter and insults from the door.

I said: "Get going, you fool."

Teeth clenched, he started the car and crossed over the Dora as if the bridge were collapsing under us. "I want to get out here," I said.

His face was half resentful, half amused. "And I want to drink," he said. "Everybody treats me like a drunk. I might at least be one."

My hands were still shaking and I kept quiet. I let him run on. But I seemed to have taken the slap myself and couldn't calm down. He's no worse than the others, I said to myself; in his circle they're all like that. I kept saying it over and over to myself and wondered if it was worth the effort to work and get where I had got and not be anything, be worse off than Momina, who at least lived among her own kind. Other times I had consoled myself by saying it wasn't what I had got but the act of getting it that made my life worthwhile. "This is a destiny like any other," I said, "and I made it myself." But my hands were trembling and I had trouble calming down.

Finally I said dryly again that I wanted to get out. I opened the car door. Then Febo began kissing me wherever he could put his lips, moaning; then he stopped. I jumped out and went off.

19. It's not easy to avoid leisured people. When I got back to the hotel, I found an invitation to a de luxe auction, with a note initialed by Morelli saying he would phone me the next day. It began to sink in on me that if I had rented a room on arriving in Turin I would never have met Morelli or anyone. Except Febo,

unfortunately. But that was the sort of life I was living—useless to lament the end of the calm disorder of my life in Rome. These things pass away by themselves. Many times in the past years I had found myself in a similar whirl. It was almost laughable: only Maurizio was left. And how long would he be left?

For several days the work in Via Po discouraged me. I was needed there all the time. I had to run around, think of everything, explore every corner of the city. Twenty years before, I wouldn't have thought it possible. Since when had I been so clever? It was as though I also were putting on a play, like the leisured people of Turin, and after all it was only proper that I should have them underfoot when I was working for them. When I think like this, I'd like to be able to get away, drop everything, go back to the workshop.

Even Becuccio had to have his say about the antique furniture. He knew a couple of cabinetmakers, father and son, who before the war had worked at the Royal Palace and had done some delicate restorations. We went to find them. They were at the back of a courtyard up a dirty, narrow alley, but inside it was an old palace; there were even some trees and a statue. The cabinetmaker, a little old man who touched his glasses suspiciously, began to chatter in the open yard. When he realized what we wanted, he said it was a shame to put beautiful furniture in a shop. Modern stuff, veneered and enameled, would do. I told him that we'd already hashed that out, that I wanted to see something. What did I want to see, he asked, since the palaces were all closed? I didn't want to see the palaces, I said, all I wanted was an idea, I wanted to orient myself. He said that if I didn't want to see, it was clear that I didn't understand anything about it, and in that case I might as well put the usual stuff in the shop.

Becuccio asked if he didn't have some work underway. The old man turned to the open shop and shouted into the dark. Somebody moved in the back.

"Do we have anything?" the old man shouted.

The other grunted.

"There isn't anything," said the old man, touching his glasses. "What do you expect? Nobody wants to work for people any more."

Becuccio was irritated and began to lecture him, and I had to drag him away too. The cabinetmaker had retreated into his shop and wouldn't answer him. We returned together to Via Po, where Febo was waiting for me to choose the materials for the walls. I told Becuccio that it was nice to live like the old man and slam the door in people's faces and work only when you liked.

"He can't have much work," Becuccio said. "Politics has gone to his head."

Then I went to the auction with Morelli, and there were some beautiful pendulum clocks and sets of tableware. Every now and then a "this would do" escaped from me; but I remembered I was there only to pass the time and give Morelli an excuse for keeping me company.

"Wouldn't you like to set up a house of your own?" Morelli asked.

"Yes . . . if some day a certain Clelia gets one for me . . ."

He enjoyed the role he played among those crystals, and the women who inspected me out of the corners of their eyes; some he said hello to. I thought how many of them must know Momina, Febo, Mariella, and the painters. Turin is pretty small.

I asked Morelli if there were any really serious people in that upper crust. He asked: Serious about what? "If they have vices," I said, "if they gamble away their inheritances, if they are as lazy as they want to be. Up to now I've found only some people a little be-spattered, or some kids . . ."

"The fact is," Morelli said, "that we're younger than the kids. They're still nowhere."

"I mean the old people like you and me, those with the time and means. Do they at least enjoy their vices? If I didn't have to work, I'd have terrible vices. At bottom I'm not at all satisfied with my life . . ."

Morelli, serious, told me that one vice I did have: I had the vice of working, of never taking a vacation. "You're worse than the industrialist fathers of families," he said, "but they at least were men with mustaches and built Turin."

"I don't have a family and I don't have mustaches yet," I said.

Morelli looked around.

"There is one who's really been serious," I said. "The Mola girl . . ."

"You think so?" he said dubiously. Then he suddenly became irritated. "Working night and day for one's family ought to mean something. If I had a daughter who played such tricks on me, I'd have shut her in a convent long ago. Once they knew how to do such things."

"I believe," I said, looking around, "that girls in convents always begin by making love together."

"But gentlewomen came out"—Morelli warmed up—"ladies, real mistresses of the house. At least they knew how to talk."

"Not that that's so bad," I went on. "A girl always falls in love with the one who's most on her toes. But here in Turin they don't even take these things seriously. They are sad and have a belly-ache."

"They talk . . ." Morelli said.

And what were we doing? The only good moments I had in Turin were really the evenings when I dropped in on a movie alone, or mornings over my coffee behind a window in Via Roma where nobody knew me and I sketched projects and imagined myself setting up some kind of shop. My real vice, which Morelli hadn't mentioned, was my pleasure in being alone. It's not young girls who are better off in convents, but ourselves. I thought of that grandmother of Mariella's who at eighty liked to see people and listen from her bed to other people's noise. I thought of Carlotta, who had led her own life. All in all, living is really putting up with someone else and going to bed with him, whether you feel like it or not. Having money means you can isolate yourself. But then why do leisured people with money always look for company and noise?

When I was a girl, I envied people like Momina, Mariella, and the others. I envied them and didn't know what they were. I imagined them free, admired, mistresses of the world. Thinking it over now, I wouldn't exchange places with any of them. Their lives seemed foolish to me, all the more so because they didn't realize it themselves. But could they act otherwise? Would I have acted otherwise in their place? Rosetta Mola was naïve, but she had taken things seriously. At bottom it was true she had no motive for wanting to kill herself, certainly not because of that stupid story of her first love for Momina, or some other mess. She wanted to be alone, to isolate herself from the uproar; and in her world you can't be alone or do anything alone unless you take yourself out of it completely. Now Momina and the others had already taken her up again: we all went together to pick her up at Montalto. Just remembering that day depressed me.

20. Rosetta returned, days later. This time too she stopped hesitatingly at the door. Becuccio saw her and said: "She's not looking for me."

That morning we were taking photographs to send to Rome and Febo turned the lights in the niches on and off, rearranging the position of a statuette that served as a model. He joked with Rosetta and told her that at Ivrea he had been seduced and deserted by two bad women. Then he wanted to photograph the two of us in front of the windows to let them know in Rome what Turin women are like.

"We need Mariella," I said.

We ended by talking about the play and Rosetta said that now Nene was preparing the set. "That's all she knows how to do," Febo said.

I asked Rosetta if she painted any more.

"It was just for fun," she said. "You can't play all the time."

"These Turin girls," Febo said, "know how to paint, act, play instruments, dance, knit. Some of them never leave off."

Rosetta looked at me sadly. Her dress reminded me that there was sun outside, a beautiful March day.

"Only the trades that hunger drives you to, you never drop," Rosetta said. "I'd like to have to earn my living knitting."

Febo said that hunger wasn't enough to make you succeed: you had to know your trade the way starving people know hunger, and practice it like gentlemen.

"Everybody who wants to doesn't die of hunger," Rosetta said, looking at us with those still eyes, "and the gentleman is not always the one with money."

Becuccio stood there listening, and the photographer—black bow tie, like Loris—rubbed his hands.

I said we must hurry. While they were shooting pictures I took Rosetta upstairs and down and showed her how the shop had turned out. She also liked the curtains and the other materials. We discussed the lighting. I was called to the phone.

"I'm leaving," Rosetta said. "Thanks."

"We'll see each other again," I said.

In the evening I saw Momina with some other people—new people, possible future clients—and there was talk of an auto trip, of going to the Riviera some Sunday. "Let's tell Rosetta, too," Momina said.

"Of course."

Some days later, Mariella and Rosetta drove up to Via Po, and Mariella, blond and fresh, shouted from the driver's seat that I should take a ride with them. "I work mornings," I said.

"Come and visit us," she said. "Grandmother wants to get to know you better."

I waved to Rosetta and they left.

The next day Rosetta appeared at the door, alone.

"Come in," I said. "How are you?"

We walked under the porticoes, talking, and stopped to look at the copper engravings and dark leather bindings in Bussola's window.

"It might almost do for a living room the way it is," I said.

"Do you like books?" Rosetta said, livening up. "Do you read much?"

"During the war. One didn't know what to do. But now I don't manage at all. I always feel I'm putting my nose into somebody else's business . . ."

Rosetta was amused and look hard at me.

". . . It seems indecent. Like opening other people's letters . . ."

Rosetta, however, had read a little of everything. She had gone to the university, she admitted with embarrassment, almost ashamed.

"How was it that Momina studied in Switzerland?" I said.

Momina was the daughter of nobles who had spent their last penny in bringing her up. Then she had married a Tuscan land-owner, and it was nice that she had never let herself be called baroness. Anyhow, she no longer had the title. Rosetta knew Neri, her husband; she had been with Momina at Versailles the very summer that Neri was courting her. It had been a wonderful summer for Rosetta, too. She had enjoyed watching Momina torment Neri, like a mouse. Four years ago. Poor Neri, he was elegant and stupid.

"Just what one needs," I observed.

But after the marriage Neri had got his revenge. After all, his grandfather had only been a steward, one of those who go around on horseback, wearing riding boots. Neri had an excuse to stay in the country to look after his lands, and Momina had left him.

"You, Rosetta, are you like Neri or like Momina?" I asked her.

"How do you mean?"

"Your father's a working man," I said. "Do you admire your father?"

"I'm more like Momina," she said without hesitation, and smiled.

So we went to the Riviera. The novelty of this trip was Nene's coming too. We took two cars, two magnificent Studebakers. I was seated between Nene and Rosetta, and some baron drove us, a young man, a donkey who didn't know the score but did know paintings. He drove all the time, half turned around to talk to Nene about plays and Frenchmen. Momina was up ahead in Mariella's car, which was full of people I had barely met. It was still dark and rain was threatening. But everyone swore the sun always shone on the Riviera on Sunday.

Rosetta scarcely opened her mouth. Again I was amazed at Nene, sculptress or painter or whatever, thick-lipped and banged, and her shameless way of laughing like a baby. And yet she was thirty at least, only a little younger than I. She was also naïve and impulsive, and when Rosetta asked how Loris was and why he didn't come too, she got confused and dropped her voice as if caught in the act. Strange girl—she seemed like a lizard. Probably she really was clever, and anyhow artists are what they are.

But I was sleepy. We had spent the evening at the baron's house having dinner and waiting for the girls so we could leave. I drowsed off. We met a strong wind in the Apennines and the rain caught us on the road deep in the woods. Then, as the day slowly brightened, the rain thinned out, until we were running along the sea in warm air with the windows open, under the last showers. Here the gardens were green and already in flower. I asked Rosetta if she were going to the sea that year. She said no, she was going back to Montalto.

Our destination was a villa above Noli, but someone said: "Let's go to San Remo."

"As for me," the baron said, "I'd like a little nap."

While they talked, we got out in the square at Noli. Momina came up. At that hour, in the early light, the square was deserted, the cafés closed.

"We're early birds once again," Momina said to me.

Rosetta, her bag hanging from her shoulder, had her back to the sea as she leaned on the railing, smoking.

"I've never seen the sea at this hour," Nene said.

"You never do unless you stay up all night," Momina said, "but it's not worth the trouble. This breeze with the smell of flowers is better than the sea."

We set out again. The baron had won. We took the mountain road and, speeding between stone walls and around risky curves, we reached the villa, which was like a huge greenhouse among the magnolias.

21.

As we walked in the garden, Rosetta told us that last year she had wanted to become a nun. We had gone off, she, Momina, and I, into a little stand of trees, up to a balustrade from which you looked out at the sea.

"But they don't want girls like me," she said.

"Why not? If you have the money?" Momina said.

Rosetta began to laugh softly and said that the nuns had to be virgins.

Momina said: "It's a marriage like any other. All one asks of a bride is that she be dressed in white."

"It's beautiful up here," Rosetta said. "But tomorrow it won't be so nice. To keep some respect for the world and people, one should do without everything. A convent solves the problem."

"And what would you have done, all alone like that? Painted

Madonnas?" Momina asked. "I wouldn't know how to get through the days."

Rosetta shrugged off Momina's allusion. I was hardly aware of it myself. But Mariella and the others were already approaching under the magnolias, and Momina murmured: "One day at a time is enough. Let's get through this one . . ."

The weather was really promising, if only there hadn't been the women, sisters and friends of the baron, and their escorts, who insisted on making a fuss and wore out the tormented old caretakers opening the house, carrying stuff, putting the verandah in order. Momina took things in hand by suggesting that they assign us women a bedroom and let us rest for an hour.

The villa was a splendor, full of heavy furniture and armchairs, but all sheeted, even the lamps. The wooden shelves were still covered in waxed paper. "It's like a medieval castle," Momina said, walking along a corridor. When the coming and going to the bathroom stopped, I sat in a wicker chair and Mariella combed her hair at a mirror, Momina took off her shoes and collapsed on the bed, Nene and Rosetta gossiped at the open window. It reminded me of those American movies about girls who lived together in one room with an older girl, quite experienced, who plays wet nurse to the others. And I thought how phony it all was: the actress who plays the ingénue is the most divorced and the best paid. I laughed to myself, and Momina, who was smoking, said: "I hope they send up a drink."

"I don't understand," Mariella began, "why Donna Paola dresses like a gypsy that way, with those earrings . . ."

They talked for a while about the earrings and the absent women. At a certain point I gave a start in my chair: I had dozed off again. I felt the coolness of the room and heard Nene's aggressive voice exclaiming: "You're nasty, nasty. I don't have to mother anyone."

"You don't need to, but you do it," Momina said.

Nene, standing in the middle of the room, shouted stridently: "Men are babies. We artists are children twice over. If you take that away from us, what's left?"

"What do you want to take away?" Momina said. "There's nothing to take away from life, it's already zero. Ah," she turned over on the bed, "you make me sick."

From the window Rosetta said: "If you like him, Nene, pay no attention to what Momina says. She does it to make you angry."

"Of course," Mariella said.

"Who are you talking about?" I asked.

"That genius Loris," said Momina, jumping down from the bed. "He won't take a bath unless someone's in love with him. I prefer Fefé."

Downstairs they rang the gong. "Let's go," Momina said. "Girls into the living room."

On the verandah we ate the lunch that the custodians had combed the countryside to scare up. Donna Paola in her scarlet gypsy cloak acted as hostess and apologized because we had to pass the plates ourselves. We had Chianti and liqueurs in brandy glasses. Mariella chattered endlessly. Toward the end of lunch the curtains had to be drawn, the sun was so bright.

It wasn't yet noon. When we got up, they talked about what to do. Someone said: "Let's go down to the sea." Some wandered into the garden. I had a fat, homely fellow beside me who wanted to point out the antiquities of Noli from above. I brushed him off. I escaped to the second-floor bedroom and sat at the window.

From the garden rose shouts and voices that I recognized; they were talking again about going to San Remo. Suddenly my door opened; Mariella came in. "Oh, it's you," she said. "Excuse me." Behind her I caught sight of the baron.

"Should I leave?" I said.

Mariella smiled broadly and closed the door in the baron's face. "I was looking for you." She came up to me. "The trouble with these trips is that there's always somebody *de trop*," she chattered. "What I wanted to say, Clelia ... let's help poor Rosetta ... You know how sensitive and intelligent she is, we were such friends before ... We've got to get her away from her morbid thinking, distract her."

I waited to know what she was getting at. I could still see the baron's bewilderment.

"You tell her, too. I know you've been seeing each other. She doesn't like to come out with me. You can't keep these girls together. How hard it is to try to put something on."

"Perhaps Rosetta has grown up," I said. "She doesn't want to play dolls any longer."

"No, no," she said, "there are feuds, petty jealousies . . ."

"She doesn't seem to have anything against Nene."

"It's not that. Ever since Momina came out against the play—Momina, too! how silly—Rosetta wants nothing more to do with it, she's dropped us."

"I think," I said, "that Rosetta tried to kill herself because she was sick of Momina, of the play, of you, of everybody. Don't you think so?"

Taken aback, she flushed and looked at me. Then she went on vivaciously. "You exaggerate. Rosetta's an intelligent and sincere girl . . ."

"Exactly," I wanted to answer. "Exactly." But someone was knocking. It was Momina.

"We're going to San Remo," she announced. Then, narrowing her eyes, she said, "I'm surprised at you."

We didn't get to San Remo. Nene began to feel sick, to flail the air, toss around on the seat, groaning. "It's terrible. I'm dying. Stop." The first car stopped too. "It's nothing," the baron said. "Car sickness. This car acts that way."

The fat fellow and a woman in the other group were sick too. We made them lean over the low wall and vomit. Nene was the most tragic: dark-ringed eyes and wild talk. They explained to me that these big American cars were so comfortable and easily sprung that they gave you the sensation of rising and falling in sea swells.

We had stopped under a rocky overhang at a wide turning, facing the sea. Irritated, Rosetta looked at the scene.

"Do you feel well enough to go on?" we asked the three.

22. They didn't feel well enough, and so Momina and I walked down among the cacti to the beach. Mariella shouted to us to wait for her.

"This is the sea," Momina said, leaning against a wall.

"Mariella thinks you go too far with Rosetta," I told her.

"Does she?" she said coldly.

Mariella, shouting "Yoo-hoo," arrived with two or three men. "Shall we swim?" they said.

"No, go collect pebbles," Momina said, "but don't put them in your mouths."

They did, in fact, go away.

"Listen," I said, impressed, "do you see much of Febo?"

"He's a presumptuous, slimy, hairy boor. Satisfied?" She laughed. "Why? Are you interested in him?"

"No," I muttered. "I wanted to know if you like only women."

"What did that stupid girl say to you?"

"I'm the stupid girl. I can't understand why Rosetta doesn't marry. It's the only thing she can do. Is she still attached to you?"

Momina looked at me for a moment there in the sun.

"I don't like women, and neither does Rosetta. That's the truth. If I did like them, you can be sure I wouldn't think twice about it. It's an idea Rosetta has got into her head. It happened three years ago, we were at the sea, like today . . . She came in a room and found me . . . I wasn't alone. It was horseplay, like Ivrea. Then she wanted to be daring, but the impression stuck and she considers me . . . something . . . like her mirror. Do you understand?"

I understood. The story was so absurd that it had to be true. But it was clear she hadn't told me everything.

"Why doesn't she get married?"

"Would that change anything?" Momina said. "She doesn't need to make her own way. She knows what a man is . . . And then they keep her under lock and key at home."

Mariella returned with her men. Up above they were calling us; they had decided to drive back to Noli. I wasn't sorry they had decided against going to San Remo, but what would we do in Noli? As for me, I decided to spend the evening in the little town square.

We had left Nene in the other car; I was sitting between Momina and Rosetta. Mariella and the baron were in front, whispering and plotting together. He turned around suddenly to ask if the car was making us sick. Then we were off like the wind.

We passed through Noli without stopping, through Spotorno and into Savona. This was beginning to get dull. I nudged Momina, motioning toward Mariella, who was pressing up against the baron, and said: "Aren't you beginning to feel a little queasy?" When the big car braked, it bounced back and forth on its springs. They turned and said: "Shall we go dancing?"

It was fun arriving at the Riviera. We drove up to a tearoom on the square and the people on the sidewalk clustered at both ends of the car as we got out and provided us with a guard of honor. We might have been a variety number.

Once inside, Momina expressed what we were all thinking. "Look here," she said to the baron, "devote yourself to Mariella. I don't feel like dancing today."

"Neither do I," said Rosetta.

"Nor I."

It was a modern place, with lattice partitions and palms. "We're going to see Savona," we told them. "Have a good time."

We went out into the street, relieved. There wasn't much to see in Savona on Sunday, but a new city always has an effect on you. There was a great sky with a few clouds, there was the sea air, we walked around aimlessly. We ate cakes in a café, looking at the women, who looked back. We went as far as the port, where we found ugly red and black ships instead of houses.

"That's the end," Momina said. "Everything ends."

We passed by the fried-fish stalls.

Momina said: "Well now, your friend Morelli would invite us to have a liter of wine. The trouble is, he can't hold it."

"Can you hold it?" Rosetta asked.

"In Rome you can do that sort of thing," I said. "That's the good thing about Rome."

"I can take the wine. I can't always take Morelli," Momina said.

We leaned on the wall over the water and lit cigarettes.

"This is how I used to get my meals," I said to Rosetta. "Not in dives like these, but at a dairy bar. Turin is full of girls who eat that way."

"It must be very nice," Rosetta said. "When I went to school, every morning I used to pass a dairy bar and in the winter through the windows you could see people warming their hands around their cups. It must be nice to be alone inside like that, when it's cold outside."

I told her that the girls don't always have time to warm their fingers in the morning. You drop your cup and run to the office, cursing somebody.

Then Rosetta asked me: "Do you think girls are fools to work? Should they sell themselves instead?"

Momina said, staring down at the water: "It looks more like a sewer than the sea. Do you suppose they wash their dishes here?"

"Going to the office is also selling oneself," I answered Rosetta. "There are dozens of ways to sell yourself. I don't know what is the most useless."

I don't know why I was saying such things, particularly to her. Especially since I didn't believe them myself.

Touched, Rosetta replied: "I know that life is hard . . ."

"Oh, drop it," Momina said. "All this political talk . . . Let's move."

Now we were walking in the middle of the street. Rosetta, reflective, kept glancing at me. Suddenly she said: "Please don't think I despise prostitutes. One does anything to keep alive . . . But isn't it simpler to live by working?"

"That's working, too," I said. "Don't think there's any other reason for it."

"I think that prostitutes are stupid," Momina said. "You only need to look at their faces."

"It depends on whom you call a prostitute," Rosetta said. "You're talking about the unlucky ones."

"It's all a matter of knowing how to look after yourself," Momina said.

Finally we got back to the Studebaker in the square, and our tearoom. Momina said: "Shall we go in?"

The other two were dancing among the palms, wrapped together like husband and wife. We stood by the bar and watched them awhile. Tall Mariella's blond head rose above the other dancers. There's one who knows how to take care of herself, I thought.

They came up to us, smiling a bit stupidly. They had had quite a few. The baron asked Rosetta to dance. They danced. Then we told him we ought to go back. Mariella, excited, said she would have liked to see Savona with us. Rosetta, very serious, said that she hadn't missed anything.

In an instant we were back at Noli and it wasn't yet evening. The sea began to take on color. We found the others in the café on the square, bored and noisy. We decided to eat there and then go back in comfort, without any more fuss.

23. The next day I had a visit from Nene at the Via Po. She wanted to see the fitting rooms and tell me what a fool she'd been to get sick. She examined the niches and mirrors, the porcelains and frames, and then invited me to a little party they wanted to give in Loris's studio. She asked why I didn't decorate the shop with something modern. She damned Febo. She discussed the Turin painters, knowingly and cleverly. I replied that I was seeing some projects through and had a lot of work these days.

The same day Mariella sent me a bouquet of white roses with a card: "In remembrance of an innocent trip." During dinner at Noli the baroness had asked us if we had had a good time in Savona. Mariella, too, invited me to an evening at her house: someone was going to read poetry. I said that I had a lot to do.

Morelli invited himself to dinner at my table. He asked why we didn't eat upstairs in my room. I replied that it wasn't proper even with a mistress.

Even Maurizio put in an appearance with a long letter; he wrote that he missed me; people in Rome were beginning to tease him about his widowhood, and I should please not come back married to a Turin football player. In short, I should tell him whether he was to confirm the renting of the villa for next summer. I suddenly realized I could no longer remember the faces of people in Rome, that I often confused Maurizio's with Guido's. But what I didn't confuse were those wild times with Guido, his fits of bad temper, his demands, and mine too, and the tranquil resignation I enjoyed with Maurizio. Maurizio was shrewd, Maurizio was in no hurry. You get things when you can finally live without them.

I talked about it with Rosetta when she came back for a visit. She appeared in her usual way, at the door, as I was going out. I told her I had been asked to Loris's party.

"Are you going?" she asked with a half smile.

"Nene wants me, Mariella wants me. When I was a girl and ate in dairy bars, such invitations would have driven me wild. But those days one used to go into the hills instead."

Rosetta asked me what I used to do on Sundays.

"I told you. To the hills. Or dancing. Or to the movies. Played around with the boys."

"Did you do that in the hills?"

"Not much. Much less than in other circles."

"Sometimes Loris used to take me to the cafés in the slums."

"Where blood flows," I said. "Have you ever seen blood flow?"

"Loris played billiards. There was often a floorshow. Disgusting women . . ."

"What do you think of those slums?"

"Those are things one does to see life. It's an existence, a suffering we can't understand."

"It's not enough just to see things. I'll bet that you got only one thing from all that experience."

"What?"

"You got to know Loris better."

Rosetta did something I didn't expect. She laughed. She laughed in her forced way, but she laughed. She said Nene was right: men are babies, and artists are doubly babies. It didn't take much to know Loris, much less than to get rid of him.

"I don't believe in this nonsense about babies," I said. "Men aren't babies. They even grow up without being mothered."

Rosetta made another unexpected response. "They dirty themselves," she said. "They dirty themselves like babies."

"What do you mean?"

"Whatever they touch. They dirty us, the bed, the work they do, the words they use . . ."

She spoke with conviction. She wasn't even irritated.

"The only difference," she said, "is that babies only foul themselves."

"Women don't foul?" I asked.

She looked at me frankly. "I know what you're thinking," she said. "I don't mean that. I'm not a lesbian. I've been a girl, that's all. But love in any form is a dirty thing."

Then I said: "Momina told me about you two. About that day

at the sea when you opened the door and found her with someone. Is that what has disgusted you so?"

"Momina," Rosetta said, blushing, "does lots of crazy things. Sometimes she is laughing at us—but she agrees with me. She says there's no water that can clean people's bodies. It's life that's dirty. She says that everything is wrong."

I was about to ask her why she went on living then, but caught myself. I told her that when I had been in love, though I knew very well—one knows these things—that we were two maniacs, that my man was incompetent and slept at home all day while I went to work, still, despite all this, one can't learn to live alone unless one has first lived with someone else. There was nothing dirty about it, only an innocence—like animals perhaps—but also an innocence of clumsy people who only in that way can understand who they are.

"Anything can be dirty; it depends on what you mean by the word," I said. "Even dreaming or riding in a car can be dirty... Yesterday Nene vomited."

Rosetta listened with a half smile, more from the lips than from the eyes. It was Momina's smile when she was passing judgment on someone.

"And when love is over," she said tranquilly, as if everything were settled, "and you know who you are, what do you do with these things you've learned?"

"Life is long," I said. "Lovers didn't make the world. Every morning is another day."

"Momina says so too. But it's sad that it should be so." She looked at me the way a dog looks at you. We hadn't stopped in front of some shop windows I wanted to see, but had reached the hotel.

"Well, come to Loris's party," she said. "Mariella's going to bring me, too."

When Momina phoned me, I told her that Mariella was right: that she, Momina, sometimes went too far with Rosetta. But one should never discuss such things on the phone. I heard Momina's voice harden. I could even see her expression when she said: "That's nonsense."

I had to explain that I was only talking about their conversations.

That Rosetta seemed unhappy enough on her own account not to have to listen to her malicious jokes. That it was very important not to touch her on her sore spot. I kept talking and knew that talking was silly. Momina didn't even have to adjust her face; she cleared her throat as she listened.

At the end she said coldly: "Finished?"

"Listen, everyone spends all day putting his nose into other people's affairs. I hope it does some good. I've said my piece."

"And that fool Mariella . . ."

"Mariella has nothing to do with it. It's our discussion."

"I don't thank you."

"And who's asking you for thanks?"

"I understand."

Then, as if nothing had happened, we talked about what we would do in the evening.

24. Every now and then Momina took an interest in the shop and asked me if we would have it done in time for a spring opening.

"I'm fed up," I said, "discouraged. It's up to Febo now."

"But you work here a great deal."

"Considering all the beautiful show windows there already are in Turin, what do you expect?"

One evening I asked Becuccio if he had a girl. He joked, not committing himself. I told him that if he wanted to keep me company, go out somewhere together, I'd let him take me. He made light of it, not trusting himself to decide.

"Of course we go dutch," I said.

He looked at me wickedly, puffing out his cheeks. He had his outfit on—windbreaker, scarf, leather wristband. He touched his chin dubiously with two fingers.

"This evening," I said. "Not tomorrow. Right away."

"I've got to shave," he said.

"I'm leaving in half an hour."

He reappeared punctually. He must have run around God knows where to get some money. His hair was perfumed.

He said: "Let's eat and then go to a movie."

"I go to the movies alone. This evening I want to make the rounds."

"Then we'll make the rounds."

He took me to eat in a little Tuscan restaurant in Corso Regina. He said: "It's dirty, but the food's good."

I said: "Becuccio, no fooling now, where do you go with your friends?"

"We'll go there later," he said.

We ate and drank, talking about the store and when the people from Rome would come up for the opening. Becuccio had never seen a fashion show and asked if men were admitted. He complained that his work always ended with the fixtures and before the last coat of whitewash. I said that we would invite him.

"They're putting up another building in the Dora suburb," he said. "The supervisor is sending me."

He told me that in the two years he had been doing that kind of work he hadn't yet seen a room finished right. Contractors were always in a hurry at the end. He told me to watch out during the last days.

He poured me some wine. I had to stop him. I asked him if he wanted to get me drunk. "No," he said, "at least I'm paying for the wine."

Then he talked about the day workers who were putting in the shelves. Becuccio laughed. "That Royal Palace cabinetmaker. I'd have him making shelves, that monarchist."

At a certain point he crushed his cigarette and said he knew why he had come out with me this evening.

I looked at him. "Yes," he said, "this is my tip."

"What tip?"

"Sunday we'll be finished. My part will be finished. And you are giving me this present."

I looked at him. He spoke good-naturedly. He laughed with his eyes, self-contented.

"I wish it had happened earlier," he said. "But you are clever. You waited till the end."

My face felt hot. "Look out, I'm drunk," I said. "I've got nothing to lose."

He touched the bottle. "There isn't any more." He called the waitress.

I stopped his hand. "Not on your life. Now we're going to your friends'."

We went out to the avenue. He asked me if I really wanted to go, really wanted to watch him play billiards.

I said: "Are you ashamed of me?"

He suddenly took my arm as we walked and said that all women were alike. They said, "I'll watch while you play," and then they didn't like it, they acted as if they're at the dentist, they got bored. "I wouldn't like to take you there. I wouldn't enjoy you or the billiards. But I can't order you . . ."

"Why? Does your girl order you?"

"Don't they do the same in Rome?" he said. "Don't you order anyone, Clelia?"

Then I said: "Make up your mind. Where are we going?"

We went to dance at the Nirvana. Nothing less. Becuccio wanted to do things properly. It was a large, colonnaded room with a four-piece orchestra. I remembered it from that night with Morelli and Momina. It would be funny to meet someone now, I thought. Becuccio, in his windbreaker, guided me firmly to the tables in the rear. For a moment I imagined what going out with him every evening would be like. We would meet on a corner of the Corso Regina and one fine day I would see him roar up on a motorcycle. He would say, proud as a peacock: "Hold on tight. We'll hit sixty." What kind of man would Becuccio be?

We danced, joking about his girl. I said: "Suppose she found you here dancing with the boss, what would you do? Which of you would yell?"

"Depends on what excuse I could think up," Becuccio said, and winked.

I had made up my mind. I wasn't drunk, but the rancor, the tiredness and malice of earlier in the evening had left. I danced and talked contentedly, warm inside. Tomorrow I would start worrying again. But tonight that scrap of music and Becuccio's scarf were enough.

"Did you ever know girls," I asked him, "even experienced ones, who did it out of anger? Or even girls who wouldn't hear of it because they have it in for men in general? Girls who are bored to have someone in bed with them?"

Of course I was talking too much, talking just like Rosetta and the others. Becuccio had me in his arms, he bent me back, he practically walked on me. He had already whispered once in my ear: "Do you want to go?"

"Girls have a lot of funny ideas," he answered. "God knows where they get them. But once in bed, they stay."

"Sure?" I said.

He took my arm and we returned to the table. He circled my waist and squeezed me tightly.

"No, Becuccio," I said, looking aside. "I like to be alone too."

"Shall we go?" he said.

Outside he tried to kiss me in the first doorway. "Good," I said. "I don't want to hurt any one."

"Let's not hurt ourselves," he said, laughing. He tried to kiss me again.

I let him. He nailed me against the wall. I felt the live shock of his mouth and the smell of his hair. I didn't open my lips.

"You're young," I said on his shoulder. "You're too young. I don't do this kind of thing in the street."

For a while we walked arm in arm, not knowing where. It seemed like those evenings with Guido when Rome was far away and I wasn't eighteen yet. It was the same sort of night, late March or September. The only difference was that Becuccio wasn't a soldier.

He went back to squeezing my middle. I wanted to kiss him. Instead I asked: "What are you thinking?"

He stopped, and stopped me. "That you should come with me," he said darkly.

"I'm coming," I said. "But it's a gift for tonight only. Remember."

25. Becuccio was a Communist and said that he had been in the war. I asked him if he had been a soldier. "I was in Germany," he told me.

Then I wondered about Carlotta, whether she was still alive

and would ever again find herself waking like me, in a hotel room in Val Salice, with a window looking out on the trees.

"We even have a trolley line," Becuccio said.

He went down to pay, and we didn't have breakfast. The owner, in pajamas and waistcoat, silently watched us walk out. I was thinking that the important things always happen where one wouldn't expect it. A miserable little hotel, a room with a pitcher and basin, sheets to get between in the dark. Outside, Becuccio was smoking in the first rays of the sun.

I went back to my hotel alone. I wasn't tired, I was calm and happy. Becuccio had understood me, he hadn't insisted on coming. I was so happy that I almost promised myself: until Sunday, you can see him when you like. But I knew I shouldn't do it; I was already bored by his way of taking me by the chin and looking into my eyes.

At the hotel, Mariuccia brought in breakfast, saw the empty bed, and her eyes popped. I imagined her expression if she had seen me an hour earlier. I told her I wasn't in to anybody, and that I wanted to take a bath.

That morning I telephoned Febo at Via Po. He wasn't there. Becuccio answered. He called me "Miss" in his usual tone. I left some messages for Febo and then was free. I phoned Momina; she wasn't in. I phoned Mariella; they had gone to a Mass for some titled woman, a relative who had died a few weeks before. I knew the church, the Crocetta.

I went out and strolled very slowly along the avenues. The first leaves were coming out, and I thought of the woods of Val Salice. I arrived at the Crocetta just as the Mass was over; the black and white announcement was still up, and the funeral decorations. I read the dead woman's name: she had been a tertiary, almost a nun. A group of girls and older women chattered beside the open doors of a large black car. A grating in front of the columns at the top of the steps closed off the loggia; someone had told me it was put there to keep out the beggars and had been paid for by a special legacy. A woman was sitting by a basket on the lower steps, selling violets.

I don't know why, but I thought I'd go in. It was cold inside and a sacristan was snuffing the last candles on the altar. I stood by a pillar. All churches are alike. I breathed the smell of incense and dead flowers. It occurred to me that priests knew something about decoration too, but it's no trouble to them: it's always the same, and people come anyway.

Two women came out of the shadows, Rosetta and her mother. We nodded; at the door they dipped their fingers in the holy water and crossed themselves. The mother wore a fur and a black veil.

Outside, we said hello and Rosetta asked me to accompany them home, only a few steps. We mumbled about this and that; the mother complimented me on the shop; she carried a small black book. Her fur notwithstanding, she had a domestic air, and even while talking she seemed amazed at everything, she sighed. They stopped before the gate of a small, ivy-covered villa.

"Come and see us," the mother said. "It's a small house, but I'm sure you won't mind."

Rosetta was silent; then she said she would keep me company as far as the trolley.

Her mother said: "Don't be late. I leave her in your hands."

We walked down the little avenue. I heard about Momina and Mariella. I asked if many people had been there.

"Don't you think," Rosetta said, "that doing funerals, baptisms, and weddings in the same way is wrong? I can understand marrying or even being born—some people enjoy them and like to talk about them—but people who die should be left alone. Why go on tormenting them?"

"Some dead people like it," I said.

"Once, at least they buried suicides in secret."

I didn't answer, I kept on walking. I said suddenly: "Don't let us torment them, too . . ."

When we stopped at the corner, I said: "Rosetta, do you love your mother?"

"I suppose so," she faltered.

"Because your mother is very fond of you," I said. ". . . Look at the flowers on that tree. They look like puffs of white silk."

That afternoon I saw Becuccio again. He had climbed a ladder to attach a chandelier, and we talked from floor to ladder.

Febo was there, and we were leafing through photographs in the salon when I realized that Becuccio had come in noiselessly. A rush of blood ran to my face and I felt my knees trembling.

"What is it?" I said.

But Becuccio said quietly that people were waiting for me downstairs. It was Morelli with some women who had come to see what was going on. I handed them over to Febo and went down to speak to the electricians. Any day now, madame might show up and let loose the avalanche of the opening. Becuccio, running up and down the stairs, winked at me as if to say: I'll do it. Febo, Morelli, and the women soon left, inviting me to tea. I said no, that I had to stay on.

I stayed to test Becuccio. As I went through the empty rooms, some in half shadow, some blindingly lit up, I expected him to appear at every step. Instead I found him at the door, putting on his jacket.

"Going home, Becuccio?"

"Oh, here you are," he said. "How about a vermouth?"

We went to the café across the street, where we had been the first day. The cashier looked at me as she had then. Becuccio said he was sore at Febo because he was talking about changing the placement of the wires and tearing up the baseboards after he had already made them redo the shelves three times. Becuccio said he had known people like Febo in the war: the regular brass. "He must know his business," Becuccio said. "He damn well has to know it. They knew theirs, too. But I don't like people who waste material . . ."

As I drank the vermouth, I raised my glass a little as a sort of toast, said goodbye with my eyes; Becuccio wrinkled his forehead and smiled. No, he wasn't a boy.

That evening I found myself with Momina and Rosetta in the rooms of the gallery where we had planned the trip to Saint Vincent. Somebody was showing some paintings, but it wasn't necessary to look at them. We three remained seated while people drifted around us. I seemed to recognize all those faces, the same faces you see in hotels, salons, and at fashion shows. The paintings meant nothing to them. The thought crossed my mind that for Rosetta and Momina I must be the same type that Becuccio was for me. I don't much like people who waste material either. Rosetta and Momina had started discussing music.

26.

Momina said she enjoyed art shows, concerts, and plays because there were a lot of people there. "Imagine being alone in a theater," she said. "Or in a gallery . . ."

"But it's the people who are annoying."

"Really?" Momina said. "These shows aren't always enjoyable —you only go when you want to see people and talk. Like going visiting."

"Music, no," Rosetta said. "You have to be alone with music. When they used to give passable concerts in Turin . . ."

I wondered what Becuccio would have said. But it was absurd even to think of him. There's nothing like spending a night together on the same pillow to understand that people are made differently and have their own road to follow.

I asked Rosetta: "Do you really like music?"

"I don't like it, but it's . . . something. Maybe only suffering."

"It must be like painting," Momina said.

"Oh, no," Rosetta said. "Painting is an ambition. But listening to music, you let yourself go . . ."

I smiled to myself. With so many things in the world, with so many things that both of them knew and possessed, they discussed music as if it were cocaine or the first cigarette.

"I don't think that artists suffer at all," Momina said. "They make whoever listens feel worse, if he takes them seriously."

"It's others who suffer and enjoy," Rosetta said. "Always others . . ."

I said: "You mean, the winemaker never gets drunk?"

"Whores never enjoy it," Momina said. "Do you know anyone who's more a whore than Nene? She's intelligent, she has her craft at her fingertips, and all the temperament a sculptress could have. Why doesn't she stick to that? But no. She has to dress like a child, fall in love, get drunk. One of these days there'll be a baby. She has the face for it . . . She thinks that others fall for her babyishness."

"You're nasty," Rosetta said.

"Momina's right," I grumbled. "It's the work you do that counts, not how you do it."

"I don't know what counts," Momina said. She looked at us almost surprised, innocent. "I'm afraid nothing counts. We're all whores."

We took Rosetta home in the car and at the gateway she asked me again, embarrassed, to come to tea the next day. She asked Momina, too.

When I arrived, Momina was already there. Rosetta's mother, in turquoise velvet, was talking to a dry woman who shook hands, looking me over from stockings to hair, and complained about wide-pleated skirts, insisting that someone or other would soon narrow them. In these cases I always say that whoever doesn't accept a style when it's in fashion will wear it the next year when it's passed. Then Momina began to argue and joke with her, and Rosetta took me to the window and told me to be patient; that woman was a pest.

The mother's hand was certainly invisible in that light and airy living room. It was cut in two by an arch. On our side were the chairs and occasional tables; on the other, a large, triple-casemented window and a long gleaming table under a chandelier. I asked Rosetta if they had lived there very long. She said no, her earliest memories were of the house at Montalto. She was born in the suburb of San Paolo, near the factory, but the apartment was probably either destroyed or damaged.

"You will want to see the garden," the mother said.

Rosetta said: "Another time. It hasn't bloomed yet."

"Show her the pictures," her mother said. The pest had stopped talking about fashion and said that even in Turin beautiful things were made. "You people don't really have to come up from Rome," she said. "Isn't that so, Rosetta? We know how to cut cloth and paint."

She left after tea, to make another call. Rosetta's mother sighed, looking at us good-humoredly. "She means well," she said. "It's bad to be left a widow."

We went to Rosetta's room, which I barely glanced at, white and blue, with a window at the far end. In the corridor she opened a wardrobe to show me a dress that Momina said was wrong for her. I caught a glimpse of the blue tulle dress.

Altogether I liked the house. The mother, poor creature, must have enjoyed it as much as she enjoyed her daughter. The maid was a little peasant girl but wore black with a little white apron; the mother wouldn't let her do anything, but served us herself.

Momina had taken off a shoe and was smoking distractedly in a chair.

After a while the father arrived, coming in cautiously with his glasses in his hand, his eyelids red. He was iron-gray, his mustache the same color; and he was stocky and a little stooped. But his expression was very like Rosetta's, impatient and stubborn.

Momina gave him her impudent smile and held out a hand from the depths of her chair. He bowed and muttered something to me, glancing at his wife. He was a man of antique cut, not like Morelli. Passing Rosetta, he touched her cheek caressingly; she shook her head.

He said he didn't mean to disturb us but that he was glad to meet me. Wasn't I the person who had come up from Rome to direct the new firm? At one time it had been Turin that opened branches in Rome. "Times change," he said. "You'll find it's not easy to stay on your feet in Turin. The war hit us hard."

He spoke in bursts, tired but positive. His wife brought him a cup of tea. He said: "At least in Rome you work?"

I said yes.

He looked around. "You have to dress. You're right. The world is made for you."

All on our feet now, we watched him holding his cup. His wife, heavy and patient in her turquoise velvet, waited. I realized that he was an old man, tolerated, and that only his work meant anything to the women. I also saw that he knew it and was grateful to us for having let him talk.

27. Rosetta told me that she didn't understand her father.

"I understand him," Momina said. "He's one of those men who used to wear beards. Then one night some woman would cut it off and they would spend the rest of their lives trying to redeem themselves."

"However, he made a Rosetta," I said.

"Probably he didn't know how to make her or not to make her."

Momina slowed down, stopped beside the portico, and none of us moved.

"Anyhow, Rosetta resembles him," she said. "Weren't you a good student, Rosetta? I'll bet your father is one of those who say: 'If I were a boy, I'd begin all over again.' "

Rosetta said, over my shoulder: "All young people are fools. And the old men, and the old women, and the dead. All of them wrong. Oh, Clelia, teach me how to earn a little money and get away to California. They say that there you never die."

I saw Becuccio through the door and signaled him. He crossed under the portico and bent down to the window. While I talked with him, Momina asked Rosetta why we didn't go up into the hills. Becuccio told me the cases hadn't arrived yet. "You've got time for a drive," Momina said.

We set off. I saw Rosetta's face in the rear-view mirror. She sat there silent, sulky, stubborn. Sometimes I thought of her as very young, a little girl, the kind you try to persuade to say "thank you," but they won't do it. If you thought about it, it was terrible to have her with us this way and talk this way, terrible but also ridiculous, comic. I tried to recall what I was like at twenty, at eighteen—how I was during the first days with Guido. How I was before, when my mother used to tell me not to believe in anyone or anything. Poor thing, what had she got for it all? I would have liked to know what advice her father and mother gave to that only daughter of theirs, so crazy and so alone.

Momina jogged me with her elbow as we were going up Sassi. Just then it struck me that Momina was the real mother, the elder sister, the demanding and evil sister of Rosetta—Momina, who threw stones openly without even trying to hide her hand, who—like me with Becuccio—had nothing more to lose.

"Rosetta," I said, "do you have any friends besides Momina?"

"What's a friend?" she said. "Not even Momina is my friend."

Momina, absorbed in the curves, said nothing. It occurred to me that every year someone breaks his neck on the Superga road. We were going fast, under the high trees. When the ascent began to flatten out, we could look off at the hills, valleys, and the plain of Turin. I had never been to Superga. I didn't know it was so high. Some evenings from the bridge over the Po you could see its rising black bulk sparkling with lights at the top, like a necklace carelessly thrown on the shoulders of a beautiful woman. But now it was morning, it was cool, and an April sun filled the sky.

Momina said: "We can't go any farther." She stopped by a heap of gravel. The radiator was steaming. Then we got out and looked at the hills.

"It's beautiful up here," Rosetta said.

"The world is beautiful," Momina said, coming up behind us. "If only we weren't in it."

"We are the others," I said, looking at Rosetta. "It's enough to do without them, keep them at a distance, then living becomes a possibility."

"It's possible here," Rosetta said, "for a moment, for the time it takes to drive up. But look at Turin. It's frightening. You have to live with all those people."

"You damn well don't need to have them in your house," Momina said. "Money means something."

There was a hedge along the road and a heavy mesh fence behind it; farther down a group of trees and a large concrete tank, a swimming pool full of muddy water and leaves. It looked abandoned; the little iron ladder for climbing in and out was still there.

"Whose villa is this?" Momina said. "Look at the shape it's in."

"That's it," I said. "Fix this place up and invite anyone I liked. Go down to Turin in the evening and perhaps visit someone. That's how I would live if I were you. I'd have lived like that since I was a girl."

"You could do it," Rosetta said. "Better than we could. Perhaps you would enjoy it."

"One doesn't do these things," I said. "It's enough to imagine them. You've got to keep moving to fill up your day. I'm no longer young enough to live willingly in the country."

Momina said: "Seeing that nothing is worth anything, one should have everything."

"If you didn't already have your loaf of bread," I told her, "you would demand a lot less."

"But I do have it," Momina cried. "I do have it, my bread. What can I do about that?"

Rosetta said that even monks in monasteries renounce everything but their meals.

"We're all like that," I said. "Eat first, pray later."

Momina drove up to a curve in the road that overlooked Turin; we pushed back the top and sat in the car, smoking. In the warm sunshine you could smell grass and the leather upholstery.

"Let's get going," Momina said. "Let's go and have a drink."

That afternoon a telegram arrived from Rome saying that madame would be in Turin the next day. The avalanche was beginning. Naturally Febo had escaped on his own business, and I couldn't get him on the telephone. I threw myself into it with Becuccio, we found two painters, it was dark and we were still hammering, checking the lights, opening and closing the curtains. The boxes arrived; shoeless like a countergirl, I dressed and redressed a window. At eight, Mariella called to remind me of the party at Loris's studio. I told her to go to the devil and went back to draping the walls, furious because I knew the work was useless, done for show; tomorrow madame would have it all done over. The agency that was to have sent the staff phoned to say that they couldn't send anyone until Monday. This was wasted time, too, because the hiring was up to madame; she wanted all the candidates there at once, to pick and choose from, according to her own notions. Becuccio ran around docilely, phoned, opened cartons. Finally—the painters had already left—I threw myself down on a carton and looked at him desperately.

He said: "I quit an hour ago. This is Saturday."

"You skunk," I said. "You, too. Go away."

"Want to have a bite to eat?" he asked.

I shook my head, looking around. Then he slowly lit a cigarette and came and put it in my mouth. Opening the cases, he had cut a hand. I told him to have it disinfected.

He came back with a package of oranges and bread. We ate seated on the cartons and while we ate we looked around and appraised the results. Everything possible had been done, the only thing left was for Febo to take a look at the salons, and then we could clean up.

Becuccio said: "We even have time for a quick trip to Val Salice."

I looked seriously at him, smiled, and said that such things don't happen twice. He came close to me and took my chin. For a couple of seconds we looked at each other. Then he let me go and went off.

I said: "There's an artist giving a party. Those girls are going. Would you like to come?"

He looked at me hard and curiously for a moment, then shook his head.

"No, boss," he said. "I don't circulate any higher than the middle classes. It's no use."

He promised to look for Febo the next day and send him around to the hotel. He kept me company up to Loris's door, then went away without insisting.

28. It was lucky that Becuccio didn't come up. They had covered a coffin with a pall daubed in black and placed four lit candles around it. They were discussing Paris, and naturally Momina was having her say. I asked what was going on. Nene, dressed in red velvet, told me offhandedly that Loris was celebrating the death of his second period and was going to give a polemic speech. But the noise was fierce, and Loris, cowering on his bed, was ruminating privately over something, smoking with his eyes closed. There was much smoke and many faces I didn't know. There was the old painter who had come with us to Saint Vincent, there was the little woman in satin with the libidinous eyes, there was that Fefé of the first evening, there was Mariella, blond and noisy. I didn't see Rosetta immediately; then I found her smoking in the embrasure of the window; a short, somewhat hunchbacked man stood in front of her and she was caressing a kitten in her arms.

"How are you?" I said. "Is it yours?"

"He came in from the roof," she said. "Nobody invited him."

The studio looked fairly neat; bottles and glasses and plates of antipasto and candy were arranged on a table near the washbowl. Everyone had a glass, either in hand or on the floor. I thought that Nene must have worked almost as hard as I that day, but for her it would all be over in the morning.

The party was beginning to sound well oiled. I kept apart, found a place to sit and drink and leaned my head on the wall. Mariella's voice dominated the rest, talking about a Parisian theater and a Negro dancer, not Josephine Baker.

"Eat, eat!" exclaimed Nene, preoccupied.

Fefé came over to light my cigarette, quizzing me with his little eyes.

"And that squire of yours?" he asked.

"I'm not a horse," I replied.

He grinned as before. He put his hands in his pockets, planting himself in front of my chair. "Too many women here," he said. "I wish you were the only one."

"No, no," I said. "You need to see people. One always learns from people."

"Ask me to your shop. Everyone's talking about it."

"Of course. Consider yourself a customer already."

But he was stupid and didn't know how to go on. He grinned and asked me if I liked cats. I told him I preferred liqueurs. He poured me a glass, kissed the rim, and handed it to me. "Drink it. Drink it, if you want," I said. He ended by drinking it.

I listened to the hunched fellow talking with Rosetta. He was an aged boy with a wrinkled face. He was talking about the Negroes who had deserted toward the end of the war and hidden out near Pisa in the pine wood of Tombolo. He was saying to her: "They were always drunk or on drugs. At night they had orgies and pulled knives. When a girl died, they buried her among the pines and hung her pants and brassiere on the cross. They went around naked," he said. "They were true primitives."

Rosetta stroked the cat and looked me over.

"Crazy things happened," he went on. "The Americans went after them but didn't succeed in driving them out. They lived in huts made of leaves. Such things never happened after any other war."

With his mouth full, Fefé put in: "It's a shame it's all over. It was a lovely picnic while it lasted."

The hunchback looked at him, annoyed.

"Are you shocked?" Rosetta said. "Did they behave differently from us? They had courage, more than we had."

"I understand the Negroes," Fefé said, "but I don't understand the women. Living in the woods like that . . ."

"They died like flies," the hunchback said. "And the men, too."

"They were murdered," Rosetta said. "By the cold, by hunger, by gunfire. Why was this?"

"Why not?" the hunchback said, grinning. "They stole. They killed one another. They filled themselves with drugs."

The cat escaped from Rosetta's arm. She bent over to pick him up and said: "The same things are done in Turin. Which is worse?"

They were screaming around the bed. Someone had lit a glass of brandy and was shouting. "Turn off the lights." Mariella's voice rose above the girls' uproar. Someone—Momina, I think—really turned out the lights. For a moment there was a confused silence.

I sought Rosetta immediately in the dark. It was like that night in my hotel room when she had turned out the lights. But everyone was saying: "How nice it is. Leave it like this." The four candles on the coffin and the little bluish flame that someone had put on the floor made you feel you were in a grotto. Then they shouted: "Loris! Speech, Loris!" But Loris didn't stir from the bed. Nene went to shake him and they struggled. I saw the two shadows moving on the vaulted ceiling, I heard Loris curse. It seems that only a few of the painters he had invited had come and he said rudely that there was no need to make a speech just for us. The funny thing was that everyone took him at his word, and they formed into groups again and someone sat on the floor. They began drinking again.

Mariella passed near me and asked if I were having a good time. She told me to look at the coffin—how theatrical it was, how surrealist—and she started again with her acting. Luckily Nene came after her right away to get her to carry around some food.

Rosetta looked upset and drank a lot. Now she was sitting with Momina at the foot of the bed in a group that was cracking jokes, pausing, and cackling over them. In the candlelight I tried to avoid Nene's eyes; I had seen that they were swollen, I felt a crisis coming on, her anger rising because the party was turning out badly. The only thing to do was to get drunk, and soon she would be; yet she was still hoping that someone would arrive and liven things up.

Somebody suggested that we take a bottle and go out and sit on the Artillery Monument steps.

"Let's go boating," a girl said.

"Let's look for some women," a boy's stupid voice exclaimed.

Even Loris laughed at this from his bed, around his pipe.

"And we'll go find some men," a woman's voice said.

We had become ugly and out of gear. Or maybe it was the effect of Loris's painting, which nobody looked at. The old man with the Chinese mustaches began: "At Marseilles, beautiful women go to the portside brothels and pay to be hidden behind a curtain."

I was thinking that I ought to go to bed, that tomorrow would be a big day. Momina said: "Pay? Why? They do the houses a favor."

Loris, Fefé, the hunchback, and the other men shouted that it was a good idea to make the women pay. Nene joined our group. By now we made one large circle, including the cat on Momina's knees. Somebody was feeling my thigh. I told him to stop it.

"Listen," said a new boy I didn't know, "we can go back over the Po and into Via Calandra. We all know," he looked insolently at Momina and me, "that no woman willingly goes down that street. So let's all go together. To the café, naturally. You can see the customers going in and out of the brothels across the street. Agreed?"

29.

Nene begged us to wait and see if anyone else might come, to eat, to sing something together. She told Loris not to be a pig. She wanted us at least to drink and wait until midnight.

"It *is* midnight," they told her. "Don't you see that it's already dark?"

"Afterwards we'll come back," Mariella said.

"Do we take the cat?" someone else said.

So that we could leave, someone turned on the lights and everyone looked confused. I lost sight of Rosetta and Momina and went downstairs with the hunchback and Fefé. The stairwell was in an uproar; Loris's voice reverberated. I thought of leaving, but Fefé was talking nonsense to me and I couldn't see the others. In short, I followed them to the café in Via Calandra.

It's not an alley and it reminds you a little of Via Margutta in Rome. Momina's car had stopped in front of the bar and inside was confusion; the customers looked unfriendly. Of course we might have been girls from one of the houses across the street, but all together, at that time of night? Having a party with our patrons? I was merely thinking all this, but the boys, especially Loris, said it out loud. I saw that it was all a farce to amuse the boys and that we women were being taken for a ride. I couldn't understand Momina falling for it. But Momina and Rosetta had already sat down at the rusty tables and we made a circle; Mariella, the painter, and Nene sat down. As each of us came in, it became a little harder to talk and imagine why we were there. The owner shooed away two little men with mustaches who were drinking in a corner and rounded us all up near the tubs of privet near the door.

Before, coming into the street—few streetlights or windows—we noticed a stand and a man in white selling *torrone* and chestnut cakes. Then little groups of soldiers, of boys who disappeared shouting into a doorway, and in front of the doorway Fefé had given a little cough. It was wide, with inner glass doors, rather dark. I smelled the mixture of piss, acetylene, and fried food I knew from outside our own house in the evening when I was a child.

In the bar Nene was already complaining that she couldn't see the street from where she was. None of us saw it; there were curtains on the lower half of the windows. To see and enjoy the action, you had to stand at the bar and crane around, look out the door; in other words, you had to move. The hunchback and the elegant boy who had brought us to the bar laughed and agreed with Loris that a decent investigation of low life could only be made by a woman with the courage to lead it. Mariella had the jitters. Rosetta was quiet and a bit drunk, her elbow on the table.

The owner wanted to know what we were drinking. The place was low-ceilinged, wood-paneled, and smelled of wine and damp sawdust. Except for our noise and the silly conversation of our men, especially Loris, it was an ordinary café of quiet people. There was even a girl behind the bar and a soldier talking to her and watching us out of the corner of his eye. A place Becuccio might have come into at any moment.

Instead of answering the owner, our boys kept on shouting. I must say I was ashamed. I tried to catch Momina's or Rosetta's

eye, to make them agree to leave. But Momina was shouting something, excited and annoyed with Loris. Rosetta didn't answer my
glances. Nene had disappeared.

They talked and argued, they wanted *marsala all'uovo*, they
said that at times like these, *marsala all'uovo* was the only thing.
The small woman in satin laughed louder than the boys, egged
them on, asked where Nene was, whether she had crossed the
street. Perhaps she had joined the boys who were going in the door.
The little woman eyed the soldier several times.

I expected what happened next. Nene returned. The wine came
—red, out of the barrel—someone had *grappa*, someone anisette,
someone Cynar. Loris said to Nene: "Madame, madame, show us
the girls. The ones we have now are little pigs."

"Look who's talking," Momina said through her teeth.

Laughing and shouting, they said we should be tested and compared and have our points entered on a score card. So they started
arguing which of us would make the best prostitute; for gifts both
of body and soul, the hunchback added. Mariella, too, was discussed and she ended by getting angry and taking the score card seriously. She nearly fought with Momina. But the old painter said
we were all meritorious, that it was a matter of time and tastes;
the real criterion should be our price and the sort of place we
worked in.

Someone tried to suggest theater and nightclub stages. "No,
no," the hunchback said. "We're talking about real whorehouse
houris." They kept it up for a while. Finally the boys were redder
in the face than Mariella. They couldn't find a place for Rosetta.
"Kid sister," they concluded. "Too innocent."

But they didn't stop there. "You've put it on the grounds of
taste," they were saying. Now it was Fefé who had the jitters.
Some of them had already gone to the door and were looking idiot-
ically from us to the street. Momina also got up and went to the
door. I heard them laughing and bitching.

"Look, look," they were saying. "An old man is going in. A
whole group is going."

"Rosetta," I asked her coldly, "are you really having such a
good time?"

Rosetta's eyes were more sunken than ever and she looked at

me with a vague smile. Nene, playing patty-cake with her neighbor, suddenly hit him hard. Rosetta put her elbows back on the table and said: "Tomorrow's another day, isn't it?"

Momina came back from the door. "Those fools," she said, "those idiots. They've gone in."

Loris, the hunchback, and another boy had gone in. They had told Nene. She shrugged, emptied her glass, and took out her pencil. She wrote "pig" on the table. She looked at us, cynical, supplicating, drunk.

This time Mariella accompanied her to the toilet and I told Fefé and the painter, who smiled good-naturedly, to pay the bill. Then we got into the car with Momina and Rosetta and left. I got out very soon at Porta Nuova.

30. The next morning Becuccio brought Febo around to Via Po. It was an empty, useless Sunday, for we spent the whole morning retouching, switching lamps on and off, and smoking in the armchairs. Madame hadn't arrived; the usual story. I asked Febo and Becuccio to lunch at the hotel so I could be quiet and rest. They began to talk politics and Febo said there was no liberty in Russia. To do what? Becuccio asked him. For example, to put up a shop like ours and furnish it the way we liked.

Becuccio asked him how many people our shop would serve. Febo said numbers didn't matter because only a small minority had good taste. Becuccio asked if we two who had directed the work had been free to do what we liked. Febo replied that in Italy an artist was still free to do what he liked because the patrons who paid him had to consider public taste.

"The public means people," Becuccio replied, "and you said the public doesn't count because only a minority has good taste. Well then, who decides?"

"The brightest decide," Febo said.

Becuccio said he knew that very well and that was the trouble. It was the last time I talked with him. He stayed a short while after Febo left, and asked if I were returning soon to Rome. I told him to let me know if he should ever pass through Rome. He didn't ask for my Rome address. He smiled, held out his hand (he had left the leather wristband at home), and left.

I was alone all day and took a walk around my old section of Via della Basilica. Now the little square, the doorways, the tiny shops frightened me less. Porta Palazzo had been renamed Piazza della Republica. Along the empty alleys and in the courtyards I watched little girls playing. Toward evening it began to drizzle, a cool rain smelling of grass, and I finally reached the Piazza Statuto under the porticoes. I went to the movies.

Madame arrived at night by car with her husband and everyone else. They always do that. The phone woke me up, I thought it was Morelli, they upset the whole hotel. I had to get dressed and have coffee with them and hear about a storm in the Apennines. It was dawn when I went back to bed: I was happy because my responsibilities were over.

They stayed on the next floor in the same hotel and I had no more peace. At mealtimes, in Via Po, in the car, I was always with someone. Madame liked the furnishings, more or less; she wanted handrails for some of the stairs, and once she suggested moving the shop to Via Roma. Then she set out for Paris with two designers and left word for me and her husband to get the opening ready for Easter. I spent the days telephoning and seeing mannequins, studying programs, acting as secretary and head of the business. Morelli appeared, and also some women who wanted discounts, favors, jobs for homely daughters and acquaintances. There was a dance at the hotel where I saw Momina and Mariella again.

Then madame returned from Paris with some new models and Febo. That damned nuisance had gone to Paris on his own, had been charming and won her over and persuaded her to put on a musical revue to present the new models. Soon musicians and impresarios began to show up at the hotel and Via Po; it wasn't Turin any more; luckily these things never went very far because the next day someone would think of something different; I stopped bothering with it and spent my days at the shop.

One day I said: "I wonder how Rosetta is?" and telephoned Momina.

"I'll come and see you," she replied. "I don't know what to say. The fool went and killed herself again."

I waited for the green car with my heart in my throat. When I saw it at the curb, I left the shop, and Momina slammed the door, crossed the portico, and said: "I've had it."

She was as elegant as ever, wearing a feathered beret. We went up to one of the salons.

"She's been missing since yesterday. Half an hour ago I phoned and the maid told me that she had gone on a trip with me."

There was no mistake. Neither Nene nor Mariella had seen her. Momina didn't have the courage to telephone Rosetta's mother. "I still hoped she might be with you," she murmured with a faint smile.

I said it was her fault; that even if Rosetta hadn't killed herself, it was her fault. I told her I don't know what. I was sure I was right and could stand up to her. I insulted her as if she were my sister. Momina stared at the rug without trying to defend herself. "I'm annoyed that they thought she was with me," she said.

We telephoned Rosetta's mother. She wasn't home. Then we drove around to all the shops and churches she might have gone to. We went back to the villa, where we intended to telephone her father. But it wasn't necessary. As I was getting out of the car, I saw her mother approaching, fat and black, under the trees along the avenue.

All that day we stayed with the shouting, distracted parents, telephoning, waiting, running to the door. I must have been deaf and blind; I recalled Rosetta's words and looks, and I knew I had known that this would happen, had known it all along, and hadn't paid any attention. But then I said, could anyone have stopped her? And I thought, maybe she has run off the way you did with Becuccio.

Then people began to come. Everybody said: "They'll find her. It's just a question of time." Mariella came up with her mother, acquaintances and relatives, someone from the police. It seemed like a reception in the big airy room under the immense chandelier, and everyone asked how anyone like Rosetta who had such a need to live could want to die. Somebody said that suicide ought to be forbidden.

Momina talked to everybody, mordantly but courteously. There was even a woman who wanted to grill me about my work and talk about the shop's opening. People in corners began to give opinions about Rosetta's story. I couldn't stay any longer. Madame was waiting for me.

All evening the mother's frightened eyes and the father's bewildered, ferocious face stayed in my mind. I couldn't help thinking how much he resembled Rosetta. Momina was supposed to telephone me but didn't. I was in conference with the designers and Febo, but I got up and telephoned.

The maid told me, weeping, that Rosetta had been found. She was dead. In a rented room on Via Napione. Mariella came to the phone. She told me in a broken voice that it was so. Momina and the others had gone to identify her. She herself couldn't; it would have driven her mad. They were bringing her home. She had taken poison again.

At midnight I learned the rest of the story. Momina came to the hotel in her car and told me that Rosetta was already at home, laid out on her bed. She didn't seem dead. There was only a swelling of the lips, as if she were angry. The strange thing was her idea of renting a painter's studio, having an armchair, no less, drawn up so she could die in front of the window that looked toward Superga. A cat had given her away—it was in the room with her, and the next day, miaowing and scratching the door, it had made them open.

THE DEVIL
IN THE HILLS

1. We were very young. I don't think I ever slept that year, but I had a friend who slept even less than I did. Some mornings you could see him strolling up and down in front of the station when the first trains were arriving and leaving. We had dropped him late at night on his doorstep; Pieretto would then have taken another walk and, after seeing the dawn come in, had his coffee. Now he was studying the sleepy faces of street sweepers and cyclists. Even he wouldn't remember the night's conversations; having stayed awake over them, he had digested them. Now he said quietly: "It's late. I'm going to bed."

Some of the others who used to trail around with us couldn't understand what we did after the movies were over, our money spent, the bars closed, and all of us talked out. They would sit on the benches with the three of us, listen to our grumbling or cackling, get excited at the idea of going and waking some girls or waiting for the dawn on the hills; then at our change of mood they would hesitate and find the courage to go home. The next day they would ask: "What did you do afterwards?" It wasn't easy to say. We had listened to a drunk, watched the posters being pasted up, explored the market, seen sheep driven through town. Then Pieretto would say: "We met a woman."

The others didn't believe it but had no comeback.

"You need perseverance," Pieretto would say. "You walk up and down under her balcony. All night. She knows it, she understands. You don't have to know her, she just feels it in her blood. Finally she can't stand it any longer, she jumps out of bed and opens the shutters. Then you place your ladder . . ."

But alone the three of us didn't much like to discuss women.

Not seriously anyway. Neither Pieretto nor Oreste told me everything about themselves. That's why I liked them. Women, the kind
who separate people, would come later. For the moment we only
talked about the world in front of us, the rain and sun, and we enjoyed ourselves so much that going home to sleep seemed like a
real waste of time.

One night that year we were sitting by the Po, on a roadside
bench. Oreste had mumbled: "Let's go to bed."

"Stretch out here," we told him. "Why waste the summer?
Can't you sleep with only one eye?"

Oreste leaned his cheek on the back of the bench and peered
up at us.

I said that one should never sleep in the city. "It's always lit up,
always day. One should do something every night."

"What boys you are," Pieretto said. "You're boys and you're
greedy."

"And what are you," I asked. "An old man?"

Oreste jumped up suddenly. "Old people, they say, never sleep.
And we walk all night. I wonder who does sleep?"

Pieretto snickered.

"What is it?" I said.

"To sleep, you first need a woman," Pieretto said. "That's why
neither you nor the old men sleep."

"Could be," Oreste muttered, "but I'm dead on my feet just the
same."

"You're not from the city," Pieretto said. "Night still means
something to people like you, means what it used to mean. You're
like watchdogs or chickens."

It was past two. Beyond the Po, the hill was sparkling. It was
cool, almost cold.

We got up and started back toward the center of town. I ruminated over Pieretto's strange ability to get on the safe side of
everything and still make the rest of us consider ourselves naïve.
Neither Oreste nor I, for instance, lost much sleep thinking about
women. I wondered for the umpteenth time what sort of life Pieretto had lived before coming to Turin.

On the benches by the station flower beds, under the meager
shadow of those little trees, two beggars were sleeping with their

mouths open. In shirtsleeves, curly-haired and bearded, they looked like gypsies. The public toilets were close by and for all the freshness of a summer night there was a penetrating stench, a sourness left over from the long day of sun and movement and uproar, of sweat and hot asphalt, of unending crowds. Always, toward evening, little solitary women came and sat on the benches—pitiful oasis at the heart of Turin—street peddlers, uprooted women of all kinds, bored, waiting, growing older. What were they waiting for? Pieretto used to say that they were waiting for something prodigious, the fall of the city, the apocalypse. Sometimes a summer storm would drive them away and wash everything clean.

The pair that night were sleeping like corpses after a battle. On the deserted square some neon signs still spoke to an empty sky, flickering over the two sleepers. "They're happy," Oreste said. "Let them teach us what to do."

He started to leave.

"Come with us," Pieretto said. "Nobody's waiting for you at home."

"No more than where you're going," Oreste said, but he stayed.

We set out for the Portici Nuovi.

"Those two," I said softly. "It must be nice to wake up with the first sunlight on the square."

Pieretto kept still.

"Where are we going?" I asked, stopping.

Pieretto took a few more steps and stopped.

"I can understand going to some place or other," I said. "But everything is closed. Not a soul around. I wonder what's the use of all these lights."

Pieretto didn't come out with his usual "And what use are you, may I ask?"—but muttered instead: "How about going to the hill?"

"It's a long way," I said.

"It's a long way, but it's got that smell."

We went down the long avenue again. On the bridge I felt cold. Then we started up the hill at a good clip to escape the familiar outskirts. It was humid, dark, moonless—fireflies glimmered. After a while we slowed down, sweating. We had been discussing ourselves as we walked. We got excited, drawing Oreste into the talk. Other times we had taken these roads, warmed by wine or the company; but none of this counted, it was only an excuse for going somewhere, climbing, having the bulk of the hill under our feet. We went on between fields, walls, villa gates, breathing a smell of asphalt and woods.

"I can't see any difference between this and cut flowers in a vase," Pieretto said.

Strange as it may seem, we hadn't ever reached the top, at least by this road. There must have been a place, a leveling off, at the top of the slope that looked from below like the last of a rising series of hedges; there must have been a balcony open to the plains below. We had already looked over in this direction from the other hills, from Superga, from Pino, in full daylight. On the horizon of a bricky sea of houses, Oreste had pointed out some dim wooded shadows, his own villages.

"It's really late," Oreste said. "This place used to be full of nightclubs once."

"They have a closing time," Pieretto said. "But the people inside go on whooping it up."

"What's the point of coming to the hill in summer?" I said. "To celebrate with the doors and shutters closed?"

"They must have gardens," Oreste said. "Fields. They probably sleep in the park."

"The parks stop after a while," I said. "After that it's woods and vineyards."

Oreste grunted. I said to Pieretto: "You don't know the country. You perambulate all night, but you don't know the country."

Pieretto didn't answer. Every so often a dog barked in the distance.

"Let's stop," Oreste said, at a turn in the road.

Pieretto came out of his thoughts. "Why should I," he said, "when even the hares and snakes have gone underground and are scared of passers-by? The master smell here is gasoline. Where is the country now that you two seem to like?"

He fastened on me savagely. "If someone were to have his throat cut in the woods," he declared in that rasping tone of his, "do you really think it would be something legendary? That the crickets would fall silent around the corpse? That the pool of blood would matter more than so much spit?"

Oreste, waiting, spat with disgust. He said: "Hold on. A car is coming down."

Slowly and quietly, a large, pale green, open car appeared and stopped without a jolt, docile. Half of it stayed in the shadow of the trees. We looked at it, surprised.

"Its lights are out," Oreste said.

I imagined a couple inside and wished we were somewhere else, on the open place, not to have to meet anyone. Why didn't they go away in that marvel of theirs, to Turin, and leave us alone in our country? His head down, Oreste suggested leaving.

Brushing past the car, I expected to hear whispers and rustlings, perhaps laughter, but instead I caught sight of a man alone at the wheel, a young man slumped back in the seat with his face gaping at the sky.

"He looks dead," Pieretto observed.

Oreste was already out of the shadow. We were walking amid a chorus of crickets; many things raced through my mind as I walked those few steps under the trees. I didn't dare turn around. Pieretto was silent beside me. The tension became unbearable. I stopped.

"It's impossible," I said. "That character isn't asleep."

"What are you afraid of?" Pieretto said.

"Did you get a good look at him?"

"He was sleeping."

A person doesn't fall asleep that way and in a moving car, I said. Pieretto's outburst a few moments before still rang in my ears. "If only someone would come by." We turned to look at the bend in the road, dark with trees. A firefly zigzagged across, like a disembodied cigarette.

"Let's listen and see if he leaves."

Pieretto said that anyone who owned a car like that could damn well do as he pleased and look at the stars. I was listening hard. "Perhaps he saw us."

"Let's see if he answers," Oreste said, and let out a howl. It was lacerating, bestial. Beginning with a bellow, the roar of a bull, it filled the earth and sky and ended in a drunken laugh. Oreste jumped away from my kick. We all listened hard. That dog started barking again, the terrified crickets stopped chirping. Nothing. Oreste opened his mouth to do it again and Pieretto said: "Ready now."

This time we bellowed in unison, long and loud, with interesting variations. My skin crawled; I was thinking of how, like a search-light in the dark, a noise like that went everywhere, up the slopes, down the paths, into hollows and roots, making everything shiver.

The dog went wild again. We listened and watched the bend in the road. I was about to say that he must have died of fright when we heard the car door being slammed shut. Oreste said in my ear: "Now comes the Road Patrol," and we waited, staring at those trees. But for a while nothing happened. By now the dog was quiet and the cricket noise was everywhere under the stars. We kept our eyes on that strip of shadow.

"Come on," I said. "There are three of us."

2. We found him on the running board of the car, his face in his hands. He didn't move. We stood looking at him a few steps away as if he were a dangerous animal.

"Don't you think he's going to throw up?" Pieretto said.

"Possibly," Oreste said. He went up and put his hand on the man's forehead as if to test him for fever. The man pressed his fore-head against Oreste's hand, like a dog playing. They had an air of shoving each other apart, and I could hear them laughing softly. Oreste turned around.

"It's Poli," he said. "I'm sure of it. They own a villa."

The other stayed seated and held one of Oreste's hands, shaking his head like someone coming out of the water. He was a good-looking, solid young man a little older than us, with bad, fright-ened eyes. Holding Oreste's hand, he looked at us without showing any sign of noticing us.

It was then that Oreste said: "Weren't you at Milan?"

"There's time to flush a few more," the other said. "Are you after squirrels?"

"We're not at the Coste," Oreste said and pulled his hand away. Then he looked at the car and said: "You have a new one?"

What's the use of talking sense to a drunk, I thought. My earlier fear had turned to irritation. Why doesn't he leave him in the ditch?

That Poli character was watching us. He was like an invalid

staring up from a bed, scared and sad. None of us had ever been in such a state. And yet he looked tanned and in every way worthy of his car. I felt ashamed of our earlier bellowing.

"Can't you see Turin from here?" he said, getting quickly to his feet and looking around. "You should be able to. Can you see Turin?"

If it hadn't been for his voice, which seemed thick, hoarse, and weak at the same time, he was now almost normal. He looked around and said to Oreste: "I've been here three nights. There's a place where you can see Turin. Don't you want to go there? It's a fine place."

Now we made a circle and Oreste asked him suddenly: "Did you run away from home?"

"They're waiting for me at Turin," he said. "*Nouveaux riches*, unbearable people." He looked at us, smiling like a shamed child. "Disgusting, those people who do everything with gloves on—even when they're making children, or their millions."

Pieretto, standing beside him, was watching out of the corner of his eye.

The man took out his cigarettes and passed them around. They were soft and expensive. We lit up.

"If they could see me with you and your friends, they'd laugh," Poli said. "I enjoy ditching people like that."

Pieretto said loudly: "It doesn't take much to amuse you."

Poli said: "I like to joke. Don't you?"

"To condemn anyone who's made a pile," Pieretto said, "you should be able to do the same thing yourself. Or live on nothing at all."

Then Poli said, looking disturbed: "Do you think so?" He said it with so much concern that even Oreste couldn't help smiling. Suddenly Poli spread his arms to take us all in, and said in a very low voice, conspiratorially: "There's another reason."

"Go ahead."

Poli dropped his arms and sighed. He looked at us humbly from the bottom of his eyes and seemed really in a bad way.

"It's that I feel like a god tonight," he said quietly.

Nobody laughed. There was a moment of silence and Oreste proposed: "Let's go see Turin."

We went down a short stretch of road to a terrace on a curve where one could see the lights of Turin glittering below. We stopped at the edge. On our way up, not one of us had turned around. Poli, his arm over Oreste's shoulder, looked at the sea of lights. He threw his cigarette away and kept on looking.

"Well. What next?" Oreste said.

"How small man is," Poli said. "Alleys, courtyards, rooftops ... From up here it looks like a sea of stars. But when you're down there you're hardly aware of it."

Pieretto moved a short way off. Watering a bush, he shouted back: "You're putting us on."

And Poli, calmly: "I like the contrast. It's only in contrasts that you feel stronger, superior to your own body. Life is banal without contrasts. I have no illusions."

"Who does?" Oreste said.

The man looked up and smiled. "Who? But everybody does. Everyone sleeping in those houses. They think they're somebody, they dream, they wake up, they make love—'I'm this person or that person'—and instead ..."

"Instead what?" Pieretto said, coming up.

Interrupted, Poli had forgotten what he was saying. He snapped his fingers, searching for a word.

"You were saying that life is boring," Oreste said.

"Life is what we ourselves *are*," Pieretto said.

Poli said: "Let's sit down." He didn't look drunk at all. I began to think that those wild eyes of his were like his silk shirt, his handshake, his fine car; things habitual with him and inseparable from him.

We chattered awhile, sitting there on the grass. I let them talk and listened to the noise of the crickets. Pieretto's sarcasms didn't seem to touch Poli, who was explaining why he had fled Turin and human society for three nights. He mentioned hotels, important people, kept women. As fast as Pieretto warmed up to him and accepted him, I drew away. I was persuading myself that he was merely naïve. I fell back to the mood I was in when his car had stopped and I'd suspected that someone inside was making love.

Suddenly I said: "Is it worth it to leave Turin only to talk about nothing else?"

"But of course," Oreste said, jumping up. "Let's go home. Work tomorrow."

Poli stood up, and then Pieretto. "Aren't you coming?" they asked me.

While we were walking to the car, I stayed behind with Oreste and asked him about Poli. He said that Poli's family owned land near his village, a large villa, an entire hill. "When he was a boy, he used to come to the country and we used to hunt together. He was strange even then, but he didn't drink like this."

He called ahead to Poli: "Are you going to the Greppo this year?"

Poli ended his discussion with Pieretto and turned around.

"Papa shut me up there last year and took the car away," he said, with no embarrassment. "People have peculiar ideas. He wanted to get me away . . . From what? I don't know if I'll go back. It might be nice to spend a day there, but not more. With a few friends and some records."

He opened the car doors hospitably. I didn't want to get in because I realized that with him we couldn't be ourselves. One had to listen to him and accept his world by following his moods. Being polite with him meant becoming his mirror. I couldn't imagine how Oreste had stood his company for days at a time.

Poli turned around from the wheel and said: "Well, are you coming?"

"Where?"

"To the Greppo."

Oreste jumped in. "Are we crazy? I want to go to bed."

I also protested that it was an absurd time of day.

"It's not day yet," Poli said. "It's three something. We'll be there at five."

We all shouted together that we had to go home. "Take us down," Oreste said. "There'll be another time."

I whispered to Oreste: "Can we trust him?"

Oreste said: "I want to go to bed. Drop us at the Porta Nuova."

We left for Turin. The car ran smoothly, sure of itself. In front with Poli, Pieretto hadn't said anything.

We were on the brightly lit and empty avenues. Oreste got off in the Via Nizza, in front of the porticoes. Standing on the running board, he said goodbye to Poli. Soon they had dropped me off, too, at my doorstep. I waved. I made a date with Pieretto for the next day. The car slid away with the two of them.

3. During the day we were sweating over some exams; especially Oreste, who was studying medicine. Pieretto and I were studying law and had put our big push off until October: as everyone knows, law is improvisation and can't be done scientifically. Oreste, on the other hand, kept at it and didn't always come out with us in the evening. But in the early afternoon we knew where to find him: being a country boy, he was renting a room and eating at restaurants.

I spent the day after that night looking for him. I found him in the restaurant, gnawing on an apple, his elbow on his briefcase and his back against the wall. It was hot in there and he asked me if I'd seen Pieretto yet.

Fanning ourselves, we discussed some plans we had made for that year. The three of us were going to spend our vacation at Oreste's village: his farm was spacious, we would enjoy ourselves. But Pieretto and I wanted to take a pack and go there on foot. Oreste said that that was pointless; we would see all the country-side and feel all the heat we wanted as soon as we got there.

"What were you saying about Pieretto?"

"You aren't thinking, I hope, that he went to bed last night."

"Maybe he's studying."

"Hardly," Oreste said. "With that character and his car around. Didn't you see how well they got along?"

Then we talked about the night before, about Poli, about the whole strange business. Oreste said there was nothing to be astonished about. He and Poli were old friends, even though Poli's father was filthy rich, a *commendatore* from Milan who owned a huge country estate and never went there. Poli had grown up on the place, from summer to summer, with ten nursemaids and a carriage and horses, and only when he had put on his first long trousers had he been able to assert himself and go out and meet people in the villages. For two or three seasons, when the woodcocks were flying, he had gone shooting with the others. He was a good kid and a clever one. But he lacked steadiness; that definitely. Halfway through something he would change his mind.

"It's the life they lead," I said. "They become like women."

"Still, he catches on," Oreste said. "You heard what he said about his own kind."

"Only talk. He was drunk."

Here Oreste shook his head. He said that Poli wasn't drunk. A drunk is something else. "Perhaps he'd been drunk for three days and made a pig of himself. But now he's worse. One likes a drunk." Oreste had these surprising opinions.

"He didn't have anything against his own kind. He had it in for people who make a lot of money and don't know how to live," I said. "You're his friend. You ought to know him."

"Going hunting together is like going to school together," Oreste said. "My father liked me to hunt."

He emptied his glass and we left. As we were passing a tenement block in the bright sun, I suggested that Pieretto must have made a fool of himself with Poli. "Pieretto has that way of laughing like spitting in your face. He isn't aware of it, but it offends people."

"Maybe," Oreste said. "I've never seen Poli offended."

Neither Pieretto nor Oreste came out that evening. I was having a bad time when I had to be alone that year. To go home alone to study made no sense; I was too accustomed to living and arguing with Pieretto and wandering the streets. The air, the movement, even the darkness of the avenues were more than enough pleasure for me then. I was always on the point of picking up a girl or sticking my nose into some alluring dive, or else making up my mind to set out along an avenue and keep going till dawn, no matter where I ended up. Instead I would circle the usual streets, passing and repassing the same corners, the same signs, the same faces. Sometimes I would plant myself uncertainly on a corner and stand there for whole half hours at a time, furious with myself.

But that evening things went better. Our late meeting with Poli had relieved me of many scruples; it let me know that in the world, night and day, there were privileged people more absurd than myself, lazy people who had a better time than I did. Because my father and mother, provincials who had moved to the city, had taught me a lesson without knowing they were doing it: that the insanities of the poor would always be open to me, but those of the rich, never. By poor, of course, they didn't mean tramps or beggars.

I spent the evening at a movie, enjoying myself but restless at the thought of Poli. I wasn't sleepy when I came out and walked down empty alleys under the stars. I had been born and brought up in Turin, but that evening I kept thinking of the winding lanes of my parents' large village, lanes that ran out to open country. Oreste had always lived in a village like that and was soon going back. Going back for good. That was his ambition. He could stay in the city if he wanted to. But what was the difference?

When I got to my door, someone called me. It was Pieretto, coming out of a shadow and crossing the street to join me. He wanted to stay and talk; he wasn't sleepy either. He hadn't shown up earlier because he had spent the whole day with Poli. They had ended the previous night by driving around the countryside; in the morning they found themselves by the lakes, in full daylight. There Poli had been sick, and had toppled from the car like a sack when he tried to get out, blinded perhaps by the sun on the water. He was full of cocaine, Poli was—poisoned with it. Then Pieretto had telephoned the hotel in Turin; someone there had told him that he ought to phone Milan. "I haven't the money," Pieretto had shouted.

Then a priest who could drive climbed into the car and they brought Poli to Novara. Here a doctor had revived him, made him sweat and vomit; then they quarreled with the priest, who kept accusing Pieretto of being his friend's evil inspiration. Finally Poli had straightened everything out, had paid the doctor, the phone and lunch bills; and they had brought the priest back home, giving him a long lecture on sin and hell.

Pieretto was completely happy. He had enjoyed Poli's lunacy, enjoyed the trip, enjoyed the priest's face. Now Poli had gone to take a bath and change his clothes; there was a woman mixed up in it, some kind of fury who had followed him from Milan to Turin and was laying siege to him at the hotel, wanted a showdown, and kept sending him flowers.

"Perhaps he's a little silly," Pieretto said, "but he's got a sense of humor. He gets good value for his money."

"He goes too far," I said. "He's irresponsible."

Then Pieretto started explaining that Poli did nothing worse than we did. Uprooted bourgeoisie that we were, we spent our nights arguing on benches, we paid for our fornications, drank wine; he had other resources, other drugs, freedom, classy women. Wealth is power. That's all.

"You're crazy," I said. "We think about things. I want to know why I enjoy my walks. For instance, you stick to Turin and I like climbing the hills. I like the smells of the earth. Why? Poli doesn't give a damn about these things. He's irresponsible. Oreste says so, too."

"Donkeys that you are," Pieretto came back, and explained that one needs experience, needs danger, and one's limits are set by one's environment. "Oh, yes, Poli says and does foolish things," he said. "Maybe he only leaves us the dry bones. But it would be pathetic if he lived the way we do."

We walked and argued, as always. Pieretto maintained that Poli was doing very well in exploring the life that was open to him.

"But if he talks nonsense," I objected.

"Doesn't matter," Pieretto said. "He works hard in his own way and touches things that the rest of you don't even know exist."

"Did he want you to take cocaine too?"

Irritated, Pieretto said that Poli didn't make a pose of his drug taking. He said very little about it. But he said things about sin to that priest which showed a keen eye and a true experience. Then I laughed in Pieretto's face, and he was irritated again.

"You're scandalized when someone takes cocaine," he told me, "and then you laugh when he discusses sin."

He stopped in front of a bar. He said he was going to telephone. After a while he leaned out of the booth and wanted to know if Oreste was coming.

"It's midnight. Oreste's asleep. His resources demand it," I said.

Pieretto shouted into the phone. He went on for a while, giggling and tittering. When he came out, he said: "We're going to Poli's."

4. The idea of spending another white night scared me. My father and mother wouldn't say anything; a word or two about the time when I came in, a dark look over the plates, cautious questions about the exams. I don't know how Pieretto may have squared it at home; but my parents' defenseless faces pained me, and I wondered what my father and mother had been like at twenty and whether one fine day I would have children so estranged. My parents were probably thinking about the courts, loose women, jail. What did they know about our midnight manias? Or maybe they were right: it's always a matter of boredom, of an initial vice, and everything grows from that.

When we were in front of the hotel with the woman Rosalba, who was pacing up and down, and Poli was maneuvering the car to take us aboard, I muttered to Pieretto: "No monkey business tonight. It's midnight already."

It was obvious that Poli wanted us with him to keep his woman from boiling over. He even made jokes to that effect. He had presented us as "the best Turin has to offer": she should listen and learn. In Poli's world, people behave badly on principle; they treat others with a cheerful brassiness. I couldn't see what Pieretto was getting out of it.

Rosalba got in front with Poli. She was a skinny woman, poor soul, with red-rimmed eyes, a stiff manner, and a flower in her hair. She couldn't keep still. Even before, while waiting, she kept giving us anxious looks, kept trying to smile, and kept looking in her mirror. She wore a pink evening gown and might have passed for Poli's mother.

He was joking and talking a blue streak. He watched the woman with dancing eyes, laughed and drove. In an instant we were out of Turin. Pieretto leaned forward and said something to him.

Poli braked suddenly. We were beyond the lights, at the base of the hills. Rosalba laughed excitedly.

"Where are we going?"

I made it clear that I didn't want to stay out all night.

Poli turned around and said to me: "I want you with us. You must trust me. We won't be late."

The woman said desolately: "Let's stop, Poli. Why do you want to drive all night? You're always so rash."

Poli started the motor again. Before putting the car in gear, he whispered to the woman. I saw the two heads together, made out the anxiety and intimacy of their voices, then saw her nod energetically. Poli turned and smiled at us.

He swung the car around and we started back toward Turin. The hill looked black in the night as we skirted it along the empty avenues of the suburbs. Then we ran along the Po under its slopes. Sassi flew by. One could see that Poli and Rosalba had taken this road earlier in the evening. She was pressing close to his shoulder. What did Pieretto find in those two? I wondered if she knew about Poli's drugs, tried to imagine them drunk together, tried to detest them. But I didn't succeed. The novelty of that drive, racing along in the night, the dark water and the black hill hanging over us, didn't give me a chance to think of anything else.

"Here! Here we are!" Rosalba shouted. Poli was already slowing in front of a lit-up villa. He swung around on the gravel and stopped in a car park. In front, facing the river, there was a shadowed open space with tables and discreet, shaded lamps. I saw the white coats of waiters.

When the fuss and embarrassment of sitting down and ordering was over—Rosalba changed her mind several times, wouldn't listen, became sulky and talked loudly; Pieretto stuck his elbows on the table, showing his frayed cuffs—I decided to let them talk among themselves and told myself: after all, it's a café like any other. I leaned back in my chair and tried hard to hear the water flowing by in the shadow.

But it wasn't just another café. A small orchestra began with a crash, then suddenly fell quiet, and in the middle of the circle of lamps a woman appeared and sang. She wore an evening dress and had a flower in her hair. One by one, couples left the tables and danced in the half shadow, clutching each other tightly. The woman's voice carried the couples, spoke for them, bent and swayed with them. It was like a ceremony, a convulsive rite between river and hill, where the woman's cry answered everyone's movements. The woman, a Rosalba in olive green, was shouting her song, rocking with her hands on her breasts and crying out, invoking something.

Now our own Rosalba was blissfully squeezing Poli's hand, and he was talking casually to Pieretto.

"The dancers should all be singing themselves," Pieretto said. "Some things we ought to do for ourselves, ourselves alone."

And Poli, laughing: "A dancer is busy enough. You must excuse them."

"Dancers are stupid," Pieretto said. "They look around for something they already have in their arms."

Rosalba clapped her hands with the convulsive joy of a child. Those bright eyes of hers were alarming. Just then the liqueurs and coffee arrived and she had to detach herself from Poli.

The orchestra began again, this time without singing. The others rested while the piano did a few showy acrobatic variations. One had to listen. Then the orchestra came in and smothered the piano. While they played, the lamps and reflectors under the trees changed color magically and we were green, were red, were yellow.

"Quite a little place," Poli said, looking around.

"Lethargic people," Pieretto said. "What we need are Oreste's sound effects."

Poli looked up, surprised, then remembered. "Our friend has gone to bed?" he said immediately. "I wish he were here."

"He's sleeping off last night," Pieretto said. "It's a pity. Some things he can't take."

Rosalba gave a start that made her look almost naked. "I want to dance," she said to Poli, annoyed.

"Dear Rosi," he said, "I can't leave my friends alone to bore themselves. It would be discourteous. We're in Turin, a well-bred city."

Rosalba reddened like a flame. I had to acknowledge then that she was both crazy and clumsy. Who knows, she may even have had children at Milan. Remembering the story of her sending flowers to Poli, I looked away. I could hear Pieretto saying: "I should be happy to dance with you, Rosalba, but I realize I can't hope for that. I'm not Poli, unfortunately." She gave him a look more bewildered than malicious.

Meanwhile the orchestra was playing and I also muttered something. I didn't know how to dance. Poli, impassible, waited for me to finish and resumed: "I'd like to say that these are very important days in my life. Yesterday I understood many things. That noise you made two nights ago woke me up. It was like a cry that wakes a sleepwalker. It was a sign, the violent crisis that resolves an illness . . ."

"Were you sick?" Rosalba asked.

"I was worse," Poli said. "I was an old man who thinks himself a boy. Now I know that I'm a man, a man full of vices, a weak man but a man. That cry has shown me myself. No more illusions."

"Power of a cry," Pieretto said. Without wanting to, I looked closely at Poli's eyes to see if they were clouded.

"My life," he went on, "I see it as the life of someone else. Now I know who I am, where I came from, what I'm doing . . ."

"But this cry," I interrupted, "had you ever heard it before?"

"You're dense," Pieretto said.

"It was the call we used to use when we went hunting," Poli said with a smile.

"You used to hunt!" Rosalba burst out.

"Yes, on the hill."

An embarrassed silence followed, during which everyone except Poli looked at his fingernails. That woman was singing again in the circle of tables. I heard Rosalba nervously beating time with her heel. That cadenced voice and the rustle of dancers on the floor made me think of the cricket chorus on the darkened hill.

"Well," Rosalba said finally, "no more stories? Would you like to dance now?"

Poli didn't bat an eyelash and didn't move. He was thinking of his hunting call.

"It's good to wake up and drop one's illusions," he said, smiling again. "You feel free and responsible. We have a tremendous force inside us: freedom. You can touch innocence. You become open to suffering."

Rosalba put out her cigarette in a saucer. When she was silent, poor woman, so thin and eaten up, she was bearable. At least for us who still didn't know, at that time in our lives, what surfeit was. Poli's cultivated voice dominated her, held her in. Rosalba twisted around as if she were naked.

Finally she said to his face: "Tell us honestly what you're thinking. Do you want to get away from Turin?"

Frowning, he touched her shoulder, took her under the armpit the way one does with someone about to fall. Pieretto leaned forward, almost as if not to miss anything, nodding encouragement. Rosalba panted, her eyes half closed.

"Shall I make her happy?" Poli asked us doubtfully. "Shall I dance with her?"

When the two of us were alone, Pieretto caught my glance and grinned. The voice of the woman in olive green filled the night. I scowled and said: "Shit."

Pieretto, happy, poured himself a liqueur. He poured one for me and took another for himself.

"They're the same everywhere," he declared. "Don't you like them?"

"I said shit."

"Even so, the boy isn't too bright," Pieretto said. "He could go a lot further with that woman."

"She's stupid," I said.

"A woman in love is always stupid," Pieretto said.

I listened to a few words of the song that was guiding the couples. It said to live live—take take—without much passion. No matter how unhappy or bored you were, it was difficult to resist the rhythm of that song. I wondered if they could hear it on the hill.

"These modern nights," Pieretto said. "They're as old as the world."

5. That night Pieretto danced too, because Rosalba was defying Poli and trying to humiliate him. I don't know how much we all drank, the night began to seem endless, but the orchestra had stopped some time ago, and Rosalba called a waiter and wanted Poli to pay and take us all to breakfast at Valentino. I could see her pink dress moving in the circle of light—the last lamp still on—and felt cold gusts coming up from the Po. But Poli had turned stubborn and insisted on arguing with Pieretto and the waiter; so Rosalba ran to the car and started blowing the horn. Then the owner came out, more waiters, late drinkers from the bar. Rosalba jumped to the ground and called Poli, Poli.

On the way back Poli drove with an arm around Rosalba's

waist, and Rosalba stretched out happily, satisfied with him. Every so often he would turn and smile back at us, almost as if we were accomplices. Pieretto was silent the whole way. The car went past the road to Turin, ran over the bridges, and burst onto the Moncalieri road. Nor did we stop there: it was obvious that we were just killing time, waiting for daylight. I closed my eyes, drunk.

I woke with a jolt, like someone dreaming himself to the edge of a whirlpool; the nightmare continued a moment, then a deep, shining sky opened up and I seemed to be falling headlong into it. I woke into a cold, pinkish light, the car was bouncing over the cobbles of a village; it was dawn. Blinking my eyes against our own breeze, I saw that everyone was asleep and that the village was empty and shuttered. The only thing alive was Poli, calmly driving.

He stopped when the sun appeared on the crest of a hill. Pieretto was cheerful; Rosalba blinked hard. Good lord, she looked old enough in that low-cut pink evening dress. I was furious at all of them and sorry for them at the same time. Poli turned around jovially and said good morning.

"I'm sorry, but where are we?" I said at that point.

"Call them up," Pieretto said. "Tell them you were taken sick."

The other two had started joking and biting each other's ears. Rosalba took the flower from her hair and, rescuing it from Poli, handed it back to me. "There now," she said hoarsely. "Don't spoil our party."

For the rest of the trip I smelled that flower and squirmed. It was the first that a woman had given to me and it had to come from a type like Rosalba. I had it in for Poli, after the night's nonsense and broken promises.

The bell tower of another village popped up. We reached the square, through a porticoed lane under rounded balconies. In the morning shadows a girl was sprinkling the cobblestones with water from a bottle.

The wooden floor of the café had also just been wet down and smelled of cellars and rain. We ate by a window in the sun, and I asked for the phone right away. There wasn't any.

"It's your fault," Poli said to Rosalba. "If you hadn't made me dance . . ."

"If you hadn't had so much to drink," she snapped back. "You were stoned, sweating cognac all over."

"Let it go," Poli said.

"Ask your friends about the things you were saying," she cried disgustedly. "Just ask them. They heard."

Pieretto said: "Important things. Innocence and free choice."

The woman who was serving us and looking askance at Rosalba said there was a phone at the post office. Then I started to get up and asked Pieretto for his wallet. Rosalba got up, too, and said: "I'm coming with you. That way I'll wake up. It smells terrible in here."

So the two of us went out on the square, she in pink, tall and lean, a spectacle. Heads poked out of windows, but the street itself was still empty.

"At this hour they're all in the fields," I said to make conversation. Rosalba asked for a cigarette. "Ordinary Macedonias," I said.

She stopped to let me light her cigarette, and while we were face to face she said with a low, forced laugh: "You're younger than Poli."

I snapped away the match that was burning my fingers. Rosalba blushed and went on: "More sincere than Poli."

I moved away, keeping an eye on her. "Well, here we are," she said. "It's my neck, don't worry . . . Now, tell me something."

She asked hoarsely what we'd been doing in Poli's company those days. When I started with our meeting, she blinked hard. "Poli was alone?" she wanted to know. "But why on the hill at midnight then?"

"He was alone, but it was three o'clock."

"How come you joined him?"

I told her that Oreste and Pieretto knew Poli better than I did. I had gone to bed, but Pieretto stayed with him all morning. Poli had seemed a little cockeyed. As always, for that matter. She should ask Pieretto; they had talked a lot.

I saw right off that Rosalba had lost no time, had already grilled Pieretto while they were dancing. She fixed me with those eyes.

I was bothered and moved away. We started walking again over the cobbles.

While waiting for the phone in the post office, I said to Rosalba, who was smoking in the doorway: "Oreste has known Poli since they were boys . . . He was with us the other night."

She didn't answer but watched the street. I came to the door, too, and examined the sky.

After I had talked and shouted to my mother in the little booth, I returned to the door. Rosalba hadn't moved. I said brightly: "Shall we go?"

"Your friend," she took up, shaking herself, "is a very sharp young man. Didn't he tell you anything Poli said?"

"They went to the lakes."

"Yes, I know."

"He was drunk and felt sick."

"No, before that," Rosalba said impatiently, and her voice trembled.

"I don't know. We found him on the hill looking at the stars."

Then with a wriggle Rosalba took my arm. Two country women passing turned to look at us.

"You understand me, isn't that so?" Rosalba said, breathing hard. "You've seen how Poli treats me. Yesterday I thought I would die. I've stayed alone in the hotel for three days. I can't even go walking without everybody recognizing me. I'm in his hands here; at Milan they think I'm at the seaside. But Poli ignores me, Poli is tired of me, he doesn't even want to dance with me any more . . ."

I looked down at the cobbles and imagined the heads on the balconies.

". . . Last night you saw him when he was happy. He can still bear me when he's drunk . . . but he gets drunk, and worse, to escape me. Now . . ." she panted more heavily, "we just live day by day."

She didn't drop my arm even when we reentered the café, when I pushed aside the tinkling curtain over the door. Poli and Pieretto had their heads together in the corner, and Pieretto called out: "What'll we eat?"

Eggs arrived in copper pans, and cherries. I tried not to notice Rosalba. Poli broke the bread and went on talking.

"The more you make up your mind, the further you fall. You touch bottom. When everything is lost, you find yourself again."

Pieretto laughed. "A drunk is a drunk," he said. "He doesn't choose his drink or drug any longer. He made a choice once and for all, millions of years ago, when he shouted the first *evoë*."

"There's an innocence," Poli said, "a clarity that comes from the very bottom . . ."

Rosalba was silent. I didn't dare look at her.

"I tell you," Pieretto interrupted, "that if you forgot what time it was last night, it was because you'd lost the power of choice."

"But that's the innocence I'm looking for," Poli said doggedly. "The better I get to know it, the more sure I am of being weak and a man. Are you or aren't you convinced that weakness is man's condition? How can you raise yourself if you haven't fallen first?"

Rosalba nibbled cherries and kept quiet. Pieretto shook his head several times and said no. I was thinking of my earlier conversation with Rosalba, not so much what we said but her voice and the pressure of her arm. My eyes were burning with tiredness. When we got up to go, I threw her a glance. She seemed calm, almost asleep.

6. We left them at the hotel door, in the squalor of a wasted morning. The sun beating on the windows hurt my eyes. I crossed the gardens with Pieretto and we didn't talk; I was thinking of Oreste.

"Be seeing you," I said at the corner.

I went home and flopped on my bed. I could hear my mother bustling in the corridor and I kept putting off our meeting. I didn't want to sleep, only to recover. My exhaustion made it easy not to think of the night, the confusion, and Rosalba's sobbing, and I sprawled into that sky I was dreaming about while dozing in the car under the cool morning light. I dawdled in the village alleys, looked up at balconies and the hills beyond. I knew them well, these little heaped-up country towns. I knew the summer vegetable gardens of the old people where my parents used to send me in the country when I was a boy, a village on the plain between irrigation ditches and rows of trees; narrow, porticoed alleys with thin slices of sky visible very high up. All I could remember of my childhood were the summers. Narrow streets opening on fields in every direction, by day and night, were the gates to life and the world. It was a great marvel when a big car, coming from God knows where, honked its way through the middle of town and on, God knows where, to new cities, to the sea, swirling dust and little boys together.

That old project of crossing the hills with a knapsack with Pieretto came back to me in the dark. I didn't envy automobiles. I knew one crossed a landscape in a car without learning anything about it. I would say to Pieretto: "You have to travel on foot, you take paths, you skirt vineyards, you see everything. It's the same difference as between looking at water and diving into it. Better to be a beggar, a tramp."

Pieretto would laugh and say there was gasoline everywhere in the world today.

"The hell with that," I grumbled. "The peasants don't know what gas is. Sickles and hoes are all they need. Before washing a barrel or cutting a tree, they still check the phase of the moon. I've seen them when hail is threatening, stretching two chains across the yard . . ."

"And they buy insurance," Pieretto said, "and they thresh by machine. And they use fertilizer on the vines."

"They make use of these things," I said. "They use them, but they live differently. They're unhappy in the city."

Pieretto laughed sardonically. "Give a peasant a car," he grinned, "and watch his dust. He wouldn't stop for Rosalba or for us, you can bet your life. He's man of affairs, a peasant is."

I thought of Oreste studying medicine. "*There's* a peasant who lives in the city," I said to Pieretto. "He knows more science than we do, but the old life dies hard. The night has another meaning for him, you say so yourself . . ."

The phone interrupted my doze. My parents called me. I thought it would be Rosalba, that the story wasn't finished yet. But it was Pieretto's sister, who wanted to know if I'd seen him— he'd been gone two days. I was with him a half hour ago, I told her. He must be on his way home. Not to scare her, I didn't mention the previous night.

She said: "What a bunch you are! Where did you sleep?"

"We didn't sleep."

"Who sleeps can't sin," she laughed.

"And who feels like sleeping?"

At the table I said we'd had a flat tire. My father said that tires can cause accidents, especially if the driver has been drinking. Then he said that one mustn't exploit one's friends; one can't ever repay a rich person.

In the afternoon I decided to study. But first I took a bath for refreshment. I thought that Poli and Rosalba were probably doing the same, and wondered if Rosalba still dared to take her clothes off in company.

Toward evening the phone rang. It was Pieretto. "Come to Oreste's," he said.

"But suppose I'm studying?"

"Come anyway; it's worth it," he said. "Those two have been doing some shooting."

We sat sweating in a restaurant with Oreste, who had just come from the hospital and had phoned the nurses twice to get news. Poli was dying: a bullet had entered his side, punctured a lung; and Rosalba was shouting to the distracted waiters: "Kill me, why don't you kill me, too?" so that they finally had to lock her in the bathroom.

"When did it happen?" I asked.

"It's the woman," Oreste said. "She shot him in a fit of anger. She'd been yelling quite a while, they heard her in the bar. Who knows what dirt's behind it?"

It happened in mid-afternoon, in the heat. Poli must have taken dope before anything happened, because he was laughing in his hospital bed, quite gay.

We discussed it all evening. At the moment, in the hospital and at the hotel, everyone was waiting for instructions from Milan. Rosalba was shut in a room; her fate depended on Poli's life and also on his father's arrival: he was the sort of man who, hating a scandal, could close the whole matter with two words, hush everything up completely. Of course there was Rosalba's revolver, a female toy with a mother-of-pearl handle, but someone was ready to substitute a more appropriate weapon.

"Power of money," Pieretto said blandly. "You can even buy up a crime or an agony."

Oreste telephoned again. "The old man has come," he said, turning to us. "Good. I wonder if he knows the woman."

Then we told him that the guilty party was Poli, that we had spent the night with the two of them and that Poli was treating her miserably. "As if he'd planned it," Pieretto said. "Rosalbas are made on purpose for that."

"I'm going back to the hospital right away," Oreste said. "They're giving him a blood transfusion."

That night I walked with Pieretto. I was worn out with excitement and lack of sleep. He ruminated and kept talking. I let him know that in the morning Rosalba had asked me about Poli. "It was obvious that something had to snap," he said. "A woman can take anything from a man except a crisis of conscience. Do you know what she told me last night? That young as he may be, Poli never turns his head to look at a woman?"

"What we'd been doing on the hill is what she asked me."

"She would rather he had made a pig of himself. Women understand these things."

Then I said that as far as I was concerned he *had* made a pig of himself. That between his drugs and his free choice it all looked pretty swinish to me. He just took people for rides—that's how it added up. Good thing he was shot.

Pieretto smiled and replied that whether Poli lived or died it had all been a great experience. "You don't agree," he said, "but what are we looking for every night in the streets? Something to break the routine, a little variety . . ."

"I wonder what you'd say if it happened to you?"

"But it's you who worry day and night about escaping from your cage. Why do you think we cross the Po? Only you're wrong; the strangest things happen in rooms in Turin, in cafés, trolley cars . . ."

"I'm not looking for strange things."

"Well," he said, "this world is made for the Polis. Believe me."

The next day Poli was still between life and death; they gave him another transfusion and he sweated in his cot. According to Oreste, who took turns with the father watching over him, the drug had worn off and he was like a frightened child on the edge of tears. The father had gone at night to find Rosalba; what they had said to each other no one knew; but they had shut her up with some nuns and nobody mentioned homicide any more. "An accident," the chief surgeon said, talking to his assistant. Pieretto drank all this in with both ears, as Oreste knew he would.

Poor Oreste, he got to the point of flunking his exams. He took turns like a male nurse at Poli's bedside. He introduced himself to the old *commendatore* and talked to him. He said the old gentleman wanted to talk about the country, about the Coste and the harvests, as if he knew the subject well. He would drive Poli's green car to the hospital himself. It was he who forced Oreste to get some sleep in the morning.

Finally we heard that Poli was out of danger. Even Pieretto went to see him. He said: "Poli's just the same, reading Nino Salvaneschi at the moment." I resolutely didn't go. We discussed it for a few days more, then Oreste told us that they had sent him to the seacoast in an ambulance.

7. That summer I spent an hour or two every day on the Po. I liked to sweat over the oars and then dive into the cold still dark water that goes into your eyes and washes them. Almost always I went alone, because Pieretto was still asleep at that time of day. If he came too, he would manage the boat while I swam. We rowed up under the bridges against the current, between the walled banks, and came out between the embankment and the trees, under the flank of the hill. The towering hill was beautiful on the way back, as one smoked the day's first pipe, and although it was June, there was still a mist around it in the early morning, a cool breath from the ground. It was on the thwarts of that boat that I developed a taste for the open air and realized that one's childhood pleasure in water and earth doesn't die. All life, I used to think on those mornings, is like a game under the sun.

But the sand diggers, standing in water up to their thighs, weren't playing; they panted as they hoisted shovelfuls of sludge and emptied them into the barges. After an hour, two hours, the barge would drift down the river, heavily loaded, and a thin, sun-blackened man, wearing a vest over his naked torso, maneuvered it slowly with a pole. He unloaded his sand in the city, below the bridges, and returned slowly; they would come back up in groups under an always higher sun. By the time I left the river, they had already made two or three trips. All day, while I was walking in the city, studying, arguing, resting, those men were going up and down the river, unloading, jumping into the water, frying in the sun. I used to think about them especially toward evening when our night life was beginning and the men were coming home to their dormitories along the river in those four-floored houses and flopping on their beds. Or nursing a drink in the bars. Certainly, they also saw the sun and the hill.

On the days when I sweated on the water, my blood stayed fresh all day, invigorated by the shock of the cold river. It was as if the sun and the living weight of the water had soaked me in one of their virtues, a blind, happy, and devious force, like that of a tree trunk or a forest animal. Pieretto too, when he came with me, enjoyed the morning. Drifting toward Turin on the current, our eyes washed by the sun and our plunges, we would stretch in the boat to dry; the riverbanks, the hill, villas, distant clumps of trees seemed cut on the air.

"If you lived this life every day," Pieretto said, "you would become an animal."

"Just look at the sand diggers . . ."

"No, not them," he said. "They only work. I mean a strong and healthy animal . . . Egotistic," he added suddenly, "with that sweet-natured egotism of someone growing fat."

"Work is no sin," I muttered.

"Who said it was? Nobody is to blame for being what he is. The blame belongs to others, always to others. We take boat rides and smoke our pipes."

"We're not animal enough."

Pieretto laughed. "Who knows what a real animal is?" he said. "A fish, a blackbird, a lizard? Or even a squirrel? Some people say every animal has a soul . . . a soul in pain. That would be purgatory."

"There's nothing that tastes of death," he went on, "more than the summer sun, the powerful light, exuberant nature. You sniff the air and listen to the woods and know that the plants and animals don't give a damn about you. Everything lives and consumes itself. Nature is death . . ."

"How does purgatory come into it?" I asked.

"There's no other way to explain it," he said. "Either there's nothing or there are souls."

It was an old argument. This was what irritated me in Pieretto. Oreste just shrugs and laughs these remarks off, but I'm not made that way. Every word with a country flavor touches and excites me. I couldn't answer at the moment, but rowed and kept quiet.

Pieretto also drank in the dripping water with his eyes. It was he who had said the year before: "But what about the Po? Why don't we go there?" and had broken through our timidity, mine and Oreste's, who didn't usually do things merely because we hadn't done them before. Pieretto had been several years in Turin, after having lived in various other cities. His father was a restless architect who kept rooting and uprooting his family on the spur of the moment. Once, in Puglia, he had even deposited them all in a monastery, leaving mother and daughter with the nuns and sharing a monk's cell himself with Pieretto while he supervised some restorations. "My father," Pieretto once said, "doesn't know what to say to priests. They scare him. He can't stand them and quarreled with them all the time, terrified that I might become a priest or a monk." Now his father, a giant in an open-neck shirt, had calmed down and was satisfied with Turin: he kept his family there while he traveled. The few times I saw him, he and his son kidded each other, gave each other advice, talked as I'd never suspected one could talk with a father. At bottom I didn't like all that freedom—the father seemed like a contemporary we didn't know what to do with.

"You were well off in the monastery," Pieretto once said to him, "because you were living like a bachelor."

"Nonsense," his father said. "You're well off wherever your soul is at peace. Look how fat the monks get."

"There are thin ones, too."

"They're fake monks, sad cases. No place for saints. Saints can't live in crowds."

"Like riding a motorcycle," Pieretto said. "It's like a monk on a motorcycle. Who believes in it?"

His father looked at him suspiciously.

"What's wrong with that?"

"Nothing," Pieretto said. "Nowadays a saint is like a monk on a motorcycle . . ."

"An anachronism," I said.

"Just a business," his father said irritably. "Religion is just another business. They know it, better than we do."

That year the father was working in Genoa, he had a contract, and Pieretto had to go there to swim on the Genoese Riviera. His sister left and Pieretto wanted the three of us to go, Oreste too, to meet some new people. But we had that old plan of visiting Oreste: for me, too many were too much, and the Po gave me an excuse for avoiding the sea. I decided to stay alone in Turin, to wait for the others to come back in August, then to take our packs and get moving.

I wouldn't have thought that I could enjoy the early summer in the city so much. With no friends around and no faces I knew in the streets, I thought about the past, went boating, imagined new things. My restless times were at night—Pieretto had debauched me, of course—the best times were around two in the afternoon when the empty streets held nothing but a streak of sky. One thing I often did was to notice some woman at a window, bored and absorbed as only a woman can be. I would look up, catch sight of the room behind, a sliver of mirror perhaps, and carry away that pleasure. I didn't envy my two friends their life on the beach or in the cafés or among tanned and half-naked girls. No doubt they were having a very good time, but they would come back; and in the meantime I was spending my mornings tanning, rowing, enjoying life. Girls also came to the Po, screamed from the boats and the banks of the Sangone; the sand diggers would look up and shout back. I knew that some day I would meet one of them and something would happen. Rowing and smoking my pipe, I was already imagining her eyes, legs, and shoulders—a magnificent woman. And when I had to stand and push with one oar, I couldn't help striking the pose of a simple-souled athlete scrutinizing the far horizon. I kept wondering if people like Poli would enjoy such pleasures or understand my life.

Toward the end of July I brought a girl to the Po, but she was nothing very novel or magnificent. I knew her already, she worked in a bookstore, was bony and nearsighted, but she had well-kept hands and a languid manner; it was she who asked me while I was turning over books how I had got so sunburned. She was very glad to come with me that Saturday.

She wore a brief white bathing suit under her skirt, turning her back and giggling as she took the skirt off. She stretched out on the cushions in the bottom of the boat, complained about the sun, and watched me row. Her name was Teresina—Resina for short. We talked politely about the heat, the fishermen, the spas at Moncalieri. She wanted to discuss swimming pools rather than the river. She asked me if I liked to dance. Her half-closed eyes made her seem distracted.

I stopped the boat under some trees and started to swim. She wouldn't swim because she had rubbed down with sun-tan oil; she smelled vaguely of the bathroom. When I came dripping out of the water, she said "*Bravo*," and walked along the bank. Her long reddened legs weren't bad-looking. I don't know why, but she bothered me. I brought cushions for her to the rocks and she asked me to get the bottle of oil and rub her back where she couldn't reach. Then, on my knees, I went up and down her spine with my fingertips; she laughed and told me to behave, rubbed my mouth with the back of her neck. Turning around, she kissed me on the mouth. Well, she knew what she was doing. I said to her: "Why did you cover yourself with that oil?"

And Resina, touching the tip of my nose with her nose. "What do you want to do, you dog? It's prohibited."

She went on laughing with those little eyes and asked me why I didn't oil myself too. Then I grabbed and hugged her. She squirmed free and said: "No, no, oil yourself."

She wouldn't do anything more than kiss, though she agreed to come into the bushes. When my first pique was over, I was glad things had ended this way. In broad daylight, on the grass, her perfume and our bodies clashed; these things you do in the city, inside a room. A naked body isn't beautiful in the open air. It bothered me, offended those places. Later I agreed to take her to a public swimming pool, where Resina happily examined the other bathers and drank soda pop through a straw.

8. I let Resina go because the oil business, the swimming pool, all the tacit rules of the game began to bore me. All in all, I was better off alone, and she hadn't been my first delusion. Which is to say that, instead of astounding Pieretto with a great adventure, I was going to have to say that there wasn't a woman worth a morning of water and sun. I knew his answer already: "Not a morning; but a night, yes."

I couldn't imagine Oreste at the sea with Pieretto. He hadn't come the year before when I went with Pieretto and his sister. He had suddenly escaped to his village in the hills. "What can he find there?" Pieretto had said. "We'll have to go." That was how our project of going on foot was born, but during the winter Oreste had argued against it, saying that it was better to spend a month in the vineyards than a month on the roads. He wasn't wrong, but Pieretto said no. He wasn't the type to stand still, not Pieretto; the previous summer he had taken me to a new beach each morning, had stuck his nose everywhere, had made friends from one end of the coast to the other. Cheap bars or grand hotels, he didn't care. Having no dialect of his own, he spoke them all. He would say: "Tonight, at the casino," and it would be some bather or shop-owner or an old landlady; he found their point of least resistance and spent the evening at the gambling casino. It made you laugh to watch him. But he didn't succeed with women. His manner just didn't work. He snowed them under, annihilated them, then lost his patience, insulted them, missed out. I wasn't even sure he much cared.

"You have to be stupid," I consoled him, "to please women."

"It's not true," he told me. "It's not enough. You have to be stupid *also*."

Pieretto was short and curly-haired, dark-skinned and dry-cheeked—he seemed born to steal someone else's girl just by laughing or looking at her. Compared to me or the big, heavy Oreste, there was no question who was the most sparkling. Still, Pieretto got nowhere, even at the beach.

"You're too excitable," I told him. "You don't let people know you. A girl wants to know who she's dealing with."

We were walking the coast road, above the sheer rock shelving, looking for a certain little beach.

"Here are the women, and here's the beach," he said.

Below, tiny in the distance, Linda and Carlotta were undressing, his sister and a friend of hers, a well-built girl, older than we were: if we'd met her on the promenade, we'd have turned around.

"Happy days," he said. "They're waiting for us."

"Linda brought her for you."

Pieretto waved in the bright sun and shouted. But the rustle of the sea that we could barely hear must have covered his shout. Then we tossed down some stones. The girls looked up and began dancing and waving. They must have yelled at us, but we couldn't hear.

"Let's go down," I said.

We got to the little beach by swimming around some rocks in the shallow green water. We played with the girls a long time on the rocks or in the spray. Then I stretched out under the heavy beating sun and watched foam running up the sand while Pieretto was entertaining his sister and her friend. I remember that we ate peaches.

They were talking about the fruit stones and bits of newspaper you find even on deserted beaches. Pieretto said there wasn't a virgin corner left on the earth. He said that too many people still found something pure and savage in the clouds and the sea horizon. He said that the old male pretense of wanting women to be virgins was a relic of the same taste—a silly mania for getting there first. Carlotta, her hair in her eyes, argued with him: she didn't see the joke and laughed resentfully.

With her, of all people, this conversation! Carlotta was the kind of girl who said: "*Mamma mia*, isn't it cute?" about the sea, a baby, or a cat. She had her friends on the beach or at dances, but she maintained that she couldn't bear to see in the city anyone who had seen her half-naked on the beach. She used to stroll arm-in-arm with Linda.

Pieretto paid no attention to these things. From the rocks where she was sunning, Linda told him to shut up. Pieretto started to talk about blood. He said that a taste for the intact and the savage was a taste for shedding blood. "One makes love to wound, to shed blood," he explained. "The bourgeois who marries and pretends he has a virgin is only indulging this wish . . ."

"Knock it off," Carlotta said.

"Why?" he said. "We all hope it'll happen to us at least once."

Linda got up, stretched in the sun, and suggested a swim.

"One goes to the mountains, goes hunting, for the same reason," Pieretto said. "Solitude in the country gives one a thirst for blood."

From that day the beautiful Carlotta was never seen again on the virgin beaches. Linda said: "You were fresh." That's how Pieretto took the girls for a ride and still was sure he had maneuvered subtly and come out on top. Then he would find new places and new people and the conversation would take a different tack. When the season was over, he would discover that he hadn't made a friend except the owner of some wineshop or some old pensioners.

I remembered that little hidden beach a long time. All things considered, so much blank and grand seascape didn't have much to say to me; I liked enclosed places with some shape and meaning—inlets, narrow lanes, terraces, olive groves. Flat on my back on a rock, I would sometimes put my eye close to an outcropping as big as a fist, until it began to look like a great mountain against the sky. That's the kind of thing I like.

Now I was thinking about Oreste visiting the sea for the first time. Pieretto wouldn't let him sleep, and I knew that together they would be capable of anything, from swimming in the nude to singing in the choir. Then there was Linda and her friends, and Pieretto's father was there in all his violence and unpredictability. I missed some of our pre-dawn expeditions and our furtive walks along the sea in the warmth of the last stars. Oreste, certainly, needed no artificial stimulants to enjoy himself. But I would dearly have liked to hear him tell me, rowing on the Po, what he had made of that Riviera world.

Instead, neither he nor Pieretto came back to Turin. Linda came back because she worked in an office; she telephoned me at the beginning of August. "Listen," she said, "your friends are waiting for you in some village. I forget the name. Come over and I'll tell you how to get there." I mentioned Oreste's hills right away. Yes, that was it. Those nitwits had gone already.

I met her before dinner in front of her usual café. She was so deeply tanned that I scarcely recognized her. This time, too, she laughed as she talked; it was her way of dealing with boys. "Are you offering me a vermouth?" she said. "It's a habit of beaches."

She sat with her legs crossed. "Horrible to go back to work in August," she sighed. "Lucky you, you never went away."

We discussed Pieretto and Oreste. "What they may have done, I don't know," she said. "I let them flounder around. They're old enough. This year I had my own friends, grownups, too grown up for all of you . . ."

"And Carlotta, the beautiful Carlotta?"

Linda laughed a big open laugh. "Pieretto exaggerates at times. We're all like that in the family. I do, too. We're tremendous that way, and we get worse every year."

I didn't say no, just gazed at her. She squirmed and made a face.

"I won't be twenty like you again," she said, "but I'm not so old either."

"The old are born old," I said. "No one ever grows old."

"That's an eighteen-karat Pieretto," Linda cried. "You took the words right out of his mouth."

I made a face of my own. "We'll coin a new one every day," I said, "until everyone has had enough."

9. Oreste's house had a rough and pinkish terrace facing a great sea of light, overlooking valleys and ravines. My train had run all morning through the plain, a plain I knew, and I could see from the windows the tree-lined irrigation ditches of my childhood—mirrors of water, flocks of geese, meadows. I was still absorbed in it when the train went in between steep banks where you could see the sky only by looking up. After a narrow tunnel we stopped. I found myself in the sultriness and dust of a little station platform with nothing in sight but chalky slopes. A fat carter pointed out the road; I had to climb and climb, the village was very high up. I threw my bag on his cart and we went up together to the slow step of his oxen.

We arrived through vineyards and burned-over stubble, and as the slope gradually leveled off underfoot, I could make out fresh villages, fresh vineyards, new slopes. I asked the carter who had planted so many vines and whether there were enough hands to work them. He looked at me quizzically, talking in circles to discover who I might be. He said: "There have always been vineyards, it's not like building a house."

Just under the heavy wall that girded the village, I was about to ask him what the idea had been in putting houses up there, but those narrow eyes in his dark face kept me quiet. I breathed a smell of moving air and fig trees that reminded me of the sea. I took a deep breath and mumbled: "What good air."

The village was a stony street from which courtyards opened, and a few villas with balconies. I noticed a garden full of dahlias, zinnias, and geraniums—scarlet and yellow predominant—and bean and squash flowers. There were cool corners between the houses, little stairways, chicken coops and old peasant women sitting about. Oreste's house was on a corner of the square, leaning out over the retaining wall; it was rosy and stained—a true villetta, discolored by creepers and the wind. It was blowing up there even at that time of day: I noticed it as soon as I came into the square and the carter pointed to the house. I was sweating and went right up the three steps to the door and hammered with the bronze knocker.

While waiting, I looked around: the rough stucco in the sunlight, a tuft of grass on the terrace against the sky, the great noontime silence. As the cart creaked off, I was thinking of how familiar all this was to Oreste. He was born and grew up here; what mustn't it all mean to him? I thought of how many places there are in the world that belong in this way to someone, who has it in his blood beyond anyone else's understanding. I knocked again.

A woman answered through half-closed shutters. She cried out, muttered, asked questions. Neither Oreste nor his friend were home. She told me to wait; I asked her forgiveness for arriving at that hour; finally she opened the door for me.

Women shot out from every direction—old women, little girls, babies. Oreste's mother, a heavy woman in a kitchen apron, welcomed me excitedly, asked about my trip, brought me into a darkened room (when the shutters were opened, I saw that it was a parlor, with china and paintings, upholstered furniture, a bamboo plant stand, vases of flowers), and asked if I would like coffee. I smelled an indoor smell of bread and fruit. She sat down and began to talk, Oreste's superior smile on her lips. She said Oreste was coming home soon, the men would soon be back, we would eat within an hour, that all Oreste's friends were fine boys, didn't we all go to the same school? Then she got up and said: "It's windy today," and closed the shutters. "You must excuse us; you'll all be sleeping together. Would you like to clean up?"

When Oreste and Pieretto came in, I already knew the whole house. Our room opened on the void, on distant hills, and we washed in a basin, splashing the red tiles. "Don't worry about spilling water on the floor. It drives away the flies." I had already been out to the terrace and down to the kitchen, where the women were working at the fireplace over a snapping fire. I had leafed through almanacs and old schoolbooks in Oreste's father's office, when he came in talking loudly. I recognized him from the photographs I'd seen in the parlor. This father wore mustaches and lit my cigarette and talked of many things. He wanted to know if I also came from the beach, if my father owned land, if I had studied for the priesthood like my friend. I was cautious and let him do the talking. After all, it wasn't such a wild idea, my being a priest.

"Did Oreste say so?"

"You know how people talk," he said, "and the women believe that sort of thing because they want to believe it. This Pieretto has a great line on the priests: he's studied them, brings up the seminary and the rule . . . My sister-in-law wants to speak to our local priest about him."

"Pieretto has a line on everything. Haven't you discovered that yet?"

"As far as I'm concerned," said the man with the mustaches, "it's all just talk. But the women lose their heads over it."

"His father says the same thing." I told him how Pieretto had lived in a monastery, that he had understood the priests, had seen them at work, that neither he nor his father were believers. "They amuse themselves, that's all."

"I'm glad to hear it," he said, "really glad. Now please don't repeat that. In a monastery! Think of it now."

Oreste and Pieretto arrived in shirtsleeves and clapped me on the back. They were brown and hungry and we went to the table immediately. The father sat at the head, the women came and went, aged aunts, little sisters. I recognized Pieretto's victim, the sister-in-law Giustina, a ruddy older woman at the other end of the table. The little girls were teasing her with a story of some altar flowers that the sacristan had put in holy water. The Feast of the Assumption came up. I was waiting for something to happen, but Pieretto seemed to have been warned: he ate and kept quiet.

Nothing happened. We talked about Oreste's vacation. I said that I had been on the Po to sunbathe, that the Po was full of bathers. The little girls listened intently. The father let me finish, then added that the sun shone everywhere but that in his day only the sick went to the Riviera. "One doesn't go for the sun," Pieretto said, "or even for the water."

"Why does one go then?" Oreste asked.

"To see your neighbor as naked as yourself."

"Even on the Po," the mother asked worriedly, "are there bathing establishments?"

"You bet," Oreste said. "And there's singing and dancing."

"Naked," Pieretto said.

Giustina sniffed at the foot of the table. "I understand men doing it," she said contemptuously, "but for young girls to go is a shame. The men should go alone."

"You mean that men should dance together?" Pieretto said. "It would be indecent."

"And more indecent for a girl to undress in public," Giustina cried. And so we went on stuffing ourselves, the conversation spinning, dropping, and surging forward. Now and then it was their own affairs, village gossip, questions of work, of crops; but whenever Pieretto opened his mouth, the landscape trembled. If we hadn't been living there together, as two representatives of the same world, I might have been amused. Oreste, anyway, watched me happily, his eyes laughing; he was glad to see me in his house. I shook my fist at him and made a walking movement with two fingers on the tabletop. He didn't understand and looked comically around the table. He thought I was bored with the long meal.

"Fine joke," I said. "Weren't we supposed to come on foot?"

Oreste shrugged. "You'll have all the walking you want in the hills and vineyards. That's why we're here."

His father hadn't understood. We explained the project of walking from Turin. One of Oreste's little sisters pretended to be amazed and locked her hands in front of her mouth. The father said: "But there's a train. What's the idea?"

Pieretto chimed in: "When everyone goes by train, it becomes fun to walk. It's a fashion, like swimming in the ocean. Now that everyone has a bathtub at home, it's more fun to bathe somewhere else."

"Speak for yourself; you were the one who went there," I said.

"What's happened to people?" the father said. "In my day, only wives were interested in fashion."

We left the table sluggish and sleepy. The women had kept my plate filled every moment, and the father at my side never stopped filling my glass. "Go and sleep while it's hot," they told me.

The three of us climbed to the torrid room. To revive a little, I washed my face in the white basin and said to Oreste: "How long does the festival last?"

"What festival?"

"They're fattening us up for the kill, the way it looks. You must eat a whole vineyard for every meal."

Pieretto said: "Suppose you'd come on foot."

Oreste laughed, mottled with light from the closed blinds. His shirt had slipped from his shoulders, showing his dark, bulging muscles. "I feel good," he said, and fell on the bed.

"Oreste's developed a taste for dancing and feeling the girls," Pieretto said. "When he dances, he looks as if he were in the deep, deep sea. He can still smell the sea every time he looks at a girl."

"This country really does smell like the sea," I said, opening a shutter. "Look down there. It even looks like the sea."

Pieretto said: "It's all right on your first day. Go ahead and moon over the panorama. But tomorrow knock it off."

I let them laugh and talk a little. "You're pretty high," I said. "What's going on?"

"You've eaten and drunk. What more do you want?" Pieretto said.

And Oreste: "Do you want to smoke your pipe?"

This conspiratorial tone in the dark room made me uneasy. I said to Pieretto: "You've already scared the women here. You'll never change. It'll end with their throwing you out."

Oreste swung upright on his bed. "No fooling, now. You're both going to stay for the grape harvest."

"What are we going to do all of August?" I muttered. I pulled my sweater over my head, and when it was off I heard Pieretto say: "Why, he's as black as a crawfish himself . . ."

"There's sun on the Po as well as the Riviera," I grumbled, and set the other two off again.

"What's the story? Are you both tight?"

"Let's see your belly button," Oreste said. I pushed down my trousers, showing a pale streak of stomach. They hooted and shouted: "Infamous! He too! But of course."

"You're still branded," Pieretto cackled in his spitting way. "You, too, will come to the cleft. No formalities there. There's nothing to hide in the sun."

10.

The next day we went. A thin stream ran down the hollow that divided our hill from an irregular upland meadow. You walked down from the vineyards, between cornfields, until you came to a steep cleft full of acacias and alders. Inside, the stream widened to a series of pools; there was one pool below a spring from which you could see only the sky above a screen of briars. During the hottest hours the sun would beat down perpendicularly.

"What a place," Pieretto said. "To take everything off, you have to go underground."

So this was their game. They left the house at noon and spent an hour or two down there, naked as snakes, broiling themselves in the sun inside this natural ambush. The point was to sun their groins and buttocks, to erase the infamy, darken everything. Then they came back to eat. They were coming back the day I arrived.

Now I understood the women's chatter and agitation. They didn't know about Pieretto's discovery, but even among men, even in shorts, sunbathing in the middle of a cornfield was a striking notion.

That afternoon I made other discoveries. The first day at a new place it's hard to sleep, even when everybody takes a siesta. While the house was dozing and flies were buzzing everywhere, I went down the stone staircase and into the kitchen, where I could hear a noise like the rocking of a cradle on a stone floor and a hum of voices. I found one of Oreste's sisters there and his mother in rolled-up sleeves vigorously slapping dough on the tabletop. An old woman was washing dishes in a tub. They smiled and said they were getting the dinner. "So soon?" I asked. The old woman turned from her tub with a toothless laugh. "You can't be too early for eating," she croaked.

Oreste's mother wiped her forehead and said: "There are too many women in this house. A few more men don't increase the work."

The little girl with the blond braids watched me, transfixed, as she poured water on the flour with a ladle. "Get busy, silly," her mother said, and went on kneading.

I stayed to watch them. I said I wasn't sleepy. I went to the pail hanging on the wall and was about to drink from the dripping ladle when the mother called out: "Dina, give him a glass."

"I don't need one," I said. "When I was a boy in the country, I drank from a pail."

So I talked about our stables, our kitchen garden, and the geese.

"It's a good thing," the mother said, "that you know the country. You're used to it, know what it is."

We discussed Pieretto, who was used to another life and knew only the city. "Oh, well," I said, "he's not suffering, he's never been happier." And I told her about his mad father who had carried him all over the place, to monasteries, villas, garrets. "Pieretto enjoys being malicious and gossiping, but it's all in sport," I said. "When you know him better, he grows on you."

The mother kneaded. "You and Pieretto will have to make do with Oreste's company. We're ignorant women."

Ignorance wasn't all. I didn't tell her so, but I was glad there was nobody in the house but older women or children. Imagine a girl our age, a sister of Oreste's, and the three of us around. Or a friend, some Carlotta or other. Instead, the oldest girl was eleven-year-old Dina, the one who clapped her hand over her mouth when she laughed.

When I asked if there was a tobacco shop in the village, the mother asked Dina to show me the way. We went out to the square together and took the street I had walked in the morning. The wind had fallen now. Along the side, in the shadow of houses, women and old men were enjoying the coolness. We passed the dahlia garden, and between the houses I could see distant hills rising level with us, like islands from the immense blank of the plain. People were eyeing us supiciously; little Dina walked beside me, neat and clean, chattering about herself. I asked her where her father's vineyards were.

"Our farm is at San Grato," she said and pointed to the yellow spine of a hill rising over the houses beyond the square. "That's one," she said, "where the white grapes are. Then there's Rosotto, with the mill," and she pointed to a slope of meadow and thickets in the valley. "Down there behind the station we have the *festa*. It's over for this year. We had fireworks. Mamma and I watched them from the terrace . . ."

I asked her who did the farmwork.

"Who?" She stopped, dumfounded. "The peasants," she said.

"I thought it was you and your sister and your papa."

Dina grinned and looked at me dubiously. "Oh, really!" she said. "We don't have time. We have to think if they've done their work. Papa orders them and then sells the crops."

"And would you like to work the earth?"

"Oh, no. You get all black. It's man's work."

When I came out of the shop, a cellar that smelled of sulfur and carobs, Dina was waiting for me very solemnly.

"So many women go to the sea to tan themselves," I said. "It's stylish to get black. Have you seen the sea yet?"

Dina discussed these things the length of the street. She said she would go to the sea when she married, not before. The sea is a place where nobody goes alone, and who would take her now? Not Oreste; he was a grown boy.

"Your mama."

Mama, Dina said, was too old-fashioned. She said you had to get married before you did anything.

"Let's go and see the church," I said then. The church was on the square, big, made of white stone, with saints and angels in niches. I raised the door curtain, and Dina squeezed by, crossed herself, and knelt. We looked around a moment, in the cool, colored

dusk. An altar glimmered in the rear like a big piece of candy—
many flowers and small lamps.

"Who brings the flowers to the Madonna?" I whispered.

"Little girls."

"You don't get black picking flowers in the fields?" I said softly.

When we came out, we ran into Giustina at the door. She moved
stiffly away, recognized me, recognized Dina, and tightened her
lips in a brusque smile. I took advantage of her confusion to go
down the steps. But Giustina didn't contain herself very long. She
turned and said to my back: "There, you did right. God is always
first. Have you met the priest?"

I stammered that I had gone in from simple curiosity, nothing
more.

"What do I hear?" she said. "There's nothing to be ashamed
of. You did something fine. Don't be bashful. It's consoled me
so much . . ."

I left her on the steps, and while we were crossing the square,
Dina told me that Giustina was always in the priest's house, at
all times of day. She dropped whatever she was doing at home—
laundry, dishes, cooking—so as not to lose a minute of what went
on. "If everybody acted like you," the mother would say, "where
would the house go?"

"To Paradise," Giustina answered.

Other things happened that day, other meetings, and in the
evening we had dinner and wandered through the village under
the stars. I thought about it all the next day, stretched naked in the
hollow under the ferocious sun, while Oreste and Pieretto splashed
around like boys. In the damp heat of the cleft I could see a sky
bleached with reflected light and feel the ground trembling and
humming. I remembered Pieretto's notion that the earth broiling
in the August sun made one think of death. He wasn't wrong. That
sensation of being naked and conscious of it, of hiding from every
eye, and soaking, blackening like a tree trunk, was something
sinister; more animal-like than human. On the high wall of the
cleft I noticed roots and filaments growing like black tentacles—
the earth's secret, inner life. Oreste and Pieretto were used to it by
now, they jumped, waded the pools, talked. They made fun of my
still pallid—infamous—parts.

Nobody could surprise us there because the noisy cornstalks would give them away. We were safe. Lounging in the water, Oreste said: "Tan yourself all over. We'll become like bulls."

It was strange down there to think of the upper world, people, life. The evening before, we had circled the village along the re-taining wall, warmed by wine and the coolness; had waved at peo-ple and laughed, talked to them, listened to singing. A bunch of young men shouted greetings to Oreste; the parish priest was walk-ing in the shade, keeping an eye on us. Later, words and jokes un-der the stars when you couldn't make out faces very well, with a woman, an old man, with one of us, elated me strangely, made me feel festive and irresponsible. Then, warm gusts of wind, the sway-ing stars, and far-away house lights stretched this feeling to take in the whole future and life itself. Children in the square chased each other deafeningly. We had been making plans, had spoken the names of villages spread out along the slopes and hilltops, discussed wines and the pleasures waiting for us, the grape harvest.

"In September," Oreste said, "we'll go hunting."

Then I remembered Poli.

11.
We suddenly began talking about him, to a cricket ac-companiment.

"The Greppo is down there," Oreste said, "under that bunch of stars. You can just make it out on the rim of the plain. When the sun is coming up, you can see the tops of the pines . . ."

"Come on, let's go," Pieretto said.

But Oreste said that it wasn't worth the trouble at night, and that Poli must certainly still be on the Riviera.

"But suppose he doesn't stay this time?" Pieretto said.

"He's all right. He must be cured by now."

"Then some other girl will have shot him."

"Does it always have to happen to him?"

"What!" Pieretto shouted into the wind. "Don't you know that what happens to you once always happens again? You always react the same way to the same thing. It's no accident when you make a mess. Then you do it again. It's called destiny."

We discussed Poli at the table the next day, after we came back from our hideout. Oreste said to the circle of faces: "Do you know who I saw this year?"

After he finished describing the shooting, and Rosalba, the green car, the expedition at night, an uproar of questions and exclamations broke out. During a baffled pause the mother said: "Such a beautiful little boy. I remember him when they used to go by in their carriage with open parasols. He had his nurse with him. She was dressed in lace, with large safety pins . . . It was the year I was expecting Oreste."

"Are you sure it's Poli of the Greppo?" the father said sharply.

Oreste began the story again, beginning with that night on the hill.

"And who is this woman?" the mother asked, looking pale.

The little girls were listening with their mouths open.

"I'm sorry for his father," Oreste's father said. "A man who once owned half of Milan. You see how money sometimes ends."

"What do you mean, ends?" Pieretto said. "On the contrary. The father fixed everything up. You can do such things in rich families."

"Not here with us," Oreste said.

Old Giustina interrupted. She had been listening intently until then, keen as a falcon, looking from one of us to the other.

"The gentleman is right," she said, darting a look at Pieretto. "People are committing these sins everywhere. Instead of letting them run around like dogs, their fathers and mothers should rule their children, keep track of them . . ."

She went on for a while. She got worked up again over dancing and ocean swimming. A word from her sister, a glance at the girls, at Dina, weren't enough to stop her. But old Sabina—a servant perhaps, or grandmother or aunt—succeeded, by blinking hard and asking from her end of the table who we were talking about.

They shouted at her. Then she said angrily in her sharp voice that the Greppo house was open, that the dressmaker's husband at the station had seen trunks going through. She didn't know about any boy, but there were certainly women up there.

That afternoon we climbed to San Grato on the ridge of the hill behind the village, where Oreste's father met us. He went there every day after his siesta. His workers were spraying sulfate along the rows of vines; bent over in the heat, they moved along in blouses and pants splashed and stiffened with blue, pumping the blue water from brass tanks on their backs. The vine leaves dripped, the pumps squeaked. We stopped above the big reservoir, which was full of clear water, deep and opaque like a heavenly eye or a piece of sky reversed. I remarked to the father that it was strange to have to spray the grapes with that poisonous mist: the peasants' hats were all eaten away by it.

"Once," I said, "they grew grapes without all this spraying."

"They may have," he said, and shouted something to a boy who was putting a bottle down in the grass. "Perhaps they did once. Now the vines are full of diseases." He looked doubtfully at the sky. "Let's hope no thunderstorm," he muttered. "It'll wash off the vines and we'll have to spray again."

Oreste and Pieretto called me from above; they were under a tree, jumping up and down. "Come up, come eat some plums," Oreste said, "if the birds have left any."

I crossed the burned stubble and met them at the top. It was like being in the sky. Below us was the village square, much diminished, and a jungle of roofs, stairways, haystacks. One wanted to leap from hill to hill, to take it all in at once. I looked to the east, where the high plateau ended, searching for the tops of the Greppo pines. But thick light swallowed everything down there, and the horizon trembled. Even squinting through the corners of my eyes, I saw nothing but a dusty haze.

Oreste's father joined us, jumping the furrows.

"It's magnificent country," Pieretto said with his mouth full. "You, Oreste, are a fool not to live here."

"My idea," the father said, glancing at Oreste, "was that this boy should go to agriculture school. It gets harder all the time to make the land produce."

"In my village," I put in, "the peasants are supposed to know more than the agronomists."

"That's good sense," the father said. "Experience first. But now everything is done with chemicals and manure. If you're going to study medicine, a thing that helps other people, you should go ahead and learn how to make the most of your own property."

"Medicine is a kind of agriculture," Oreste said brightly. "A healthy body is like a good field."

"But if you don't smarten up, young man, I won't give you the fields."

"Do vines get many diseases?" Pieretto said.

The father turned to the farm below and ran his eye along the rows of vines and the innocent little clouds of spray. "They do, yes," he said. "The earth gets tired. It may be true, what your friend says, that the land once was more healthy, but the fact is now, if you turn your back a minute, tomorrow there's a new disease ..."

I could feel Pieretto grinning without looking at him.

"The earth is like a woman," the father went on. "You're still young, but you'll find out soon enough. A woman has something new every day: a headache, a backache, her periods. Of course, it *must* be her monthly, the moon that waxes and wanes ..." He winked at us gloomily.

Pieretto grinned again. "You, though," he attacked me suddenly, "what's all this about the country having changed? Men make the country. Plows, sulfate, gasoline ..."

"Of course," Oreste said.

The father approved. "There's nothing mysterious about the country," Pieretto said. "Even the mattock is a scientific instrument."

"I never said the country had changed," I objected.

"Good God," the father said, "you'll see how little a mattock counts when a field has run to brambles. You wouldn't know it. It's like a desert."

It was my turn to look at Pieretto. I laughed and said nothing.

He said: "The cleft is different."

"From what?"

"From these vines, for instance. Man reigns up here, and down there the toad."

"But there are toads and snakes everywhere in the country. And crickets," I said. "And moles. And trees are the same everywhere. By day and by night. The same roots grow in wild country as here."

The father listened abstractedly. Turning around, he said at one point: "If you want to see what wild country really is, go to the

Greppo. Good God, all day I've been thinking of that boy and his father. Now I understand certain things. An estate that bought only olive oil and salt when the grandfather was alive. It's a bad thing to own land and not live there . . ."

12. Every day we went down to the cleft, and in the morning we mostly explored, argued and laughed. We looked for fields beneath certain slopes when they were still wet with dew; sometimes the ground in the cleft was still damp and nocturnal under our backs and legs when the place was already steaming hot. By now I knew every twist in the hedges, every change of light, every sound and rustle of the morning. A thick white cloud would come over at the height of the sultriness, the water would grow opaque, and afterwards the reversed images of cliff, flower, or sky would be all the more brilliant.

That sunbath had become almost a vice, though by now we were tanned all over. On the first Sunday we didn't go down but spent the noon hour in front of the church in the festive crowd, listening to Mass from the doorway amid a confusion of boys, organ music, and bells. But I greatly missed being naked and flattened out between the earth and the sun. I didn't tell anybody what was going through my mind.

To Pieretto, who was looking sardonically at Oreste's neck, I whispered: "Can you imagine these people naked in the sun like us?"

He didn't bat an eye, and I went back to my thoughts. I had a discussion with Oreste (we were spending the afternoon at San Grato, and Pieretto was off somewhere that day): whether in the country there were still a nook, a bank, a piece of wild land where no one had ever set foot, where from the beginning of time the rain, sun, and seasons had followed one another without man's knowledge. Oreste said no, there isn't a canebrake or square foot of woods that some man's hand or eye hadn't disturbed. At least the hunters, and before them the bandits, had gone everywhere.

But the peasants, the peasants, I said. Hunters didn't count. The hunter lives off his game. I wanted to know if the peasants as such had gone everywhere, if everywhere the earth had been touched by some hand. Or rather, violated.

Oreste said: "Who knows?" but he didn't understand me. He shook his head and gave me one of his mother's quizzical looks.

We were sitting at the edge of the vineyard, where one could look up and see the vine shoots moving in the wind. To look up from below at a vineyard climbing into the sky is to be out of the world; at your feet are chalky clods and heavy, contorted stocks; above, you watch a fugue of green festoons and rows of canes touching the sky. You breathe and listen.

"That carter I met at the station," I said at one point, "told me that the vines have always been here."

"Oh, my, yes," Oreste said, "even when they used to tie them up with sausages and milk ran out at the bottom."

"Still," I said, "even cities have always existed. Maybe dirty, maybe built of straw, only three huts, a cave; but man means city. You must admit that Pieretto is right."

Oreste shrugged. It was his way of discussing things—as good as any other.

"I wonder," he said, "how he feels when my mother bolts the door at midnight. In the city that's when he begins to live."

"We'll have to go out some night," I said. "I'd like to see the hills under the moon. There was a sliver of moon last night."

"We went swimming by moonlight at the beach," Oreste said. "It was like drinking cold milk."

They had never told me. I felt a sharp sadness. I felt shut out and jealous.

"Time is passing," I said. "These grapes will never ripen. When are we going back to Turin?"

Oreste wouldn't hear of it. He asked me what more I could want; I was eating, I was drinking good wine, I was doing nothing all day . . .

"But that's just it. And your mother works. Everyone works for us."

"Are you bored?" Oreste asked. "Do you think you're too much trouble? Aunt Giustina loves you." (I was the one who had wanted to go to Mass, out of consideration for the family, nothing else.)

"Aren't we going to the mill today?"

Each day we would go down to the hollow where the other

farm sheds were: we would follow the peasant around the threshing floor; the father would stick his head out of the archway and
offer us a drink. But the best thing at Rosotto was the haymowing,
the deep clover fields, the flocks of geese. Toward evening we would
play a round of *bocce* with the boys, Pale and Quinto. And Oreste
went to the station on business.

"In my opinion," Pieretto said, "something is beginning to
smell. At Genoa he was mailing letters every day."

Oreste, when we brought it up, shook his head and laughed.
And he gave us the same smile when we were passing in front of a
house with geraniums on the windowsills next to the railroad
tracks. He shouted a greeting, and the fresh, cheerful voice of a girl
replied. He told us to keep going; we turned the corner.

"So," Pieretto said when Oreste arrived in the yard, "it's the
stationmaster's daughter."

Oreste laughed again but didn't say a word. But in that hollow
of the mill there was something propitious in the sky. Even at the
level crossing, where the carts stopped and the animals relieved
themselves, one breathed a special gentleness: the small houses
and station flower beds made one think of the outskirts of a city,
on May evenings when girls go strolling and hay-smelling gusts
invade the city. The boys of Rosotto too, no matter how shirtless
or shoeless, felt the presence of the trains and gossiped about beer
and bicycle races.

But we drank wine, not beer, in the evenings after mowing.
Oreste's father had said: "Come up before sunset," and started up
the path with his jacket over his shoulder. There was something
festive going on at the station, and Oreste had to ask our pardon
for a longer absence than usual.

One bottle came up from the Rosotto cellars, then another. It
was a wine that left your mouth always a little drier. The three
of us drank under the archway that opened on the fields. I didn't
know if so much sweetness was passing from the wine into the air,
or vice versa. One seemed to drink the perfume of the hay.

"It's strawberry wine," Oreste said, "from my cousins at Monbello."

"We're fools," Pieretto said. "We look day and night for the
secret of the country, and we have it here inside ourselves."

Then we wondered why we had not got tight since we had come to the village, although we were fond enough of drinking in Turin.

"We'll have to go out some night," I said. "After all, we can't get drunk in your house."

"Pour it down," Oreste said. "We're at home now."

The talk turned to horses. At Rosotto there was a covered single-seater, just right for the three of us, and Oreste said that all we needed was to hitch up the horse and go.

"Let's go to my cousins in Monbello," he said. "I want to see them. Those people are smart. We can leave early and get back in the evening."

"We'll miss our sunbath," I muttered. "I missed it this morning."

Pieretto grunted. "Who gives a damn? I'm sick of seeing you naked."

"That's your loss," I said.

"But you're so ugly," he said. "I can't stand the sight of you any more unless I'm drunk."

Oreste filled our glasses.

"That's one thing," I said, "that can't be done—stripping naked in the woods and filling up with wine."

"Why not?" Oreste said.

"No more can you make love in the woods. In real woods. Love and drinking are civilized things. When I went boating . . ."

Pieretto interrupted: "You've never understood anything."

"When you went boating . . ." Oreste said.

"I had a girl with me, and she was willing. It could have happened. Well, I couldn't do it. I mean, *I* couldn't. It seemed like offending somebody, or something."

"It's because you don't know what a woman is," Pieretto said.

"But you don't mind being naked in the cleft," Oreste said.

I confessed I didn't, but it was with my heart in my throat. "I feel like a sinner," I admitted. "Maybe that's why I enjoy it."

Oreste nodded, smiling. I realized we were drunk.

"The proof is," I went on, "that we do these things secretly."

Pieretto said that one does any number of secret things that aren't sins. It's a question of custom and good manners. Sin is when you don't understand what you're doing.

"Take Oreste," he said. "Every day he visits his girl on the sly. Only a short way from here. They don't do anything obscene. They talk in the garden, perhaps they hold hands. She asks him when he is going to get his degree and she will have him all to herself. He answers that it's a matter of another year and after that his military service, then his practitioner's license: three years. All right? And he fondles and kisses her hair . . ."

Oreste, bright scarlet, shook his head and grabbed the bottle.

"And you think all this is *sin*?" Pieretto snorted, moving away. "This little scene, this social game, is sin? At least he might trust us and tell us about it. He's no real friend. Tell us something, Oreste. At least her name, at least her name."

Oreste blushed and smiled. "Another day," he said. "Let's drink tonight."

13. But I had already learned everything from Dina. One day I found her sitting on a stool on the terrace, sewing.

"Well now, you'll be getting married soon," I said.

"It's your turn first," she came back. "You're a big boy now."

"But boys have time," I said. "Look at Oreste, who isn't even thinking about it."

A little game of jokes and answers followed, and Dina enjoyed my amazement. In a low voice, slyly, she let the cat out of the bag. She said that Oreste was talking to Giacinta: Cinta's parents knew, but nobody here at home did. Cinta was the daughter of the road-maintenance man and worked for the dressmaker; she was clever, she made her own clothes and rode around on a bike. Dina even knew that Oreste had to pretend in the village to be only flirting, because Cinta's father had to till his own fields by hand.

"Is she nice?" I asked. "Do you like her?"

Dina shrugged. "Oh, I like her all right. It's Oreste who has to marry her."

It was Dina who found out that we had got drunk the day of the mowing.

"Last night we talked about Cinta with Oreste," I whispered to her on the stairs, where we were sitting under a slice of moon.

And she, fixing me with her big eyes: "Did you open a bottle? How many?"

"How do you know?"

"All during dinner you covered your glass with you hand."

I wondered what kind of woman little Dina would become. I watched the elders, Giustina, the others, Oreste's mother. I compared them to the village girls one saw at work, with their thick legs, brown, seamed faces, heavy blood. It must have been the wind, the hill, their thick blood that made them so hard and leathery. Often while eating or drinking—thick soups, meat, pepperoni, bread—I wondered how it might have affected my blood to eat that crude and rich diet, those earthy juices, the same essences one smelled in the wind. Dina, however, was blond, tiny, a wasp. Cinta too, I thought, would be slim and fragile, a vine. "Perhaps she only eats bread and peaches."

A thunderstorm, luckily without hail, swept by, beating down the countryside and pitting the roads. It was the morning we were supposed to set out in the buggy. We spent it indoors, from window to window, among women and children running and groaning at the lightning flashes. The father put on his boots and left early. The crackling of twigs in the fireplace threw a reddish light around the kitchen, made fantastic reflections on the festoons of colored paper, on the battery of copper pans, on the prints of the Madonna and the olive branch on the wall. Pieces of bloody rabbit on the chopping board gave out a smell of garlic and basil. Windowpanes shook. Someone upstairs called out to close the windows tighter. "And Giustina's out in this," they shouted up the stairs. "Don't worry"—I heard the mother's voice—"that woman always has somewhere to go."

A moment of strange solitude, almost of peace and silence, occurred during the downpour. I stood at the bottom of the stairs and looked up at rain streaming over the darkened skylight. You could hear the almost solid mass of water falling and rumbling. I imagined the steaming and running landscape, our cleft boiling over, roots laid bare, the most private cracks in the earth penetrated and violated.

It ended the way it began, suddenly. When we went out on the terrace with Dina and the other women—one could hear people shouting all over the village—the leaf-covered pavement was already showing dry spots. A frothy wind blew up the valley; low clouds galloped over. The ocean of almost black hills, streaked with whitish clay, seemed nearer than usual. But it wasn't the clouds or the horizon that struck me. I was overcome by a rich damp smell of branches, of crushed flowers; sharp, almost salty, a smell of lightning and rootstocks. Pieretto said: "How delicious!" Even Oreste breathed deeply and laughed.

That morning we didn't go to the cleft, Oreste's father called us to San Grato to see the damage. Fruit had been laid waste up there, and a few roof tiles broken. We joined the girls in collecting big baskets of spattered apples and peaches. We retied some beaten-down vines. It was charming to see tiny flowers clinging to half-dissolved clods of earth raise themselves delicately, miraculously, in the sun. The earth's thick blood was capable of this, too. Everyone said that the woods would soon be full of mushrooms.

But we didn't look for mushrooms. Instead we went to visit Oreste's cousins the next day. The little horse, taking the left-hand fork at the station, pulled us up a faint rise covered with stretch after stretch of Indian corn—a small stand of trees, and then more corn. The morning sun had done wonders already. If it weren't for the holes in the road or the smell of the wind, no one would have thought of the day before. We drove between fields, along the very gradual slope, now in a light shadow of acacias, now boxed in by cornstalks.

The farm was at the end of the high plain, between low hills, lost among giant reeds and oak trees. As we came up, I kept turning around because shortly before, as we emerged from a stony pass, Oreste had pointed upwards and said: "There's the Greppo." Climbing into the sky above the vines was an enormous wooded slope, dark with humidity. It looked uninhabited, not a field or a roof.

"Can that be the estate?" I muttered.

"The villa is on top, hidden by trees. One can see the villages of the plain from up there."

A dip in the road hid the Greppo, and we reached the farm while I was still trying to find it among the trees.

At first I couldn't understand Oreste's enthusiasm for his two cousins. They were grown men, one even grizzled, dressed in checked shirts and corduroy trousers, and had large hairy hands. They came into the courtyard and stopped our horse without showing surprise.

"It's Oreste," they said.

"Davide! Cinto!" Oreste cried, jumping down. Three hunting dogs surrounded us, growling a little and leaping on Oreste. It was a big yard of reddish-brown earth, like the vineyards we'd just crossed. The house was stone, shaded with the green of some espaliered vines. There was a dark and empty window on the ground floor.

The first thing was to bring the horse to the shade of the oaks and leave it to paw and calm down. "All of you doctors?" Davide asked, looking up. Oreste explained warmly who we were. "Let's go where it's cool," Cinto said walking away.

The day ended with our drinking again, and August has long days. Every so often, one of the cousins would get up, disappear in some kind of grotto, and return with a darker glass. It ended with our going down to the cellar ourselves, and here Davide filled our caked glasses at the barrel, making a hole in the mastic with his finger and then plugging it. But this was in the afternoon. Meanwhile we had explored the house and vineyards, eaten a meal of polenta, salami, and melon, catching sight of some women and children in the dark interior of the house. The room was low, as rustic as a stable: we went out and saw clouds of starlings rising from fields dotted with oak trees.

Next to the stable was a well, and Davide drew up a pail of water, threw in some bunches of white grapes, and invited us to eat. Pieretto, sitting on a stump, laughed like a child and talked with his mouth full. Cinto, the younger of the two, circled the well, listened to our talk, and looked complacently at the horse.

We discussed everything that day, I mean everything about crops, hunting, the storm, the past year.

"You must be shut in here all winter," I had said. "You're in low ground."

"We go up when we need to," Davide said.

Oreste said: "Don't you know that winter is their season? Do you realize how fine it is to hunt in the snow?"

"It's fine all year round," Davide added, "when your day goes well."

It seemed as if the dogs understood. They had got up and were watching us restlessly.

"But nobody checks on you here," Pieretto said. "I can imagine how many hares you slaughter in August."

"Say that to Cinto." Davide broke out laughing. "Tell that to Cinto; he shoots pheasant."

Oreste raised his head as though catching a scent. "Are there always pheasant at the Coste?" He looked searchingly at Davide, then at Cinto. "Did you know that Poli of the Greppo was shot at—like a pheasant?"

The pair listened in silence. While Oreste was telling the story, Davide poured him a drink. I was aware by this time that the old story had begun to sound false with retelling. What did it have in common with that wine, that land, those two men?

When Oreste was finished, he looked at the brothers and looked at us. "You didn't tell them that he takes cocaine," Pieretto added.

"Oh, yes," Oreste said. "He's not exactly right in the head."

"He must know what he's doing," Davide said. "Good thing he's back on his feet."

"We don't know whether he's back on the Greppo," Oreste said.

"He is, yes," Cinto said quietly. "They do their shopping at Due Ponti."

"What does the caretaker have to say?" Oreste said, surprised.

Cinto grew cagy and showed his teeth; Davide spoke for him: "There was a fight about the canebrake. With all the poaching we've done on his land, that man has to worry about his canes. Well, you know how it is . . . It's something we don't discuss."

14. We left under a pale moon, in the cool early-evening air. I was sorry to leave that island, that immense red landscape, and the thin black vines under the oaks.

"Let's go before it gets dark," Oreste said.

The little horse set off like a hunting dog. As he ran under an apple tree, Pieretto reached up and pulled down a hail of fruit. "Wheeee!" we shouted.

"Have you ever drunk so much wine?" Pieretto said, "or held it better?"

"When you drink in the open air and in the right place," Oreste said, "you can't get drunk."

Then they turned on me and said: "You who don't like to drink or make love in the country, what do you say now?"

I brushed off the question like brushing off a fly. "I like those two," I said into the breeze of our running.

Then we discussed Davide and Cinto, the wine, the grapes in the pail, how good a genuine life is.

"The great thing," Pieretto said, "is the way they control their women. The five of us outside drinking and telling stories, the females and brats in the kitchen not bothering anybody."

The low sun raked the vineyards and dug out a redness, a rich shadow, from every clod and every tree trunk.

"Meanwhile they work," I said. "They've made this land what it is."

"What a fool you are, Oreste," Pieretto said. "To hell with Turin and anatomy classes. You should marry that girl and work your lands in peace . . ."

Fixing his eyes on the horse's neck and following the curve of the road with his chin, Oreste said calmly: "Who said I don't intend to do that? Give me time."

"What people you are," I observed. "One of your fathers wants his son to be a monk, the other an agronomist. You won't hear of it, you tell them off: and you'll end up, you Pieretto, an atheist monk, and you Oreste, a farmer doctor."

Pieretto smiled complacently. "Everyone should help his father," he said. "You have to teach him that life is difficult. After that, if you happen to become what he wants you to be, you have to convince him that he was wrong to want it, but that you did it anyway, for his sake."

"Are you really going to marry the girl?" I asked Oreste.

"Don't answer, don't answer," Pieretto said. "We're drunk, so that's your excuse."

The moon was beautiful, a very pale yellow in the evening, and

I began to think of its nightly shining over the immense landscape, on open ground, on the hedgerows. I remembered the Greppo's slope but saw it disappear into the pure air behind our backs.

"Was that the Coste, where we were?" I was about to say, but just then Oreste spoke.

"Her name is Giacinta," he said, without looking at us. Then, shouting and waving his whip: "Jesus Christ, I'm going crazy this year."

The night before, he and Pieretto couldn't sleep and started going over their month on the beach. Oreste had said that the low hills we were driving through now had seemed like an ocean horizon to him since his childhood—a mysterious sea of islands and distances as he looked down from the terrace and let his imagination run wild. "How much I wanted to go, to take the train, to see and do. Now I'm happy here. I'm not even sure I like the sea."

"Oh, but you took to it like a fish," Pieretto said.

We were singing when we arrived, and after the last bit of road on foot we meant to go on drinking. Women understand these things; they had set a table on the terrace with a bottle. "But of course," the mother said. "You're taking the moon cure. The moon's heard plenty already."

The wind had died, the village was asleep, all we could hear were dogs barking in the distance. It was Oreste's night; he told us all about Giacinta. When the moon had set and the cock crew, Pieretto said: "You miserable dog. You've made even me jealous."

The next day was Sunday. How the weeks pass! Again we walked around the square, among the clowning men and veiled girls who made one think of the great sun and the cleft. We watched Mass as before, looking up at the sky. I wondered if the two Monbello cousins were the type to celebrate, if they would ever interrupt their life—farmyard, land, wine cellar—to mix with other people. Their celebration was the hunt, the patient waiting, the twilight solitude. When the church emptied, I looked from face to face to see if I could find another look, another expression as composed, as shrewd and wild as theirs had been. Our women came out. Giustina looked us over avidly, pulling the girls away and starting to argue.

She wanted to know why we went to Mass and then missed it by standing outside holy ground.

"What's holy ground?" Oreste said.

Pieretto was worse. He explained that the whole world is God's church and that even St. Francis kneeled in the woods.

"St. Francis was a saint," Giustina barked. "He believed in God."

The people in church, Pieretto said, are those who don't believe in God.

"Don't tell me that the head priest believes in God—with that face," he declared.

Around us everyone was talking about the holidays and the fairs to come, because the end of August is an empty time when the countryside, between grain harvest and grape harvest, has a breathing spell, and the peasants move around, make deals, enjoy themselves, and let things slide. There were festivals everywhere and the talk was all about going.

"The liturgy," Giustina was saying, "the liturgy. If you don't respect the ministers of the liturgy, you're neither Christians nor Italians."

"Religion," Oreste's father said, "isn't merely going to church. Religion is a difficult thing. It involves raising children, supporting a family, living in peace with everyone."

And Giustina to Pieretto: "All right then, you tell us now what religion is."

"Religion," said Picretto, standing still, "is understanding how things work. Holy water is no use. To talk to people you have to understand them, know what everyone wants. Everyone wants something in life. They want to do something they never know very well. Still, there's God in this desire, for everybody. It's enough to understand and help others to understand."

"And when you're dead," Oreste put in, "what have you understood?"

"Damned gravedigger!" Pieretto said. "When you're dead, your desires are dead."

They kept it up at the table and afterwards. Pieretto said he admitted there were saints, that in fact there are only saints, because each person in his intentions is a saint, and if only he were let alone he'd bear fruit. Instead, the priests cling to the most famous saints and say: "Act like this one. He can save you," forgetting that there aren't two drops of water alike, that every day is another day.

Giustina was silent now, giving him only black looks. At four we were sitting on the terrace drinking coffee. Tired voices, rustlings, puffs of wind came up from the burning sea of the countryside. We could look out from the shade where we were sitting to long valley slopes, like the flanks of resting cattle. Each hill was a world, made up of successive places, some tilted, some level, seeded with vineyards, fields, and woods. Houses, stands of trees, horizons. After so much looking, one could still find new things—an unusual tree, a turn in the path, a farmyard, a color not yet seen. The setting sun threw every detail into relief, and even the strange sealike corridor, the vague cloud of the Greppo, was more tempting than usual. We would have to go there next day in the buggy, and meanwhile anything we said would help pass the time.

15.

The hill of the Greppo was also a world. You went there through the Coste, through hollows and by lonely slopes, beyond the country of the oak trees. When we were underneath, we could see the dark and luminous pines of the crest against a clear sky. From a bend halfway up, Oreste had shown us the extent of Poli's land in the country we had just traveled. We left the buggy, which followed at our own pace, and walked a road much wider than the earlier lane. This wide road—still asphalted in places—had been dug into an unkempt hillside thick with brambles and trees, dramatic with outcroppings and sheer falls. But the striking thing was the tangle, the sense of abandonment: after several wasted vineyards full of weeds, there were woods that had been invaded by fruit trees—fig and cherry overgrown with creepers; willows and acacias, plane trees and alders. At the beginning of the slope there was a stand of tall ironwoods and shadowy cold poplars; then, as we came gradually into the open, the vegetation lightened, but mixed with the familiar kinds were trees like oleanders,

magnolias, a few cypresses, and some odd trees I'd never seen before, in a disorder that made the few clearings seem all the more
exotic.

"This must be what your father meant?" I asked Oreste.

He replied that we had already passed the real waste, the wood-
land and plowland where everyone in the neighborhood pastured
and cut wood as they pleased. The land up here was meant to be
a hunting preserve. Look at the road they put in. In Poli's grandfather's time, whole brigades of rich guests used to come up. But in
those days the lowland was worked, and the old man would patrol
the place day and night with a gun and whip. Oreste's father knew
the old man; he had come from down there himself.

The air was heavily scented, a mixture of hot vegetable fer-
mentation, sun and soil, and the breath of broiling asphalt—a
smell suggestive of sports cars, speed, coastal roads, and gardens
over the sea. A hedge of prickly pear dangled its pale fruit from an
embankment over the road.

We came out among bushes at the top, and here the undergrowth gave way to a real park, a pinewood screening the villa.
Now we had fine gravel underfoot and could see sky between the
trees.

"It's like an island," Pieretto said.

"A natural skyscraper," I added.

"The way it is now," Oreste said, "it's no use to anyone. There
should be a sanatorium here, a modern sanatorium, with the latest
equipment. Two steps from home—what do you say?"

"It already smells of death," Pieretto said.

The rotten smell came from a pool on a level with the ground,
about ten meters square, with an accumulation of stuff in the middle and green, stagnant water sprinkled with small white flowers.

"You've even got a swimming pool," I told Oreste. "You can
throw your dead in there and pull them out alive."

The whiteness of the villa glimmered between the pines. "Let's
stop here," Oreste said. "I want to explore."

We stayed with the horse. I hoped that Poli wasn't there, that
no one was there, that we could explore the park and then go
home. The smell of the pool reminded me of our hollow and filled
me with nostalgia for unknown country. All I really wanted was

another look, going down, at the woods in their beautifully wild state of neglect.

"Who do you want?" asked a clear voice.

She had approached among the trees, quietly, in a blouse and white shorts, a blond girl with hard eyes.

We exchanged glances. Her breeding was obvious in her voice. I immediately felt ashamed of our horse and buggy.

"We're looking for Poli," Pieretto said with a smile. "We're . . ."

"Poli?" The woman raised her eyebrows, almost offended. Not to stare at her legs, I had to look aside; I felt shabby in every sense.

"We're friends of Poli," Pieretto said. "We met him at Turin. Tell us how he is."

The woman didn't like that either; her frown changed into a bored smile and she glanced at us impatiently.

Just then Oreste shot out of the road, exclaiming excitedly: "Poli and his wife are here. Who'd have thought he was married?"

He stopped, seeing the girl.

"Did you find him?" Pieretto said quietly.

Oreste blushed and said that the gardener had gone to find him. He looked from us to the woman. He hesitated.

"We're trying to keep up a conversation," Pieretto said.

Suddenly the blond girl warmed up. She eyed us skeptically and held out her hand. She dropped her reserve. "My husband's friends are mine, too," she said, laughing. "Here's Poli now."

I have thought many times about that meeting, about Oreste's blushing, and the days that followed up there. The girl Giacinta came to mind immediately—I don't know why—but Giacinta was dark. And the idea that Poli should have a wife disturbed me at first. All our previous experience with him would be out of bounds, a nuisance. What could we talk about now? We couldn't even ask how his father was.

But Poli welcomed us with that faintly absurd, exaggerated warmth of his. He didn't seem much changed, a little fatter, the same soft, infantile expression in his eyes. He was wearing a short shirt outside his trousers and a thin chain around his neck. He told us immediately that we had to stay, must be with him day and night; long talks were just what he needed.

"But aren't you on your honeymoon?" Pieretto asked.

Husband and wife looked at each other, then looked at us. Poli smiled an amused smile. "Honey gives him the hives," the woman said briskly. "All that is ancient history. We're here to be bored. I keep him company and nurse him a little."

"The wound must be healed," Oreste said. Pieretto smiled.

Then Oreste caught on, bit his lip, and stammered: "Quite a man, your father. But you're giving him gray hair . . ."

The woman said: "You must be thirsty. Show them the way, Poli. I'll join you soon."

So, in the high, glassed-in room full of curtains and armchairs, Poli continued to welcome us and sigh with pleasure, and to Pieretto's question whether or not his wife knew the whole story he very simply said yes. "There was a time when Gabriella and I discussed everything. She helped me a lot, poor child. We've done plenty of crazy things together, as all the world knows. Then life separated us. But this time we agreed to spend the summer together like the children we once were. We have memories in common . . ."

Pieretto stood listening with evident courtesy. But Oreste couldn't contain himself and burst out: "But what were you doing in Turin if you were married?"

Poli looked at him in disgust, almost with fear. All he said was: "One doesn't always do what others might like."

Gabriella came in and opened the liquor cabinet. It was lined with glass and lit up when opened. We talked about the Greppo. I said it was very beautiful up there and that I could understand spending my life exploring the woods.

"Yes, it would be pleasant," she said.

"What do you do from morning till night?" Pieretto asked.

Gabriella stretched her long brown legs in the armchair. "We sunbathe, we sleep, we do exercises . . . We don't see anyone." I couldn't get used to her surprising face, deeply tanned and rather scornful. She was very young, must have been younger than Poli, but now and then her voice had hoarse inflections that struck me. From drinking, I thought, or from other things?

"We're having a cold lunch," she said, laughing. "Crackers and marmalade. The serious meal will be tonight."

We protested that they were waiting for us at home. The horse was waiting. We had to get back before nightfall.

Poli grew pensive, irritated. He told Pieretto that having us with him was like being on a holiday, he had so much to tell us. He asked his wife to have the maid prepare rooms for us upstairs.

We argued good-naturedly, but didn't yield. His insistence annoyed me, and looking at Oreste, I thought of the road back, the girl waiting for him at the station, the twilight. Poli said: "What does it matter where you live? Why are you treating me like this?"

Gabriella raised her glass urbanely, looked at him with surprise, and said to us: "Do you find cows and public dancing so interesting?"

Even Poli laughed. We agreed to come back the next day and stay a while.

16.

It took us two days to persuade Oreste's family to let us go back. "Aren't you well-off here with us?" the father asked. The women glowered and held high counsel at the table. Only the news that Poli was married pacified Oreste's mother, and then the conversation turned to the new aspect that Poli's adventure was assuming, and they wanted to know if his wife wasn't duty-bound to be overcome by distress but at the same time be strong, resolute, unyielding.

"She doesn't give a damn. She sunbathes," Oreste said.

"That's what happens when you separate."

"But if two people separate," his father said, "there's always something behind it."

Oreste, annoyed, concluded that it was all the fault of money. "If you don't have too much money, then you study or work and don't have time to be a fool. Well, are we going, or aren't we?"

We left in the buggy without deciding whether Oreste would stay or not. During our goodbyes three days before, Gabriella had said that it was a pity not to come and pick us up in the car, and Poli added, very quietly, that his father had taken the car away to keep him out of danger and make him rest in earnest. We crossed the same landscape, the stands of oak and broken hedgerows. I saw the ironwoods and the sloping woods. Everything was bright and dripping in the morning air. The great hill spread its bushy wildness around us, solitary in its bee hum, like a mountain of other days. I kept looking for abandoned clearings. Pieretto said it was unfair for an entire hill to belong to a single man, as if we were still living in an age when villages were named after single families.

On the level ground near the pines, we found something new. Lounging chairs, bottles, and cushions were abandoned on the grass. The gardener busied himself with our horse, took him to the stable: Pinotta, a red-haired, sulky girl who had served us at the table the time before, stood by the doorway and watched us without coming into the sun.

"They're asleep," she answered, looking up. A sound of water on zinc came from the greenhouse nearby.

"What a lot of bottles," Pieretto said, to conciliate her. "They drank like pigs. Was there a party last night?"

"A mob came from Milan," the girl said, pushing back her hair with her arm. "They danced until dawn and fought with the lawn cushions. What a mess! And you, are you staying?"

"Where are the Milanese now?" Oreste asked.

"They came and went in their cars. What people! A woman fell from a window."

It was cool there among the pines. We smoked a cigarette and waited. No one stirred in the house. I leaned against a pine and examined the plain. We drank the lees of a bottle and asked Pinotta to open the verandah for us.

That was where Poli and Gabriella found us. They announced themselves noisily, Pinotta ran upstairs, we heard voices, bells, a slamming of doors. Finally Poli came down, in pajamas, with tousled hair. He complained that we had made him wait three days, he held us by the hand; standing like that, we discussed whether guilt for excesses lay with the seducer or with those who let themselves be seduced. "Good friends," Poli said. "They gave me a taste of Milanese life. Let's hope they don't come back. We should be by ourselves."

Gabriella came in, cool and fully dressed. "Come on. You must want a bath. Leave them alone, Poli. You can talk later." I'd forgotten the blond honey of that head, her bare, sandaled feet, and her air of always being on the verge of leaving for the beach.

Taking us upstairs to our rooms, she said: "Let's hope that none of those nuts slept up here."

At this point Oreste stoutly declared that he was going to sleep at home: he was leaving us on the Greppo and would come back on his bicycle, if at all.

"Why?" Gabriella frowned. "Mama doesn't want you to get lost?" Then, laughing: "Well, do what you like. You know the road."

When I went down to the parlor, I found them with Oreste. Pieretto had stayed to wallow in his bath.

Reentering the glassed-in room, I still wasn't resigned to the adventure. By then Pinotta had finished straightening vases of flowers, collecting plates and glasses, putting ashtrays away, and the room was a delectable place with its light, clear curtains. Other rooms showed more rustic accumulations from the age of the hunting grandfather—carved wooden chests, elaborate chairs, heavy oaken tables, even a canopied bed—but here in the parlor one felt the hand of Gabriella and Poli. Or of Rosalba? I wondered. I couldn't seem to forget Rosalba or the bloodstains or the empty-headed bitterness of those days. The embarrassment I felt at walking on rugs, behaving politely, and seeing poor Pinotta called and ordered around with that cheerful hardness, was increased by remembering Rosalba, by knowing that such things happened amid so much cleanliness and civility.

We talked about the woods that morning. Oreste happened to say that I liked the country so much that I'd given up the sea to come here, and Gabriella began immediately to talk about the sea, about a beach near a little port where they had friends and the olive trees went down into the water. It was a private sea, an enclosed, off-limits beach, and had a pool for use on windy days, and none of the ordinary vacationers could get in, none outside their circle. Poli damned the taste of the owners, who, he said, dressed their servants in broad sashes and stocking caps and made them masquerade as fishermen.

"Stupid, they did it that one time, at the party," Gabriella said with a sharpness I didn't like. I caught a flash of malice as on our first meeting the other day.

Oreste said: "You say the trees went into the water?"

"They're still there. These things don't change." She had

relaxed again but was keeping an eye on Poli's movements as she talked. He was smoking and smiling abstractedly.

"Gabriella danced to Chopin among those trees," he said, looking vacantly at his cigarette smoke. "Classical dances, with a veil, under the moon. Don't you remember, Gabri?"

"A shame," she said, "that your friends weren't here yesterday."

She called Pinotta and told her to open the glass doors. "It still stinks from last night," she muttered. "Erotics and drunks leave a place looking like a run-down zoo. That odious paintress of yours who smoked Havanas!"

"I thought the orgy took place under the pines," I said.

"They're like monkeys," she burst out. "They went everywhere. Most likely there's a pair of them still in the woods."

Poli smiled at something that crossed his mind. "Isn't Pieretto coming down?" he said.

When Pieretto entered the room, Gabriella had already told Oreste and me that one lived in perfect freedom on the Greppo, one came and went, and anyone who liked to be alone would do well to keep to himself. "You come down, I go up," she said to Pieretto. "Be good, children." She had disappeared at the same moment during our first visit: Poli had told us she was sunbathing. We had discussed it in the buggy and Pieretto had said: "She has the stigmata, too . . . Shall we ask her to the cleft?"

At this point I would have liked to leave the others and take my time investigating the hill until lunch. But instead I took Oreste's arm and we walked under the pines. Poli and Pieretto, behind us, had begun arguing.

17. Toward dusk Oreste left in the buggy, annoyed, and night fell on the Greppo. I managed to be alone under the pines waiting for dinner to begin. Pieretto and Poli were talking near the pool. Poli, who had gone about all day with a tired and swollen face, spoke softly—reminding me of the night on the hill, the night of Oreste's howling. I could catch Pieretto's outbursts across the hedge, his peremptory witticisms. Poli was complaining, talking about himself, about his body. "When I realized I had to heal, that I had to remake myself like a child . . . Some things one never really knows. Dying didn't scare me. It's hard to live . . . I'm grateful to that poor girl for teaching me this."

He spoke slowly, fervently, in his low, distinct voice. ". . . At bottom there's a great peace in us, a joy . . . All of us are born out of this. I understood that evil and death . . . don't come from us, we don't make them . . . I forgive Rosalba, she wanted to help me . . . Now everything is easier, even Gabriella . . ."

Pieretto interrupted with a growl. He said: "Bunk," I think to his face. The two voices struggled for an instant and Pieretto's won.

"What brass," he was saying. "It cuts no ice with me. Rosalba had no intention of helping you and you have no right to pity her. You were two pigs . . . Drop all this innocence business."

Poli kept talking in a low voice. ". . . It was all fated. It isn't we who give ourselves death . . ."

The voices trailed away under the moon. I sniffed the piny smell in the still warm air—pungent, almost marine. All day we had wandered in the scrub, going halfway down the hill. Gabriella led us to a little grotto under an overhang, ringed with maidenhair fern, where some water was stagnating. We found peaches on a tree in a hollow, as ripe as honey. Oreste had been darkly gay. He let out some of his bellows to scare Gabriella. Toward evening I realized that you didn't hear farm noises on the Greppo—creakings, barking, crowing. You dominated the plain up there as if from a cloud.

After dark we sat down to dinner at the gleaming table, set in the main room by Pinotta. Pinotta feared Gabriella's glances and was on her toes. "The table is sacred," Gabriella had said. "As long as you can, you ought to make each mouthful a celebration." She even demanded that flowers be scattered around on the tablecloth. She came down in sandals, but dressed for the evening. "Do sit down." I tried not to look at Pieretto's cuffs.

We discussed Oreste and his secretive mood, talked about when he and Poli used to beat the woods for game. We compared city and country living. We discussed Poli as a boy, and the need for solitude that sooner or later takes hold of everybody. Gabriella chattered about trips she had taken, the annoyances of the fashionable world, strange meetings in mountain inns. She was born in Venice. We confessed to being only students.

Pinotta served us, always, in her peculiar gait of someone walking barefoot. I had the impression that somewhere, in the kitchen perhaps, there must be someone, maybe a cook, who was the true mistress of the house. I looked at the flowers, the white tablecloth, I chewed noiselessly, kept an eye on Gabriella. I still wasn't quite convinced I was there, that a house like this could rise like an island from a region of peasants. I was still thinking of the festoons of colored paper over Oreste's chimney, of the yellow ears of corn over the threshing floor, of the vines, the faces at doorways. Gabriella ate modestly, Poli was bent over his plate; we listened to an endless monologue by Pieretto about how he liked to walk at night.

I watched Gabriella out of the corner of my eye and wondered if Oreste hadn't been cleverer than we had. With a fine show of manners Oreste had gone home to sleep on it, to be alone and think it all over from a distance. He knew Poli better, knew things we didn't, and had made up his mind he didn't want to stay on the Greppo. He hadn't escaped merely to see Giacinta. Days before, on the road, we had been wondering whether Gabriella was worthy of coming with us to the cleft. But what are they doing in the country, these two, we asked ourselves. If they came alone to make peace, why should they want us? And, we said, what does Gabriella know about Rosalba? She certainly seemed wide-awake. Did they take cocaine together at night?

"Believe me," Pieretto told us, "those two detest each other."

"And why do they live together then?"

"I'll find out."

It was a good thing that Poli never stopped filling our glasses at dinner. Gabriella drank too, in tasteful sips, turning her head aside afterwards like a bird. I thought: perhaps if they drink enough they will grow more sincere, younger, and Gabriella will tell us that in spite of everything she loves her Poli. Poli will tell her that Rosalba was ugly, vicious, a madwoman, and that meeting us was what cured him, our meeting and Oreste's cry. This will be enough, I kept telling myself, to make us more friendly; we'll let

Pinotta off and go walking or go cheerfully to bed. Life on the Greppo would be changed.

"You'll be bored," Gabriella said. "We have nothing here at night except crickets. Your friend did well to get away..."

"The crickets, the moon," Poli said, "and us."

"So long as they're happy," Gabriella said, toying with the rose in front of her. She looked up, intent. "I hear that you used to go to night spots with Poli at Turin?"

She looked at us an instant and burst out laughing.

"Come come—who died?" she exclaimed. "We're all sinners. Misfortunes make one younger and nobody is guilty. We lost a son and a son is given back to us. Let us kill the fatted calf."

Poli looked up and snorted. "Madame," Pieretto cried, "I toast the fatted calf."

"What's this 'madame'?" she said. "We might even call each other by name. We have enough common acquaintances."

Poli clouded over and said: "Listen, Gabri. At this rate we'll end like last night."

Gabriella smiled faintly, maliciously. "There's no music," she said, "and no one is drunk tonight. So much the better; we can talk sincerely."

Pieretto said: "We can drink afterwards."

"If it's music you want," Poli said, getting up, "I can put on a record."

I saw her slender hand squeeze the rose she had dropped and didn't dare look her in the face.

Poli had sat down again without putting on the record. "Music needs cheerfulness," he said. "Let's drink some more first." He held a glass out to her, she nodded and drank. We all drank.

While we were lighting up in the silence, Gabriella breathed out smoke, looked us over and started laughing. "We haven't understood one another," she said mockingly. "Sincerity is no crime. I hate crimes of passion. I only want somebody to tell me if Poli was very funny that night in the car—when he discovered the sincere life..."

18.

"Let me talk," Gabriella grumbled. "We talk so little when there are only two of us and we already know all the answers. It's like being alone . . . I only wish that someone would tell me if that night . . . you two were there . . . if Poli explained his innocent life to the assembled company. He found it in Turin; this I know. But I'd like to have seen the faces, the faces of everyone listening. Because Poli *is* sincere," Gabriella said emphatically. "Poli is as naïve and sincere as any man should be, and doesn't always understand that crises of conscience aren't always convenient for others. It's his charm"—and she smiled—"this being simple. But tell me what the others looked like."

She fixed us with hard, laughing, malicious eyes.

Poli took this turn in the conversation with composure. He had an air of having expected something very different. It was Pieretto who said: "A blue fury . . . with foam. One heard the grinding of teeth. Someone had seven devils inside him."

I didn't like Poli's face; he was looking down, his eyes swollen, half closed.

"*Quos Deus vult perdere* . . ." Pieretto went on, "well, it happens." Gabriella looked at him, surprised, and laughed softly, a silly laugh. She changed her tone quickly and suggested: "Shall we go outside for some air?"

We rose in silence and went down the steps. We were met by the song of crickets and a fresh night smell.

"Let's go look at the moon from the woods," Gabriella said. "Then we'll have coffee brought out."

Later Pieretto came to see me in my room. I was stirred by the thought of sleeping in that house and waking tomorrow and then going downstairs, finding those two again, talking to them, having dinner and passing another evening with them. Our session under the pines and the moon had lasted until late: Gabriella had made no more allusions to the past; she'd been relaxed and let us talk about ourselves. But just this stuck in my throat: the tension, the suspicion, the things not said. Now I knew they were all alike, Poli and Gabriella, too—all of them ready to turn themselves inside out merely to pass an evening. Those trees and the moon must have seen dark things the night before. Why so much innuendo, draped like ivy to hide a cesspool, when everyone knew the cesspool was there?

I said as much to Pieretto as we were smoking our last cigarettes. "Can you tell me what we're doing in this house?" I said.
"These aren't our kind of people. They have money, friends, all the
time in the world. Have you ever seen people eat with flowers on
their plates? Oreste's vineyard was better, the cleft was better.
Oreste caught on right away . . ."

"Still, you like Gabriella," he interrupted.

"Gabriella? When she fights all the time? She's sized us up
from head to toe. She has no idea what to do with us. Look at
Oreste . . ."

"Oreste will come back, you'll see," Pieretto said.

"Well, I hope so. Tomorrow . . ."

"Keep your voice down," Pieretto said. "I'm not leaving even if
they throw me out. It's too good a comedy . . . while it lasts."

Then we discussed Poli and his peculiar fate—that gift he had
for exasperating women.

"He's a real wonder," Pieretto said. "He ought to be a hermit.
He was born to live in a cell and doesn't know it."

"Conceivably. But he can pick his women."

"And what does that mean? Only that they pursue him like
furies."

"Yes, but he doesn't mind. Gabriella's his wife. It's not you who
sleep with her."

Pieretto gave me that special look of his, half foolish, half
amused.

"How stupid you are," he said. "Gabriella doesn't sleep with
Poli. Anybody can see that. All you need is a pair of eyes."

After relishing my amazement, he went on: "Neither of them
even thinks about it. I don't even know why they stay together.

"For that matter," he went on, "it's possible they never ask
themselves why."

I slept well in that soft bed with the silk eiderdown. Being alone
after days and weeks of sleeping in a room for three rested and
refreshed me like the sky I saluted at the window the next morning. Everything was awake, alive, and sparkling; sunlight flooding
the plain beyond the pines and the vast horizon reassured me
that there would be much to do on the Greppo, pleasures of the
woods, gossiping, games—this kingdom to be absorbed with one's

whole body—hollows, clearings, many long afternoons, Gabriella's grotto.

Oreste arrived at midmorning, ringing his bicycle bell like the postman. Pinotta was with him on her way back from shopping at Due Ponti. The funny thing was that he was really bringing the mail, postcards for us. Gabriella shouted to him from the window: "If it takes mail to bring you here, I'll tell all my friends to write."

We sat down inside with her to wait for Poli. Oreste, in high spirits, said that he had seen some birds on his way, heard some whirrings and chirpings that promised early hunting.

"Do you enjoy shedding blood so much, Oreste?" Gabriella exclaimed. "Listen," she said, "isn't it better to use first names? One comes to the country to be free, no?"

Oreste went on about hunting and said that Poli shouldn't sleep so late. "The time for hunting in summer is before dawn, the earlier the better . . ."

"Not with dogs," Gabriella cried. "The dogs don't like it. The dew drowns the scent." She laughed at Oreste's surprise. "You don't know, I guess, that when I was a girl I used to vacation on the Brenta among the lark hunters. You used to hear nothing but shooting and barking dogs . . ."

"Where is Rocco's old dog?" Oreste asked.

"He must be dead," she replied. "Have you asked Poli? Incidentally, Poli doesn't want to do any more killing. Did he tell you?"

Oreste looked at her questioningly.

"He doesn't enjoy it any more," Gabriella explained. "It doesn't agree with his new life." She smiled. "But he eats steak anyhow."

"I suspected it," Pieretto groaned.

Oreste didn't understand our cheerfulness and looked at us one by one, puzzled.

"Last night we were discussing Poli," Gabriella said. "You really must stay with us. Here everything happens at night."

Gabriella disappeared shortly afterwards. We circulated around the rooms near the verandah—there were books, old, rebound books, card tables, a billiard table. I liked the green light of the pines against the windows. In a corner I found novels, illustrated magazines, and Gabriella's workbox. Muffled thumps came up from the kitchen. I still hadn't seen the gardener.

"All this land you own," Pieretto said to Poli, "why don't you try to cultivate it?"

At Poli's vague smile, Oreste said: "He's not exactly the type, is he? It'll end with his father selling everything. He doesn't even use it for hunting."

"Why should he work his land?" I asked Pieretto, looking up from my magazine.

"A person in crisis always works his land," Pieretto said. "It's our common mother, who never deceives her children. You should know that."

"However," Poli said, "in September you can hunt . . ."

No one spoke. I was thinking that September was close, ten days away, and wondering if it were right to stay so long. It seemed understood that we would stay. I said nothing and reopened my magazine.

At lunchtime Gabriella came down in a negligée, smelling of sun. Laughing in the shade of the window shutters, Oreste went on talking about hunting.

19. So Oreste stayed to live on the Greppo. Occasionally he left on his bicycle and came back later. The hill seemed to cook in the August sun; honeysuckle and mint surrounded it with an invisible wall. It was fun to bushwhack in the undergrowth, and coming to a clearing, to dart back in again like an insect or a bird. It was like catching your claws in bird lime, in that perfumed sunshine.

In the afternoons we went down in a group, those first days, down steep slopes to the vineyards suffocated with weeds; and once we circled the entire hill and found a small black kiosk among the brambles and looked at the sky through holes in the battered roof. But there was no trace of hedges or paths; the slope was all waste, whatever garden may have been there once, with the present ruin its pavilion. Oreste and Poli called it the Chinese pagoda and could remember when it was still covered with jasmine. Now, as we approached among thistles, we could hear a rustle of mice or lizards —they had taken over the hill. But the scrubland seemed so virgin, so wild that the effect wasn't depressing. Our voices couldn't touch it. The idea that the great summer sun in the woods tasted of death was true. Here no one broke ground to get something out of it, no one lived here: once they had tried and then gave up.

Pieretto said to Gabriella: "I don't see why you two don't spend the winter in this kiosk. You could eat roots. You would find the peace of the senses . . . The country is disgusting in summer, it's a sexual orgy of pulp and juices. Winter is the soul's only season . . ."

"What's got into you?" Oreste said.

And Gabriella, nastily: "Oh, you're crazy."

Poli smiled. And Pieretto went on: "Let's be honest. The country in August is indecent. Why all these sacks of seeds? It stinks of coitus and death . . . and the flowers, the animals in heat, the dangling fruit."

Poli laughed. "The winter, the winter," Pieretto insisted. "At least the earth is hidden. You can think of better things."

Gabriella looked at him and looked at Poli and smiled fleetingly. "The winter is something I can take in my stride," she murmured, "and I like this indecent odor."

While Poli and Pieretto were spending a lot of time together during those first days, the rest of us would go halfway down the slope in the evenings to sit where we could see far off, smoke a cigarette, and look at the minuscule trees on the plain.

Unlike Poli, who never said a word about the villages, roads, or churches, Gabriella was interested in everything and made Oreste her guide. She wanted to know how the peasants lived, where Oreste had spent his boyhood, where they had hunted. I especially enjoyed looking down on the oak country, Monbello of the red earth, where the two brothers lived. We were talking about it once when Gabriella, curious, asked me if Oreste's girl lived there. I said that there was something better than that: two smart men who kept their vineyards and were sufficient to themselves. Oreste was silent. Praising Davide and Cinto was like praising him. Gabriella had said: "But why, if they own the land, do they work it themselves?" I started explaining that this was the beauty of it, that you only deserve to live off your property if you work it yourself, and everything else is slavery. I saw her smile with faint irony, her lips as rosy as her cheeks were burnt. "Obviously they are made that way," she murmured.

Strolling with them in the odor of mint and parched earth, I couldn't get it out of my mind that we were a horizon up there for the vineyard at San Grato, an island in a marine sky. I don't know if the thought had occurred to Oreste; he wasn't the type to think it. I said jokingly: "If you'd been born on the Greppo, this would have been your horizon," and I pointed with my finger to clusters of houses glimmering white below. "Don't you want to go voyaging any more, to circle the globe?"

"Nothing but rice fields in that direction," he said, "and then Milan . . ."

"Oh, Milan, don't run down Milan," Gabriella groaned. "I've got to go back there in a day or two."

During those early days I was still sure I liked Gabriella, that there was no harm in being with her. Alone, with her and Oreste, we could talk, without the shadow of Poli making us uneasy. We forgot Poli and Rosalba; if any hint of those Turin days came up, Gabriella was the first to smile. But most of the time we said little: Oreste was silent as usual, I was unsure of my ground. I sensed a withdrawal in her, an unnecessary pretense, even when she laughed and clapped her hands. Perhaps Pieretto could have stood up to her, but he was also being cautious. What I liked most, after all, was turning things over in my mind, the simple thought that we were living with her on the Greppo, that she was breathing the smell of the thickets in our company. The best thing we did was climbing down to the grotto or the vineyards, eating some wild fruit, throwing ourselves on the grass, roasting in the sun. There was always a slope, a turning, a cluster of trees I hadn't yet seen, touched, absorbed. That vaguely brackish August smell was stronger here than elsewhere. There was the pleasure of remembering it at night under a broad moon that thinned out the stars, of hearing at our feet, in every direction, the hill living its own secret life.

Oreste named the animals of the Greppo for us—magpies, jays, squirrels, field mice, hares, and pheasants. Crickets and cicadas were already singing in my blood day and night, giving voice to the summer. Sometimes their racket was loud enough to make me shudder—it must have penetrated underground to the roots and snakes. I wondered if the masters of the Greppo, not so much Poli and Gabriella, who didn't count, but the hunting ancestor and earlier caretakers, had loved this wild mountain as much as I seemed to love it. They had certainly possessed it in better style than we.

Gabriella's presence had helped me understand one thing. I used to discuss it with her in my mind, as I sometimes discussed things *sotto voce* with Pieretto. That abandonment, that solitude of the Greppo were symbols of the mistaken life she and Poli were leading. They were doing nothing for their hill; the hill was doing nothing for them. Their waste of so much land and so much life could bear no other fruit than restlessness and futility. I thought of the Monbello vineyards, of the sharp face of Oreste's father. To love a piece of land, you had to work it and sweat over it.

We went back the next day to the kiosk where Pieretto's idea that the country smelled of coitus and death made me smile. Even the insects amazed me with their buzzing. As did the summer coolness of the ivy, the whistling cry of a partridge. I left Gabriella and Oreste on the sagging floor, shouting and stamping to flush the partridges, and went outside in the sun.

20.
We would pass our nights on the verandah, drinking, listening to records, playing cards.

"Who is more useless?" Gabriella would say. "I can't even amuse all of you?"

She would dance a turn with one of us and go back to her chair. The first evenings we would listen silently, following the dancers and the movements of her blue skirt.

"Who's more useless than I am?" she said one night, stretching in her chair. "I'm tired of living."

"She sounds serious to me," Pieretto observed.

"Tired of everything," she said. "Of getting up in the morning, of dressing to come down, of your bright discussions. I'd like to go to a tavern and get drunk with porters."

"Masochism," Poli said.

"But of course," she said. "I'd like some man to strangle me. It's all I deserve."

"Oh, oh, we're in crisis!"

"Precisely," Gabriella snapped coldly. "We're in a crisis. It's the fashion up here. Watch out, Oreste, or you'll collapse like the rest of us."

"Only he?" Pieretto said.

Gabriella's mouth twisted. "Compared to him, we're filth," she said. Her glance took me in as well. "He's the only one of us who's sane and sincere."

Oreste looked at her so sharply that we all had to laugh. Gabriella smiled, too. "Isn't it true that you don't have crises of sincerity?" she asked him. "Have you ever in your life told a lie, Oreste?"

"There are crises and crises," Poli began.

"How true," Oreste said contentedly. "Who doesn't tell fibs once in a while?"

Then Poli began to complain and accuse us all, Gabriella, people in general, of stopping at the surface of things, of reducing life to a pointless drama, a senseless succession of acts and manners. People acted in heat and exercised their consciences over the most material and foolish things. Some were fixed on their work, some on petty vices, some on the future. Everyone floundered around and filled his days with talk and vanity. "But if we want to be sincere," he said, "what do these trivia matter? Certainly we're all filth. So what then *is* a crisis? Surely not getting drunk with porters, who aren't worth a finger more than we are. The only thing is to dig down into ourselves and find out who we are."

"Just talk," Pieretto said.

"What's the point of all the rest?" Poli said stubbornly. "Everything else you can buy, or people can do it for you . . ."

"Everyone doesn't have the money," Oreste interrupted.

"And so? I said that people can, not that they do. There are always things that don't depend on ourselves. The only thing that no one else can tell you is who you are . . ."

"But if we're filth," Gabriella broke in. ". . . Oh, Poli, didn't you agree that we're filth?"

"Poli is saying something else," Pieretto observed. "That we all tend to satisfy ourselves with manners, with the going thing. It's not enough to know we're filth, it's too little. We have to ask why, have to understand why we can't be anything else, that we too are made in the image of God. There's more fun in it that way."

Gabriella went to put a new record on. At the first notes she turned, held out her arms, and groaned imploringly: "Who wants me?"

Oreste stood up and the rest of us continued arguing. Now Poli was saying that if God was inside us he couldn't see why one should look for Him in the world, in action or in works. "If we're supposed to resemble Him," he murmured, "then it must obviously concern our inner selves."

I was following the blue dress with my eyes and thinking of Rosalba. I was on the point of saying: "This scene has happened before," but I saw a strange smile lighting up Pieretto's face.

"Are you sure that's not an old heresy?" he said.

"I don't care," Poli said sharply. "I'm satisfied enough if it's true."

"Are you dead set on resembling the Eternal Father?"

"What else is there?" Poli said emphatically. "Do the words frighten you? Give Him any name you like. My God is absolute freedom and certainty. I don't speculate whether God exists: I'm satisfied with being free, certain, and happy, like Him. And to reach that point, to be God, it's enough for a man to touch bottom, to know himself down to the ground."

"Drop it," Oreste shouted over Gabriella's shoulder. We ignored him. Pieretto said cheerfully: "And have you touched those depths? Do you go down there often?"

Poli nodded, unsmiling.

"I used to think," Pieretto went on, "that the best way to know yourself was to pay with one's own person. Have you thought about what you would do if another flood came?"

"Nothing," Poli said.

"You didn't understand me. Not what you would like to do, but what you would do. Would you run? Fall on your knees? Dance with sacred joy? Who can pretend to know himself unless he's been in real danger? Conscience is only a sewer; health is in the open air, among people."

Poli kept his eyes on the floor and said: "I've been among people since I was a boy. First college, then Milan, then life with her. I've had a good time, I don't deny it. I suppose everyone does. I know myself. And I know people . . . This isn't the road."

"I wouldn't want to die," Gabriella said, dancing past, "because I wouldn't see people any more."

"Stick to your dancing," Pieretto called out. "Still, she's right," he said to Poli. "Do you see God in the mirror perhaps?"

"Meaning?"

"Matter of logic. If the world doesn't interest you and you carry God in your eyes, so long as you live you see Him in the mirror."

"Why not?" Poli said. "No one knows his true face." He spoke so calmly that I was impressed.

The music had stopped. We heard crickets through the open windows.

"Anguish again," Gabriella said, arm in arm with Oreste. "We're sick of you people."

We all went out under an enormous moon and strolled down the road. "There ought to be a nightclub down there." Pieretto said, "a place to go." Gabriella, ahead of us with Oreste, said to him: "Stinker! Don't you dare mention the flood again."

I walked between the two pairs, drinking in the earth smell, the moon, and the honeysuckle. We passed under the overhanging prickly pear. Bushes and trees on the open slopes made a thousand patterns in the moonlight. A gentle wind seemed like the breathing of the night.

Ahead of us, Oreste was chattering about his experiences on horseback. And Poli was talking to Pieretto: "There's a value in the life of the senses, in sin. Few men know the limits of their own sensuality . . . know that it's an open sea. That takes courage, and one can free oneself only by touching the bottom of it."

"But it has no bottom."

"It's something that goes beyond death," Poli said.

21. I was kidding Oreste for not having gone home for three days, for sleeping in a room on the ground floor next to the cook's. "I trust him," Gabriella had said.

Oreste came up to wake me in the mornings and we smoked at the window.

"I've been walking in the woods all night," he told me.

"Why didn't you whistle for me? I'd have come."

"I wanted to be alone."

I made the face Pieretto would have made and was immediately sorry. Oreste looked like a scolded dog.

"Is there someone mixed up in this?"

Oreste looked at his cigarette and said nothing.

"Let's go out to the terrace," I said.

One reached the terrace by a small wooden ladder that ended below a trap door. We had never been up. At noontime Gabriella usually sunbathed up there.

We crossed the corridor on tiptoe. The ladder creaked damnably under our weight. Oreste went through first.

It was a sort of loggia open to the sky and full of cool morning sun. A low brick wall closed it in, and on top of that were light columns supporting wooden beams to make a pergola. Pots of scarlet geraniums were set on the wall and the whole was surrounded by the dark tops of pines.

"Not bad, not bad. This woman knows how to live."

Oreste looked around, perplexed. Stools and dressing gowns of toweling and a beach chair were folded against the wall. One couldn't see more than the sky and the geraniums from the beach chair, I thought to myself.

"No need to take her to the cleft, my friend," I said to Oreste. "She must be better cooked than we are."

"You mean she tans in the nude?" he stuttered.

"Did she invite you up here, too?" I smiled, and was sorry again. Oreste couldn't take his eyes off the dressing gowns.

"Happy ants, happy hornets!" I said. "Let's go down."

Whose fault was it, that morning? Mine, for kidding him? When I think of it now, I still blame the Greppo, the moon, Poli's ideas. I should have said to Oreste: "Let's go home," or discussed it with Pieretto. Perhaps Pieretto could still have saved him. But the all-wise Pieretto was blind to everything those days.

Furthermore, I was enjoying the game. Midday approached and Gabriella, who had walked around all morning in shorts, chattering, slamming doors, making Pinotta run—Gabriella suddenly disappeared, leaving us under the sunny pines or on the quiet verandah to read or listen to each other by turns. Oreste and I exchanged quick glances—it was our secret now—and that hour of sun passed in suspense: buzzing, endless. One morning when Poli went up and we didn't see him for a while, I saw Oreste grow pale. I wasn't jealous of Oreste: I wasn't thinking seriously of Gabriella; but neither did I suspect that he was. I just enjoyed the game, that's all; it was a bit like the other secret of the cleft, as harmless; nevertheless, I was careful not to let Pieretto understand. He was the type to discuss it at the table.

When I got around to asking Oreste if Giacinta wasn't expecting him, I saw that it was too late. It was the morning when Oreste didn't answer my customary wink; he was no longer himself. Gabriella had spoken to him. They had gone out at dawn together, after the thunderstorm of the night before. From the window I watched them coming back laughing through the long grass. Just that morning Poli hadn't left his room: I found Pieretto and Pinotta whispering together and Pinotta gave me a nasty look. Pieretto said we were back to normal now. Pinotta had been to clean vomit from the blankets.

"Has it happened before?" Pieretto asked.

"Every time they drink too much," Pinotta said.

The evening before, we had drunk only orangeade: but the heavy air and the first flashes of lightning had made us restless, bad-tempered, which in me became uneasiness, a real sense of trouble; turning the conversation to our long stay on the Greppo, I said that now was the time to go. They all jumped on me—she, too—and told me that everything was fine, there were so many things still to do. "The only one with a right to complain," Poli said, "is Pinotta. But Pinotta isn't allowed to complain." Then (lightning was flashing behind the pines) I'd said that I couldn't understand why they came there to be alone and then needed our company. "O presumptuous one..." Gabriella said, but a clap of thunder sent us indoors and the conversation ended.

Now Pieretto followed me into my room and we discussed Poli's relapse.

"I expected it. That idiot is serious," he said. "It's why his father wants to keep him in the country. He'll be out of bed in an hour," he went on. "This is what being a son of God amounts to."

"We have Oreste too, if we need him," I said.

Pieretto made a face. He was thinking about Poli. "He's a vicious boy," he said. "The guilty party is this world where the fathers make too many millions. So, instead of starting from the shore like the rest of the animals, their sons find themselves in deep water before they know how to swim. And then they start drinking. Do you know the sort of life they made him lead as a boy?"

He told me an ugly story of maids and governesses whom his father and mother had kept around him on the Greppo until he was thirteen or fourteen. They had taught him all kinds of nonsense, the worst being that the rich are born that way and that it was right for other women to bow to his mother. As children of God, to be sure, they were all equal. In fact, one of the maids had taken him to bed when he wasn't yet twelve and had sucked his strength for months. Not content with that, she took him into the woods, where they played games, so that Poli was a libertine before he became a man.

"This is what life is for him," Pieretto said. "He used to steal his mother's sleeping pills to drug himself. He chewed tobacco. He would slap the serving girls as an excuse to grab them and be grabbed . . ."

"He's a pig," I said impatiently. "What has money to do with it? Not all the rich are like him."

"They are like him," Pieretto said. "But he's different in this —even though his wife does say so—he's more naïve than the others. And he's serious, you know. If he doesn't die, he'll become a Buddhist."

Just then I saw Gabriella and Oreste through the window, laughing and coming up. They were sliding around on the grass.

I said to Pieretto: "And Gabriella? She doesn't take cocaine?"

"Gabriella takes us all for a ride," he said. "It amuses her."

"But why do they stay together?"

"They've grown used to fighting."

"Couldn't it be that they love each other?"

Pieretto cackled as usual and gave a whistle. "These people," he said, "have no time to lose. Their problems are simpler. They always come down on the side of money."

Then we went down to the verandah and I saw Oreste and saw her. Gabriella had already seen Poli, who had a room separate from hers, and had said when she returned: "The sick man has risen." No one mentioned the drug. Gabriella's and Oreste's eyes were so happy that we forgot Poli. We went on discussing our plans to go to a village festival the next day and dance. It was a village famous for its fair at the end of August. When Gabriella disappeared at noon, I glanced quickly at Oreste and realized then that he wasn't going to respond. He sat in a corner, absorbed in himself. But his eyes were still shining. Then I thought seriously about Giacinta.

22. Oreste went home to get the buggy to take us to the fair, but it held only three and Poli had a headache and down there in the village one had to dance. Then I said I would also stay on the Greppo because I'd grown fond of it and a day off is always pleasant.

"Stinkers that you are," Gabriella said, already seated between Oreste and Pieretto. "But it's still a shame."

They left, waving and laughing. I spent the morning by the grotto of the maidenhair fern. Just there the brow of the hill rose against the sky and a canebrake hid the plain. The canebrake was a souvenir of earlier times; perhaps there had been a vineyard. I stretched out naked at the mouth of the grotto and sunned myself. I hadn't done so for a long time. I was shocked to see myself so dark, almost as dark as the stems of maidenhair. I thought of many things as I looked lazily around. Someone might emerge from the undergrowth that bounded the clearing, but who? Not the cooks, not Poli. Spirits of the cliffs and woods perhaps, or some little animal of the Greppo—beings as naked and wild as myself. In a clear sky, above the canes, the white sickle of a moon gave a magic, emblematic quality to the day. Why is there a rapport between naked bodies, the moon, and the earth? Even Oreste's father had joked about it.

At noon I went back to the villa among the pines. I circled behind the villa near the greenhouse; I saw Pinotta's red head through a window as she leaned over her ironing. While I was looking at flowers through the greenhouse door, old Rocco came out and muttered something. We started talking; he complimented me on my color.

I said that the air on the Greppo was good to breathe; if Poli was so healthy and lively, didn't he owe it perhaps to the years he had spent on the Greppo? Pinotta stopped her work to listen, as surly as ever.

"Yes, yes," Rocco said. "There's air."

All we needed, I thought, was for Poli to sleep with Pinotta too.

I had to smile at the dubious way Rocco was looking at me. Then he spit his cigarette butt into his hand, a large black hand, and muttered something.

He griped about the weather. He said that there wasn't enough water in the pool and he had to carry more in by hand. Once there had been a pump, but now it was broken.

Then I asked where our drinking water came from. "Well water," Pinotta said from the window. "And who draws it?" The red head shook itself fiercely: "I do, I draw it."

I wanted to talk to Rocco, have him tell me about the woods, the old life, but Pinotta's round eyes never left me for a moment.

So I asked if anyone took baths on the terrace and with what water. Pinotta snickered: "Madame takes sunbaths on the terrace."

"I thought perhaps you carried water up."

"I'm not a convict. I haven't murdered anyone yet."

She worked up the courage to ask me why I hadn't gone to the fair. The subject interested Rocco, too. They looked at me hopefully, like eavesdroppers.

"There wasn't room in the buggy."

Old Rocco shook his head. "Too many people," he grumbled, "too many."

Poli, who still looked debauched from the previous day, came down for a brief lunch, then went upstairs again and reappeared only at dusk. We hadn't exchanged ten sentences during the day; we didn't know what to say; he smiled a tried smile and puttered around. I spent the afternoon leafing through old books in the game room—yellowed albums, old encyclopedias, and illustrated sets. When Poli came in at sunset, I looked up and said: "Are they coming back for dinner?"

Poli's look brightened. "Meanwhile let's have a drink," he suggested.

So we drank, sitting among the pines.

"Time passes," I said. "Even up here, where everything seems to have stopped. Fundamentally you're well-off alone, Poli."

He smiled. He was in shirtsleeves, wearing his chain. "Why," he began, "don't we use the friendly *tu*? We're old friends of Oreste's."

So we did. He asked politely about my life in Turin, what I would do when I returned. We talked about Pieretto; I told him how Oreste's women had taken him for a theologian, which amused Poli greatly. He said Pieretto was worth more than that, but he had a defect, he didn't believe in the deeper forces, in the unconscious innocence we all have.

I asked him if he were spending the next winter on the Greppo. He nodded silently, looking intense.

"I keep thinking," I said, "that being in this place where you spent your childhood must have a certain effect on you. Everything must say something to you and have a life of its own. Especially right now."

Poli was silent, listening with his eyes.

"... Even I was moved when we arrived up here," I said. "You can see why. I'd never been here. But this mixture of abandonment and roots—not simple countryside, but something more—impressed me very much. Was it the same when you used to live here?"

He looked at me doggedly.

"The house was the same," he said. "There were more people, more servants, but they haven't changed it."

"I wasn't thinking of the house. I mean the woods, the unkept vineyards, the air of wildness. This morning I sunned myself at the grotto and it seemed to me that the hill was alive and could speak or bleed ..."

I saw him pull himself together.

"... You've been here a long time. Have you ever had such thoughts about the Greppo?"

I talked and was telling myself meanwhile: *If you're a lunatic, then here's another.* Perhaps some day we might agree on something.

369

But Poli spun his glass in his fingers and said: "Like all boys, I was crazy about animals. We had dogs, horses, cats. I had Bub, an Irish trotter, who later broke his back . . . I like the laziness of animals. They're more free than we are."

"Perhaps what I'm trying to say about the hill, you found in animals. Do you like the wild ones, hares or foxes?"

"I don't," Poli said firmly. "I used to talk to my animals the way I talk to you. You can't talk to wild animals. I liked Bub because he let me use the whip. I liked the cats because I could hold them on my knee. Do you understand?" he said, his face clearing. "It was like being with a woman, with my mother . . .

"Mother, she was something else again," he went on. "Poor soul, she made me suffer. One winter she went to Milan and I spent Christmas alone, with the servants and the snow. I stood in the dark room looking through the window at the snow and when the women called me I didn't answer; it drove them crazy . . ."

"There's a winter memory for you," I said.

"Mother is gone," Poli said. "You're right. It's always winter for me now in the country."

So the evening went by, and at midnight we had to eat. Pinotta watched us, the two of us at the table, and seemed to be thoroughly amused. She clattered in and out of the room. I was more anxious than Poli. We drank a good deal and for some reason I brought up Rosalba. I asked him where she was, how it had ended.

"Oh," said Poli sadly, "she's dead."

23. When the three of them arrived in the buggy halfway through the morning, I was hoarse and half out of my mind. All night we had talked about Rosalba's death. Poli didn't know much about it. She had killed herself in that boarding house of the nuns —poison, some narcotic—when he left for the sea. We had walked under the pines, around the pool, and talked continually in low voices until the daylight came. Poli kept repeating that death is nothing, it's not we who make it. Inside us there's joy and peace and nothing else.

Then I asked him if cocaine could add to the peace of the soul. He said that everyone took some kind of drug, from wine to sleeping pills, from nudism to the cruelty of the hunt. "What has nudism to do with it?" Oh yes, it was part of the picture: people go naked into company to brutalize themselves and defy convention.

The night wasn't long enough to make him admit that there was a difference between suicide and death by sickness or accident. Poli discussed Rosalba in the shaky voice of an excited boy; he spoke tenderly of the moment when he was on the edge of death; nobody was guilty of anything; Rosalba was dead; they both were well-off.

All night long, almost as if to prove him right, we drank, argued, and smoked. The first sunlight found us in armchairs, and a rumpled Pinotta made us coffee. A moon was still showing above the pines. Now we were talking about hunting and the poor animals; Poli was saying that, of all drugs, he couldn't understand the shedding of blood. Rosalba had taught him this, that blood has something diabolical about it. "Now Oreste wants to go hunting. He doesn't understand that a man may feel repugnances. Let him go, and leave others in peace . . ."

Daylight calmed me a little, but I couldn't sleep for tension, tiredness, and dumb anger. When I heard happy voices coming up to the villa, an anger with Pieretto took hold of me because he certainly knew and had told me nothing, and I didn't come down right away. I stared vaguely at the ceiling and thought that Rosalba, cocaine, spilled blood, the hill, were a dream, a joke; that all of them had agreed to take me for a ride. All I had to do now was go down, pretend that nothing was happening, not allow the game to continue. To laugh in their faces; that certainly.

A noise, a gunshot, made me jump from the bed. I ran to the window and saw them pour laughing from the buggy. Oreste was brandishing a smoking shotgun. Her hair blowing in the wind, Gabriella had caught her dress on an armrest and was shouting: "Help me down."

Pinotta and the cook ran out; Poli went out. Greetings and discussions followed. Wine, the fair, the ditches. "We've never laughed so hard," they said. "We went by Oreste's village." The horse pawed the ground with his head down.

I came downstairs and it was noon before the excitement subsided. Sprawled in armchairs, they sighed and went noisily from one subject to another. The festivities had created a special understanding among them. They knew how to celebrate, those country people. What villages! And Pieretto had been thrown in a ditch after a fight with a tavern-keeper. Then they rang bells in a church, made the sacristan run out. They had stolen grapes from a vineyard. "And so," Pieretto said, "are your guns ready, Poli? The rest of us will be your dogs."

Quiet returned at noon. Gabriella went upstairs to wash. I looked at Oreste; he was calm and happy. His growing intimacy with Gabriella was lurking in his eyes. No need to ask him any questions.

I couldn't make Pieretto out; he had started joking again with Poli. They were talking about a peasant who had known his grandfather and about how many wives the old man had got pregnant in the country nearby.

"It's an old family custom," Poli said. "Country people enjoy it."

Then Pieretto said: "It's a shame Gabriella loves you. She could liquidate the family debt. You should send her to these fairs more often."

Whatever Pieretto had in mind, it was Oreste who exploded inarticulately. Poli just looked bewildered.

Oreste was on his feet in front of Pieretto but didn't say a word. They glared at each other a moment, both crimson. But Pieretto had already got hold of himself.

"What's eating you?" he said brusquely. "Target practice make you sick?"

Oreste looked him slowly up and down, the same with Poli, and then left without a word.

As soon as we were alone on the stairs, I asked Pieretto if he knew about Rosalba. He answered quietly that he had known for some time; he'd expected it ever since those days in Turin. "What else would a woman do in such a situation? A woman has no retreat. They're incapable of abstract thought . . ."

"Poli's a thoughtless bastard . . ."

"Didn't you know that?" he said. "Where have you been?"

I could have punched him. I bit my tongue. At that moment

Gabriella fluttered by in the corridor, tossed us a salute, and disappeared.

"What's this new mess?" I muttered. "Which one of you seduced her?"

"You mean, who *thinks* he seduced her. That cock robin hasn't yet been born."

"Still, one of you is taking it seriously."

"That may be so," Pieretto cracked. "Is that the advice you've been giving him?"

I realized then that Pieretto was more innocent than I. I took his arm—something I'd never done before—and we went to the window.

"It's been going on for three days," I told him, "and could end in a real mess." I told him it was best for us to leave. "As far as I'm concerned, they can do anything they want. I don't care about Poli . . . But Oreste does matter."

"What are you scared of? The gun?" Pieretto said, ready to laugh.

"Anyhow, I see you've been thinking it over too. What scares me is how one can't talk to Oreste . . ."

"Is that all?"

"And I don't like Poli's expression. I don't like the way he talks. I don't like this Rosalba business . . ."

"But you like Gabriella."

"Not when she falls drunk in ditches. These people aren't like us . . ."

"But that's the beauty of them," Pieretto exclaimed. "That's the beauty of them."

"You said yourself that they hated each other."

"Stupid," Pieretto said. "At least people who hate each other are sincere. Don't you like sincere people?"

"But Oreste's supposed to marry Giacinta . . ."

We went on until they called us to lunch. We found Poli puzzled and annoyed, Oreste cantankerous, and Gabriella with her hair washed, chattering about the red tassels on the oxen and the abominable smell of acetylene lamps.

"I like the smell of acetylene," Pieretto said. "It reminds me of carnival in Turin, winter booths, and the horns."

24.

I wanted to talk to Oreste. Not that he was avoiding me, but he had an air halfway between sarcastic and offended that put me off. I stopped him on the stairs and asked him to show me his gun.

"Can we come hunting with you?" I asked.

He had thrown his gun and game bag on a sofa in the billiards room.

I took a red shell from the bag and said: "Do you intend to kill Poli with one of these?"

He took it out of my hand and muttered: "What the hell do you mean?"

Then I asked him to let me talk. In a low voice (the others were on the verandah) I said that now we all knew Poli so well we had to treat him as a friend. Did he think he was treating him as a friend? Fifteen days before, if Poli had hung around Giacinta, who wasn't even married, what would have happened? At least he and Gabriella should hide it better. After a while even Poli, no matter how bored, how crazy, how innocent, wouldn't be able to keep his eyes shut any longer. Wasn't it better for us to leave right away? To go home and keep a pleasant memory? What did he expect to get out of it?

Oreste listened and blushed and was several times on the point of interrupting. But when I stopped, he smiled a stubborn smile and kept silent, looking me up and down.

"It's not the same thing," he said finally. "I'm not stealing anything. And we don't want to hide either. She agrees with that."

"It's obvious that she agrees. She's a woman. But how will it end? Have you any idea?"

He gave me his sour-lemon look again. "They've been apart for more than a year," he said. "She didn't want to see him any more. It was Poli's father who sent her here. To keep him in order, so he wouldn't make any more messes. Have you noticed how Poli treats her?"

I didn't answer that one doesn't cure an invalid by making him drink, making him furious, or making love under his nose. It was useless because Oreste was talking indignantly, with that stubborn flush that means "now or never."

"She's an amazing girl," Oreste said. "You should have seen her dancing, laughing at the fair, kidding the musicians . . . She gets along with everybody . . ."

"And she told you that you're her man?"

Oreste made an effort and looked at me, glanced at me sidelong with a pitying air. His eyes were shining. Days later, when it was clear that the game was out of control, I realized that his look was an effort to avoid insolence, not to offend me with his happiness. Things like this had always shamed us. We didn't know how to discuss them.

"As far as that goes," Oreste said, "even Poli knows. After the Turin affair . . . she was already living alone . . ."

"Did she tell you that herself? Well then, what are they doing here together?"

We went on like that until they came and interrupted us. I couldn't manage to get under his skin or break his obstinacy. Gabriella must have realized that we were discussing her because she came and took us both by the arm and said: "All right, you wind-bags," looking closely at me.

We went hunting that afternoon. Poli came too. "We'll talk and they'll shoot," Pieretto said to him. It seemed to me that Poli was amusing himself watching Gabriella and Oreste. He would stop every so often, would hold back Pieretto or me, would tell us how good it was that of all the people he had met recently nobody understood him as we did. I let Pieretto talk; once I grew impatient and dodged behind some bushes. I knew that Gabriella and Oreste would have to go down as far as the vineyards to find pheasant. I knew that Gabriella wasn't thinking about pheasant, nor was Oreste, nor Poli. So I made up my mind to stay apart and find a bank, a canebrake, a view. That's what I did and lit my pipe.

Yes, I missed Gabriella, missed her talk and wished I were in Oreste's place. I wondered if I'd shown any envious spite in my last talk with him. Just the thought that she might be glad to go with one of us through the woods, perhaps into the kiosk, and that together, in plain daylight . . . I remembered the Po, the cleft. Where was the summer smell of death now? And so much chatter, so many conversations?

A gunshot reverberated. I cocked an ear. Voices followed, Pieretto's very clearly. Another shot. I jumped up and looked for a puff of smoke among the vines. They were far down, almost to the ironwoods. Those clods, I grumbled, they're really shooting pheasant. And throwing myself back on the grass, I listened to the rustling and buzzing, the echoes of those shots, the Greppo life I now could enjoy peacefully in all its subtleties of terrain.

We went back when the shadow of the Greppo already filled the valley. They had killed a dozen sparrows, which they showed me, caked in their blood, among the shells in the game bag. Gabriella gave her arm to Oreste and Pieretto and made a face at me; they asked me where the devil I'd been. "Next time they'll shoot you in the back. Watch out!" Poli said in his mildest tones.

At the table we discussed the hunt and pheasant and different kinds of shooting. Oreste was more excited and positive than I'd seen him for a long time. Gabriella kept her eyes on him, looking puzzled and distant.

"Davide and Cinto have been poaching on your land," Oreste said. "Why don't you change your gamekeeper?"

"All the better," Poli said. "Hunting is a game for boys."

"And for princes," Pieretto said, "and feudal lords. Just right for the Greppo."

Then Gabriella curled up in her chair to listen to us talk and didn't ask for either cards or music. She smoked and listened, looking at us one by one and apparently smiling. Drinks came and she didn't want any. I watched Poli's face and wondered what evenings on the Greppo had been like when he and Gabriella had been alone. We would have to leave sooner or later. So would they. What was the villa like on winter evenings? I felt a sudden pang at the thought that the Greppo summer, Oreste's love, our words and silences, we ourselves, everything would soon be over.

But Gabriella jumped up, stretched and yawned like a baby, and said, without looking at us: "Turn out the lights. Isn't it true, Oreste, that you have to put the lights out before you can see the bats?"

They went out to sit on the steps, the rest of us behind. There were more stars than crickets. We talked about the stars and the seasons. "The last star of the morning appears down there," Oreste said. They walked, he and Gabriella, among the pines; they were very close, cheek to cheek; we listened to their rustling. It was odd to see Poli sitting there with us. For a moment it seemed to me as if he were the only sane person around; the three of us were quiet and anxious. And Poli said: "It seems like the night we looked down on Turin."

"Something is missing," I murmured.

"The hunting cry."

Then Pieretto—I heard him taking a deep breath—threw out that howl, macerating it in his own style, and cackling. We heard noise in the house, a creaking of doors, and, from the distance, Oreste's voice answering weakly.

"Let's hope that Gabriella doesn't catch cold," Poli said.

"Aren't we drinking?" Pieretto said.

25. "How I'd like to march into a bar," Pieretto said when we went back to the steps with a bottle, "or walk past a movie house or have a night on the town. How about you two?"

"At times," Poli said, "I wonder if women understand anything. If they understand what a man is ... Women are always either chasing you or running away to make you chase them. No woman can stand still."

"You can meet that kind at one in the morning," Pieretto said.

"Once I used to think they were sensual," Poli said, staring at the ground. "This at least I thought they would understand. But no. It's only skin deep. No woman is worth a pinch of drugs."

"But doesn't it depend on the man as well?" I said.

"The fact is," Poli said, "that they have no inner life. They have no freedom. So they're always chasing someone and never finding him. The desperate ones are the most interesting, the ones who can't enjoy themselves ... No man satisfies them. There are true *femmes damnées*."

"In the convents," Pieretto said.

"Nonsense," Poli said. "On trains, in hotels, everywhere. In the best families. Women shut up in convents and jails are women who've found a lover ... The god they pray to or the man they killed never leaves them for a moment. They're at peace ..."

I pricked my ears at a rattle of gravel. I hoped that Oreste and

Gabriella would come back, that it would all be over. But it was a pine cone or a lizard.

"This conversation doesn't concern you," Pieretto said. "Or would you like to kill someone?"

Poli lit a cigarette and his face flared out, eyes half closed. He seemed taken aback. He said from the dark: "I'm not enough of an altruist to do it. It's not a pleasure that attracts me."

"He lets people kill themselves," I said to Pieretto.

We were silent a long time, contemplating the stars. In the coolness of the pines the hill smelled sweetly. I remembered the jasmine of the kiosk; once, in the shade of the little grove, they must have looked like so many stars. Had anyone ever lived in that kiosk?

"Animals," Poli said, "understand men. They can be alone, better than we can . . ."

Gabriella came tearing up, calling, "You can't catch me." Oreste arrived more calmly. "Your flower," he said to her.

"Oreste sees in the dark like a cat," she laughed. "He even uses *tu* with me in the dark.

"Listen," she said. "Why don't you all use *tu* and stop the nonsense?"

We were relaxed when we went back in and lit up. We scattered around the room. Gabriella hummed and looked through the records. She put an oleander into her hair. She threw herself into an armchair and listened to the record. It was a sweet blues, syncopated, a penetrating contralto. Oreste stood silently by the record player.

"It's beautiful," Pieretto said. "I've never heard it before."

Gabriella smiled, absorbed.

"Is it one of Maura's?" Poli asked.

So ended that evening, and we went to bed. I slept badly, a heavy sleep. Pieretto came in and woke me up when the sun was high.

"I've got a headache," I told him.

"You're not the only one," he said. "Listen to them, they're at it already."

The voice on the record, the contralto, was filling the house. "They're mad. At this time of day?"

"It's Oreste greeting the beautiful one," Pieretto said. "The others are asleep."

I dunked my face in the basin. "Isn't Oreste overdoing it?"

"Nonsense," Pieretto said. "It's Poli I don't understand. I didn't expect him to complain. But one would have thought that he wouldn't relish his horns."

I was combing my hair and stopped. "If I've understood rightly," I said, "Poli is tired of women. He said that they didn't let him breathe. He prefers animals, or us."

"Not at all. Don't you see how he suffers when he talks about women? He's a fool in love . . ."

When we went down, the song had been over for a while. Pinotta, dusting the room, told us that as soon as he put the record on, Oreste had left in the buggy, saying he'd be back at noon.

"He's lost his grip," Pieretto said. "Now we're in for it."

"He'll come back on his bicycle."

Pieretto laughed at that, and even Pinotta gave me an impertinent look.

I couldn't restrain myself. "I wonder what effect the station will have on him."

"It'll be good for his health, good for his health," Pieretto said, rubbing his hands. Then he said to Pinotta: "Did you remember the cigarettes?"

At eleven, unable to resist any longer, I went upstairs to knock on Poli's door. I wanted to beg an aspirin. "Come in," he said. He was in bed under the canopy, wearing handsome, claret-colored pajamas, and Gabriella was sitting by the window, already in her shorts.

"Forgive me."

She looked at me, amused.

"This is visiting day," she said.

It was embarrassing. I didn't like their faces.

She got up herself to get me the medicine. She crossed the polished red tiles and rummaged in a drawer.

"If I'm not mistaken . . ." she said, laughing into the mirror.

"It's in the bathroom," Poli said.

Gabriella slipped out of the room.

"I'm sorry," I said. "We didn't sleep much the night before last."

Poli looked at me without smiling, bored. I had the impression that he didn't see me. He moved his hand and only then did I notice that he was smoking.

Gabriella came back with the aspirin and gave it to me. "Let's go down right now," she said.

I spent the morning at the grotto with my headache. I wondered if Gabriella could see the canes, my present retreat, from her loggia. I thought of old Giustina and Oreste's mother and what they would have said if they had known what was going on at the Greppo. But I felt calmer that morning; the worst seemed to be over and accepted; perhaps everything could still be straightened out. That imbecile, I thought, he already has a girl. Obviously he's made that way.

There was nobody there when I climbed back up, and I stayed under the pines. Had Oreste come back? The valley between the trees was lost in haze. Every time I returned from one of my walks, I expected it to be the last. But if Poli didn't throw us out it must mean that he still could bear us; if Pieretto were right, he would have swept us out long ago. He was always the same, Poli; he put up with Oreste to have Pieretto and me nearby to talk to. Out of sheer laziness and his usual malice.

Oreste, unfortunately, had arrived. Pieretto told me so. "They're sunbathing on the terrace," he said innocently, and Poli by his side didn't seem worried. But Poli didn't seem to have slept very much. I could see his hand trembling as he smoked.

"Upstairs, they're sunbathing?" I asked, alarmed. They gave me the kind of look one gives bores. They went on talking about God.

But at lunch Poli said something. He complained about whoever it was who had had the bright idea of playing a record at seven in the morning. He also blamed Gabriella for having waked him. He said sharply: "There's a time for everything."

Gabriella looked at him ferociously. But Oreste's conscience got the better of him and he admitted his guilt with a joke.

We all fell silent, and Gabriella glanced around hotly. She was really furious. "To have to live with lunatics and children!" she said with disgust.

Then Oreste, red in the face, threw down his napkin and went out among the pines.

26. A painful afternoon of silences followed. Oreste's absence killed the hunting party; Gabriella retired to write letters; Pieretto said: "That idiot," and went off to take a nap. The only calm person seemed to be Poli, who stayed in the parlor leafing through magazines, a bottle of cognac beside him. Seeing me pass the window like a soul in torment, he asked me why I didn't come in for a drink and call Pieretto. Then I went out in front of the house, called Pieretto, and escaped.

I went down to the ironwoods and beyond, the farthest I'd been. I found myself on a dusty red lane leading to the plateau, dodging cow droppings. A swarm of yellow butterflies danced overhead. That warm smell of clover and dung was pleasant; it told me that the world didn't end on the Greppo. Mustering all my accumulated irritations, I made up my mind to announce later in the evening that I was going back to Turin.

As I went back up the lane, I looked at the hill for the last time. From below, you could see only pines and broken, brushy slopes. It was a true island, the Greppo, a wild and useless place. At the moment I would have liked to be far away, planning my ordinary life. So much had the hill got into my blood by now.

I met Rocco coming slowly down the road. He said they were looking for me up there. "Who's looking for me?" All four of them, according to him, and they were very quiet, having tea under the pines. "The doctor, too?" The doctor, too.

They're crazy, I thought, and approached the top cautiously. Gabriella, in a red skirt, shouted when she caught sight of me, shouted that I shouldn't be unfaithful to her, that I shouldn't desert them as I had the day before. I shrugged and drank my tea. Oreste, as if nothing had happened—he was still holding his gun on his knees—was again explaining certain fine points of shooting. Then we left.

This time we all went down in a group. I touched Pieretto's elbow and questioned him with my eyes; he hunched up and looked at the sky.

"But hadn't they fought?" I whispered.

"She went into his room," he answered.

Then I walked up to Oreste and asked him where this hare was that we were supposed to slaughter. But Poli spoke to him, he turned around, and Gabriella looked at me sidelong with the trace of a smile. We had already left the road, so a bush was enough to hide us from the others. I asked her nervously: "Can I talk to you?"

"*Pardon?*" she said gaily.

"This won't do, Gabriella," I said. "I wanted to talk to you about Oreste."

We had stopped. I could see her eyes very well; she was serious but also laughing.

"Oreste's a great trial," she groaned. "Oreste is mean."

She shrugged off my glance and moved away. Her voice was hard. "You must tell him so yourself, if he'll listen to you. I think you've been good friends. He mustn't go on with this foolishness. I'm not afraid of people like you two . . ."

We walked among the trees and bushes, not far out of sight of the others. Pushing some branches aside, Gabriella took my wrist and breathed at me: "You don't know how fond of him I am . . . Nobody knows. So serious, so funny, so young . . . Don't you dare tell him I said it . . . But he's got to obey me and not be ridiculous . . ."

We came into the sun, followed by the others. Something brushed past my head and a shot rang out. I heard Pieretto shouting, and Gabriella—all of us. Oreste had shot at a duck—a wild duck, he told us—and missed.

"That was brilliant. Shooting at our heads," Gabriella said. "You might have flattened us out."

But Oreste was happy. "It's only birdshot," he said. "You'd have to hit a man point-blank to kill him."

"Give me the gun," she said. "I want to shoot."

Poli had stayed at the edge of the clearing, almost as if to divorce himself from this game. We waited for another bird to come over, Gabriella holding the gun over her arm, Oreste looking from her to the sky, restless and happy. After a while, when nothing happened, Poli suggested going on to the kiosk.

At the table that evening we were making merry over the wild duck. "You need a dog," Oreste was saying. "First you need a hunter," Pieretto said. They were talking excitedly, with their mouths full.

"You haven't lost your appetite," I said to Oreste.

"Why shouldn't he be hungry?" Poli said. "He's a hunter."

"He's a growing boy," Pieretto said.

"What have you all got against Oreste?" Gabriella burst out. "Leave him alone. He's my man."

Oreste looked at us, puzzled and gay.

"Watch out," Poli said to him. "She's a woman.

"Have you noticed that Gabriella is a woman?" he went on lightly, mockingly.

"That's not difficult," she laughed. "I'm the only one."

"The one and only," Poli said, with a wink and a smile.

Pieretto seemed to be taking it all in and enjoying himself. Oreste was bent over his food as if he wanted to hide. And Gabriella watched him a moment without dropping that penetrating smile.

How long had Gabriella been smiling at him like that? She smiled at me too, finally at Poli. Our first hours on the Greppo seemed to have come back. She and Oreste would disappear together, upstairs to the terrace or into the woods. They seemed to be playing; why should they hide? I think they could have met and talked under our noses, even under Poli's: Gabriella was the kind to do it. Sometimes I would have said that she was laughing at us, that Oreste was a pretext for relieving her feelings at all our expenses. When we met around the table for dinner, Oreste looked surprised, frequently stunned. Neither Pieretto nor I could shake him, not even by making him discuss Poli. And anyway, what did it matter? For Gabriella he was only a pastime. I told him so one evening when I noticed him frowning. He shook his head as if to say, "You don't know the half of it."

Now and then they would quarrel with silences and angry looks. On mornings when Poli was late coming down and Gabriella found Oreste everywhere underfoot, she would tell him to go play with us, to look for flowers, to accompany Pinotta to Due Ponti. "Out of my way, you big baby," she said, annoyed and smiling quickly as she passed through the rooms. Oreste would go down under the pines, desperate. But then Poli would come down, Pieretto would come down, and Gabriella would call him curtly, insisting that he come, and would take his arm. Oreste would obey under Poli's sarcastic glance.

27.

"I don't like this pine grove very much," Pieretto said one evening as he walked up with Poli. "It isn't wild enough. No toads or snakes."

"What's got into you?" I said.

"I'll bet," he said, "that you're having a good time." He laughed derisively. "The cleft was better. Here nobody can go naked. Too respectable."

"I can't see that," Poli said. "We live like peasants."

Gabriella appeared and looked at us suspiciously.

"Plots?" she asked.

"If only!" Pieretto said. "Here's Poli, who's convinced he lives like a peasant. To me, we seem to eat and drink like pigs. Like gentlemen, I mean."

"Gentlemen?" Gabriella said angrily.

Then Pieretto sneered at her. "People have peculiar ideas," he said. "Do you imagine that you're earning your living?"

But Poli said: "If you want to strip naked, you're quite free to do it."

"Impossible," Pieretto said. "One feels too civilized here."

"Do you want to strip?" Gabriella said. "Why not? But peasants don't act that way."

Pieretto looked at me then. "Did you hear her? The lady has your ideas."

"Don't call me a lady."

"The truth is," Pieretto went on stubbornly, "that nobody succeeds in being as naked as an animal. I wonder why..."

Gabriella smiled faintly.

"Understand, I mean living naked, not stripping for fun," Pieretto said.

Oreste appeared among the trees, looking offended.

"I think we're all naked without knowing it," Poli said. "Life is weakness and sin. Nakedness is weakness, it's like having an open wound... Women know it when they lose blood..."

"Your god must be naked," Pieretto muttered. "If he resembles you, he must be."

We sat down to dinner, embarrassed. Even Pieretto was humorless that evening. Oreste seemed the most innocent as he looked gloomily at Gabriella. Something from that conversation under the pines stayed in the air and shamed us. Suddenly I realized that Poli and Gabriella were exchanging looks, hard, rather anxious, honest glances. My old impatience took hold of me; I wanted to be alone. It was Pieretto who spoke this time.

"We've reached the dregs of the pleasures of the Greppo," he said brusquely. "What do you say, Oreste?"

Oreste, caught in a tender look, raised his head. But no one smiled. Poli and Gabriella made no objection. Clearly something was happening.

"Hunters, the season is over," Pieretto said then.

Oreste smiled timidly.

"There's still the autumn hunting," Gabriella suddenly burst out with surprising energy. "Woodcock. Partridge." She grew sulky. "First you have to bring in the grapes."

We talked it over once more, this thorn in Oreste's side. He and his father had agreed that we should be there at the vintage of San Grato. We had discussed it at the time, and as always when the subject came up, Oreste glowered.

"It's a shame that the Greppo vineyards will be harvested only by thrushes," Poli said, eyeing him closely. "Console yourself, Oreste. You go down there, and we'll wait for you."

But strange to say, it was the very uneasiness that weighed on the dinner that kept our glances free of malice. In the silence that followed, we heard a loud automobile horn. A sudden light flooded the windows. Gabriella was already on her feet, excited, calling out: "It's them. They've come back." Cries and shouts outside. Poli got up angrily. Pinotta ran across the room to escape to the kitchen. At a certain point I found myself alone with Oreste, poured myself a drink while the noise and laughter outside were increasing, put my hand on Oreste's shoulder and said: "Courage."

So began the night that was to have been our last. The mild starry air outside was thick with the scent of pines and ripe countryside. Harsh light from the two cars threw the white gravel and the black trees into startling relief against the empty plain. The Milanese seemed to come from every direction. Gabriella introduced me at random; blinded by the headlights, I shook hands, Pieretto shook hands. When we went back in, I didn't know anyone.

Our dinner was convulsed. Pinotta, who usually just served us in an apron, reappeared wearing her cap. They threw open the liquor cabinet. Girls and men collapsed into armchairs, protesting and laughing; some had eaten already, some had been drinking. Baskets were brought in from the cars, a flood of things, bottles, desserts. Corks popped. I counted three women and five men.

The women were in traveling clothes, with scarves wrapped around their hair, an arabesque of colors and bare legs. None could touch Gabriella. They chattered, begged lights for their cigarettes, stared us in the face. Names were flying around. I caught the name Mara. There was a lean young man with a demonic face and a strange jacket that ended at his waist. They called him Cilli, and when he came in, he gave Pieretto such a stare that everyone laughed. Another took Gabriella by the arm and they dropped on a sofa. Another joined suavely in the uproar from the sidelines.

While the reunion was in progress, other conversation had to stop. The news of Milan, the repartee, the general excitement transformed even Poli, who made a cheerful fuss over the women, winked and talked volubly. A flushed Gabriella was arguing in a group of her own. The grand topic was a chorus of protest over the hermetic life the two of them were leading, the immoral egotism of love in the country, of deliberately cultivated boredom. A man in a light-colored suit with a strong, sarcastic face—a certain Dodo, about forty, as I learned later—took advantage of a moment of silence to announce coldly that one had affairs with other people's wives, never with one's own.

Pieretto sniffed the atmosphere like a hunting dog. I noticed that Oreste had disappeared. So had Gabriella. They came back immediately, carrying a small table. Pinotta came in timidly with crushed ice. Gabriella laughed and clapped her hands—she had changed into a blue dress in the meantime—and invited anyone who wanted to go upstairs and wash up. We stayed on the verandah in fours or fives, and a thin woman was sitting next to Poli.

28. The thin woman said to Poli: "I want you to tell me right away why you're living up here."

"Don't you know?" Poli said. "Papa is holding me prisoner."

The woman made a face. She wasn't as young-looking then. She reached out a hand with a glass in it and said: "Drink, please." Her voice was dry and hard and her fingers covered with rings.

"Papa or Gabriella?" she said, laughing foolishly.

"Same thing," a shaggy young man said from the edge of a sofa. "Family obligations."

Then Pieretto opened up: "You couldn't get the secret out of him in a whole evening."

Everyone ignored him. The hairy young man went on: "But we want to amuse you. We said: perhaps he's not drinking enough alone. We're here to give you scope. Dodo was betting us that you don't even know what they're dancing in Milan this year."

"This," Poli said solemnly, and beat the time with a finger.

"No!" they all laughed and yelled. The thin woman coughed helplessly into her glass. That ironical Dodo with the gold teeth came back into the room.

"You're a year behind the times," the hairy youth said when he could make himself heard.

"Not more than three months," Dodo corrected him blandly, like a master of ceremonies. "Poli's had a three months' arrested development."

Dodo was a cold-eyed, deeply tanned person who spoke carelessly and confidently. I remembered Poli's irritation when we heard them arriving, and the first looks they exchanged. Now the signals had been reversed; all I could see were friends milling around, pouring into the room from the stairs, well-bred faces. Gabriella was the last to come in, just as the phonograph began to scratch.

I was standing up, leaning against a windowsill and wanting to disappear, to flee to the woods. The imperturbable Pieretto had already begun chattering in the center of a group. No one was dancing yet. The lean Cilli was amusing himself alone by wolfing down sandwiches with great bobs of his adam's apple. Oreste had disappeared again. I watched Gabriella for him. She was saying something to Poli while the rumpled young man pulled her by the wrist. She laughed and chattered and let herself be dragged away. She was beautiful in that dress. I wondered how many of those men had touched her, how many knew her as well as Oreste did.

I didn't like the other women. They were so many Rosalbas. Slumped in their armchairs, blond or dark, they laughed coldly and exchanged toasts. The thin one, more beringed and made up than the others, hadn't moved yet. With her little innocent and corrupt face she was listening to the conversation of the men, curled on the sofa with her legs underneath her.

Then suddenly they were all dancing. The contralto was singing those blues. Oreste was still missing. Gabriella and Dodo were intertwined, but he was as cool as ever. It seemed obvious to me that he was the man for her. Grizzled and sarcastic, he whispered to her, and Gabriella laughed against his cheek.

I crossed the room to pour myself a drink and found Pieretto chewing ice. "Are you still upright?" I asked him.

He looked at me tolerantly.

The strange Cilli approached through the dancers; I expected a joke, expected him to make faces or crow like a rooster. Instead he reached out a hand.

"Delighted," he said in a silly voice.

"Nice atmosphere," he winked.

"Is this your first visit?" Pieretto asked.

"I'm not too sure where we are," he said with that voice. "We were at the club playing poker and some friends came by and picked us up. I thought we were going to the casino, then I saw Mara, who told me: 'We're going to Poli's.' And who still remembers Poli? They told me he'd gone mad." He rolled his eyes like a lunatic. "How's the maid?" he whispered. "That redhead—edible?"

"Like ice cream," Pieretto said.

"What do they say about Poli in Milan?" I asked him.

"Who knew he was still among the living? It was an excuse for a ride."

He had turned toward the door, preening like a turkey. He pulled his jacket tight and left.

"Elegant and sincere," I murmured to Pieretto.

Pieretto shook his head and looked at the table of couples. "They're all sincere," he said firmly. "They eat, they drink, and they attack each other. What do you expect? That they will teach you how to behave?"

"Where's Oreste?" I asked.

"If you were one of them, you'd act the same."

I gulped down another drink and left.

It was very pleasant to go outside and stop on the brow of the hill. The music and muted uproar behind me shut me off with the emptiness of the countryside.

I went back and found Gabriella. "Oreste is out there waiting for you," I said.

"If that boy is crazy . . ."

"I don't know which of you is crazier," I said. "But for me nobody is waiting."

Then she laughed and ran out.

Now and then a circle would form and Pieretto would hold forth, laugh and flirt with the women. No one had yet proposed going out en masse under the pines. The tireless phonograph was singing. On the whole, it was easy to mix with those people. The women and Dodo wanted only to have a good time. You only needed to enjoy their company. The morning was still far off.

The most constant dancers were Poli and the thin woman of the rings. There came a time (I don't know how long Gabriella had been outside) when the phonograph stopped playing. Poli and his woman, tightly enlaced, also stopped. The others made a circle around Cilli, who, kneeling on the carpet, was whimpering and prostrating himself in front of a little portrait of Poli that they had propped on the floor. Pieretto was in the circle, still unsatisfied.

Then Cilli began the litany. Mara, Dodo's blond friend, dried her eyes and begged him to stop. The others were applauding. Poli weaved over and even he was laughing.

But Pieretto said something. He said that any self-respecting god should be wounded in his side. "Let the accused bare himself," he declared, "and show us the wound."

There were a few more feeble laughs, then silence. The thin woman, now outside the circle, panted: "What's going on? What are they doing?" I didn't dare look at Poli; the other scarlet face was enough.

Someone put a record on; couples formed immediately. I found myself drinking with Dodo, who was looking around for somebody. "She isn't here," I said. "She'll be back right away." He raised his glass and almost winked. I nodded very solemnly. We understood each other.

I was exceedingly drunk. The noise and music began to fog my mind. I saw Poli seated at the far end of the room. Someone was talking to him—Pieretto was still there—and he seemed calm enough, a bit faded. He was pale, but by now everyone looked pale.

Gabriella and Oreste came in.

29.

Many of them had moved out under the pines by now. They were talking about going hunting down the hillside. They were looking for someone, I think it was Poli and the woman of the rings. The music had stopped. I went inside to get another gin.

Oreste came by and slapped me on the shoulder. He was happy for some reason or other.

"Things going well?"

His hair was rumpled too.

"These donkeys," he said. "If only they would go."

"What does Gabriella say?"

"She can't wait to send them packing."

Just then Gabriella left with Dodo. "Good," I told Oreste. "Now you should drink."

Cool, almost cold air was coming in the window (the plain had begun to be veiled in fog both mornings and evenings). Pinotta walked in front of the magnolias with a tray and somebody in the shadows grabbed her; it was Cilli. She escaped with a sharp jerk that sent the glasses flying. A chorus of cheers among the pines greeted the crash.

"You see," I said to Oreste, "they're letting loose tonight. Where's Pieretto?"

"I wish they'd go," he said.

We moved to the verandah. "You can tell me tonight," I murmured behind my glass. "Were you on the terrace with her? Did you do it?"

Oreste looked at me frankly and barely moved his lips. I leaned forward. He smiled, shook his head, and left.

I heard someone coughing on the staircase and low voices talking. That was the way to the bedrooms. They may have been going to mine. I was curious and went to the door. No one. Then I went upstairs, ready to smile casually. The lights blazing everywhere made one seem especially alone. Nobody, not even up there. Then I went to my room, closed the door behind me, turned the lights on and off. No one was there. I sat in the dark in front of the window and smoked. I could hear shouting, faint voices, rustlings below among the pines. I thought of the no longer virgin Greppo.

Footsteps in the corridor startled me. I went out and saw the blue skirt turning on its way downstairs. I joined her halfway down.

We descended together and Gabriella only made a face at me.

I said: "Tired?"

She shrugged. I didn't mention Dodo.

I went outside too. I could hear feminine squeals and Pieretto's piercing laugh. "They're having a good time," I said.

Subsiding on the steps, Gabriella took my hand and pulled me down hard. "Stay here a minute," she said more intimately than usual.

"Suppose Oreste should come," I muttered.

"Would that bother you?" She smiled. "Do you want a drink?"

"Listen," I said. "What have you done with Oreste?"

She kept my hand in hers but didn't reply. I could hear her breathing and smell her perfume. I put my cheek against hers, then turned and kissed it.

She pushed me away. She said nothing and pushed me away. I hadn't touched her mouth. She hadn't answered me. My heart was beating fast now and she must have heard it.

"Stupid," she said coldly. "You see? That's what I did with him."

I was angry and desperate. I hung my head and listened.

"You're boys," she said. "Oreste too, and that other one. What are you looking for? We're friends; what more do you expect? That's all there is. This winter you go back to Turin. Oreste, too, must go back. You should tell him so. Oreste has a girl, let him marry her. I don't come into it."

She stopped.

After a while I murmured: "Are you jealous?"

"Oh, stop it. That's the end."

"Then it's Poli who's jealous?"

"Don't talk nonsense. You should only tell Oreste that I'm not free to do what I'd like. Will you tell him?"

"What's the matter? Crying?"

Her voice was thin. "Yes, tell him I was crying. He must understand that Poli is sick. I only want him to get well."

"But Oreste says that you don't know what to do with Poli. You were separated. Where were you when Poli was in the hospital?"

I was ashamed for having said it. Gabriella was silent. My heart started pounding again.

"Listen," she said, "will you believe me?"

I waited.

"Will you believe me or not?"

I looked up.

"I love Poli," Gabriella whispered. "Does that seem absurd to you?" she demanded.

"And he? Does he love you?"

Gabriella stood up and said, "Think it over. You must tell Oreste. When you go, you must repeat it every minute . . . You're a dear."

She went off under the pines. My head was spinning. When I got up, I felt like running down the Greppo, I wanted to walk till dawn, as far as Milan, anywhere, as I used to walk during those manic nights at Turin. Instead I went back inside to drink some more.

Then Poli came in from the hallway. He had two jackets thrown over his shoulders, and eyes like ashes, like live coals among ashes. I expected him to be drunk, but not this way. He told me to stay with him, to sit and smoke with him. He said it quietly but insistently.

I asked him if he had known these friends for long. And then I saw that he wasn't drunk, not with alcohol at any rate. His eyes were the same they had been that night we first met him.

"Poli," I said, "don't you feel well?"

He looked me over and gripped the arms of his chair.

"It's getting cold," he said. "Let's hope that it snows. Oreste might be able to kill something . . ."

"Are you angry at Oreste?"

He shook his head, unsmiling.

"I would like you all to stay. Aren't you enjoying yourself tonight? You don't really want to go?"

"Your Milanese friends will be leaving tomorrow morning."

"They bore me," he said. "Old people who don't know how to talk." He heaved as if to vomit and looked grim. Then he dropped his eyes and went on. "It's incredible," he said, "that the oldest thing in us is the youngest, the soul we had as a boy. It seems to me I've always been a boy. It's the oldest habit we have . . ."

Some idiot below sounded the horn of one of the cars, and the raucous, strangled noise made Poli jump.

"The trumpets of judgment," he said darkly.

Dodo came in, saw us, and stopped. "That beast Cilli," he exclaimed, "he's stolen someone's panties. He makes you sniff them and says: 'If you can guess whose they are, the woman is yours.' I ask you . . ."

Poli looked at him with two dead eyes.

"Are you drunk?" Dodo said. "Is he drunk?" He resumed his sarcastic look. He rubbed his hands and went to the table. "It's getting cold," he announced. "I don't know what's come over the girls." He emptied his glass and clicked his tongue. "Nobody upstairs?" Poli gave him the same dull look. "Have you seen Gabriella?"

When Dodo had gone, Poli went on: "It's good to cry out like that, in the night. It seems like a voice from underground. It seems to come from the earth, or from the blood . . . I like Oreste."

30.

Dawn found us all in the parlor in twos or threes or slumped alone in armchairs. Cilli and another man were sleeping. Someone was staring at a window, another chattering aimlessly. Pieretto and Dodo were sipping *grappa*.

We had straggled back one by one from the bushes, the woods, the brow of the hill. Pinotta, whom I had waked by knocking on her little door, was making coffee for us.

Our faces grew livid, then pink in the light of dawn, and the electric light faded. When we turned it off, we looked around, dismayed. The women were the first to come alive.

They left in clear daylight, over damp gravel that barely crackled. Old Rocco watched them leave, near the pool, where he was drawing water.

"We'll be back," they called out. "It's fast on the new highway."

"We'll be coming to Milan," Gabriella shouted from the top of the road.

Poli had gone back in. We strolled listlessly on the gravel, looking around. A checkered scarf hung from the low branch of a pine. I kicked a glass across the gravel. Now, in the familiar morning light, I didn't dare meet Gabriella's look. Oreste was silent too, his hands behind his back.

"Stupid people," Pieretto said. "Milanese."

Gabriella smiled tiredly. "Don't be banal. Perhaps they're saying the same about us."

"It's the men's fault," Pieretto said. "You can judge a man by the women he puts up with."

Oreste said: "You don't put up with any at all."

"Listen," Gabriella said, "settle it among yourselves. I'm going to repair the damage. Peace."

She went off in the bright air. We returned to the room. I couldn't imagine our taking up our former life again. Something had changed. Who could have spoken the word? It was as though we had also left.

The messy room smelled of stale people and stale flowers. Also stale candle wax. A cigarette was guttering in an ashtray.

"I found Pinotta crying in the kitchen last night," Oreste said, "because nobody ever takes her dancing."

We stayed in the armchairs. I was expecting a headache and I got one.

"Hair of the dog," Pieretto said, "that's what we need." He poured out a glass.

Then we talked about going shopping at Due Ponti. The idea was attractive. "We'll help Pinotta that way."

I went up to my room to get my jacket. While I was going down the corridor—bright with sun and curtains—I heard coughing, hawking, groaning. It came from Poli's room. I put my hand on the knob and the door swung open. Poli looked up, sitting on his bed and breathing heavily. He had a bloody handkerchief in one hand which he held to his mouth.

I had hesitated and stopped and Poli was looking at me out of swollen, helpless eyes.

"I don't understand," he stuttered, breathing heavily.

He made a gesture as if to hide his hand, then opened it instead. It was bloodstained, too. "It's not vomit," he said. "Gabriella . . ."

I found her in her room. She ran out, slipping on a wrap. Poli still looked surprised when she came in, looked like a punished child. "It doesn't hurt," he said. "I've only spit it up."

We called Oreste, we called Pieretto. Gabriella moved quickly and nervously around the room, round Poli's bed. All the looks, words, and gestures of those days burned in her eyes like a fever. She never lost her hardness.

Oreste, silent and obliging, examined Poli, biting his lip.

"We'll go," I said to Pieretto. "Let's leave them alone."

"Did you know he was tubercular?" we asked each other on the verandah.

"Considering the life he leads, it's not surprising," I said. "Probably he knew it . . ."

"Like hell," Pieretto said. "When you know, you take care of yourself."

He was naïve sometimes, Pieretto. I told him that one didn't always think of one's health when it was a question of doing or not doing something. I said that Poli, crazy as he might be, was a melancholy man, a solitary man, one of those who by force of thinking about it know in advance what will happen to them.

"Did you know about Gabriella?"

"What about her?"

"That she's deep in love?"

He admitted it was so. But then he said: "What little bird told you?"

They all came downstairs, Poli too. His eyes sunk in an ashy face, he seemed more fed up than anything else. He told us in his normal voice that there was no reason to change his habits, that the world is full of people who bleed through the nose, that those who want to live live the way they want to.

Oreste explained icily that the disease must have been well established, that he couldn't see why they hadn't recognized it at the hospital. He spoke without looking at Gabriella. "You've got to go back there right away," he said. "You've got to go to Milan."

Then Gabriella said she was going down to Due Ponti to telephone.

"I'll take the bicycle," I suggested.

"Take me too," Gabriella said. "I want to talk to his father."

But I didn't know how to carry a passenger downhill, so it fell to Oreste, as it should have. They left, with Oreste holding her in his arms, with his cheek on her shoulder.

"Shall we drink on it?" Poli said, going back inside. "So much for that."

He sipped from his glass, leaden-faced and smiling. I was thinking of that night on the hill when the green car slid out from among the trees.

"My father . . . that's the last straw," Poli said. "All the better that it'll soon be over."

Pieretto told him not to talk nonsense.

"Will it change anything?" Poli said, depressed. He coughed and touched his mouth. He pulled out a cigarette.

"Put that down," Pieretto said.

"You too," Poli grumbled, but he did put it down. "These are the little sins that make one's day. You gamble your life on baby sins, on little nothings. It's a whole world to discover."

"The world is immense," Pieretto said, and swallowed his drink.

When Oreste and Gabriella returned, we were a little high and Poli was saying that life is easy when you know how to get rid of your illusions.

Oreste advised him to rest before the trip. Gabriella took the glass from his hand and told him to lie down. Then they started to circulate through the house, she and Pinotta, to send us here and there, to empty drawers and pack up. Oreste followed her with clenched teeth.

The car arrived a little after noon, the green car, driven by a uniformed chauffeur. The *signor commendatore*—he said it respectfully—was away from Milan. Gabriella made him carry the luggage.

We ate in silence. Gabriella had to leave the table to speak to old Rocco. Alone, I went to sit on the brow of the hill and look down on the plain, on the wild slopes. Large white clouds moved slowly in a soft sky; there was a smell of fruit in the air.

We got into the car. We three sat in back. Poli didn't say a word and I was surprised that he didn't take the wheel. Oreste had slung his gun over his shoulder and held his bicycle on the running board.

At the base of the Greppo I forgot to turn around. We were arguing about the right road for the chauffeur to take. After a few minutes of bouncing and jouncing, we were at the station among the flowered houses, facing the familiar hills. I seemed to have known them always. We got off at the level crossing. The branch road began there, with its curbstones and hedges, paved and white. We exchanged a few words, we joked. Gabriella's hard face smiled an instant. Poli waved his hand.

Then they left and we went to the mill to drink.

OTHER NEW YORK REVIEW CLASSICS*

For a complete list of titles, visit www.nyrb.com or write to:
Catalog Requests, NYRB, 435 Hudson Street, New York, NY 10014